Praise for
A Scarlet Cord

"A second chance at love, a devastating disappearance, and a moment of selfless surrender, all inextricably bound by Raney's lilting style and her trademark mastery of emotion. Readers of *A Scarlet Cord* are going to love this one!"

—DEBORAH BEDFORD, best-selling author
of *The Story Jar* and *When You Believe*

"I couldn't turn the pages fast enough! *A Scarlet Cord* had me holding my breath in suspense and hope. You won't soon forget Melanie and Joel. Deborah Raney has written another winner."

—ROBIN LEE HATCHER, best-selling author
of *Firstborn* and *Speak to Me of Love*

"*A Scarlet Cord* is further proof that Deb Raney has a talent for telling stories of the heart. Deb's faithful fans will not be disappointed. This is perhaps her strongest work yet."

—KAREN KINGSBURY, best-selling author
of *One Tuesday Morning*

"I love Deb Raney's books, and *A Scarlet Cord* is no exception. Her warm portrayal of abiding faith in the lives of those who've suffered loss speaks to the heart and soul, and gently reminds us that God's grace is always sufficient. Another winner from the pen of a perennial favorite who grows each year in her craft."

—LISA SAMSON, author of *Church Ladies*
and *Women's Intuition*

"Deb Raney has crafted an incredibly compelling, fast-paced story of intrigue that runs the gamut of human emotions. *A Scarlet Cord* is a heartrending cry for love, both human and divine. A must-read!"

—YVONNE LEHMAN, author of *His Hands*

a Scarlet Cord

DEBORAH RANEY

WATERBROOK
PRESS

A Scarlet Cord
Published by WaterBrook Press
2375 Telstar Drive, Suite 160
Colorado Springs, Colorado 80920
A division of Random House, Inc.

Scripture quotations are taken from the *King James Version*. Scripture quotations are also
taken from the *Holy Bible, New International Version*®. NIV®. Copyright © 1973, 1978,
1984 by International Bible Society. Used by permission of Zondervan Publishing House.
All rights reserved.

The characters and events in this book are fictional, and any resemblance to actual persons
or events is coincidental.

ISBN 1-57856-577-4

Library of Congress Cataloging-in-Publication Data
Raney, Deborah.
    A scarlet cord / Deborah Raney.— 1st ed.
        p. cm.
    ISBN 1-57856-577-4
    1. Witnesses—Protection—Fiction. 2. Mothers and daughters—Fiction.
3. Widows—Fiction. I. Title.
    PS3568.A562S28 2003
    813'.54—dc21
                                                    2003003993

Printed in the United States of America
2003—First Edition

10 9 8 7 6 5 4 3 2 1

For David and Lori Keazirian,
with love and appreciation.

Wishing you God's richest blessings for the future.
Jeremiah 29:11

∿

Jockeying for position beside the jaded businessmen and -women who lined the curb on 42nd Street, Melanie LaSalle hesitated, then stepped onto the pavement and raised a hand half-mast to hail a taxi.

The brisk November air filled her nostrils with an intoxicating mix of aromas—fragrant steam from a pretzel vendor's offerings, a hundred different colognes wafting from the crush of bodies; even the exhaust from a million automobiles added its own pungent spice to the mix that was uniquely New York.

The morning sun was just beginning to peek over looming skyscrapers and high-rise apartments. Excitement rose in her at being here in the city again. Shading her eyes from the glare, she looked down the street.

Half a block away, a tall man stepped off the curb and opened the door of the Yellow Cab that had pulled up. Melanie's heartbeat quickened as she watched him. The man's confident demeanor, the tilt of his head, and the way his hair curled defiantly into his collar stabbed at a place deep inside her. If she didn't know better, she could almost imagine that she knew that athletic bearing...knew how the coarse, sand-colored curls would feel against her fingertips.

Wanting to banish the unwelcome thoughts, she watched the man slam the door as his taxi eased into the flow of traffic. If she could just get a look at his face through the cab window, she could put it out of her mind.

It had happened often at first—after the letter. She would be stopped dead in her tracks by a familiar posture, an identical square jaw in profile. The shock— when the face, head on, turned out to be unknown—had overwhelmed her those first months after Joel had disappeared. Once, she'd chased a man through a congested parking lot after a concert, only to be thoroughly embarrassed when it was a stranger who turned to answer her insistent cries.

She had long ago learned to quell those unrealistic hopes, and yet now she still felt compelled to take one look at the man's face.

The cab rolled slowly up the street toward her. Melanie strained her eyes as the passenger inside leaned forward to give the driver instructions. As he settled back against the seat, he turned his head slightly in her direction.

Patterns of light played on the darkened windows of the cab. The glare fashioned distorted images of towering buildings and triangular patches of blue sky on the glass, but as the taxi moved into shadow, for a brief moment the face of the man inside was clearly visible. The dim light revealed a thin gash of a scar creasing his right cheek.

Melanie's breath caught in her throat. *No! It can't be!*

The man shaded his eyes and turned to look out the window. For one haunting second their eyes met, and recognition flowed both ways. Then he turned away quickly, leaning forward again to speak to the driver.

Her hands grew clammy and in spite of the chill autumn breeze, perspiration seeped through every pore. *It is him!* Even after all these months, there wasn't a shred of a doubt.

It was Joel.

One

Silver Creek, Missouri, two years earlier

Melanie LaSalle looked up from her computer and leaned back in her chair as she kneaded her stiff neck with the tips of neatly manicured fingers. Her small loft office space—like a crow's nest tucked between the rafters of the former warehouse—afforded a bird's-eye view of the open, modern layout of the graphic design studio she managed.

In the waning hours of the late winter afternoon, thick shafts of sunlight poured through the wide expanse of antique leaded glass windows, painting angled patches of saffron on the brick walls of the old building. The light might have been intrusive had it not been filtered through a jungle of flowering plants and the gaily colored, kite-like sculptures that hung from thick oak rafters and danced in the updrafts. As it was, the sun bathed the towering space in a golden warmth that was almost palpable.

She remembered how this building—and the charming St. Louis suburb—had captivated her when she first came to work in Silver Creek. By Design had been brand new then, the brainchild of Jerry LaSalle, the man who would become her father-in-law.

She stood and tried unsuccessfully to brush the wrinkles from her linen skirt. Hearing a commotion in the foyer beneath her, she went to the sturdy wrought-iron rail that guarded the loft against a thirty-foot drop. She knew, without leaning over to look, that Jerry had just

3

made his grand entrance. She watched, amused, as he walked through his small kingdom—issuing greetings, admiring sketches, cracking jokes—leaving secretaries and designers laughing in his wake.

The supposedly retired owner of the design firm made an appearance nearly every afternoon. "Just to keep my foot in the door," he often told Melanie. "You never know when I might get bored with golf and sailing and traveling the world."

She smiled to herself. Only Jerry could get away with such blatant bluster about his ultracomfortable lifestyle. At sixty-two, Jerry LaSalle had just missed the hippie era. He always said he'd been born a decade too soon, and Melanie was inclined to agree. Even now, he wore his shock of white hair in a neat ponytail, wire-rimmed spectacles rode low on his bronzed nose, and a tiny gold stud bedecked his left ear.

Melanie chuckled to herself thinking how different the son had been from the father. Her beloved Rick had been as preppy as they came—his dark hair always trimmed well above the collar, his face clean-shaven. In an industry thick with artsy, avant-garde types, Rick LaSalle's button-down dress shirts and conservative ties had ironically set him a world apart.

It was good, she realized, to be able to feel joy over a memory of her late husband. Two months ago, the first day of winter had marked the fourth anniversary of Rick's death. Strange how the time crawled in one sense, yet some days it seemed as though she would walk into the house after a long day at work to find him waiting for her, wearing that charming, crooked smile and singing her snippets of love songs.

She felt that familiar ache again. She was grateful when her thoughts were interrupted by Jerry's footsteps on the winding open staircase that led to her office.

"Here she is," he boomed, peeking over the top landing. "The girl who kicked me out of my office."

"Hi, Jerry."

He took the last steps two at a time, and Melanie grinned and leaned to receive the requisite kiss on the cheek.

"Is it as nice out there as it looks?" She nodded toward the west where a bank of windows framed an inviting view of the river.

"Even nicer. It must be at least sixty degrees. Not bad for February, huh? Everything going okay?"

"Just fine. Would you have time to look over a couple of ads for the Milton account?"

He looked at his watch. "I'll make time. I'm supposed to meet Erika at 5:00 though. Don't let me get carried away."

"Everything is on Suzanne's desk. Why don't we go down there?"

He nodded. Melanie went to her desk and punched in the senior designer's extension.

"I think you're going to like what she and José have done with this," she told him while she waited for the call to go through. Suzanne's voice came on the line, and Melanie signaled Jerry to wait. "Hi, Suzanne. Hey, can Jerry and I come down and take a look at the Milton stuff?… Okay. Give us five minutes." She dropped the receiver into its cradle and turned to Jerry. "Now wait a minute…if you're meeting Erika at 5:00, when am I supposed to get my baby back?"

"I was getting to that." His pale blue eyes twinkled. "I don't suppose we could borrow her for a couple of extra hours? Grandma has a surprise up her sleeve… Something about a new Easter dress, I think."

"That could probably be arranged," she laughed.

Jerry opened his mouth, hesitated for half a heartbeat, then cocked one eyebrow. "Maybe you could find yourself a date for the evening?"

She held her palm up and shot him a wry warning glance. "I've got plenty to do without complicating things, thank you very much." She knew Jerry only wanted her to be happy, but she didn't appreciate his meddling in her love life—or more accurately, the lack thereof. But it was true: She had all she could handle managing the firm and raising a daughter on her own.

"We'll feed Jerica and bring her home right after dinner," Jerry said.

"Thanks, Jerry. She'll love that." A twinge of guilt pinched her conscience as she thought of her daughter. She'd put in far too many hours at the office the last few weeks, and Jerica had suffered the brunt of it. Melanie's eyes went to the framed portrait on her desk. Now almost five, the little girl looked remarkably like her father—painfully so, Melanie thought sometimes. But it was her grandpa LaSalle's spunky personality the little girl had inherited, and taming her spirit was sometimes a challenge. Jerica had been only four months old when cancer robbed her of a father, and with Melanie's own parents retired and living in California, Melanie was thankful that Jerica had doting grandparents close by—and appreciated the loving support system they offered her.

Melanie put her computer in sleep mode and turned to Jerry. "Ready?"

He nodded and let Melanie lead the way down the steep spiral of stairs, past the accounting offices on the mezzanine level, and to the ground floor where the design team worked.

While Jerry exclaimed over the vibrant illustrations spread out on Suzanne Savage's desk, Melanie's pulse quickened. She breathed in the excitement that always seemed to permeate the air when a project came to fruition. Sometimes she missed working in this wing of the building where the flow of creative juices was almost palpable.

She had come to By Design as a graphic designer fresh out of college. Jerry had introduced her to Rick, who, just out of school himself, was training under his father to manage the firm. The mutual attraction had been immediate, and they'd married a year later.

Melanie still treasured the memories of those early days with the company. The excitement of finding success in the career of her choice, the thrill of being newly in love, the introduction of Jerry and Erika—mentors both—into her life.

And though she still loved her work at By Design, the new pressures placed on her since Rick's death sometimes weighed heavily. Four years ago she never would have dreamed that she could develop the business acumen it took to manage a firm this size with efficiency and authority. Yet she had done just that. And in spite of the aching sadness over the tragic blow life had dealt her, Melanie usually found deep satisfaction in the life she had made for herself and Jerica.

Jerry had been wonderful to come out of retirement to carry the bulk of the burden after Rick's death. Financially he had been more than generous. Between Rick's insurance, her salary, and the fact that she would someday inherit a share of the firm, she would never have to worry about money. Still, she sometimes thought she would trade it all in for a chance to return to that earlier carefree time.

"This is topnotch work, Suzanne, José. I'm impressed." Jerry's enthusiastic voice prodded Melanie from her reverie. He nodded at the two young designers in turn, then shrugged. "What can I say? You guys are the best."

Melanie gave her designers an I-told-you-so smile. "I think we'll be seeing this front and center at the Addys next year," she said, referring to a coveted advertising award.

By Design had received more than its share of regional and national recognition over the thirteen years the firm had been in business. Melanie's own office sported an impressive array of design and advertising awards. Several of her pieces had been selected for inclusion in national and international design annuals, so her praise carried more than a little weight with these employees.

José Lorenzo ran a hand through thick, jet-black hair. "I'm just a little worried about how these colors will translate to print," he ventured.

"I agree," Suzanne said. "It might be worth sending it to Hadley's this time."

Jerry didn't hesitate. "You guys do whatever it'll take. This one is worth doing right—even if we have to eat some of the costs. What do you think, Mel?"

"Definitely," she agreed.

Melanie could read the relief and victory in the two designers' eyes.

"Good work, guys." Jerry looked at his watch. "Whoa! I'd better fly. Till tomorrow…" He saluted them and headed for the wide front doors.

"Now, don't forget to bring a certain little someone home to-night," Melanie called after her father-in-law, only half joking. She missed her daughter terribly during the day and usually looked forward to their reunion each afternoon. But today a few extra hours of peace and quiet did sound pretty good.

Sighing, she turned to go back up to her office. Rounding the corner of the partition that enclosed Suzanne's work space, she collided with a man who was headed for the front entrance. His hands flew to her shoulders, steadying her.

"Oh! Excuse me! I'm so sorry…" Embarrassed, she backed away from the impromptu embrace.

He smiled broadly and Melanie noticed that a thin scar creased his right cheek just above his jaw line.

"My fault entirely," he said, arms still outstretched. "I saw you coming but I couldn't toot my horn quickly enough to warn you." He spoke in an accent that Melanie thought had roots somewhere in the East.

"Well, I should have been watching where I was going," she told him, clutching a hand to her chest.

"No harm done," he assured her, straightening his suit coat.

They both laughed nervously, and then said farewell. He hurried on through the front lobby. Wondering what had brought this handsome stranger to By Design, she stood and watched his broad back disappear through the door.

Two

Jerica LaSalle sat forward on the velvet cushion of the church pew, fidgeting and swinging her white-stockinged legs back and forth in a noisy rhythm. Melanie laid a warning hand on the little girl's knee, thinking wryly that her almost-five-year-old daughter wasn't the only restless worshiper. From the kitchen area beyond the sanctuary, mingled savory and sweet aromas wafted over the congregation. Judging by the number of people checking their watches and glancing toward the fellowship hall, the enticing smells threatened to upstage the speaker at the lectern.

But Joel Ellington had the advantage. Not only was the man a newcomer to the congregation—and a good-looking one at that—but he spoke with such a thick East Coast accent that it required their studied attention to translate his English into something their Midwestern ears could understand. Halfway through his speech, Melanie realized why the new Christian education director seemed so familiar: He was the one she'd almost mowed down at the office last week.

As Mr. Ellington addressed the congregation, Melanie smiled down at her daughter, who was decorating the bulletin with purple tulips. She retrieved a stray crayon from the pew cushion, handed it to Jerica, and turned her attention back to the front of the church.

There was no denying that the Lord had put this particular man in an attractive package. Tall and athletic, with an olive complexion

9

and startlingly green eyes, he wore his sandy brown hair cropped close, except at his neck where it sprang into short, unruly curls. The thin two-inch scar that marred his smooth-shaven cheek only served to give a rugged handsomeness and a touch of mystery to his face. His large hands had long tapered fingers. He gestured expressively as he spoke, reminding Melanie of the man who sometimes signed for the deaf in the eight o'clock service.

She watched those hands with fascination, equally charmed with the rounded *As* and the slightly nasal intonations of his Eastern brogue.

Jerica looked up at her mother and wrinkled her nose, apparently amused by the peculiar accent. Melanie put a finger to her lips, suddenly afraid that her daughter would laugh or point.

Now Joel Ellington stepped from behind the podium and stretched his arms wide. "I look out across this sanctuary, and though I've never met most of you before, I feel somehow that I know you because I see God's love written on your faces."

According to a blurb in this morning's bulletin, Ellington had previously held a teaching position at a small private college in New York. Melanie wondered what had prompted him to this rather drastic change in careers. And why the Midwest? Finding himself so far away from the home and friends he knew must be difficult.

Melanie forced herself to focus on his speech. He was telling the congregation how it had blessed him to travel a thousand miles across the country and find the same devotion to God among the people here as he had known in his church "back home."

"It's wonderful to realize that God's people can feel quite at home even when they are far from home." He pronounced the words without benefit of the letter *R: even when they ah fah from home.* "Thank you all for making me feel so welcome. I count it a privilege to serve the needs of this congregation," he concluded.

The "amen" of the closing hymn had scarcely died away when the double doors leading into the fellowship hall were opened and there was a small stampede toward the source of the delectable aromas.

Melanie fell in line with the other young mothers. She helped Jerica get settled at the children's table, then made her way to the end of the long serving line to fix her own plate.

Joel Ellington came in from the foyer where he'd been greeting church members and almost timidly took a place behind Melanie.

"Hello," he said, a question in his voice. "I think we've met, but I can't quite put my finger on your name."

She smiled. "We, um…bumped into each other at my office the other day."

His furrowed brow told her he still didn't remember. "I'm sorry… I've met so many new people this week…"

"You were leaving By Design—the graphic arts firm where I work."

He grimaced comically. "Ooh…you meant that 'bumped into' literally. I remember now. I'm so sorry. I practically knocked you off your feet."

Oh, if you only knew how true that was. She felt her skin flush at the impulsive thought and quickly pushed it from her mind. She held out her hand. "I'm Melanie LaSalle."

"Nice to meet you, Melanie." He let go of her hand and dipped his head sheepishly. "I hope there wasn't any permanent damage."

"I think I'll live," she said lightly, still smiling.

He turned and craned his neck toward the buffet table, looking genuinely worried. "Do you think there'll be anything left by the time we get up there?"

"I have never yet gone away from one of these dinners hungry," she promised. "I don't think you have anything to worry about."

As the line crept forward, Melanie struggled to think of something to say. "I enjoyed what you had to say this morning, Mr. Ellington," she said finally.

"Well, thank you. I am feeling very welcome here. And please… call me Joel. I'm not one for formalities. Have you attended this church for long?"

"Since the very first Sunday we held services."

"A chahter member, huh?"

She couldn't hide a grin.

"Did I say something funny?" he asked, clearly puzzled.

"I'm sorry. It's just…your accent. It's charming," she added quickly, "but that East Coast twang is pretty rare in this part of the country."

Now it was his turn to laugh. "And I thought y'all were the ones with the accent," he said in a bad Southern drawl.

"Us? Y'all have obviously never been down to Texas—or Alabama, for that matter." She attempted the Southern belle inflection, painfully aware that she was flirting with him. She cleared her throat and reverted to her normal voice. "To answer your question, yes, I am a charter member. My husband's parents were good friends of Pastor Black. He's the one who started Cornerstone. My husband and I followed them here as newlyweds. Maybe you've already met my in-laws? Jerry and Erika LaSalle? Jerry is one of the deacons."

"I'm sure I have, but I confess I'm terrible with names."

"Me, too," she admitted. "Oh, there's Jerry now." She waved at her father-in-law across the room, and Jerry waved back.

"Oh, sure… I met him during my second interview here. You'll have to reintroduce me. I'll be anxious to meet your husband, too. Or maybe I've already met him, as well?"

She cringed inwardly. "I'm sorry. I should have explained. Rick—my husband—died several years ago. I'm…I'm still very close to his parents. Jerry owns By Design, and I manage the company."

"Oh, so it was the boss I ran into the other day?"

"Quite literally," she laughed, grateful he'd not felt it necessary to express sympathy. "So what brought you to By Design?"

"Don—Pastor Steele—sent me to have business cards made up."

"Oh, of course. We design all the church's stationery."

"Is that right? I'll have to remember that. Don's put me in charge of the capital campaign for the new Christian ed wing, and I've been thinking about some ideas for a logo…maybe even a newsletter…you know, just to keep people updated on how the fund-raising is going. I'll talk to Don and see what the budget looks like."

"Oh, don't worry about that. By Design does all the church's design work gratis."

"Really? That's great. So, do you only handle the business end, or are you a designer as well?"

"I started out as a designer. My degree is actually in commercial graphics. Since I became manager I haven't had time to do as much design work as I'd like, but I do still take on an occasional project—especially when it's for Cornerstone."

"Well, it sounds like a great place to work. The building is certainly impressive. Not at all what I expected to find out here on the frontier."

She laughed. "That's Jerry's creative touch. He's definitely not a frontier boy."

His gaze traveled across the room to where Jerry was holding court at a long table. "No. I can see that."

She tipped her head. "Jerry's a sweetheart, though. Don't let that brash exterior fool you. I don't know what I'd do without him and Erika. And they are wonderful grandparents."

"Oh, you have children?"

"A daughter. Jerica's almost five." She pointed proudly in the direction of the children's table. "She's the little brunette in the red polka dots."

Jerica chose that moment to jump up and let out a loud squeal as an older boy tried to swipe a cookie from her plate.

"She's the one with the mouth," Melanie said, hanging her head and shielding her eyes in mock embarrassment.

"She's cute."

"She's my joy," she said with genuine emotion. "But she is a little spoiled. She was just six months old when Rick died, and Grandma and Grandpa LaSalle have—" She had been about to blame her in-laws for overindulging Jerica but caught herself midsentence. "Well, we've *all* spoiled her a little."

They had reached the food-laden buffet tables by now, and Joel looked over the spread in front of them. "Wow. So much food, so little time... Any recommendations?"

"Oh, right here," she said, picking up a serving spoon from a large casserole. "You have to try Margaret Unruh's vrenika. It's heavenly."

"Vrenika? I've never heard of it."

"I hadn't either until I met Mrs. Unruh. It's an old Mennonite dish...German, I think...a little like a dumpling but with a cottage-cheese filling and the most wonderful gravy..."

He wrinkled his nose. "Sounds...um, interesting, but I think I'll pass."

"Your loss." She shrugged, and scooped a small serving onto her own plate.

"Cottage cheese has never been a favorite of mine," he said.

"You can't even taste it. Honest."

"Then what's the point?" His smile was rather smug. "Thanks anyway, but I think I'll go for something a little more familiar." He reached for the spatula in a pan of lasagna and dished up a generous serving. "Now, this looks good."

"Don't say I didn't try." She put another dumpling on her plate.

They moved on to the end of the long stretch of tables where an impressive array of desserts awaited them. She took a small slice of cherry pie and snaked her way through dozens of tables as she looked for an empty place.

As she went by the children's table, she checked to make sure Jerica was behaving. The Breyer sisters, eleven and thirteen, had unofficially taken charge of the younger children. Jerica was seated between the two adolescent girls, happily licking the frosting from a sugar cookie.

Melanie spotted some friends at a table near the double doors, but all the chairs were taken. The only available seats seemed to be at a large table where several young married couples had congregated. She started for the empty seats.

"Hey, Melanie," several voices chimed, accompanied by the screech of chair legs as they adjusted to make room for her at the table.

Reluctantly, she deposited her plate on the table beside Norm Arnett.

"Hi, Melanie." Rita Arnett leaned around her husband's burly form and greeted her with a smile, but Melanie didn't miss the possessive arm that went around Norm's shoulder.

She arranged her Styrofoam cup and plastic utensils near her plate. After four years it was still difficult to watch happily married couples interact. As much as they tried to include her, eventually their conversation would turn to marriage and family life, and she would be left out. It was a painful reminder of all she'd lost.

With her place saved, she went to check on Jerica again. When she returned, Joel Ellington had taken the seat across the table from her. Introductions were made all around, and the talk turned to Joel's move to the Midwest.

"Have you succumbed to culture shock yet?" Marti Stinson asked.

"Well, I do miss my classical radio station. All I can seem to get around here is country-western."

"Kinda hard to sing about pickup trucks and hound dogs with an East Coast accent, huh?" Norm joked.

"Not to mention gee-tar pickin'," Joel laughed good-naturedly.

By the time they got to dessert, it was obvious that Joel Ellington was going to fit in well here. Melanie relaxed a little, enjoying the amiable give and take and feeling happy that Joel was being made welcome. He was warm and personable, and she found herself more than a little attracted to him.

She shook her head as if to chase the thought away. *This is ridiculous. Why am I thinking such things? I don't even know the man.* She forced her attention back to the conversation.

When she pushed away from the table and excused herself a few minutes later, Joel looked up and gave her a smile that caused her heart to beat an erratic rhythm. "It was nice to meet you, Melanie. I'll be calling you about that logo."

"Oh, sure...that'd be great." Feeling uncharacteristically shy, she gave him an awkward wave and went to collect Jerica and gather the now-empty pie plate and casserole dish she'd brought.

~

The following Thursday evening, Melanie was putting the last of the day's dishes into the dishwasher when the doorbell rang. Drying her hands, she went into the foyer and looked through the peephole. One large, heavily-lashed dark brown eye stared back at her. If the familiar lilting laughter of her daughter on the other side of the door hadn't given them away, the friendly yapping of Biscuit, the LaSalles' little bichon frise, would have.

Melanie opened the door to find Jerica sitting atop her grandfather's shoulders. He was loaded down with shopping bags like a packhorse. Erika cradled the small dog in her arms.

"Hi, sweetie!" Melanie reached up to catch the kiss her daughter blew her.

"Hi, Mommy. Did you see my eye?"

"Is that what that was? I thought it was a big black spider. I was almost too scared to open the door."

Jerica giggled, and Melanie closed the door behind them.

"Did she wear you out?" she asked Jerry and Erika as she led the way through the foyer to the living room.

"No more than usual," Erika said, depositing the little dog on the floor. "We can't stay long, but I do want to see the fashion show."

Melanie clapped her hands. "Oh, you must have found the dress." Jerica and her grandmother had been shopping since after Christmas for the perfect Easter dress.

"Finally. It was worth waiting for, though. Just wait till you see." Erika pointed an impeccably manicured nail toward Jerica's bedroom. "Run and try on your new dress for Mommy, sweetie. And don't forget—"

"I know…I know, Grammy," Jerica interrupted. "The tag goes in the back!" She lugged the largest shopping bag down the hallway, singsonging all the way. "The tag goes in the ba-ack. The tag goes in the ba-ack…"

Biscuit pattered behind her, his dog tags jangling. Jerica turned and, backing down the hall, shook a pudgy finger at the dog, a nervous waver in her voice. "No, Biscuit! Stay! Bad dog. Stay." Her voice climbed an octave. "Mommy?"

"Just go, Jerica. He won't hurt you," Melanie said, shaking her head in exasperation.

"Biscuit! Come," Erika scolded, clicking her tongue. Biscuit complied, and Jerica ran back to her room and slammed the door against the tiny dog. Since she had been a toddler, Jerica had feared canines of all breeds. She tolerated Biscuit—all three and a half pounds of him—only when he was under the watchful eye of an adult.

"Come here, baby," Erika cooed, scooping up the dog, then slumping onto the sofa with an exaggerated sigh. "Oh, for half the energy of your little dynamo! She's a treasure, Mel. A real treasure."

"And you're not one bit prejudiced, Erika," Melanie teased.

The elder Mrs. LaSalle laughed, looking at least a decade younger than her fifty-eight years. Her smooth platinum-blond hair was styled in a chic, short pageboy, and her olive skin bore only faint crow's-feet. She had a dancer's build and wore her extensive wardrobe beautifully.

Jerry LaSalle plopped onto the sofa beside his wife, feigning exhaustion. She put a hand on his knee. "One quick glimpse of the little princess in her new duds, and then we'd better get you home to bed, Grampa."

"Well, you'd better hurry, or you may have to carry me."

"Poor baby." Erika patted her husband's cheek affectionately.

They made a handsome couple, and Melanie knew that theirs was a happy and satisfying marriage—one that had been strong enough to weather the tragic death of their only child. Though at times Melanie felt smothered by their acute interest in her life—and Jerica's—she also felt blessed that she'd been able to offer them the gift of Rick's child. Jerica was a precious antidote to their loss. And Melanie knew as well that they had come to love *her* as their own daughter.

Now Jerica skipped back down the hallway and turned a pirouette in front of the fireplace. The frilly hem of her new tangerine-colored dress swirled about her thin legs, and she curtsied before them.

"Ooh, don't you look pretty," Melanie said. "I hope you remembered to tell Grammy thank you."

"Did I, Grammy?"

"Of course you did, pumpkin."

"Looks pretty sharp, squirt," Jerry said. "You'll have to beat the little boys off with a stick."

"Grampa! Don't!" Jerica stamped a tiny foot and furrowed her brow in irritation.

"Oops, sorry. I forgot." He turned to Melanie. "I was informed this afternoon that Miss Jerica is not, has never been, nor will ever be interested in B-O-Y-S."

"I see," Melanie said with mock seriousness. "Well, maybe I'd better get that in writing. It could come in *very* handy about ten years from now. Do you think this aversion could possibly last until she's out of college?"

"Don't count on it, Mommy…don't count on it," Jerry sighed. "It will probably—" The shrill ring of the telephone interrupted him. "Go ahead and get that, Mel." He motioned toward the phone. "We need to be going anyway."

She went to the table in the hallway and lifted the receiver.

"Hello?"

"Melanie?"

"Yes?"

"This is Joel Ellington, the new CE director…"

"Oh, hi, Joel. How are you?" From the corner of her eye she saw Jerry and Erika exchange glances. Aware that they were listening intently to her end of the conversation, and acutely conscious of the heat that suddenly rose to her cheeks, Melanie turned her back to them.

"I'm fine, thanks," Joel said. "Listen, I hope you don't mind me calling you at home. I wondered if we could set up a time to visit about the logo for the capital campaign."

"Oh, sure. When would be a good time for you?"

"Well, I assume beggars can't be choosers. I'll make time whenever it's convenient for you."

"We're kind of swamped right now. Do you mind working on Saturdays?"

"Not at all. Do you mean this coming Saturday?"

"I think that would work. Hang on, let me check my calendar." She carried the cordless phone to her desk and flipped through her Day-Timer. "Yes, I think that would be fine. Why don't you meet me at the studio around 10:30? Does that work for you?"

"You bet. Is the office open on Saturday?"

"Well, not officially, but there's usually somebody in the building. I'll wait in the lobby for you and make sure you can get in."

"Great. I'll see you Saturday, then."

She put the receiver back in its cradle and turned to face her curious in-laws, feeling the color rise in her cheeks.

"Was it good news, dear?" Erika asked coyly.

"Oh…it was Joel Ellington—you know, the new Christian ed director at church?"

"Oh?" The older woman waited for Melanie to explain.

19

"I'm going to work on a logo for the capital campaign for the new CE wing."

"How nice." Erika said. "Do you want to bring Jerica by while you're at your meeting?"

"You wouldn't mind?"

Erika waved her question away. "Of course not."

"That would be great. Thanks, Erika."

Jerry hauled himself up from the deep sofa, took his wife's hand and drew her up beside him. "We'd better get out of here, dear, so a certain little girl can get ready for bed.

"Do I get a kiss?" he asked, puffing out one cheek and kneeling to offer it to the child.

Jerica ran to him and planted a noisy kiss on his face. "G'night, Grampa."

"Good night, sweetheart. I love you."

"My turn," Erika said, handing Biscuit to Jerry and bending to repeat the ritual.

Melanie walked them to the entryway, said good-bye, and locked the door behind them.

"Okay, sweet pea," she said, scooping Jerica up and hoisting her over her shoulder like a sack of potatoes. "I don't know about you, but I'm starving."

With Jerica perched on a stool beside the counter, Melanie fixed a quick supper of scrambled eggs and jelly toast. By 8:30, stories had been read, teeth brushed, and prayers said, and a worn-out little girl was sound asleep under the pink ruffled canopy of her bed.

Melanie was tempted to join her, but as it always seemed to be for a single parent, these were the hours reserved for laundry and cleaning and, if she was lucky, perhaps a stolen moment for a soak in the bathtub and a chapter or two of a bestseller before her head hit the pillow in exhaustion.

Three

Melanie typically used Saturdays to balance the checkbook, catch up on errands, and shop for groceries. Today she ignored the checkbook and left the dry cleaning to be picked up another day in favor of getting her hair done before her 10:30 meeting with Joel Ellington. She drove to the LaSalles' and dropped Jerica off. The little girl was bubbling about Grampa's promised trip to McDonald's for hot cakes.

Darlene Anthony was ready for her when she walked into the salon. While the hairdresser worked her magic, the two of them caught up on each other's lives.

"So how's that little girl?" Darlene asked, massaging shampoo into Melanie's scalp. "Will she start school next year?"

Melanie nodded underneath Darlene's hands. "It doesn't seem possible, but I'm afraid it's true."

"I saw her a couple weeks ago when Erika picked her up. I couldn't get over how tall she's gotten." Jerica spent mornings at the day care center at Cornerstone, where Darlene moonlighted as the church secretary.

"You should try keeping her in clothes. It seems like every time I turn around she's outgrown another pair of jeans."

The older woman laughed. "I remember those days. Of course, I could hand Jeanette's clothes down to Mary and Beth." Darlene turned the sprayer on high and began to rinse Melanie's hair.

"Mmm, that warm water feels great."

"My mother always says a day at the hairdresser is better than a day at the shrink."

"Well, I've never been to a shrink, but I can't imagine it'd be any more therapeutic than this," Melanie said. "How is your mom getting along? I've been wondering about her."

Darlene sighed heavily. "Oh...about as well as can be expected, I guess. We won't really know if they got all of the tumor for a couple more weeks."

"Well, Jerica and I have been praying for her."

"I know you have. And I appreciate it."

"Jerica has really missed her." Darlene's mother, Jeanne Hines, taught Jerica's Sunday school class when her health allowed.

"Thank you..." Darlene's voice trailed off, and she was silent as she finished rinsing Melanie's hair. She turned off the spray and wrapped a towel around Melanie's head.

"So, how do you like working with Mr. Ellington?" Melanie asked.

"Oh, that man is a doll, that's all there is to it." Darlene seemed to welcome the change of subject. "I'm probably old enough to be his mother," she said, lifting Melanie's head from the sink and bringing the chair upright in one smooth motion, "but I'll tell you what, if I were twenty years younger, Joel Ellington would make my heart go pitterpat. Pastor Steele says we haven't had so many singles attending church since Jeffrey Franzen was the youth pastor. Of course, I wasn't working at Cornerstone back then, but I hear he was a real looker too."

Melanie laughed nervously. Catching her reflection in the mirror, she hoped the pink that colored her cheeks would be blamed on the pungent chemicals in the highlighting solution Darlene was preparing.

Darlene didn't seem to notice. "All I can say is, it's a good thing they hired someone else. As fast as the membership is growing, we're going to overflow the classrooms before you know it. They sure are gung-ho on this new building project. I don't think I've ever seen Pastor Steele so excited about anything." She chattered on as she combed out Melanie's wet hair.

Melanie tried to keep her attention on what the woman was saying, but her thoughts were tugged to what she'd come to think of as "the Jeffrey Franzen fiasco." Jeff had served a brief internship as Cornerstone's youth pastor. He had come to Silver Creek two years after Rick's death. She'd actually been cautiously pleased to discover that she was attracted to him, having been told by everyone, from her brother to her best friend to her in-laws, that it was time she "come out of mourning and get on with her life." Barely three weeks into Jeff's tenure at the church, he had asked her to dinner. They enjoyed each other's company from the beginning, and for the first time since the death of her beloved husband, Melanie had felt hopeful again. Jeff was a wonderful Christian man, and he adored Jerica. He seemed perfect.

But things moved too fast for Melanie. That Christmas, only four months after they had begun dating, Jeff declared his love for her. She wanted to reciprocate, but when she came home that night and stood in front of the closet in the master bedroom—the closet where all Rick's clothes still hung—she suddenly felt as though she were suffocating. She called Jeff, crying, not wanting to hurt him, but knowing that she wasn't ready for another relationship. It was too soon.

Though Jeff claimed to understand and offered to give her all the time she needed, things had never been the same between them. They'd continued to date until he finished his internship, but when his term was up, he took a church in Oklahoma and told her good-bye. She hadn't heard from him since, nor did she wish to.

Now, two years later, Rick's clothes still hung in that closet, and once in a while, on an especially difficult day, Melanie would burrow her face into his shirts and imagine that they still carried the faint

23

scent of him. Her rational mind knew that it was emotionally unhealthy—maybe even a little neurotic—to have held on to his things for so long. But the truth was, there never had been anyone who'd inspired her to box up those reminders of him and risk loving again.

Hers and Rick's had been an extraordinary romance, and when she thought about her life ten or fifteen years into the future, she knew she wanted to know that kind of love again someday. She wanted Jerica to grow up with a father's love. She wanted more children. But the whole thing with Jeff had scared her. And she wasn't about to make the same mistake again.

"Earth to Melanie." Darlene was standing over her, scissors in hand, an expression of amusement on her thin face.

"Oh, I'm sorry, Darlene… I was a million miles away."

"I could see that. Is everything all right?"

She forced a smile. "Fine. I just have a lot on my mind. I'm sorry. Now, what were you saying?"

"Just wondered how you want me to cut your hair this time. Same as usual, or are we going for something different today?"

"No, the same, I think. It's been working pretty well for me."

"Good. I think this style really flatters your heart-shaped face."

Melanie emerged from the salon with bouncy, shiny hair, the few strands of grey that had prematurely begun to plague her transformed for now into auburn highlights.

She caught her reflection in the salon window as she stepped off the curb to get into her car. Darlene had done a good job. Her hair turned under in a smooth wave just above her shoulders. The style did flatter her—and de-emphasized the fine lines that had begun to appear at the corners of her eyes. She wouldn't have minded being three inches taller and—well, at least five pounds lighter—but for someone who was now on the other side of thirty, she supposed she couldn't complain.

Other than her every-six-weeks haircuts, she seldom gave her appearance a second thought. Why was she fussing about it today? She shook off the thought and climbed into the car.

When she pulled into the By Design parking lot at a quarter after ten, Joel Ellington was already waiting for her. She parked beside him, surreptitiously checking her lipstick in the rearview mirror before she stepped out of the car.

"Good morning," he said, turning the key in the door of his white Taurus. He walked around to the other side of the vehicle.

"Hi, there. I can see that you are definitely a big-city boy."

He looked puzzled.

She inclined her head toward the keys dangling from his hand. "This is Silver Creek, Missouri. Nobody locks their cars here."

"Seriously?"

"Not in daylight anyway."

"Wow. That's refreshing."

"It is," she said. "I guess I take it for granted." She rummaged in her purse for the keys to the studio. "Well, are you ready to get to work?"

"Sure." He let her lead the way. "I sure appreciate you taking time out of your Saturday."

"No problem. I enjoy these on-the-side projects. It keeps my creativity percolating."

"That's good to hear"—he put a finger to his temple—"because I guarantee you there's not a single creative spark perking in this brain."

They entered the expansive lobby, and Melanie smiled to herself as Joel Ellington did what every visitor to By Design seemed compelled to do. He craned his neck to gawk at the leaded glass windows high above them. "This is just incredible," he told Melanie. "Even more impressive than I remembered from my first visit."

"It is beautiful, isn't it?"

He nodded, still taking it all in.

She guided him through the labyrinth of stylish work spaces on the first floor. Suzanne was at her computer, and Melanie stopped to make introductions. "Suzanne Savage, I'd like you to meet Joel Ellington. Joel's the new Christian education director at my church. Suzanne is our senior designer." Suzanne extended a hand, and Joel shook it warmly.

"Is anyone else working this morning?" Melanie asked the young woman.

"Not that I know of. Actually, I'm about ready to leave. Do you want me to turn the lights and fans off before I leave?"

"No, that's all right. I'll get them."

Melanie's shoes tapped a pleasant staccato on the hardwood floors as she led the way to the service elevator that went to the mezzanine level and beyond to her office.

"The building looks old," Joel said.

"It used to be a brick factory," she told him. "But it sat empty for years. Jerry could tell you the whole history."

"Well, he's done a great job with the place. I'm impressed."

"Wait till you see the view from my office." Turning a key in the door, she waited for the intricately latticed gates to open, then motioned for Joel to enter ahead of her. She pushed the button for the upper level, and they rode up in silence, gazing out through the latticework to the space below. A few seconds later, the doors glided open to reveal Melanie's office.

"This is it. Come over here." She went to the railing that overlooked the main-floor studio.

He followed her, whistling under his breath as he looked out over the rail. Below them, two dozen Casablanca fans whirred lazily, ruffling the kite-shaped sculptures and the vines that trailed over massive hanging pots. "I bet it's hard *not* to get inspired here."

"That's true."

"How do they water all the plants?" he asked, gazing over the thirty-foot drop to the floor.

She pointed to the north wall. "You can see the pulley system over there...don't ask me how it works—one of Jerry's inventions again. It's pretty ingenious, actually."

"I'll say."

They stood side by side, elbows on the railing, appreciating the view. After a minute, Melanie turned to him. "Well, shall we get to work?"

"I'm ready when you are."

"Could I interest you in a cup of coffee?"

"That sounds great. I haven't had mine yet this morning."

She pulled out two tall stools near the high, slanted drafting desk by the railing. "Here, have a seat. Coffee won't take but a minute." She went into the tiny kitchenette off the opposite side of the room, rinsed the coffeepot, and refilled it with cold water from the sink. "Hey, we're in luck," she called. "Somebody brought up some leftover Danish." She lifted a flimsy bakery box as proof. "If you don't mind day-old."

"Are you kidding? Danish is Danish."

She served the pastries on napkins, and while they waited for the coffee to brew, she asked him about his ideas for the logo.

"Like I told you," he said, "I truly do not have a creative bone in my body. I was hoping you would have some ideas."

"Well, tell me what you want the logo to convey. Hang on." She slid off her stool and grabbed a notepad and pen from her desk. "Is this something that will go out mostly to church members, or were you wanting it to serve as more of an advertising piece for fund-raisers and such?"

He thought for a minute. "Well, actually, we'll probably use it both ways. Is there any way to make one design work for both?"

"Sure. That probably makes the most sense anyway."

She poured coffee, and they set to work. Joel looked on in silence as she flipped through a portfolio of samples.

"I like those," he said finally, pointing to an ad campaign the firm had done for a large credit union.

"Okay." She slipped the ad slick out of its plastic sleeve and handed it to him. "What is it that you like about this one? The colors, or the graphics, or just the overall feel the design conveys?"

He stared at the piece for a long minute, then gave an awkward laugh. "You are asking questions I can't answer, Melanie. Seriously, I guess I just don't think this way. I…just like the way it looks. I'm not sure I could tell you why."

"All right. The client on this project was a large financial institution. We were going for an image of security and conservatism…stability. Does that sound like what you're wanting to convey?"

"Yes…" He nodded slowly and a twinkle came to his eye. "Throw in just a hint of adventure, and I think that's very close to what we want to say."

She smiled up at him. "*Now* we're getting somewhere. A hint of adventure, huh? Okay… What about something like this?" She dashed off some quick sketches, using a rough variation on the design Joel had selected, but incorporating a stylized letter *C* for *Cornerstone.*

"Yes…yes. I like this one especially." He pointed to the sketchpad. "It's really remahkable how you can just draw that, without tracing or anything."

Melanie smiled, charmed all over again by the East Coast in his voice.

She scanned the sketches into her computer and tweaked them a bit.

Joel watched over her shoulder in obvious fascination. Finally, he stretched and looked at his watch. "Do you realize it's past 11:30 already? I really ought to let you get home." He put out a hand. "Thank you for all your help, Melanie. I'm excited about your ideas."

"I think we can come up with something really nice. I'll do up some thumbnail sketches from these preliminaries, and we can go from there. Give me a week or two. I'll give you a call when they're ready."

"Well, hey, no rush. The capital campaign has been without a logo for this long; I doubt it'll hurt to wait a few more weeks."

He turned toward the elevator, but Melanie said, "Let's take the stairs. You get a neat view from there, too. Let me just turn out some lights first."

He waited while she shut down her computer and closed the office, then she descended the curved staircase behind him. They chatted idly as they walked through the main studio, Melanie turning off fans and lights and checking locks as she went.

She had enjoyed their time together immensely and almost hated to have the morning end. In the parking lot, they stood by their cars, still chatting.

"Have you found a permanent place to live yet?" she asked as he unlocked his car door.

"Well, right now I'm in the Manor Haven apartments over on Crestview, but I wouldn't mind finding a small house eventually. You don't know what's available around here, do you?"

"Hmmm…I really don't. But I have a friend who's a Realtor. She might be able to show you around. I think I have one of her cards at home. I'll bring it to church tomorrow."

"That'd be great. Thanks." He looked at his watch again. "Good grief, it's almost lunchtime."

There was an awkward moment when Melanie thought he was going to invite her to lunch. Instead, he climbed into his car and drove off with a friendly wave.

She got in her own car and turned toward Jerry and Erika's, but as she thought about the morning, she had to admit that she wouldn't have minded a lunch invitation from Joel Ellington. "Stop it, LaSalle," she chided aloud. "You've been down this road before, remember?"

And it led nowhere.

Four

Joel Ellington rolled onto his back and plumped the pillow beneath his neck. Beside him on the nightstand, the digital numbers of his alarm clock glowed red in the semidarkness. He turned his head and watched them change minute by minute, marching toward 5:00 A.M. His thoughts swirled like mist, carrying him back to a time that was painful to revisit. He floated on vapors of memory into a dreamlike trance, feeling powerless to change the course of his thoughts.

He was in his dorm room at Hartwick with its peeling paint and battered desks. He was studying, trying to concentrate on a particularly boring chapter in his world civilization textbook, when his roommate, Brent Payne, hung up the phone complaining loudly that his parents and younger sister were in town and making an impromptu visit to the campus. They planned to stay over the weekend, effectively putting his party plans on ice.

Listening to Brent's grumbling, he kept silent, but that afternoon he watched with envy as Brent's parents embraced their son and bombarded him with questions about campus life. He was angry at Brent's irritation with his family. His own parents had been dead for several years now, and his brother was three thousand miles away, attending college on the West Coast. He would have given anything to have a family to intrude on his life once in a while.

But the weekend had turned out to have one great redeeming

quality. That was when Victoria Payne had walked into his life. Brent had always painted his kid sister as a brat, but Brent was wrong. She was incredible. At eighteen and a high school senior, Tori, as she liked to be called, was mature beyond her years. And beautiful. They'd hit it off immediately.

"It's like we've known each other forever," Tori told him that Sunday night before she climbed into the car to go home with her parents. As he watched their car disappear through the campus gates, he realized he felt the same way. There were many more weekend visits that spring. Victoria entered Hartwick the following year, and after that there'd never been anyone else for him.

The memories floated disconcertingly through his mind. Joel rolled onto his side and stared at the bare wall of his bedroom. His eyelids grew heavy, and he felt sleep trying to overtake him. He struggled against it, knowing that the dreams would follow. The minute he closed his eyes, the familiar scene flashed before him. He fought it, but the pull was too strong. Like a drowning man, he finally ceased struggling and gave in to the nightmare. It dragged him under, suffocating him as surely as any murky depths of water. The dream played like a film on a continuous loop. Victoria was there…so beautiful…so beautiful. It all seemed real…as though it were happening all over again…

The main dining room of Ciao! was bathed in warm candlelight. Strains of Mozart offered a soft accompaniment to the hushed voices of a few late evening diners, punctuated by the faint clatter of dishes that drifted from the kitchen each time the wide double doors parted to let a tray-bearing waiter pass through.

He thrust his hand deep into the pocket of his suit jacket and nervously fingered the small square box hidden there. Across from him at the linen-clad table, Victoria Payne was intent on the steaming plate of pasta in front of her. He studied her delicate features in their frame of golden curls.

31

She took a sip from her water goblet, but when she caught him staring at her, she set the glass back down and flashed him a quick smile. "What?"

"Nothing…" He stifled a grin and turned his attention to his own entrée. But he had trouble keeping his eyes off of her. She had never looked so beautiful. In the flickering light of the single taper on their table, her porcelain skin was flawless. The cream-colored dress with its high ruffled collar and long lacy sleeves made her look almost like an angel. Or a bride.

Suddenly nervous, he wrapped his hand tightly around the box in his pocket and willed his heart to slow down. He was certain she would say yes. Almost *certain*.

A crash from the kitchen made them both jump. Victoria laughed at their skittishness and put another bit of pasta on her fork. He'd wanted everything to be perfect tonight. He had tried to secure a table away from the noise of the kitchen, but it was late, and the other sections of the restaurant were closed for the day.

Now the dining room was nearly empty, the only other diners two businessmen at a nearby table. A lilting Mozart air faded away, and the room filled again with the sweet strains of a Handel sonata.

Victoria looked up, fond remembrance in her gaze. "Oh, listen. I used to play the flute part for this piece—with my high school symphony. It's so beautiful." She closed her eyes, listening, obviously enraptured.

He took a deep breath. It was now or never. He took the velvet box from his pocket and set it casually on the linen tablecloth.

A sudden commotion at the lobby entrance was followed by a loud shout and a stream of curse words from the older man at the table near them. Then, as though it all happened in slow motion, he and Victoria stared in horror as a fashionably dressed man stood calmly at the nearby table, pulled a gun from beneath his suit jacket, and methodically fired six shots into the angry diner's chest.

The ring box was forgotten. They froze in their chairs, unable even to breathe, unable to believe that what they had just witnessed was reality.

Then, seeing the horror in Victoria's eyes, he forced himself to act. He lunged across the table and covered her body with his, then pushed her down to the banquette beneath it. He scrambled toward the kitchen on all fours, pulling Tori along with him, until they sat trembling against a wall.

The gunman turned then and strode quickly toward a rear exit. As he passed, hard, deep-set eyes glared at Victoria.

Less than six feet away from the man, he frantically memorized the dark eyes, the wavy brown hair, and the jagged-edged port-wine birthmark on the left side of the gunman's face. Though only three or four people had actually witnessed the shooting, the few workers remaining in the restaurant quickly learned that the gunshots had left a corpse at table 4B.

Panic took over. In the kitchen, a woman sobbed hysterically. The headwaiter shouted, trying in vain to calm the small group now being herded toward the exits. Several cooks and a trembling waitress peered cautiously through the steamed-over window. As he and Victoria sat on the floor just outside the kitchen, he watched them, fear clenching his stomach.

"He's gone, man…he's gone now," a waiter whispered, shaking his head in apparent disbelief. "But that guy ain't goin' nowhere." He motioned toward the table where the dead man sat, still slumped in his chair, his eyes staring unseeing at the blood-splattered white linen in front of him.

The man's dining partner had disappeared.

Now the distant wail of sirens pierced the eerie silence that enshrouded the restaurant. Almost without exception, those who had not already fled stood like statues, covering their faces with trembling hands, their eyes horror-stricken as they stared at the victim.

He had the odd sensation that they were playing roles in a movie. Surely at any moment a director would yell "Cut!" and the man would get up and begin to wipe the greasepaint and fake blood from his face and clothing.

But as police officers stormed the building from front and rear entrances, they realized that what they had just witnessed was very real.

Putting his arms around Victoria, he gripped her hands tightly, and she turned to look up into his eyes.

Her face was ashen, her lips bled of color, and her eyes held a dazed, glassy expression. "What…what happened? Joe? Oh, Joe…"

The haunting sound of Tori's voice caused him to thrash in the bed. The sheets were soaked with his perspiration. Barely conscious, he struggled to open his eyes before the next scene of the nightmare could overtake him. But there it was—a ball of fire, exploding, blinding him. The silence that followed was equally deafening.

He sat up in bed, battling to untangle himself from the sheets. "Tori!" he yelled, his own voice bringing him instantly awake…and instantly aware that it was futile to call for her.

"Tori…" Her name came out on a whispered sob, torn from his throat against his will.

Shaking, he swung his legs over the side of the bed and sat, head in hands, trying to orient himself. He hadn't thought of himself as *Joe* in months. He crawled from the bed and went to the window. The sun was just coming up; the scene outside his window reassured him. The traffic in front of the apartment on Crestview was light on a Sunday morning, but the parking lot of the donut shop across the street was a hive of activity. He was in Silver Creek. Everything was all right. He was safe now. This was the town where no one locked their doors.

He took a deep breath and stumbled into the bathroom. Peering into the mirror, he scratched at the dark stubble on his jaw and instinctively traced the thin scar that ran along his cheek.

Why did this have to happen now? Why this vivid dream—this *memory* of Victoria? Why now, just when he was finding happiness here in Silver Creek?

He remembered his meeting with Melanie LaSalle yesterday, and thought then that he had his answer. Melanie reminded him of Victoria somehow. Physically, they were as different as they could be—Tori's fair hair and complexion, and her statuesque elegance, contrasted with Melanie's dark-haired beauty and petite stature. But something about the effect Melanie LaSalle had on him reminded him of Victoria. Melanie had the same easy grace, the same intelligence and no-nonsense attitude.

But the dream was a stark reminder that he could never again have what he'd had with Victoria. That part of his life was over, and he couldn't pretend otherwise. He must be grateful that he had this new chance at life at all.

"Thank you, Lord. Thank you for a new day." It was not a heartfelt prayer, but one uttered out of sheer obedience and willful self-discipline. He stepped into the shower and let needles of hot water pelt his body, trying in vain to wash away the sweat, the tears, and the terror of the dream.

Five

"Hey, sunshine. Time to get up and get ready for church." Melanie sat down on the fluffy pink comforter beside her daughter and patted the thin arm that flopped over the edge of the mattress.

Jerica stretched, opened her eyes, and immediately began whining, "I don't wanna get up. I don't feel good."

Melanie put a hand to her daughter's forehead. It didn't feel especially warm. "Come and eat some breakfast, and you'll feel better." She pulled the quilts back and stroked Jerica's arm briskly. "Come on, baby…"

"Noooo," Jerica whimpered.

For a minute, Melanie was tempted to stay home and let her daughter sleep. But the thought of seeing Joel Ellington again spurred her to ignore Jerica's cantankerous mood. Besides, she'd promised to give Joel the number of Dana Landon's realty company.

"Come on, sweetie," she coaxed again, brushing a dark tendril of tangled hair away from the little girl's forehead. "Let's go eat, and then you can choose your outfit for Sunday school."

Jerica stuck out her bottom lip and gave one last bleat of protest, but she climbed out of bed and padded behind her mother to the kitchen.

Melanie set Frosted Flakes and juice on the table for Jerica, then rummaged through the junk drawer until she found one of Dana's business cards. Her friend had helped her and Rick find this house five years ago, and since then, she had steered several By Design employees Dana's way. She tucked the card in her purse, poured milk on Jerica's cereal, and went back to her room to get dressed.

An hour later, Jeanne Hines greeted a much happier Jerica at the door of her Sunday school classroom.

"Jeanne! It's so good to see you here," Melanie said. "I thought you were still in the hospital. How are you feeling?"

"I'm…I'm doing okay," she said weakly. But Darlene Anthony's mother was thin and pale, and it was obvious that it was an effort for her to be here. Melanie was glad to see that Selina and Kimmy Breyer were helping out in the classroom today.

Kimmy came over and steered Jerica to a group of children coloring at a low table. Confident that Jerica was happily settled, Melanie thanked Jeanne and went down the hall to her own class.

When she walked through the door, half a dozen people were already helping themselves to coffee and donuts at a table in the corner.

"Good morning!" Karen Dixon waved a half-eaten maple long john at Melanie.

"Hi, Karen," Melanie said. "Hey, we've missed you guys. I take it the kids are over the chickenpox?"

Karen puffed her cheeks in an exaggerated sigh. "Finally."

"Well, we've been praying for you. It's good to have you back." Melanie touched the young mother's arm sympathetically, then went to pour herself a cup of coffee. She picked up a small cinnamon roll and looked over the room, scouting out a seat. This class was made up mostly of married couples—*as the entire world seems to be,* she thought wryly—and it was always tricky to find a spot in the circle of chairs that didn't split up a couple or leave an odd number of chairs open.

She took a seat facing the door and self-consciously occupied herself with juggling her Bible and the sweet roll and brimming Styrofoam cup. Finally settled, she took a sip of coffee and looked up to see Joel Ellington walk through the door. His gaze caught hers, and he nodded a greeting before heading for the refreshment table. A minute later, he took the empty chair beside her, wrestling with his own coffee and roll.

"Good morning,"

"Hi, Joel."

"This is the eating-est church I've ever seen," he told her over a mouthful of pastry. "If I don't learn to 'just say no,' I'm going to end up fat as the proverbial pig."

"I seriously doubt that a little cinnamon roll and a cup of coffee are going to do you in," she told him.

"Yes, but you didn't see the two extra-large muffins I had for breakfast."

"Don't you know you're not supposed to eat breakfast before you come?" she teased. "That's one thing I love about Sunday mornings: Somebody else does the cooking."

"I'll remember that," he whispered, motioning toward the front of the room where Mike Dixon was clearing his throat and waving his arms, trying to get the class's attention.

Throughout the class period, Melanie was uncomfortably aware of Joel's presence beside her. She felt like a silly schoolgirl with her first crush. She struggled to concentrate on Mike's lesson until one of his comments launched a discussion about grief. Her interest in the topic outweighed her juvenile reaction to the man beside her, and she finally relaxed a little.

Half an hour later, Mike dismissed them with prayer, and the room broke into a pleasant buzz of conversation. Melanie remembered the business card she had for Joel, dug it out of her purse, and handed it to him. "This is the Realtor friend I was telling you about yesterday," she explained, seeing the question on his face.

"Oh, sure…thank you." He gave the card a quick perusal before tucking it into his breast pocket. "I'll have to give her a call when I get ready to start house shopping."

An awkward silence followed, and Melanie gathered her Bible and purse and started toward the door. But Joel put a tentative hand on her arm. "Hey, Melanie? Um…can I ask you something?"

"Sure," she said, turning back toward him, her heartbeat quickening at the warmth of his hand on her skin.

He paused as if he wanted to say something, then his gaze dropped to the floor and he tucked his hands into the pockets of his pants. "I…just wondered if you ever attend the singles class here."

She hesitated. Cornerstone had a thriving singles ministry, with its own Christian education class that met during this hour. "Yes…I've gone a few times," she hedged. "Why do you ask?"

"I'm trying to get a feel for where we need to improve in the CE department. I was thinking you might be able to give me the lowdown on the singles ministry. I assumed you would attend that class. I was surprised to see you here…that's all."

She hesitated. "Well…to tell you the truth, I've always felt a little awkward and out of place there."

He flashed a crooked grin and looked around the room. "More awkward and out of place than you feel in this hotbed of marital bliss?"

She followed his gaze. All around them, little duos and quartets made up of married couples buzzed in easy conversation.

"You know…I guess in a lot of ways I don't *feel* single." She couldn't believe she was being so candid with him. "I know this will make me sound like I'm in some kind of delayed denial, but I still feel somehow a part of the couple that was Rick and Melanie LaSalle."

"Really?" His gaze was warm, full of genuine interest, and instead of making her feel self-conscious, it comforted her.

She tried to explain. "It's just that after Rick's death, so little changed in the day-to-day pattern of my life. I stayed at the same company, even took over Rick's position. I still live in the same house, I attend the same church, and I see my husband's parents almost daily. And, of course, there's Jerica. It's almost as if Rick is simply away on an extended business trip or something." What she told him was true, and yet, didn't the cold, empty pillow beside her head on the bed each night contradict her comments?

Suddenly she was desperate to change the subject. "I don't mean to badmouth the singles class. It really is a good class, Joel. Milt does a wonderful job with the lessons, and I know that a lot of the people who attend wouldn't miss it for anything."

"Well, that's good to hear. I've thought about trying it myself, but for a few months at least, I need to sit in on each of the other classes, so I have an idea of what we have to offer and what we need to add. Actually...I've thought about teaching a class myself somewhere down the road."

"Really? That would be wonderful. I know they're always looking for teachers."

He started to say something, then paused, clearing his throat and glancing at his watch. "We'd probably better go if we want a seat in the service."

She looked around the now-empty classroom, then glanced at her watch. "Oh, my! Jerica's teachers probably think I've abandoned her!"

"Well..." He put up a hand in farewell. "Have a good morning."

She returned his wave, and they hurried in opposite directions down the corridor.

∽

The alarm clock buzzed annoyingly. Without opening his eyes, Joel reached over and fumbled with the buttons. Tuesday morning was his day off, and he was tempted to sleep in, but he'd planned to finish organizing his apartment today. He forced himself to roll out of bed and pulled on yesterday's jeans and T-shirt. Sidestepping a stack of half-empty moving boxes, he headed for the kitchen.

Most of his personal belongings had yet to arrive, but he knew from past moves that it might be weeks before they were shipped. He couldn't complain. The apartment was furnished, and his clothes, small appliances, and computer and stereo equipment had been delivered Saturday. He had everything he needed. But standing in the tiny kitchen, looking out over the open combination living-dining area, he was struck by how clinical and austere the space was. The only things that set this unit apart from the two hundred other apartments in the complex—that marked this as the home of the man called Joel Ellington—were the small framed snapshots of his family.

The photographs sat side by side on an end table near the low-slung sofa. The one of his family had been taken the summer before his parents' plane went down somewhere in Africa. The other one showed him and his brother, Tim, arm in arm on the Foxmoor campus the first year Joel had taught there. He had a smaller copy of that one in his wallet, along with Victoria's college yearbook photo. They were all he had left to remember his past by—those fragile pieces of paper and colored inks. He had hand-carried the frames all the way to Silver Creek, unwilling to risk having them among his possessions that seemed to mysteriously disappear every time he moved.

Joel crossed the room and picked up the frame that contained the likeness of his parents, his brother, and himself. They stood arm in arm in a row, Mom and Dad in the middle, he and Tim flanking them, wide smiles on every face. He couldn't remember now who'd taken the picture. It didn't matter. As far as he was concerned, it was just the four of them. His world. They'd been so happy then.

A crushing sense of loneliness came over him, and he replaced the frame carefully on the table and went back to the kitchen. Taking a loaf of raisin bread from the counter, he popped two slices into the toaster and went to the refrigerator for butter and orange juice.

Soon the smell of toast filled the kitchen. His mother had baked homemade bread twice a week when he was growing up. The faint aroma of cinnamon offered him a moment of pleasure. Closing his eyes and breathing in the familiar scent, he could almost imagine that he was back home in New York.

Home. That word and all it had once meant to him had been perverted, changed forever—first with his parents' deaths, then inexorably sealed the day he'd lost Victoria.

He took the bread from the toaster, spread a thick layer of butter on each slice, and shook off the memories that encroached. He perched on a barstool at the kitchen counter and, out of habit, bowed his head and gave thanks before he took the first bite.

When he finished eating, he put his dishes in the dishwasher and went to tackle the boxes in the bedroom. As he put away the rest of his clothes and the few books that had been packed among them, he practiced the new attitude he had determined to embrace. He spoke the words aloud like a mantra: "Thank you, Father, for this place of refuge. Thank you for a new beginning. Thank you."

He *was* grateful for the safe haven Silver Creek provided. He could be going out of his mind in a run-down hotel in some unknown city.

He could be dead.

Six

Melanie went to the drafting table where a dozen miniature logo sketches were neatly aligned on a piece of art board. She straightened the images one last time and smiled to herself. She still had the touch. And even though Cornerstone's account didn't add to By Design's profits, she felt a tremendous sense of satisfaction in having created some attractive and unique designs.

She went to her desk and dialed the church's number. Darlene Anthony answered on the second ring. "Hi, Darlene, it's Melanie LaSalle. Is Joel in the office today?"

"Oh, hi, Mel. He sure is. Just a minute… I'll get him."

Melanie tapped a pen nervously on her desk while she waited. Her heart lurched when Joel's voice came on the line.

"Good mahning, Melanie. What can I do for you?"

That gorgeous accent again. *Good grief, LaSalle. Get a grip!* "Hi, Joel." She inhaled slowly and forced a businesslike tone. "I have some sketches for the CE project ready to look at. I was wondering when might be a good time to get together."

"Wow, that was fast. Well, let's see…my schedule is probably more flexible than yours. Why don't you just name a time?"

"Does Pastor Steele need to be in on the meeting?" she asked. "Or any of the rest of the committee?"

"I guess not. Don keeps telling me this is my baby. I'll want the committee's input on the final design, of course, but it looks like I'm on my own for the preliminaries."

"Okay… I don't suppose you could come by this morning? I just finished the sketches, so they're all laid out on my drawing table. I have a meeting later this afternoon, but if you could come in anytime before noon, I'd have time to show them to you. Or we can do it another day this week…"

"I can be there in fifteen minutes if that works for you."

"Oh…great…perfect. I'll just have the receptionist send you on up when you get here."

"Sounds good. I can't wait to see what you've come up with."

She hung up the phone and turned to her computer. Opening the art files one by one, she printed them out in a larger size for Joel to take back with him. She examined each one as it came from the printer, and slid the pages into a folder. She realized that her palms were damp. She still got a little nervous before presenting her work to a client, but it wasn't as if Cornerstone were a make-or-break account.

She glanced at the clock. Joel would be here any minute. She went into the small rest room off her office, checked her lipstick, and fluffed her hair. Then she went to look over the layouts one more time.

Joel followed the receptionist to the elevator and thanked her as the doors glided shut. A minute later, he was standing in Melanie LaSalle's office.

"Hi, there." Melanie met him with an outstretched hand and that warm, open smile she always seemed to wear. "Thanks for coming on such short notice."

"Not a problem," he told her. "I'm anxious to see what you have for us."

"They're right over here." She started toward the drafting table where they'd sat together the day she gave him a tour of the building. He followed and took a seat at the high stool she indicated. She perched on a stool beside him.

"Now, on this first row"—she motioned toward the drawings on the table—"I used variations on the lettering…using the initials as a design element; mostly text, very little artwork on these. With the rest, I tried to incorporate some of the architect's drawings like we talked about."

He'd expected to see rough pencil sketches and vague ideas, but the samples she was showing looked like finished artwork to him. Not that he knew much about art, but still he was impressed. He spent several minutes studying the drawings, then looked up to see Melanie watching him. With her hands clutched in front of her and her eyes wide, she reminded him of an anxious child. He smiled at her. "These are beautiful, Melanie. How in the world am I supposed to choose just one?"

She laughed, relief obvious in her voice. "I'm glad you like them. What I usually suggest is that the client just go with first impressions. Pick out two or three that really grab you. Then we can work from there narrowing it down, incorporate ideas from more than one logo into the final design, even go back to the drawing board…"

He held up a hand. "I can tell you right now that *that* won't be necessary. Every one of these are great."

She beamed, then looked almost embarrassed. "Well…I'm glad you think so." She was silent for a few minutes while he looked over the drawings, then she handed him a folder. "I made some larger copies of the thumbnails if you'd like to take them with you. I can e-mail you digital files, too, if you like. Then we can iron out the comps and start working with layouts."

"Whoa!" He held up a hand. "You are speaking a totally foreign language there, but…whatever you say."

"I'll walk you through it," she laughed. "I promise." She spent a few minutes explaining the process—this time in layman's terms.

Finally, she looked up from the drawings and glanced at the over-sized clock on the wall across from the railing.

"I've kept you long enough," he said, taking the hint.

"Oh no. No problem. My meeting isn't until 2:00."

"Could I take you to lunch?" The words were out before he could even think through the ramifications.

To his dismay, she seemed flustered by the invitation.

"Lunch? Well...I suppose..."

He thought he understood. Hadn't she told him just a week ago that she felt out of place in the singles world, that she still felt married? Yet that was exactly why he'd felt comfortable asking her. He wasn't looking for a relationship either. But she couldn't know that. She probably had to fend off men all the time, and here he was making her do it again.

He cleared his throat, feeling compelled to explain himself. "I...I just wanted to thank you for everything you've done..."

He motioned toward the drafting table and her designs. "For the work on this project, for making me feel so welcome here, all of it."

She looked at him as if trying to assess his sincerity. "I'd love to have lunch with you, Joel. Thanks for asking."

He tried not to let his relief show. "My car is parked in the front lot," he said, fishing his keys from his jeans pocket.

She hesitated. "Just so I'm back by 1:30. I'll turn into a pumpkin after that."

"No problem, Cinderella."

She laughed at his joke, and it somehow warmed his heart. That hadn't happened in a long time.

∼

Melanie had been thrilled at Joel's invitation to lunch, but now, after just a few minutes in the car, they'd seemed to run out of things to talk about. Uncomfortable with the silence, she reached up to touch a length of red silk cording that was draped over his rearview mirror. "Ah, you must have been an honor student?"

He turned to her, his eyes questioning.

"It looks like the honor cords that graduates wear," she explained. "You know—on your cap or gown—if you graduated summa cum laude or were valedictorian or whatever? Not that I've ever seen one up close." She laughed nervously, feeling silly now that the words were out.

He batted at the cord. "No, it's—" He looked at his lap, seeming embarrassed.

"Ah, I get it… It's a souvenir from an old girlfriend?"

When he didn't respond, she cringed. "Oh…or maybe a not-so-old girlfriend?"

At that he laughed and shook his head. "No, nothing like that. It's just—a reminder…of a Scripture passage, actually. One that… means a lot to me."

Curious, she arched a brow in his direction, but he ignored her questioning gaze and changed the subject. "Where would you like to eat?"

Okay, I can take a hint. "I'm not picky," she told him. "What sounds good to you?"

"I really haven't been here long enough to know what's available. Why don't you decide? I'm open for anything."

"Okay. How about Larkspur? It's nice…kind of a bistro atmosphere."

He rolled his eyes and laughed. "Spoken like a true woman: Never mind the food, how's the ambiance?"

She cocked her head and grinned. "Oh, excuse me, did I mention they have great sandwiches?"

"No, you didn't. But don't mind me. I'm just giving you a hard time. Anything's fine with me."

When they walked into the restaurant's lobby, the hostess met them with menus in hand.

"Would you care to sit on the patio?" the model-thin young woman asked. "We have the burners going, so it's really quite comfortable out there."

Joel raised his brows, tacitly leaving the decision with Melanie.

"It'd be fine with me. I'm dressed plenty warm," she assured him, rubbing the sleeves of her wool-blend jacket. "And I love dining alfresco."

"We'll take the patio," Joel told the hostess.

"Right this way, please." She led them through the large dining room to the patio outside. Several other diners had already been seated at the umbrella-canopied tables. With the trees still leafless, they had a clear view of the river and the town's spare winter skyline. The tall radiant burners on either side of their table kept the air temperature comfortable, and the hostess adjusted the table umbrella so that the sun warmed their shoulders.

When they were settled and the hostess had gone, Joel turned to Melanie. "So you've been at By Design for how many years now?"

"Going on seven—not counting the months I took off when Jerica was born. It's the only place I've worked since I graduated from college."

"That's kind of unusual."

She shrugged. "I guess I don't know anything else. I take it your work history is a bit more checkered?"

He appeared startled by her question. Then he smiled and took a sip of his ice water. "Just a bit," he said.

"Where did you work before coming to Silver Creek?"

He took several gulps of water and wiped his lips on the linen napkin before answering. "I...I taught English." He cleared his throat.

"Oh yes. I remember reading that."

"You read it? Where?"

"In the church bulletin, I think."

"Oh yes...of course."

"Where was it you taught?"

"At a small college. You…probably wouldn't have heard of it. It was back East."

"Ah, back where your English made sense to them?"

He warmed to her teasing. "Hey! My English is impeccable."

"In the East, maybe." She grinned at him and knew she was flirting again. What was it about Joel Ellington that brought out that annoying coyness in her? She pushed aside the thought that she had business lunches with male clients all the time and never felt the need to flirt as shamelessly as she was doing now.

A college-age server appeared at their table. "Good afternoon. My name is Alec, and I'll be your server today." *Ah, saved by the waiter.* "May I get you two something to drink?"

"I'll have coffee, please…black," she told him.

"The same," Joel said. The waiter left, and Joel turned to Melanie again. "So, how's your little girl? Jerica, isn't it? That's an interesting name."

"She's named after Jerry and Erika," Melanie explained, warming to her favorite subject.

"Oh, sure. That makes sense." He nodded his understanding. "She's five, did you say? Does that mean she's in kindergarten?"

"She'll turn five in April. She won't start school until next year. She attends Cornerstone's preschool during the mornings."

"Oh, I've probably seen her, then. The preschool kids keep things at the church pretty lively."

"I'll bet," she laughed. "That's another thing in favor of the new wing—it'll move the kids a little farther from the administrative offices."

"I really don't mind the noise. It's kind of nice, actually. Reminds me what this work is all about."

"That's a good way to look at it."

The waiter came and poured coffee. Melanie took a sip and asked, "So, are you starting to feel at home now?"

"In the job, you mean?"

"Well, the job, the town…the whole thing. Are you getting used to the Midwest? That was probably the biggest adjustment. A bit of culture shock, I'd imagine."

"You could say that. The other day I told someone I was going to get a soda, and they seemed to have no idea what I was referring to."

"And just what *were* you referring to?" she joked.

"Apparently what you people call 'pop.'" He pronounced the word with a nasal twang, laughing.

She was growing to love the sound of his laughter. "Ah, yes, pop. You ask for soda around here, and you'll get baking soda. Where exactly did you live back East?"

His smile faded, and he lingered over a sip of coffee before replying. "Several places, actually. Most of them in New York State. But my parents were part-time missionaries, so we sometimes spent summers out of the country with them."

"Oh, really? Where?"

"South Africa. The Philippines. Those are the two I remember best."

"What a rich childhood that must have been. Are your parents still doing mission work?"

He looked at his plate. "No… They were…killed in a plane crash…several years ago."

"I'm so sorry, Joel. I can't imagine…" She could sense that the wound was still tender and grasped for a way to change the subject. "Do…do you have brothers or sisters?"

He brightened a bit. "I have a brother. He's two years older than I."

"And is he on the East Coast too?"

Joel nodded. "Yes. He is." He seemed lost in thought, and Melanie felt terrible for opening such a tender issue.

"How about you, Melanie? Do you have other family—besides your in-laws, I mean?"

"Well, my parents are out in California. My folks are older. Mom was forty-two when I was born. Dad had a couple of heart attacks about twelve years ago, so he retired early, and they moved out to San Diego. My brother and his family live in New Jersey...in Bergen County."

"Wow. You have family scattered from coast to coast."

She nodded. "Matt—my brother—married my best friend. In fact, I'm the one who set them up."

"A matchmaker, huh?"

"Yes, and proud of it. Karly is like the sister I never had. They have two adorable little boys now."

"Do you get to see them often? Your family?"

"Not nearly as often as I'd like. Jerica and I get out to see my folks once a year, and I'm able to see Matt and Karly a little more often since I'm in New York on business occasionally...but it's hard being so far from all of them. I suppose you know how that is."

"You must really appreciate having your in-laws close by. I visited with Jerry a little bit at the elders meeting the other night. He seems like a nice guy."

"He is. I'm sure I take Jerry and Erika for granted sometimes. They're the greatest. I owe them a lot. After Rick died, Jerry trained me to manage the business. Even though Rick had a nice insurance policy, I'm not sure I would have made it without Jerry's generosity. Of course, he had an ulterior motive."

"Jerica?"

She smiled. "Uh-huh."

"Typical grandparents."

"Maybe a little...um...beyond typical," she said wryly. "Rick was their only child, so Jerica is extra precious to them."

"I can imagine. Well, it's nice that they've been so good to you. It's obvious that you love the family business."

"I really do. Well, most of the time. I wish I could be home with Jerica more. She's growing up so fast, and sometimes I worry that I'm missing out on half her life."

"I suppose that's something every working mother feels."

She nodded. The waiter brought their lunch then, but they talked more than they ate, and when Melanie finally looked at her watch, she was shocked to see that it was almost 1:30.

At her gasp, Joel looked at his own wrist. "Oh!" He slapped the palm of his hand to his forehead. "And here I promised to get Cinderella home before the clock struck midnight."

"Well, it's certainly not your fault, but…I'd better go. I really can't miss this meeting. I'm sorry, Joel," she said, looking at the half-eaten sandwich on his plate. "I'd be glad to call a cab so you can at least finish your lunch."

He waved off her offer. "No…no, I've had all I want. Don't worry about it." He motioned the waiter over and explained their situation. He left enough cash on the table to cover the tab and tip, then ushered Melanie quickly back through the restaurant and out to the car.

"If we hit the lights right all the way through town, you should be okay," he said, checking his watch again.

"It'll be fine. Thank you for lunch. I really enjoyed it. I wish we hadn't had to rush."

"Me, too. Would…would you like to have dinner some evening?"

She tried not to let her surprise show on her face. "I'd like that." Surely he could hear her heart thumping.

"Saturday night? This Saturday… Is that too short of notice?"

"No…no, that'd be fine."

"Will seven o'clock work for you?"

"I think so…as long as I can find a sitter."

"I understand. How about if I call you Saturday morning just to make sure it's still going to work."

"Okay."

They rode in comfortable silence the rest of the way, and five minutes later, Joel dropped her off in front of By Design.

"Thanks again, Joel."

"Thank *you*." He patted the folder of drawings tucked on the dashboard. "These are wonderful."

She waved away his praise.

"I'll talk to you Saturday, then?"

"Okay." She stood in the parking lot and watched as he drove away.

The prospect of dinner with Joel Ellington sent a shiver of—something—up her spine.

What had she gotten herself into?

Seven

Saturday afternoon as Melanie drove to pick Jerica up from a play date at Ami Dixon's house, she found herself caught in a strange tug-of-war between anticipation and dread. Joel had called this morning and their date was on. Since Jeff Franzen, she had stopped entertaining the idea of another man in her life. With the responsibilities of the design firm—and with Jerica to think of—she hadn't been willing to waste her free evenings with someone who was certain not to measure up to Rick.

Now she was almost afraid to admit that Joel Ellington seemed different. She couldn't quite put her finger on what it was about the man that had so quickly foiled her determination to stay uninvolved, but even as she felt anxiety about tonight, there was a sense of anticipation, too.

She pulled into the Dixons' drive and rang the bell. Mike Dixon answered the door. "Hi, Melanie. Come on in."

She stepped into the foyer.

"Are you sure we can't keep Jerica for a few days?" Ami's father asked.

"You've got to be kidding."

Mike laughed. "Seriously, she was an angel. Karen said the girls didn't have one argument. She hardly knew they were here."

"Are we talking about the same Jerica?"

"And the same Ami."

"Well, wonders never cease." Melanie heard a clatter on the staircase, and as if on cue, the two little girls appeared on the landing.

"Do I have to go home now, Mommy?" Jerica asked, peering over the stair rail into the foyer.

"Afraid so, punkin. Get your coat, though. It's chilly out there." Mike reached into the closet and handed Melanie the jacket. She held one sleeve open, waiting for Jerica to slip into it. "Did little Brendon survive the day?" she asked Mike.

"I think they wore him out. Karen's thrilled. She's putting him down for a nap now."

"Wanna go see him, Mommy?" Jerica piped.

"I saw him this morning, sweetie...remember? We don't want to wake him up. Besides, we need to get home. What do you tell Mr. Dixon?"

"Thank you," Jerica singsonged dutifully as they started out the door.

Melanie turned to Mike. "Thanks so much for having her over. We'll have to invite Ami over sometime soon."

"Tonight, Mommy? Can Ami spend the night tonight? Please?" Jerica bounced on spindly knees in front of her.

"Oh, honey. I'm sorry, but it's not going to work tonight. Mommy has—"

A sharp bark split the air, and a large yellow Labrador retriever came bounding around the side of the Dixons' house and up onto the porch. Jerica let out a blood curdling scream and clawed frantically at Melanie, trying to climb her like a tree.

"Jerica! Stop it." She tried to pick her daughter up, but with her arms flailing, it was like trying to hold an octopus.

"Butch! Down, boy. Down." Mike snapped his fingers and grabbed the dog's collar. "He won't hurt you, honey," he spoke soothingly to Jerica. "Butch is a nice doggy. He just wants to play."

His assurances were drowned out by the little girl's hysterical screaming.

"I'm sorry," Melanie explained, embarrassed. "For some reason she is just petrified of dogs."

"Hey, I understand," Mike said. "My wife got nipped as a child; she won't admit it, but she has a bit of a dog phobia to this day."

Jerica quit screaming, but she buried her face on Melanie's shoulder. "I'm sorry," she told Mike over Jerica's head. "I sure hope she outgrows this before she gets too big to carry. Hey, thanks again for having her over to play." She looked down at Ami. "You'll have to come and play at our house soon, okay?"

Ami had knelt to hug Butch. She nodded shyly, acknowledging Melanie's words, but her eyes were fixed on Jerica.

Melanie carried Jerica to the car and helped buckle her seat belt in the back. For as long as Melanie could remember, Jerica had had an irrational fear of dogs. As far as anyone knew, Jerica had never been bitten or attacked. The only dog she tolerated was Erika's little Biscuit. And even that was a tentative alliance. She thought about what Mike had said about Karen Dixon. She hoped Jerica's phobia wouldn't last into adulthood.

Jerica was silent as they backed out of the Dixons' driveway and headed down the street. Melanie watched her in the rearview mirror. Jerica seemed composed now, gazing out the window—probably feeling grateful for every block that separated her from Butch.

When they pulled onto the highway, Jerica leaned forward and tapped her on the shoulder. "Mommy?"

"Yes, sweetheart?"

"Can we get a baby too? Like Ami?"

Melanie took a deep breath. "Oh, honey. I... I'd love for you to have a little brother or sister someday, but..." She let her voice trail off. How did one explain this to a five-year-old?

"Hows come I don't have a daddy like Ami does?"

Melanie checked the traffic, then turned in her seat to meet Jerica's questioning gaze. The longing etched on her sweet features broke Melanie's heart. She would rather face a thousand ferocious dogs than this. They'd had this conversation before, especially since the birth of Ami's baby brother, but Jerica seemed to need to hear it over and over.

Melanie turned her eyes back on the road and answered carefully. "Honey…you know the answer to that. Your daddy died when you were just a tiny baby."

"Like Brendon?"

"Yes, but you were even tinier than Brendon."

"But I don't remember my daddy."

Oh, help me, Lord. Help me say what she needs to hear. "I know, honey," she sighed. "Tiny babies don't have very many memories. But *I* remember. Oh, your daddy loved you so much. He would hold you in his arms for hours…and he talked to you and made up funny little songs for you. He could make you smile faster than anybody else. Oh, Jerica… You had the best daddy in the world."

"Could I get another daddy…someday?"

"I…I don't know, honey. Only God knows that. Hey, you know what?" she said with false brightness. "I have a surprise for you. Guess who's babysitting tonight?"

"Kimmy?" Jerica said, a smile in her voice.

"Yes. Kimmy." Melanie stifled a sigh of relief. How quickly moping could turn to glee. "We're going to go pick her up right after we drive through McDonald's for a Happy Meal."

Ah, bribery will get you everywhere, she thought ten minutes later, as Jerica munched contentedly on chicken nuggets and soggy fries. By the time they pulled into the driveway with Kimmy Breyer in tow, the two girls in the backseat were singing together at the top of their lungs.

Jerica managed to hoodwink the teen into playing Candy Land with her, while Melanie went back to her bedroom to change clothes. Melanie had always known that she would have to explain Rick's death to her daughter someday, but she hadn't counted on having to answer the same difficult questions over and over again. She ached anew every time she saw the pain in her daughter's eyes as Jerica watched her little friends with their daddies or with their brothers and sisters. Jerry and Erika went out of their way to keep Rick's memory alive for their granddaughter. *And for me,* Melanie thought. But a memory, no matter how vivid, could not sing songs or play catch or pass out good-night kisses.

Standing in front of her closet, trying to decide what to wear, Melanie's gaze fell on the row of shirts at the far end of the closet. Oh, how it hurt that Rick wasn't here to share in raising their daughter. She fingered the sleeve of a pale blue oxford shirt. It hung there with the others, as though ready for him to come, fresh from the shower, and put it on. Some of his shirts still had the paper slips from the cleaners pinned to them, others were fastened to the hanger by just one button—an indication that Rick had worn them only a few hours and deemed them still wearable. Melanie knew exactly which ones still held the faintest scent of his cologne. They hung there now, accusing her.

She pressed her fingertips firmly against her eyelids to stave off the tears. She didn't have time to redo her makeup. *Come on, LaSalle...think about something else. You've got a hot date tonight, remember.*

She closed the closet doors with a sigh and finished dressing. After she touched up her hair, she went to peek into her daughter's room. Jerica and Kimmy were still bent over the Candy Land game. Jerica's gingerbread man had already traversed Gumdrop Pass, while Kimmy's marker sat in the Molasses Swamp. Melanie heard the sitter patiently trying to explain the rules, while Jerica insisted sweetly that she already knew the rules.

They both looked up as Melanie came into the room. "You look pretty, Mommy."

"You do look nice, Mrs. LaSalle," Kimmy echoed.

"Well, thank you, girls," she said, pleased with their assessment.

The doorbell chimed. Feeling as nervous as a teenager on prom night, Melanie went to answer it.

Eight

Joel stood on the porch, looking as handsome in chinos and sweater as he ever did in his Sunday suit coat and tie. He was freshly shaven, his hair still damp, and as he stepped closer, Melanie caught a heavenly whiff of aftershave. "Hello, Melanie. I hope I'm not too early…"

"Hi, Joel. Not at all. Come on in. Let me just tell Jerica and the sitter good-bye, and I'll be ready to go."

She went back down the hall and stuck her head into her daughter's room. "I'm leaving now, Jerica. You be a good girl for Kimmy, okay? Kimmy, my cell phone number is on the desk in the dining room. Jerica can show you how to use speed dial if you need anything."

"Okay. See you later, Mrs. LaSalle."

"Bye-bye, Mommy." Jerica scarcely looked up from the game. She gave a halfhearted wave and went back to moving her gingerbread man along the brightly colored spaces on the board. Confident that her daughter was in for a pleasant evening, Melanie fended off the tiny nudge of guilt she always felt when she left her daughter with a sitter, and took a deep breath before joining Joel in the foyer.

"All set," she told him, picking up her purse and jacket from the hall table.

Outside, he opened the passenger door of his Taurus for her, and she slid into the seat. As he backed out of the drive, he glanced up through the windshield, taking in the view of her house. "Nice place you have."

"Thank you." The tidy Tudor cottage stood proudly on a landscaped hill, and Melanie was happy to accept the compliment. "Dana Landon helped us find it. Landon Realty… I gave you her card," she reminded.

"Oh, sure." Joel nodded.

"We really do love the house. Not too much yard to mow, but plenty of room for Jerica to play. Mostly I love the neighborhood. We know everybody, and I never worry about Jerica playing outside."

"And don't tell me," Joel said, "I bet you never lock your doors."

She smiled, remembering how she'd teased him about being a city boy. "Well, we do lock ourselves in at night, but if I just run to the grocery store or go for a walk…nope."

"I still can't get over that."

"A little different than where you come from, huh?"

"A lot different than where I come from. Where do you want to eat?"

"Oh…well…do you like Mexican food?"

"Love it," he said, patting his belly.

"How about Pedro's?"

"Sounds good to me. Just tell me how to get there."

She navigated for him, and within minutes they parked in front of the popular restaurant on the south edge of town.

They were greeted by a perky Britney Spears wannabe. "How many tonight?"

"Two, please," Joel told her.

"Name, please?"

"Um…LaSalle," Joel said, spelling the name for her.

Melanie thought it a bit odd that he'd given her name instead of his own, but her curiosity was squelched when a waiter bearing menus approached the hostess's stand. He led them to a cozy corner booth, and soon they were snacking on chips and salsa. Raucous music scratched from the speakers overhead, and the flickering candles in the otherwise dark room made her feel bold before him.

"So, Mr. Ellington, do you always work this fast when you move to a new town?" She laughed lightly, but she was only partly joking. He'd been in Silver Creek less than a month, and he'd certainly wasted no time in asking her for a date.

He opened his mouth, but the words seemed to stick there. Her face grew warm at the realization that perhaps Joel didn't see this evening as a date at all.

But after a minute he looked at her, and she caught a spark of mischief in his green eyes. "Melanie, would you believe me if I told you that I have not had a date in almost two years?"

She wasn't sure how to answer, but—relieved that he did indeed count this as a date—she opted to stay with the teasing tone. "I'm not sure I buy that," she said. "The words 'Would you like to have dinner with me?' tripped just a little too easily off your tongue."

A slow grin curved the corners of his mouth. "That's because I rehearsed about fifty times before I asked you."

"Really? You rehearsed?"

"I told you…I'm seriously out of practice."

"Then why me?" she risked.

"Why did I ask you out?" He seemed taken aback by her question. She nodded.

"Hmmm…" He rested a hand on his chin. "Well, let's see… You were easy to talk to. I liked what you said in Mike's class that Sunday—about grief."

Melanie struggled to think what she'd said.

"It surprised me to hear you make light of your grief," he said. "Even though you're right—everyone will experience grief at some point in their life. But I knew that you…that you'd lost your husband. That's a pretty big one."

"It's been four years, Joel. I've worked through a lot. I don't see any reason to pout about something I can't change. And I'm *not* the only one who's known pain. I…I guess I've tried to move on…" She pushed away the sudden vision of her closet, bulging with her dead husband's shirts.

"That's good. I'm glad," Joel said.

"I still have my moments—pity parties, my brother calls them—but they're fewer and much farther between now. Time really does heal all wounds," she said.

"No. I'm not sure I believe that." There was a hard edge to his voice.

His abruptness startled her. "You…you know something about those wounds."

He shrugged. "Yes."

"Do you want to talk about it?"

He shook his head. "Not first date material." Words that hinted at heartache, but he smiled when he said them.

The waitress came to refill their drinks, and they fell silent. But the silence didn't feel so uncomfortable now.

Absently, he ran a tapered finger over the scar on his cheek.

When the waitress left, Melanie traced a finger along her own cheek in the same spot where Joel's finger still rested lightly on his scar. "Mind if I ask what happened?"

"Also not first date material."

"Oh?" She might have been stung by the rebuff, but he brought his hand from his face and put it lightly over hers across the table. He gave her a smile that melted her heart. "So how about a second date?"

"Bet you didn't rehearse that one," she said, smiling.

"Is that a yes?"

"Okay," she said simply.

⁓

Joel awoke on the morning of March 15 to the ringing of the telephone. He groped at the phone on the nightstand, clearing his throat. "Yes? Hello."

"Hey, little brother! Happy birthday!"

"Tim. Good morning. You forget I'm an hour behind you these days." He sat up on the side of the bed and squinted at the clock radio: 6:00 A.M. "Hey, it's early even for you. What's up?"

"Nothing much," his brother said. "I've got a long day of meetings at the central office. I was afraid it might be too late to call when I got in tonight. Just didn't want you to think I forgot."

"Forgot?"

"Your birthday. Did *you* forget?"

Joel gave a humorless laugh. "I'm just not awake yet, I guess. Thanks, man. I appreciate that."

"Everything going okay out there?"

"Yeah, everything's going good. Really good, I think."

"I'm glad. You let me know if you need anything, okay?"

"I will. Thanks again, Tim…for calling."

"Well, I knew you couldn't exactly celebrate today, but I…I didn't want you to think nobody remembered."

"That means a lot, man." The lump that lodged in his throat embarrassed him. He ran a hand through his hair. "You have a good day."

"Yeah. You, too."

He hung up the phone, turned off the alarm clock, and staggered into the bathroom. This was always a tough day. His birthday. Not the one that was on his driver's license or his résumé or his social security card. But the anniversary of the day he was born, nevertheless. He'd learned to blow out the candles and eat the cakes that came his way every tenth of May, but both dates were ones he'd just as soon see stricken from the calendar. He couldn't celebrate either without some guilt.

It seemed that a part of his true self died a little bit every time he perpetuated the deception. And though he had little choice in the matter, he hated the lies his circumstances compelled him to sustain. He hated them with everything that was in him.

◯

A second date turned into a third and then a fourth and fifth, and by the end of April it seemed to Melanie as though Joel had always been a part of her life.

One evening as they drove home from a concert in St. Louis, Joel asked, "What was your marriage like, Mel?"

She looked over at him, surprised that he'd brought up the subject. "Well…we were only married two and a half years before Rick got sick. And then he died a year later. But we had a happy marriage. Very happy, I'd say. It was sometimes hard living so close to his parents—working with Jerry and all… That was what we argued about when we argued. But we always worked things out. And I think Jerry and Erika kind of backed off after the first year. I don't know if Rick talked to them or if they just figured it out themselves, but things were much better toward the end. And then, when he got sick—and especially after he died—I was grateful to have his parents nearby."

Joel reached across the seat and captured her hand. She felt sympathy and understanding in his touch, and she went on, "Sometimes—after he was gone, when Jerica was still tiny—I felt so utterly alone. I just didn't see how I could raise her on my own. It seemed impossible."

"You've done a beautiful job."

She gave him a grateful smile. "The truth is, I haven't had to do it alone. The Lord has been with me every step of the way, and he's filled our lives with wonderful people. It's been amazing really—" She stopped abruptly, and swallowed the lump in her throat.

She'd never shared her feelings about Rick so openly with Joel before. It felt a little strange…talking to him about the man she'd loved, the man whose child she'd borne. Now, watching his profile in the intermittent light from passing cars, her heart overflowed with an emotion that felt achingly familiar. She'd almost forgotten. This was how she'd felt when she looked at Rick. Could she already be in love with this man she'd known for such a short time? Or was it just that he somehow seemed to understand the grief she'd faced in her life? She didn't want to make the same mistake she'd made with Jeff Franzen. But she was certain she'd never felt this way about Jeff.

Joel turned to her, concern on his face. "Are you okay?"

She nodded and squeezed his hand, her throat full. "You talk for a while. I've been doing all the talking."

"No, please. I want to hear it—all of it."

"Are you always such a great listener, Mr. Ellington? I feel like you know exactly what I'm talking about."

He didn't answer right way. Then, with a sigh, as though he'd suddenly made a decision, he said, "I do understand a little, Melanie, because of...because of what I've been through myself."

She waited, and when he remained silent, she said, "Tell me about your family, Joel. Please. You hardly ever talk about yourself."

He waved her off. "There's not much to tell."

"Tell me about your parents. It must have been hard to lose them."

He hesitated, as though deciding how much to say. Finally, he looked away, and his voice grew quiet. "I was eighteen when Mom and Dad were killed. Tim, my brother, was away at college, but I was still living at home. It was my senior year in high school." He recited the facts as though he were detached from them.

She put a hand to her mouth. "Oh, Joel! I had no idea they died while you were still at home...still so young. I'm so sorry." Why hadn't he mentioned before how young he'd been when he lost his parents? Surely this had been one of the defining events of his life.

Letting go of her hand, he gripped the steering wheel. He gave her a sidelong glance, then turned his eyes back to the road and began to talk. It was as though an ice floe had melted in the spring thaw and now the icy river waters underneath—the stories of his past—gushed forth unrestrained.

"They were flying home from Africa...coming back from a

short-term missions trip," he told her. "It was something they did every year for as long as I can remember. Sometimes they went to the Philippines, but usually it was somewhere in Africa. But they…they always came back. I just took it for granted that they'd always be back. Even after all this time, I still sometimes can't believe it happened," he said, his voice low. "It never crossed my mind to worry that they wouldn't return. Tim told me once that he did worry…that every time they left, he was terrified they'd never come home again."

Joel shook his head and gave a small laugh that was incongruous with the anger that had crept into his voice. "I don't know which was worse: Tim's worst fears coming true or my incredible shock because I never once gave it a thought."

"That must have been terrible, Joel. Were you just…on your own after that? I mean, did you stay in your home or…?"

"Tim quit school and came back home. The term was almost up, and I was headed off to college the next year, but it…it was never the same. Home, I mean."

"Oh, I'm sure it wasn't. It must have been awful."

"It wasn't easy. We sold the house a couple years later. Neither one of us could stand to be in it without Mom and Dad there."

"Oh, Joel…I'm so sorry. Tell me about your parents," Melanie said gently, attempting to coax happier memories. "What were they like?"

"Dad was more serious—our solid rock—the glue that held us all together. My mom was…comic relief." His laugh was warm with remembrance. "She was always teasing and playing jokes on us. She never failed to get us on April Fools' Day. Tim and I would try to outwit her, and every year she beat us to it. She'd freeze plastic bugs in our ice cubes, put salt in the sugar bowl—once she put our underwear in the freezer overnight—anything to get a laugh out of us."

When Joel turned to Melanie, there was a faraway look in his eyes, but a soft smile painted his face. "You would have liked her, Melanie. She was a lot like you in some ways. She had a sense of humor like yours. But she could be moody, too."

Melanie wrinkled her nose at him. "Are you saying I'm moody?"

"You are."

"What? I'm not moody!"

"Yes, you are," he declared.

"Joel Ellington, I am *not* moody. When have I *ever* been moody?"

"Trust me," he said. "You are very moody. In fact, I think you might possibly be the moodiest woman I've ever known."

She stared at him, mouth agape. "Define *moody,*" she said finally.

"Subject to being in moods," he deadpanned.

"As in *bad* moods?"

He gave a little laugh now and leaned forward, looking pointedly out the windshield. "Isn't that the most beautiful sky? Just look at all those stars."

"It's foggy, Joel. There is not one star in that sky. And quit trying to change the subject."

"Whoo," he whistled under his breath. "If I didn't know better, I'd think you were all of a sudden in a mood."

She turned defiantly toward him, ready to give him a piece of her mind. One look at his Cheshire-cat grin told her she'd been had.

She gave a little growl of frustration. "I think Joel Ellington took after his mother," she said, slugging his arm playfully.

He made her laugh, and it was wonderful to laugh with Joel. But she realized with dismay that she had effectively dammed the river of communication. The moment passed, and Joel shared no more about his family or his past.

But when he walked her to the door, he took her face in his hands and stroked her cheekbones gently with his thumbs, studying her face with a light in his eyes that made her feel like the most beautiful woman in the world. She trembled a little beneath the warmth of his touch. And when he leaned to place his lips softly upon hers, nothing else mattered then but the joy of that moment.

Nine

Joel pushed away from the table and rubbed his belly. "I've eaten some fine lasagna in my day, Ms. LaSalle, but that was some of the finest."

"Hey! I helped too," Jerica pouted from her place across the table.

"You, too, Little Miss LaSalle. It was delicious."

Jerica beamed, and Melanie said, "Well, thank you, Mr. Ellington, but I hope you saved room."

"That depends. For what?"

Melanie scooted her chair away from the table and arched a brow. "You'll see. Sit right there. Come help me, Jerica." She took their empty plates, and Jerica skipped after her into the kitchen. He could hear them whispering and rummaging around in the cupboards, and soon the sulfurous odor of a lit match wafted under his nose. "What are you two up to in there?" he hollered.

"Okay, close your eyes, Joel," Jerica shouted from the doorway of the kitchen.

He complied, wondering what in the world these two had up their sleeves.

"Now don't peek," Melanie warned. He felt her brush against him, then a rush of heat and the smell of burnt sugar assailed him.

They must have cooked up a Cherries Jubilee or Bananas Foster or whatever those flaming desserts they always served in restaurants were called.

"Okay," Jerica singsonged. "You can look now."

He opened his eyes, and his heartbeat faltered. On the table in front of him, a two-layer birthday cake blazed with candles. Melanie and Jerica burst into the "Happy Birthday" chorus.

A flush of shame washed over him. "How…how did you know?" he stuttered, when the last note died out.

"It was in the church newsletter, silly," Melanie said. "I can't believe you went through the whole meal without saying something. You didn't think we'd just let your birthday go by, did you?"

Joel didn't know what to say.

"Joel?" She eyed him, her forehead creased with astonishment. "Did you forget your own birthday?"

"I…guess I did," he said, forcing a smile. That much at least was true. "You guys are something else. Thank you."

"Blow out the candles!" Jerica begged.

"There're too many! You help me, okay?" he said, pulling her up to sit on his knee. "Be careful now." He scooted her close to him and brushed a soft strand of hair away from her face. She felt light as a little bird on his lap.

"You'd better hurry," Melanie laughed, "before the whole cake goes up in flames."

"Wait!" Jerica turned to him, her face serious. "You have to make a wish first."

He closed his eyes and swallowed the lump in his throat. *Oh, Lord Jesus, let me be worthy of their love.* He opened his eyes and counted. "One, two, three." Together they blew, and finally the last candle was extinguished.

Jerica bounced on his lap. "What did you wish? What did you wish?"

"Huh-uh," Melanie scolded, shaking her finger. "He can't tell us, or it won't come true."

Melanie went to the sideboard and brought out a package from behind a vase of fresh flowers. She set it in front of Joel.

He looked up at her, his heart so full he was afraid he would weep. "For me?"

"You're the birthday boy, aren't you?"

Again, guilt pierced him.

"Open it! Open it!" Jerica sang.

"Okay." He shook the box gently. "Do you know what's in here?" he asked Jerica.

She shook her head, eyes wide.

Slipping off the shiny ribbon, he carefully peeled the tape from one end of the silver paper.

"Oh, good grief," Melanie laughed. "You are worse than any woman. Just *open* it!"

Laughing, he ripped the gift-wrap and held out the package for Jerica to finish the job. Inside the box, nestled in white tissue paper, was a set of wind chimes fashioned with a pinecone motif. He held them up, and Jerica batted at them gently. They sounded a lovely and haunting melody.

"I hope your neighbors won't mind," Melanie said, "But I remember you said you'd always liked wind chimes."

He didn't recall when he had told her that, but it was true, and he was touched that she remembered. "Thank you, Melanie."

Jerica gave him a special birthday card she'd made herself. Joel hid a smile as he opened the envelope. The card must have contained half a pound of glitter and nearly that much Elmer's glue.

Melanie sent all but two small slices of the birthday cake home with him. He drove back to his apartment with a car full of goodies and a heart overflowing with love.

For the first time, the tenth of May seemed like a day he could truly celebrate.

∾

The July sun beat down on the dusty baseball diamond, and the sweaty little girls in the outfield shaded their eyes against its glare.

"Go, Comets!" Melanie yelled from the bleachers. "Get ready, Jerica! Batter's up."

From her spot in left field, Jerica brushed off her mother's words with a wave of her glove.

Sitting beside Melanie in the stands, Joel shouted, "Back up a little, Jer. This one's a slugger, remember?"

Jerica flashed him an ear-to-ear grin and promptly took three steps backward.

"Oh, brother!" Melanie rolled her eyes in Joel's direction. In truth, she was thrilled that Jerica was so obviously proud to have Joel there watching her play.

A ponytailed batter stepped up to the tee and wound up the miniature bat as though this were the majors. She took one mighty swing, and the ball sailed over the third baseman's head straight toward Jerica.

Joel leapt from the stands and started yelling. "Catch it, Jerica! You got it, babe. Get under it! Get under it!"

The ball dropped in front of the droopy glove and bounced out of reach. By the time Jerica chased the ball down and got it back to the pitcher, the home-run batter was exchanging high-fives with the rest of her team in the dugout.

The game went downhill from there, and it was a dejected five-year-old who climbed into the backseat of Joel's car at the end of the afternoon.

Joel helped Jerica with her seat belt, then knelt by the open door. "Hey, sport, tough luck, huh?"

"I stink," she pouted, arms folded tightly in front of her.

"Hey, I don't want to hear you talk like that," he told her firmly. He tipped her chin, forcing her to look at him. "You did your best.

You weren't the only one who made mistakes out there. Tonight just wasn't the Comets' night. Besides, that team you played was really good. I'd be willing to bet they haven't lost a game all season."

From her perch in the front passenger seat, Melanie watched the exchange with a full heart. Joel was so tender and wise with Jerica. When she'd been dating Jeff Franzen, she had sometimes resented Jeff's attempts to have a hand in Jerica's nurturing or discipline. But Joel's interest in Jerica seemed natural, seemed to spring from true love and affection, not from a sense of obligation or an effort to impress Melanie with what a good father he would be.

Now he tousled the little girl's sweat-damp hair. "You okay?"

Jerica nodded, tears threatening.

"Come on, babe. Let me see a smile." He blew a kiss her way and waited for the halfhearted giggle that followed.

Joel chucked her under the chin, carefully shut the door, and walked around to the driver's side. "Anybody feel like ice cream?"

Those magic words brought Jerica out of her doldrums in an instant. "Yeah! Chocolate chip!"

"Mmm, orange sherbet here," Melanie chimed, giving Joel a grateful smile. "A double dip."

As they headed for Baskin-Robbins, Jerica leaned forward in her seat. "Mommy, I need a rubber band. My ponytail holder broke, and my hair is hot on my neck."

Melanie searched her purse without success. "Sorry, honey. I don't have anything with me. Where's your hair ribbon? Maybe we can get your hair up off your neck with that."

"I lost it…at the game."

Melanie turned in her seat to look at her daughter. "Sorry. We'll be home soon…"

"Hey, Joel?" Jerica pointed to the braided cord that swung from the rearview mirror. "Can I use your ribbon?"

Melanie hadn't asked Joel about the cord since the first night he'd sidestepped her questions, and neither had he volunteered any information. She was curious and waited with interest to see what his response would be.

He fingered the cord, keeping his eyes on the road ahead. "Sorry, Jerica, but this is kind of special to me. Maybe they'll loan us a rubber band at the ice cream store."

"Just what *is* so special about this mysterious red ribbon?" Melanie ventured after Jerica was occupied again, singing to herself in the backseat. "You said it reminds you of a Bible verse?"

He nodded, avoiding her gaze. "It... It's just a Scripture passage that has been a comfort to me."

"Oh?"

His silence was deafening.

"Any chance you're going to let me in on this secret verse?" she pressed, attempting a light tone.

He reached over and patted her knee. "I'll tell you someday, I promise." He met her gaze, but his smile didn't quite reach his eyes, and somewhere in the back of her mind a tiny alarm went off.

∼

After Jerica had been tucked into bed, Melanie and Joel sat on the deck in her backyard, sipping iced tea and watching a hundred fireflies flicker in the branches of the mimosa trees. Two citronella candles gave off a pungent scent that kept the mosquitoes at bay.

Melanie kicked off her sandals, leaned back in her chair, and propped her suntanned legs on the umbrella table. "Thanks for cheering Jerica up, Joel," she ventured. "I never dreamed preschool sports could be so cutthroat."

"She'll get thicker skin after a while. It's a good lesson, though: You can't always be a winner."

"I'm afraid she hasn't been allowed to lose very often. Between Erika and Jerry and me, she's always gotten just about everything she ever wanted."

"She's a great kid, Melanie. And you're a good mom. I don't think she's spoiled rotten. Just…loved an awful lot."

"None of us really mean to spoil her, but…well, I guess we're all trying to make up for the fact that she doesn't have a daddy. Jerry's great with her, but he dotes on her a little too much. I wish my dad and my brother lived closer. Matt is such a great dad to his two little guys. And Jerica adores him. I wish you could meet him, Joel."

"I'm sure I will someday."

"You know, I was thinking…maybe sometime…when I have business in New York, you could fly out with me. You could meet Matt and Karly and maybe even drive up to Connecticut to see Tim—" She stopped short, afraid her suggestion might seem too forward.

"Maybe…"

The silence that followed was not the comfortable quietude they'd come to enjoy with each other. Joel shifted in his seat and fidgeted with the edge of the table. Melanie mentally kicked herself for bringing up the idea of a trip to New York. But Joel's next words surprised her.

"My memories of…of back home aren't the greatest, Melanie."

"You mean because of your parents?"

"Not just that…"

"Oh? What else?" She'd learned not to push him, but hope bounded in her heart because he finally seemed on the verge of opening up to her.

"I just… I don't like to dwell on the past. I'm happy now. I'd rather concentrate on that."

"But Tim's there. Don't you ever go visit him?"

"I have," he hedged. "But usually he comes to see me. He travels quite a bit anyway."

"I'm so anxious for you to meet Matt and Karly. And their kids." She put a hand on his arm. "You know, they say the best way to erase bad memories of a place is to create new memories there. Maybe—"

"Maybe sometime, Mel…" Joel shook his head. "Just not…not right now." A hard edge had come to his voice.

"Do you…want to talk about it?"

"Maybe sometime," he said again.

He seemed glum, and she was ready to apologize for pushing him when Joel reached for her hand across the table. "Tell me about Rick, Melanie."

Relief washed over her. Maybe this was why he'd seemed so quiet and evasive. Thinking about the husband. She could imagine how that must feel. If Joel had been married before, she would have worried that he was making comparisons. Most dead spouses had been nominated for sainthood. She tried to read Joel's expression in the semidarkness. "Dead husbands aren't exactly the topic of choice when you're trying to fall in love with someone else."

"Are you?" he asked, raising an eyebrow, his gaze piercing her. "Trying to fall in love with me?" His tone held a trace of—was it hope?

Until now, she'd been afraid to let him know just how deep her feelings for him ran. But seeing him with Jerica today, something had given way inside her, and she could no longer think of a reason to hold back.

"I didn't have to try too hard, Joel. You make it pretty easy…"

He scooted his chair closer to hers so their shoulders were touching. His hand found hers again, and he brought it to his lips and kissed the soft skin on her knuckles. The air had cooled a bit, and all around them cicadas chirred a happy melody.

"So what exactly are you trying to say, Ms. LaSalle?" She heard the amusement in his voice, but he brushed his thumb roughly over her fingers.

"I'm not *trying* to say anything. I *am* saying it." Her voice quavered. "I…I think I'm in love with you, Joel. There, it's out. Are you happy now?"

He leaned forward in his chair and squeezed her hand, planting a kiss in her hair. "You have no idea, lady," he whispered. "No idea at all." He took a ragged breath and untangled his fingers from hers. Brushing her hair off her face, he kissed her tenderly, then drew back to gaze into her eyes. "I love you too, Melanie. More than you can possibly know."

Her heart soared. She hadn't realized until now how she had longed for them to exchange these words, how she longed to be the reason for his happiness.

Joel stayed late, and they talked for hours.

"Do you ever wonder why God allowed things to happen the way they did...in your life?" Joel asked, looking up toward the cream-colored moon that had risen over the trees.

"All the time. Sometimes none of it makes sense...Rick dying when I—when *we* needed him so much. I used to wonder why God allowed me to get pregnant when he knew I wouldn't have Rick to help me raise Jerica. We weren't even trying to have a baby. But I look at Jerica and think how much it helped me to have her then. And how precious she is to Jerry and Erika—the only connection they have to their only child—and I realize all over again that God knows what he's doing."

"I had the same thoughts when Mom and Dad died. I don't suppose I'll ever know what God's purpose in that was, but I do know that some good came from that horrible time in my life."

She tilted her head and looked up at him. "Like what?"

"Well, for one thing, I can empathize with people who are going through similar tragedies...because I've been there. There was a kid in one of my classes at Langston who lost his dad his freshman year. It was hard to watch, because it brought back everything that had happened to me, but I was looking at it with a few years' perspective behind me, and I really think I had something to say to Seth that nobody else could. Very few others could honestly tell him, 'I know exactly what you're feeling.'"

"That's so true," Melanie said. "I'm sure he'll never forget that either. Do you still keep in touch with him?"

Joel shook his head and looked away. "No. That happened the first year I was at Langston. But…there were other kids like Seth through the years."

"Sounds like you were as much counselor as you were teacher."

"Sometimes. My department head always told me that would get me in trouble one day. But Barbara didn't practice what she preached." He laughed softly. "She always had a string of kids in her own office pouring out their hearts to her too."

"I wish I'd had a confidante like that when I went away to college."

"Yeah. Me, too."

Melanie wanted the evening to last forever. She felt honored that he had chosen to tell her the stories of his past that he'd shared tonight. And yet there was still so much she didn't know, so many missing pieces of the life he'd led before she met him. She wanted to spend a lifetime getting to know him.

Later, when Joel took her face in his warm hands and caressed her cheek with such exquisite tenderness, when his kiss eagerly claimed her lips, the promise of all that lay in store for them filled her to overflowing. She realized that she hadn't known such happiness since she had loved Rick—and been loved by him.

After Joel left, Melanie shut the door behind him and stood with her back against the door frame. She closed her eyes and pressed her fingers to her lips as though she could somehow preserve his kiss. A warm flush of happiness washed over her, and she smiled to herself. Finally, with a little sigh, she went down the hall to check on her daughter.

Jerica had thrown off her covers and was sprawled on her back, arms over her head, her breath coming so gently it was almost unde-tectable. *Oh, to know such peace and security,* Melanie thought, brushing her hand over the cherubic cheek. She swallowed the lump of joy in her throat and pulled a light blanket up over the slight form.

She closed Jerica's door and walked through the house, turning off lights and checking the locks. Then she went to the bathroom off the master bedroom to take a quick shower. She slipped into a nightshirt and robe, ran a brush through her hair, and flipped off the bathroom light. Going to her closet, she hung her robe on a hook. But as she turned to close the door, the faint scent of Rick LaSalle seemed to waft from the shirts that hung at the far end of the closet. A veil of bittersweet longing fell over her.

She sighed. It was time.

Before she could change her mind, she gathered Rick's shirts into an unwieldy bundle and pulled them off the rod. Flopping them across the foot of the bed, she took them from their hangers one by one, fingering each sleeve and carefully folding each shirt into a neat rectangle, the way Rick had folded them when he was packing for a business trip. The act seemed almost sacred, and her tears came easily.

"I loved you, Rick," she whispered, stopping to bring a shirt to her face one last time. "Oh, how I loved you, darling. But I have to move on. It's time for me to let you go." For a moment the pain was as raw as the night he had died. But she knew she was only doing what she should have done long ago. She allowed herself a good cry then. It hurt to say such a final good-bye. But she slept under a blanket of peace that night and awoke to the sound of a mourning dove's familiar, plaintive cooing in the tree outside her window.

Ten

Joel leaned back in his chair, propped his feet on top of his desk, and leafed through the notes he'd scratched out on a yellow legal pad. Pastor Steele was surprising his wife with a weekend getaway, and he'd asked Joel to preach the sermon Sunday in his place. Don had begun a series on the psalms, and Joel accepted the assignment with enthusiasm. But that was before he'd read the Scripture passage Don Steele wanted him to highlight: Psalm 101. Now, two pages into his first draft, Joel was stumped. He wasn't sure he could look his congregation in the eye and preach on these verses. He reached for his Bible and read the words again: *I will behave myself wisely in a perfect way.... I will walk within my house with a perfect heart.* His eyes traveled down the page, each verse piercing deeper. *He that worketh deceit shall not dwell within my house: he that telleth lies shall not tarry in my sight.* Joel rubbed his eyes with his fists, suddenly feeling as though the metaphorical log were blurring his vision.

Putting his head in his hands, he whispered, "Lord, how can I deliver a message like this when I am a deceiver above all things... when I am *living* a lie? It doesn't seem right—"

A rap on the door interrupted him. In one smooth motion, he sat upright and put his feet on the floor. "Come in."

The door opened a crack, and Darlene Anthony stuck her head

in. "Sorry to bother you, Joel. Bill Randolph is here to see you…
something about the building fund. Do you have a minute?"

"Sure." He stood and came from behind his desk.

Darlene put up a hand. "I can send him down."

"That's okay. I need a change of scenery anyway. I've been sitting
here too long."

He followed Darlene down the hallway to the front office. Somehow Bill Randolph always seemed to be the bearer of bad news where
the building project was concerned. Joel hoped that wasn't the case
today. A new wing for the youth had been on the church's wish list
for years now, and they'd finally gone through the process of hiring
an architect, but one thing after another had conspired to thwart the
actual construction of the addition. Last week it had been major
problems with the architect's drawings, and the week before that, a
scare about the zoning of the land the addition would occupy.

Joel spotted Bill at the end of the hall. "Thanks, Darlene." Joel
nodded at her as he hurried by to greet the man.

"Morning, Joel." Bill shook his hand. "I hope I'm not catching
you at a bad time."

"Not at all. What's up, Bill?"

"Not bad news this time, I promise. I just need your signature
on a couple of checks."

"That, I can probably handle." He indicated the front office. "We
can use the desk in here…"

Joel bent over the desktop to sign the two checks Bill presented.

"I didn't count on a simple addition being so much trouble," Bill
said. "Did you ever work on anything like this in your last position?"

His pen stopped in midscrawl. As always, Joel found himself
weighing his words carefully. "You mean the building project? No…
This is my first experience with anything like that—and I hope
my last."

"Oh, that's right," Bill said. "I forget you weren't in church work
before you came here. Taught English or something, wasn't it?"

Joel nodded. "Not much experience with architects in that line of work, I'm afraid."

"You know, my daughter teaches English. Used to teach high school, but she just took a job at a junior college in Iowa. Seems to like it a lot. Whatever made you decide to quit teaching and take on a job like this? It sure wasn't the pay."

Joel forced a laugh, then tensed and rubbed the toe of his shoe over an invisible spot on the carpet. "No, I just…needed a change. Say, Bill, have you had a chance to look at those revised blueprints?"

Bill harrumphed and launched into an account of the most recent meeting with the architect. When the older man left fifteen minutes later and Joel headed back down the hall to his office, it struck him anew how ingrained his evasiveness had become. Four years ago it would have been the most natural thing in the world for him to eagerly compare notes with Bill about his daughter's teaching experience and to explain in detail his reasons for changing jobs.

But then four years ago he'd had nothing to hide.

◇

Melanie absently plucked a yellowed leaf from one of the geraniums on her front porch and looked at her watch again. "Do you think his flight was delayed?"

"He'll be here, Mel," Joel said from his seat beside her on the stone step. "Just be patient." But Melanie thought there was more than a twinge of concern in his voice.

"I'm hungry, Mommy," Jerica whined from her perch on the porch railing.

"I know, honey. We'll go eat just as soon as Joel's brother gets here."

Tim's flight was to have arrived in St. Louis at ten o'clock, and he was renting a car and driving to Silver Creek. But it was almost noon now, and Melanie watched Joel's eyes anxiously scan the street beyond her cul-de-sac. She had been rather surprised to find that Joel didn't intend to meet his brother at the airport. But he brushed her off, saying something about Tim wanting to have a car to drive while he was in the area.

The plan was to take Tim to Silver Creek's annual Septemberfest. Melanie was nervous that a city boy like Tim would find the small-town family festival rather boring. But she was encouraged by the fact that Joel had finally invited his brother for a visit. It was a small sign that he was offering her an opportunity to get another glimpse into his life, into his past.

The sound of a car pulling into the cul-de-sac brought Jerica to her feet, clapping. "I bet that's him! I bet it's him!"

The car slowed and pulled into Melanie's driveway. She didn't miss Joel's sigh of relief as he hurried down the walk. Melanie followed at a distance, wanting to give the brothers a chance to have a private reunion. The man who stepped out of the rental car was a taller, blonder version of Joel. The two men greeted each other with a bear hug and wide smiles that Melanie thought still held a hint of the tragedy they'd shared.

With an unexpected lump in her throat, she watched them. After a minute, Joel turned and beckoned her over to where they stood. "Melanie, I'd like you to meet my brother, Tim. Tim, this is Melanie LaSalle."

Tim took her hand. "Hi, Melanie. I've heard so much about you."

"And this is Mel's daughter, Jerica," Joel said.

Tim stooped to Jerica's eye level. "Hello there, Jerica. What a pretty name."

"I got it from my Grammy and Grampa," she told him.

Tim looked up at Melanie, a question in his expression, and she explained to him about Jerry and Erika.

"Well, it's by fah the nicest name I've heard in a lawng time," Tim said.

Jerica looked up at him, wrinkling her button of a nose. "You talk like Joel," she said.

The two brothers laughed, and Tim chucked Jerica under the chin. "Are you in school yet?"

Jerica shook her head, then chewed her lip and studied her shoes intently, suddenly shy.

"She'll start kindergarten next week," Melanie explained.

"Oh, kindergarten is great. You'll love it."

Melanie liked Tim immediately. The soft voice with the heavy accent made her realize how much of his Eastern accent Joel had already lost since moving to the Midwest.

"Did you have trouble finding us?" she asked.

He shook his head. "Drove right to it, no problems at all." Tim looked at Joel as he said it and some unspoken message seemed to pass between them. "This is sure a pretty little town."

Jerica tugged on the hem of Melanie's blouse. "I'm hungry, Mommy," she said in a stage whisper.

"Silver Creek is having its big fall festival this weekend," Melanie explained. "We thought we might hit the food court there for lunch and show you some of the sights of our little city."

"That's what Joel said. Sounds great to me," Tim said.

"Do you want to come in and freshen up first?" Melanie offered.

Tim shook his head, then winked at Jerica. "It sounds like I've kept this little lady waiting long enough. My car will be okay here, won't it?"

"Sure," Melanie nodded.

"Then I'm ready to go whenever you are."

Jerica cheered and raced for Joel's Taurus, which was parked on the other side of Tim's car on the driveway. Fifteen minutes later they were in line at the food pavilion on the festival grounds. Joel ordered hot dogs and Cokes for all of them, and while he and Tim waited for the order, Melanie and Jerica searched out the only empty picnic table in the crowded park. They flagged Joel and Tim down, and Joel squeezed in beside Jerica, helping her unwrap her drinking straw. That done, he started to sort through the wad of change the hot dog vendor had given him.

"Wait a minute," he said, unfolding several bills. "Didn't that sign say hot dogs were a dollar-fifty apiece?"

"I think so. Why? Did they shortchange you?" Melanie asked.

"No. I think the guy gave me back too much. With drinks and chips, our total should have come to"—he counted on his fingers, looking perplexed—"at least seventeen-fifty. I gave him a twenty and he gave me back four-fifty." He extricated himself from the cramped picnic bench. "Hang on… I'll be right back."

"Where are you going?" Melanie asked.

"I'm just going to take this back." He creased two dollar bills between his fingers.

"Joel, look at that line! You'll be there forever. It wasn't your mistake. Maybe the chips came with it or something," Melanie said.

He waved her off. "It won't take long," he said, already weaving his way through the crowd.

"Your food will be cold, Joel…"

"Don't waste your breath, Melanie. That's just Joe for you," Tim said, taking half of a hot dog in one bite. "Honest as the day is lawng."

Melanie couldn't hide her amusement. "Goodness, Tim…hearing you speak reminds me all over again how thick Joel's accent was when I first met him." It had almost sounded as if he'd called his brother Joe.

They ate without speaking for a few minutes, the clamor of the festivalgoers around them providing background music. Then Tim swallowed and wiped his mouth with a crumpled napkin. "So, you think my brother is losing his accent, huh?"

"Well, a little," she admitted, winking. "We can *almost* understand him now."

"Well, then it's high time I talked him into heading back East with me."

"Don't you dare," Melanie warned.

"Don't you dare what?" Joel asked, appearing out of the crowd and sliding back onto the bench.

Melanie patted his hand. "Never mind."

By now, Tim and Melanie had almost finished eating, and Joel's hot dog was anything but hot. He ate it anyway, and when he was finished, the four of them strolled through the midway at the festival. Melanie held Jerica's hand and trailed behind them, enjoying the brothers' banter and their obvious joy at being together again.

With one ear to Jerica's constant questions and running commentary, Melanie eavesdropped on the men's conversation.

"So you're liking your job at the church?"

"I like it a lot, Tim. I think it suits me."

Tim clapped Joel on the shoulder. "I can see that. You look good, Joe."

"You're not looking too bad yourself."

Tim patted his firm torso. "I took a few pounds off this summer. Hard work, that."

"Worth it, I'd say. So how's the real estate market in Connecticut these days?"

"Well, we've seen better times. It's a buyers' market right now, but we have some things in the works that I think might pan out pretty well."

Melanie relished the East Coast that tinged each of their voices and smiled to hear Joel's accent thicken in his brother's presence. The tenderness she saw between the men was yet another new side of Joel, and it made her love him all the more.

Later that evening, they all sat around the umbrella-covered table on the deck in Melanie's backyard, enjoying a rare cool breeze and laughing at Jerica's antics. When Melanie finally told Jerica that it was time for her to get ready for bed, Joel pushed back his chair and went to the cooler for another can of Coke.

"Hey, Joe!" Tim called. "Bring me one of those, will you?"

Melanie looked up in time to once again see something she couldn't decipher pass between the brothers. The expression on Joel's face almost seemed to be a warning directed at Tim.

Tim cleared his throat and toyed with the coaster on the end table beside him. "Coke, Joel...if you have it."

Melanie cocked her head and watched them. This time, Tim had clearly pronounced Joel's name correctly—almost as if it were deliberate. But at least twice today Tim had called his brother Joe. Maybe it was a childhood nickname that Joel despised. She could understand if Tim was calling him Joey or Jo-Jo, or something equally childish, but Joe was certainly not a name that should cause him embarrassment. Something about the whole exchange made her vaguely uneasy. She brushed the feeling aside, not wanting anything to cloud the happiness of the occasion.

ᔕ

Melanie saw little of Joel for the rest of Tim's visit. She knew the two rarely got to see each other, and she didn't begrudge Joel a moment of time with his brother.

However, the following week when Tim had returned to Connecticut and she finally got Joel to herself for a day, he was unusually quiet, and she thought he seemed a little down.

It was Friday afternoon and they'd taken the day off work and driven to the Missouri Botanical Garden. They were enjoying the first hint of autumn in the air as they strolled along the winding pathways of the lush gardens.

Pulling her sweater around her, Melanie cleared her throat and ventured, "Is everything okay, Joel? You've been awfully quiet."

"I'm fine." He shrugged. "Just a little tired, that's all."

"Did you and Tim catch up on all the news?"

"I guess so... There's not a lot to catch up on."

"After all those months of not seeing each other?" She tried to make light of it, but he shrugged her off. Something was wrong. "So what did he think of Silver Creek?" she pressed.

"He liked it, I guess. What's not to like?"

Frustrated, she clammed up. They walked through the English Woodland Garden in silence. The trees still wore all their leaves, but now they were tinged with the faintest colors of autumn. The turquoise sky was unmarred by clouds. It would have been a perfect day.

"Now you're the quiet one," he said abruptly.

"Well, I wasn't having much luck getting conversation out of you," she countered. "I thought maybe you just wanted some peace and quiet."

A boisterous group of senior citizens came down the pathway ahead of them, and Joel was silent until they passed. "I need… I want to talk to you, Mel. There…there are some things we need to talk about."

"I'm listening," she whispered, not liking the apprehension in his tone one bit.

"Would you mind if we leave now? Go someplace quiet?"

Her heart seemed to stop beating. Numb, she nodded and let him steer her back to the parking lot in silence.

They got on the interstate, and Joel headed back toward Silver Creek. In the waning afternoon, the sky turned pewter and the air felt thick with rain, though no drops fell. The sky matched Melanie's mood, as a feeling of dread settled over her. Something was terribly wrong.

They drove for thirty minutes, neither of them speaking. Joel turned off at the Silver Creek exit, but instead of driving into town he turned the opposite way, taking a deserted country road. They came over a shallow rise and an old stone church loomed on the horizon, standing sentinel in the middle of the plains. She remembered coming out here years ago on a photo shoot for By Design. The place remained unchanged. In spite of the well-tended cemetery to the east of the building, it didn't look as though the church itself had been in use for a long time. The prairie grasses had grown up around it, and now bright spatters of autumn's last wildflowers were daubed among bearded wisps of brome and wheatgrass.

Joel slowed the car and pulled into the churchyard. He turned off the ignition and swiveled in his seat to look at her. Taking her hand, he let out a deep sigh. But just as quickly, he loosed his fingers from hers and raked them through his hair, turning back to hunch over the steering wheel. "I don't even know where to begin, Melanie."

"How about at the beginning?" she whispered. Her heart was beating rapidly now, the seed of fear taking firm root.

"I'm not sure…where the beginning is." Now he looked into her eyes, and what she saw there was an expression of anguish. "I haven't wanted to keep anything from you, Melanie. There really wasn't any reason not to tell you this…but now so much time has gone by that I feel like I've been— Oh, man, Mel, I'm messing this all up."

"Joel, please tell me what you're talking about. You're scaring me."

He gave a humorless laugh. "It's nothing to be afraid of."

"Then tell me…please."

"Can we…walk or something? It's…stuffy in here," he said.

She nodded, and he got out of the car and came quickly around to open her door. As she climbed out of the car, he took both of her hands in his, his grasp as urgent and stiff as his words. "I want to ask you something, but…there's something you need to know first… something I should have told you a long time ago…"

Eleven

Melanie stared at him, waiting.

Joel let go of her hands. He paced in front of her, then stopped to lean against the car beside her. When he finally spoke, his voice was so soft she had to strain to hear him.

"I was in…a very serious relationship…before. I was almost engaged. I…had the diamond. We'd talked about marriage, but Tori—" He stopped abruptly and swallowed hard. "She…died before I could give her the ring," he said, his voice flat.

In the agonizing wait for Joel to spit out whatever it was he was trying to tell her, a thousand possibilities had gone through Melanie's mind, but what he had just told her wasn't even in the ballpark. And in spite of her distress that he was just now getting around to mentioning this fact, the thought that overrode her dismay was what came to her lips now.

"Oh, Joel. She died? How could that be? You… You've lost so much…everyone you ever loved." She turned to him and took his hand, overcome with compassion. "What happened? How did she die?"

He stroked his thumb over her fingers. "There was a fire," he said. "Tori—Victoria—lived in an apartment over a huge old house. It caught fire, and she…she couldn't get out."

She drew back in alarm. "Oh, Joel. How awful! I'm so sorry. Why…why didn't you tell me?"

"I *should* have told you before, Melanie. I'm sorry." He gently disentangled his fingers from hers and looked into her eyes. "That's how I got this," he said quietly, running his index finger along the thin line that creased his cheek.

"I don't understand." Tenderly, she reached up and traced the path of his finger.

"When I got there, the house was still burning. The firefighters had already brought Tori out… She was"—his Adam's apple bobbed in his throat—"already dead. But I didn't know that. Someone told me she was still inside."

His voice wavered as he continued, "I…I ran up on the porch just as the roof collapsed. They said a falling beam hit me. I don't remember any of it. I woke up in the emergency room."

"I don't know what to say. Oh, Joel, nobody should have to deal with everything you've been through."

"It was a very bad time in my life, Melanie. The hardest thing I've ever gone through. I was angry for a while…very, very angry. But I'm…better now. Now, it seems like it happened a lifetime ago."

He reached out to stroke the back of his hand along her cheek. "You couldn't know it, but you are part of the reason I've been able to work through it all. You didn't just lose someone you loved; you lost a husband, your child's father. And still you've managed to go on and find real joy in life. You've shown me that I'm not the only one in this world who's suffered."

The huge lump in her throat wouldn't let her answer.

Joel drew her into his arms. "I feel so blessed that God has put you in my life. The Lord has been closer to me these last few months than I could have ever imagined. He's given me the gift of someone to love again. It's you I love, Melanie, and I'm…I'm muddling through this like a bumbling idiot…"

Now Melanie broke down and sobbed, her tears dampening the shoulder of his shirt. "Oh, Joel. I'm the one who's been given the gift of someone to love again." She pulled away to gaze into his eyes, and reached up again to trace her finger lovingly along the scar on his cheek—a hero's badge. "I love you…so much, Joel."

Gently he pushed her from him. He looked down and rolled a tiny stone under his shoe. "There's a reason I needed you to know this, Melanie. Maybe this is too much, too soon… Maybe you need time to sort this out?"

"What is it, Joel? Please, tell me what's going on?"

He took her face in his hands and his gaze pierced her. "Melanie," he breathed, "will you marry me?"

Joy rippled through her like the breeze over the prairie grasses. "Joel… Oh yes…a thousand times yes."

He drew her to him again. His tender kiss was a healing salve. Finally, he ran a warm hand down her arm until he found her fingers and knit them with his own. They began to walk slowly, hand in hand, their fingers entwined, as their hearts had become. Her heart soaring, Melanie leaned her head on Joel's shoulder, contemplating how hallowed a gift his love was.

They walked along the deserted country road until the light waned. Together they mourned the sorrows each had known. Yet Melanie rejoiced that this day that had had such a rough beginning had become a memory she would cherish forever.

◦◦◦

Joel was invited to supper at Melanie's the following evening, and before he left her house, he knelt with Melanie in front of Jerica, and together they shared their happy news.

"We have something to tell you, Jerica." He smiled as Melanie's eyes shone with tears of happiness.

"What is it?" Seeing them both on their knees, the little girl giggled, but the tight knit of her thin eyebrows told him she knew something out of the ordinary was afoot.

Melanie looked at Joel, then to her daughter. "Joel asked me to marry him. And I said yes."

Through the window of the little girl's wide-eyed gaze, Joel could almost see the wheels turning. She looked from him to her mother, mouth agape. "You mean…I'll have a daddy now?"

"Yes, you will, sweetie," he answered, surprised by the catch in his own voice.

Jerica flung herself at him, almost bowling him over. "You'll be my daddy! Daddy…hey, Daddy…" She practiced the unfamiliar appellation. The sound of it on her lips sent a thrill through the core of his being.

Melanie put a warm hand on his cheek and looked at him with such love in her eyes. "You'll have the most wonderful daddy in the world."

He pulled Jerica closer and nuzzled the top of her head with his chin, his eyes locked with Melanie's. "Yes, I'll be your daddy, sweetheart. And the only thing that makes me happier is that I'll be your mommy's husband." He leaned to plant a kiss on Melanie's cheek, sandwiching Jerica between them. "We'll all be a family—together."

The joy in their laughter warmed his heart like nothing had in many years. He kissed them both good-night—these beautiful girls who would soon belong to him—and drove back to his apartment. In the shadow of darkness, he tried to ignore the terrible truth that nagged at his conscience. But it wouldn't go away.

He had made a decision months ago. It had seemed right at the time, but now he found himself wrestling with the question all over again. Melanie was going to be his wife. Didn't he owe her the truth? He'd asked that question a thousand times since the day he realized he was in love with her.

Voices warred in his head, and a chill went up his spine as he recalled the stern warnings of John Toliver, inspector with the U.S. Marshals Service. "You want to stay alive, Bradford? *You tell no one.* You got that? We've never lost a man who followed the rules. Never. But you do the Lone Ranger thing, and all bets are off."

But he was out of the Federal Witness Security Program now, no longer compelled by the rules of the U.S. Department of Justice. He argued with himself. In this little Midwestern town where people didn't even bother to lock their doors, who would believe him if he did tell the truth? The whole scenario would likely be met with bemused skepticism. It was the stuff movies were made of. If people knew anything about the witness protection program at all, they had the notion that WITSEC existed to protect Mafia thugs—criminal rats who agreed to squeal on their mob buddies in exchange for life outside of prison and a guarantee that they wouldn't meet up with a hired assassin in a dark alley some night. For the most part, the perception was true. But the sad fact was that, of the more than six thousand witnesses to whom the program had offered sanctuary over the years, something like six percent were innocent, law-abiding citizens like himself. Men and women who'd had the misfortune of being in the wrong place at the wrong time—unwilling spectators to crimes that now demanded justice.

Joel wished with everything in him that he wasn't a walking encyclopedia of Justice Department statistics—that he wasn't himself a statistic. His had been a long journey—one for which he had no desire to keep a scrapbook. As it was, he revisited the terrible events far too often in his dreams.

Bile rose in his throat as his mind toyed with the memories. The reward for his sacrifices had been a hung jury. An evil man had gone free, and Joel's testimony no longer held any power. The attorney for the defense was apparently confident that the prosecutor would not ask for a new trial.

Thankfully, Silver Creek was the end of the line for him. He'd had no contact with the U.S. Marshal's office since before he'd moved to Silver Creek. Though he would always use the identity WITSEC had provided, he no longer reported to the inspectors. For all intents and purposes, he was out of the program, and he didn't care if he never heard the term WITSEC again as long as God gave him breath. His unsolicited association with the agency had tied a thousand knots in his life. And he feared that he would never be completely untangled from the mess. Nothing—not even the very name with which he'd been christened—would ever be the same. He couldn't go back.

True, there wasn't a price on his head anymore. No one was looking for him now. Tim had seen to that. But God forbid something should change and they should trace him to Melanie…

A vision of Victoria Payne floated before him, and he shuddered involuntarily. If Melanie was ever faced with being interrogated on his account, Joel didn't want her to be able to answer one question. He didn't want her to even know the name of the man being hunted. And in truth he wasn't that man. Not anymore.

Melancholy settled over him like a cloak. He fought to shake it off, scrambling to recall the scriptures that had offered him comfort and justification in the beginning—Old Testament stories of godly men and women who'd found themselves in circumstances like his and had been commended for their necessary deceit. The prophet Elisha, who lied to the Syrians when they came to his doorstep to kill him. The mother of the infant Moses, who hid the child and served as his wet nurse under false pretenses. Jonathan, who deceived his father to defend the life of his friend David. And Rahab, the prostitute whose guile had saved the Israelite spies. Joel thought of the braided cord that hung from the mirror in his car, much as the scarlet cord had hung from the window of Rahab's house in the biblical story. That cord had been a symbol of her faithfulness. It had gained her favor with God and saved her life and the lives of those in her household. Rahab's actions had earned her a place among the parade of the faithful in the New Testament book of Hebrews. Joel had taken that scarlet cord as his own reminder that God had not abandoned him. No, God had *spared* him.

But spared him for what? he wondered now. A life of loneliness? of never feeling he could be close to anyone? A lifetime of keeping secrets from the people he loved most? What kind of life was that?

He shook his head. He should be grateful. Today of all days he should feel God's favor on his life. After all the tragedy, all the sorrow, he'd been given a fresh start, a precious daughter-to-be and a woman who loved him.

It was for her own sake that he couldn't tell Melanie. He pounded the steering wheel with the palm of his hand. He would not dwell on the past. His past—the history of Joseph William Bradford—had died so that Joel Ellington might go on living.

He'd known enough of death in his lifetime. Living was what he intended to do now.

 ∽

Sunday night, Melanie called to give her parents the happy news. She ended up crying like a baby on her end of the line while her mother sobbed with joy on the other.

"Oh, honey, we're so happy for you," her mother said through her tears. "Have you called Matt and Karly? What does Jerica think? Have you set a date?"

"Whoa! One thing at a time, Mom," Melanie laughed. "I'm calling Matt as soon as I hang up. Jerica is over the moon. And we're thinking about April for the wedding. Things will settle down a little at work for both of us by then, and we thought that would give everybody plenty of time to schedule flights."

"Well, you know your dad. He'd be out there on the next red-eye if that's what it took."

"I don't think that will be necessary." Melanie smiled into the phone.

Erika LaSalle, too, burst into tears when Melanie announced her news after dinner at the LaSalles' the following evening, but Melanie wasn't altogether certain that these were tears of joy.

"Erika, what is it?" Melanie pushed her chair back from the table in the formal dining room and went to stand beside the older woman's chair. Feeling awkward and helpless, she put a tentative hand on Erika's arm. She was thankful that Jerica had already been excused to play outdoors. And thankful that she'd decided not to invite Joel today. She had suspected that her news might be somewhat bittersweet for her former parents-in-law—reminding them as it would of her and Rick's happy announcement seven years ago. But she hadn't expected such a strong reaction from Erika. She turned to Jerry for help, but the look on his face was one of equal gloom.

"I'm sorry, Mel." Erika fluttered a slender hand, tacitly asking Melanie to wait for a new wave of tears to pass. Finally she composed herself. "I'm happy for you, honey. Truly I am. I just... I don't want to lose you—either of you. You're all we have." She broke down again.

"Melanie, we want you to be happy..." Jerry interjected.

"It's just that...already we don't see you nearly as much as we used to. And now Jerica's talking about changing her name and—"

"What?"

"Jerica told us that...she's going to be an Ellington now," Jerry explained.

"Oh no... You misunderstood. Yes, Joel and I told her that after the wedding we would be a family, but I would never take the LaSalle name away from her. Jerry, I would never do that." She pulled out a chair and sat down beside Erika. "Nothing could ever change the way I feel about you two. I'll always be grateful for the short time Rick and I had together, for the fact that he gave me Jerica. I'll always be grateful for my happy memories of him," she said tearfully, "and especially for the fact that Rick brought you both into my life."

Erika dabbed with her dinner napkin at the rings of mascara under her eyes. "I'm sorry, Mel. Just...just give me a little time to adjust to this news. Since Rick died, you and Jerica have been the only thing keeping me going. I know I'm being selfish, but...I just can't stand the thought of losing either one of you. And now...I feel like I'm losing you both at once!"

Melanie thought she understood. And she couldn't deny it. The truth was they hadn't eaten a Sunday dinner with the LaSalles in six weeks. Her Sundays had belonged exclusively to them before Joel came along.

She had intended to invite them to dinner with Joel some even-ing, but her time with him was so precious that she kept putting it off. She didn't know what to say now. There was no denying that things would be different once she and Joel were married. Already they had talked about moving to the other side of town, closer to the church and Jerica's school. And they wanted children together; they were both certain of that. Of course, those children wouldn't have the same connection to the LaSalles that Jerica did. The new family she and Joel and Jerica formed would compel new loyalties and would consume much of Melanie's time.

She hadn't considered how these things might make Rick's par-ents feel. Now she realized that, in a way, it must feel almost as if they were losing their son all over again.

"Oh, Mom..." Melanie had rarely used the endearment since Rick's death, but it came naturally from her lips now.

She put her arms around her mother-in-law. "Of course you won't lose us. I'll still be at By Design. And you will always be Jerica's Grammy... Nobody could ever take your place."

She looked to Jerry, sought to include him in her tribute. "Jerica loves you two more than anything in the world. I would never try to keep her from you. Never!"

Jerry scooted his chair back and stood to embrace her. "We're happy for you, Mel. We truly are. It's just a little hard to remember…" He cleared his throat, and Melanie saw tears glistening in his eyes.

Erika rose now and put an arm around Melanie. Biscuit pattered into the room, his toenails clicking on the wood floors. The dog cocked his head and stood looking up at them as if to ask, "What is wrong with you people?" Looking down at his bewildered eyes, they all laughed, and the somber mood was broken.

But as Melanie drove home later, she realized that she had been far too wrapped up in her own little world these past weeks. She had more than just herself to think of. Rick's parents were an important part of Jerica's life, of her heritage. Erika was right. Her and Jerry's memories of the past and all their hopes for the future were wrapped up in the precious little girl who shared their name. She must remember to respect that. And she must be certain that Joel understood and honored it as well.

Twelve

As the holidays approached and the year came rapidly to a close, By Design was deluged with work. It seemed that every client had decided that this was the year to do an elaborate more-than-just-a-card Christmas greeting. In addition, one of the company's largest accounts was doing a major revamp of its corporate identity and had chosen the holiday season to unveil the new look. Every designer was working overtime to meet the deadlines, and when the designers were swamped, Melanie was doubly swamped.

She hated the extra hours Jerica was spending at the day care center, and she hated that her time with Joel had become so rare. However, one mixed blessing of the firm's workload—aside from the financial boon—was that there were many candidates for entry in the annual regional design competition. It had always been Melanie's task to select the pieces they would enter each year, and she spent many an evening at the office helping fill out entry forms and assemble displays.

Amidst all this, Christmas seemed to get lost in the rush. The holidays came and went in a whirlwind, and when Melanie went back to the office after New Year's Day, she breathed an audible sigh of relief as she and several of the designers enjoyed the luxury of milling leisurely around the coffee pot.

"Isn't it great not to be on deadline?" Suzanne Savage joked.

"The only thing we have to worry about now is what to wear to the Addy awards."

Silver Creek didn't offer many opportunities for glitz and glamour, so the advertising awards presentation—known as the Addys— was a highlight of the year for the By Design crowd. It was a chance to dress to the nines, mingle with designers from other St. Louis area agencies, and for many of them an opportunity to strut their stuff professionally.

Melanie glared at Suzanne and pulled at her hair in mock distress. "You had to remind me? Couldn't you just let me enjoy one measly day in oblivion before bringing that up?"

"Sorry, Melanie," Suzanne laughed. "I take it you don't have your dress yet?"

"Are you kidding? Last year I was still shopping the morning of the Addys."

"I don't think my nerves could handle that," Sena Baker said.

They chattered on about the sales the local department stores were having, and finally, the staff meandered back to their posts. Nursing a cup of black coffee, Melanie went up to her office daydreaming about the upcoming gala.

$\backsim$

"Wow! You look gorgeous!"

Melanie twirled in front of Joel, basking in the compliment. The sleeveless above-the-knee velvet sheath she wore was simply a dressier version of the little black dress every woman was supposed to own. But she was pleased with the way she had turned out tonight. Darlene had done her hair in a sleek upsweep. And with simple diamond earrings and strappy heels, she felt very feminine and pretty.

"You don't look so bad yourself," she told Joel, reaching out to straighten his bow tie.

"Well, I feel like I'm headed for my high school prom," he

lamented. "I'd like to get hold of the guy who invented these zoot suits!"

She laughed and her spirits soared in anticipation of a glamorous evening in the city with Joel.

"I can't wait to show you off," she told him, as he pulled the Taurus onto the interstate, headed into St. Louis.

"Same here," he said, giving her another appreciative once-over. "Did I mention that you look ravishing tonight?"

She giggled. "Only about a hundred times."

When they arrived at the America's Center where the event was being held, Joel let out a low whistle. "Good grief, valet parking? What have I gotten myself into?"

"Hey, you're a big-city boy. You should be able to handle this," she teased.

He turned the keys over to the attendant and came around to escort Melanie. The night was cold. Overhead the lights of the city shivered in folds of navy silk, as though they, too, had dressed for the event. Joel and Melanie followed the crowd to the hall where the awards ceremony was being held. They checked their wraps and fell in line with the crush of other attendees at the buffet table.

The room was elegantly decorated, with pillar candles under glass chimney lamps providing the only light on the dining floor. Already the room was choked with cigarette smoke, which swirled artfully in the flickering light. In front of the stage, a small band played mellow jazz.

A six-foot-high ice sculpture served as the centerpiece on the buffet table. Joel's eyes sparked when he saw the intricately carved ice dragon, which had somehow been rigged to breathe a continuous flow of water. "Well, look at that," he said, inspecting the piece.

"Pretty impressive, isn't it?"

"No...I mean, yes...it *is* impressive. It's just that it looks so much like this fountain that was on the campus...at Langston."

"Where you taught?"

He nodded.

"Really? Isn't that interesting? Oh, here…" She handed him a fancy buffet plate and a napkin embossed with the stylized flame that was this year's Addy logo. "Do you want something to drink?"

"Sure… Whatever you're having is fine."

She got them ginger ales from the bar, and they stood along a wall, searching the room for their table.

Soon Melanie spotted a bejeweled hand waving from a corner of the room.

"Oh, there's Suzanne…and Jerry and Erika…over there…

She waved back, and balancing her plate of hors d'oeuvres and drink, she nudged Joel in the direction of the LaSalles and the others from By Design.

"I wonder how we rated a table up by the platform," she whispered as they wove their way through the crowd.

Along the way, Melanie spotted a designer she knew from a St. Louis agency with his wife. "Hi, Steve, Margo. Isn't this lovely?" She took in the decorations with a toss of her head. "I don't think you've met my fiancé. This is Joel Ellington. Joel, Steve and Margo Kieffer."

"Margo…nice to meet you." Joel nodded politely and juggled his plate in order to extend a hand to Steve Kieffer. "Steve, is it? Very nice to meet you both."

Melanie winked. "Steve's firm is our toughest competition tonight."

"Ah, so I gather we won't be *leaving* the premises on quite such friendly terms," Joel joked.

The Kieffers laughed, obviously charmed by her handsome escort, and Melanie flushed with pride.

They continued through the crowd to their table. Jerry spotted them and pushed back his chair and stood to kiss Melanie's cheek. She gave him a hug and leaned to embrace Erika, too.

"You look lovely tonight," Erika said.

"Thank you, Erika. So do you."

Setting her plate at an empty spot, Melanie slipped her evening bag off her shoulder and put it on her chair. She waved across the table. "Hi, Suzanne. Oh, José, I don't think you've met my fiancé." She turned to introduce Joel, only to find that he had disappeared. She glanced around the room and spotted him three tables away, speaking with a man she didn't know.

She rolled her eyes and laughed. "I've lost him already. Sorry... I'll be right back."

She moved to join Joel, but stopped in her tracks when she got close enough to get a glimpse of his face. His lips were white as chalk, and he looked as though he might be sick. The paunchy, middle-aged man with whom he was speaking had a stricken look on his face as well. "Man, I'd heard you were dead!" the man said loudly, shaking his head.

What in the world was going on? The man seemed to know Joel, but Joel only shook his head and held up a hand. "No, I'm sorry, you must be...mistaking me for someone else."

The man returned to his table and took a seat with his back to them, but Melanie heard him tell his dining companions, "Well, I guess I made a fool of myself, but he's a dead ringer for a guy I knew back in New Yawk." Melanie started as she realized the man spoke with the same East Coast accent Joel did.

Joel seemed dazed, and stood there with his drink tipping precariously. Melanie took the glass from him. "What was that all about?"

No response.

"Are you all right?" she asked, putting a hand on his arm.

"I'm...fine." He moved toward their table.

She motioned to the table behind them. "Who was that?"

"I...I don't know. He thought he knew me. I guess...I must look like somebody he knows."

"Someone from New York? That's strange."

"Yes."

She shrugged and led the way back to their table to introduce Joel to the By Design crew who hadn't yet met him. José wielded his camera and had them pose for several shots. Joel pulled Melanie close and they smiled into the camera.

Later, while they waited for the awards ceremony to begin, Melanie watched Joel surreptitiously. He fidgeted in his seat like a little boy, avoiding her eyes and seeming preoccupied.

Several times throughout the social hour, Melanie caught Joel looking furtively over his shoulder toward the table where the stranger with the East Coast accent sat. Granted, the encounter had been odd, but it struck Melanie that Joel seemed overly disturbed by the exchange.

"Is everything okay?" she whispered, as the lights dimmed.

He nodded and tucked her arm in his, but the smile he gave her was tight-lipped.

The program began and in the excitement of the awards presentations Melanie put aside her concerns. By Design cleaned up, taking home top honors in five different categories and garnering several honorable mentions. Melanie was in high spirits as they left the banquet hall, exchanging high-fives with colleagues and modestly accepting congratulations from rival agencies.

It was well after midnight when they were finally on the interstate headed back toward Silver Creek. Joel was silent, and Melanie soon drifted to sleep in the passenger seat beside him, dreaming of the glowing headlines that would appear in tomorrow's newspapers.

∽

"No!"

Melanie stepped back, mouth agape. "Joel? Why not?"

Sitting across from her on a barstool in her kitchen, he held up a hand in apology. "I'm sorry, I didn't mean to shout, but...no, I don't want the picture in the St. Louis papers."

She stared at him. "Joel, what is wrong with you? It's our engagement. You can't publish an engagement without a picture."

"You can put it in the *Chronicle* if you want to, but we don't…we don't need to put it in the bigger papers. We don't even know anybody in the city, Mel."

"Joel, half the people in Silver Creek take the *Dispatch*. And *you* might not know anyone in the city, but a lot of the designers and clients I work with won't even notice it if we publish it without a picture. And you know my mom will want to put it in their papers out in California."

She stood up and went around to rub his shoulders, trying to humor him, pouting just a little. "I'm proud of you, honey. I want to show off your handsome face." She reached around his neck and patted his cheek affectionately.

But he shook his head and pulled away from her touch. "I'm sorry, Mel. Please don't send pictures to the bigger papers."

"Would you just explain why?" She picked up the photographs that were lying on the counter. They were candid shots that José Lorenzo had taken the night of the Addy awards. She'd laughed when José brought her the small stack of snapshots at work. Joel looked like a deer caught in the headlights in the first two shots, but then she had flipped to the next print and fallen in love with him all over again. The camera had captured that smile Joel reserved for her alone. It was a wonderful picture of both of them, and she had known immediately that she wanted to use it for their engagement announcement.

She walked back around the bar so she could see Joel's face, search his eyes for a clue to his peculiar behavior. She knew he'd been under a lot of pressure at work with the building project, but surely it didn't warrant the reaction she was getting now.

"Joel?"

"I…I don't want to discuss it any more," he told her, refusing to meet her gaze. "I don't think it's a huge request to make of you."

"Well maybe I could agree if I had even a clue what your reason is."

"I just don't want my picture in the paper, okay?" He spat out the words like bullets, practically shouting now. "Put *your* picture in if you want to." His voice softened a bit. "Don't they sometimes do that…just use the bride-to-be's picture?"

She stared at him. Her easygoing sweetheart had suddenly turned into a paranoid, raving madman. Why wouldn't he tell her what was eating at him? Her tone was icy as she answered him now. "Joel, I don't know what is going on, but there is something you're not telling me."

With his eyes downcast, he rubbed his fingertips in aimless circles on the countertop.

"Joel? What is it? Talk to me. Please."

He shook his head, then kneaded his temple with two fingers. He still would not look at her.

A chill went up her spine. Something was terribly wrong. "You… you don't need to worry, Joel…" Her voice began to quaver violently. She swallowed hard and started again. "You don't need to worry about me putting the announcement in any paper because… because I don't think there's going to be anything to announce!" She burst into tears and fled the room.

"Melanie…Mel, listen to me." He ran after her, catching up with her in the hallway and grabbing her arm, pulling her to himself. "I… You're right. I'm sorry." He leaned away and met her gaze, stroking her cheek with the back of his hand. "I'm sorry, Mel. I'm acting like a jerk. I can't…I can't explain why I feel this way. It's just…"

She looked him in the eye. Agony was written on his face. "Joel? What is it? Are you…are you having second thoughts?"

"What? About us? About getting married? No! No, of course not." He pulled her close again, stroking her hair. "I love you, Melanie. Nothing will ever change that."

"Then what is it? Something is wrong. I know it."

He swallowed hard and shook his head. "It's nothing. I'm sorry. I just… I went crazy for a minute. Please…forgive me."

She paused, searching his face, his eyes. He seemed sincere, and suddenly she felt foolish. She had been acting more than a little irrational herself. Maybe they both just had a bad case of prenuptial jitters. "I forgive you. I'm sorry I made such a big deal out of it."

His eyes softened, and his demeanor changed. "Hey," he told her, leaning down to kiss her forehead, "you put that announcement in any paper you want to. Shout it from the rooftops. Shoot, put it on CNN if you want to."

She laughed then, but the laugh he gave in return rang hollow—like the emptiness that had begun to grow low in the pit of her stomach.

Thirteen

Rain pelted the roof of Joel's Taurus. He cut the engine and cracked the driver's side door far enough to slip his closed umbrella through the gap. Popping open the canopy, he slid from behind the steering wheel and huddled beneath the black umbrella while he fumbled with his keys, trying to lock the car. Melanie still teased him about it, but he never had grown comfortable leaving his doors unlocked, even here in Silver Creek, Missouri.

As he ran across the parking lot, dodging puddles, the wind drove shafts of cold rain at him. He wondered if the umbrella had been worth the trouble. Yanking open the wide front door of By Design, he shook off as much water as he could and left the open umbrella upside down in the foyer to dry. He wiped his feet on the mat and tried to brush the rainwater from his hair, then stepped into the reception area in front of the main design studio.

"Good morning, Joel."

"Hi, Patty." He smiled at the petite, blond receptionist and looked up at the mammoth clock on the wall behind her. "I hate to tell you, but it's afternoon already."

She swiveled her chair and followed his gaze. "Oh…oops. My mistake. Good afternoon, then. Is it raining hard enough for you out there?"

"Plenty, thanks. I shouldn't complain though. It could be snow. It is February, you know."

"Well, now that you put it that way, I take back everything I said at eight o'clock this morning when I was trying to blow-dry my clothes in the ladies' room."

Joel laughed, then motioned with his head toward the loft. "Is Melanie in her office?"

"I think so. Let me ring her." She reached for the intercom.

Joel held up a hand. "That's okay. I'll just go up. She's expecting me."

"Well, here…you better take the elevator." The receptionist reached into her top desk drawer and handed him a key on a thick wooden dowel. "Melanie nearly fell going up the stairs this morning. Her shoes were wet, you know. Those stairs do get slippery as all get out. I keep telling Harold not to wax them like he does, but you can't tell that man anything."

"Thanks, Patty." He started toward the service elevator at the end of the long studio.

"You two have a nice lunch," Patty called after him.

The elevator was at the top, so he turned the key in the lock. The century-old gears ground and grated, and the large car descended and settled on the ground floor with a shudder. The doors slid open, and Joel got in.

He rode to the top and stepped into Melanie's office.

She greeted him with that smile he knew was reserved only for him. "Hey, you. I'm glad you took the elevator. I about killed myself coming up those stupid stairs this morning. My shoes were slick, and I lost my footing, and then I dropped my keys and just about went headfirst down the stairs trying to retrieve them." She glared in the direction of the steep spiral staircase around the corner from the elevator.

"That's what Patty said."

"Oh, she told you?"

He went to her desk and leaned over to kiss her. "Well, I don't think her version was quite so dramatic"—he ran a finger playfully down the bridge of her nose—"but I got the general idea."

She captured his hand and kissed his knuckles. "Where do you want to go for lunch?"

"You don't have anything to eat here, do you? It's nasty out there." He looked out over the rail to the opposite wall where rain cascaded down the grid of leaded glass windows.

"Hmmm. It wouldn't break my heart at all not to have to go out in this. I might have some instant soup. I know I've got crackers. Here... I'll go check. You put some water to boil in the microwave."

"I think I can handle that."

He took off his topcoat and spread it over the railing to dry, then followed her into the tiny kitchenette. She handed him a ceramic teapot. He filled it with water, put it in the microwave, and punched in four minutes. Gathering up napkins and plastic spoons, he took them out to her desk.

"Do you want chicken noodle or French onion?" she hollered.

He went back to the doorway. "I'm not picky...chicken noodle, I guess." While he waited for the water to heat, he stood with his back against the doorjamb and watched her as she emptied soup packets into heavy mugs and arranged everything neatly on a rattan tray. He marveled at how her mere presence could turn a simple instant soup lunch into a feast. He loved her so much.

She turned and caught him staring at her. "What?"

"Nothing," he smiled. "Just enjoying the scenery." He lowered his voice. "Just thinking how much I love you."

She set the tray down on the counter and curved a finger at him. "Come here."

He went to her and took her in his arms, cradled her head gently to his chest, feeling a delicious warmth spread over him. "Mmm..." he murmured into her hair. "Who needs lunch?"

The *ding* of the microwave broke the spell.

"Saved by the bell," he deadpanned.

She gave a breathy laugh and disentangled herself from his arms.

While the rain continued outside, they sat together at her desk, savoring the warm soup, laughing and talking, and enjoying just being together.

Finally Melanie dropped her spoon into her empty mug and stood to brush the cracker crumbs from her skirt. "Here, if you're finished, I'll take your dishes."

He crumpled his paper napkin and put his dirty dishes on the tray. "I'll get these. You go wash up or fix your makeup or whatever it is you women do after lunch."

"Thanks," she laughed. She closed the door to the rest room, and he heard the water running.

He took the dishes to the kitchenette, found some soap under the sink, and squirted a little into the mugs. Rinsing them, he set them upside down on the counter to dry and went back out to Melanie's office to wait for her.

Below, he heard the quiet *whoosh* of the main door opening in the lobby and, a few seconds later, felt the draft it created reach the loft. Walking to the rail, he looked down through the plants to the receptionist's desk. A tall potted plant blocked his view, but something about the voice that drifted up from the lobby made him take notice. The visitor stepped closer to Patty's desk and the top of a balding head came into view. Joel could see a black umbrella clutched in the same hand as the man's briefcase.

"Could you tell me where I might find the manager?" the man was asking. His voice held an unmistakable New York accent. Joel heard Patty tell him the manager was at lunch, but through the branches of the ficus tree, he watched her punch a button on her phone.

Joel started as the phone on Melanie's desk rang. "I can get that," Melanie hollered from behind the closed rest-room door.

Joel watched as the visitor stepped back from the desk and did what every visitor to By Design did: He tilted his head and looked up, taking in the impressive view thirty feet up. Now with a clear look at the man's face, Joel's heart jumped, and he sucked in a tight breath. It was Larry Cohen, the man he'd run into at the Addy awards. *What was he doing here?*

Cohen was the father of one of Joel's former students at Foxmoor College. Joel had only met the man on a couple of occasions, but he did recall now that the family owned an advertising agency. The day after the Addy awards, disconcerted by his encounter with Cohen, Joel had looked up the name in a St. Louis telephone directory. A few discreet calls confirmed that St. Louis was, indeed, where Larry Cohen had relocated his business.

The family had moved from New York before Joel had had to leave Langston, so apparently the news of Joseph Bradford's demise had traveled as far as St. Louis. The thought terrified him.

Melanie's phone rang again, and Joel had to force his feet to propel him away from the railing. Frantically, he tried to decide what to do.

Melanie came from the bathroom, her lipstick fresh and her hair neatly brushed. She barely glanced his direction and hurried to pick up the phone.

"Yes? Hi, Patty. Okay… What did you say his name is? Oh yes. The Cohen Group. In St. Louis, right?"

From his stance near the rail, Joel could hear threads of Patty's end of the conversation, including Larry Cohen's name, and he felt the blood drain from his face.

"No, that's okay. We were finished." Melanie flashed Joel a smile over the receiver. "Sure. Bring him on up. Thanks, Patty." She put the phone back in its cradle and gave Joel an apologetic smile. "Sorry, but I probably should see this guy—" She stopped short and peered into his face. "Are you all right, Joel? Your face is white as a sheet."

"I…I don't think that soup agreed with me," he said. "I think… I'll go home and lie down for a while."

She came to him and put the back of her hand on his forehead. "You don't feel hot." Reaching up, she put her warm palm on the side of his face and planted a kiss on the opposite cheek. Her forehead wrinkled. "I hope I didn't give you food poisoning. That soup mix has been around here for a while."

The old elevator clanked, and Joel heard the grind of gears as the car descended to the main level, apparently at Patty's command.

"I'm going now," he told Melanie, starting for the spiral staircase.

"Why don't you wait for the elevator, Joel? I'm serious… Those stairs are treacherous."

"It's okay. My feet are dry now," he said. His heart raced as he heard the elevator hit the first floor, then begin its thirty-foot climb a few seconds later.

"Just be careful," Melanie warned. "I hope you feel better. I'll call you."

"Thanks."

Hurrying to the steps, he grabbed the railing and started down. His heart lurched as he heard the door slide open and Melanie's business voice ring out. He stopped midway down and stood stock-still, listening as Patty introduced Melanie to Larry Cohen.

"Hello, Mr. Cohen. Nice to meet you. Please, have a seat…" Then her voice rose an octave. "Oh! Patty…Joel left his coat!"

Joel froze. He heard Melanie's voice again. "He just took the stairs. Would you mind seeing if you can catch him, Patty? Take the elevator, though."

Again, he heard the elevator doors glide open and the gears grind to life.

He descended the last few steps and walked to the foyer, careful to keep his head down. While he shook out his umbrella, Patty came jogging down the corridor with his coat over her arm.

"I wondered where I left that," he told her lamely.

"You need a wife," Patty laughed.

He knew she expected him to tease her back, but his mind could not come up with the appropriate retort. Instead he nodded and busied himself with the buttons on his topcoat.

The phone rang, and Patty went to her desk to answer it.

Before Joel went out into the rain, he risked one glance up toward Melanie's office. Larry Cohen stood beside Melanie at the rail, smiling and pointing out toward the colorful sculptures that hung from the rafters. But before Joel could look away, Cohen turned in his direction, and for an instant their eyes met. Again, Cohen's eyes flashed a spark of recognition. And something that hadn't been there before. A trace of suspicion, perhaps?

Joel shivered involuntarily and walked out through the wide doors into the pouring rain.

Fourteen

Joel Ellington shook out the society section of the *Post-Dispatch* and pondered his own face staring back at him. Beside him in the newspaper photograph was a radiant Melanie. Their engagement announcement, set apart in a box at the top of the page, filled him with conflicting emotions. His love for Melanie surprised him all over again each morning when he awoke to the realization that she was in his life and that she loved him in return.

And he couldn't help but smile as he thought of the little girl who had already begun to call him Daddy. He had never dreamed that hearing that word from Jerica's little Cupid's-bow mouth would do such strange things to his heart. He didn't believe he could have loved her any more had she been his own flesh and blood.

He folded the page carefully and put it with his briefcase to take home. He knew Melanie would want extra copies. A flush of heat came to his face as he remembered the ridiculous scene he'd made over their engagement announcements. Even if anyone still had a reason to come after him—which they didn't—they sure wouldn't be sitting around scrutinizing the society pages of obscure Midwestern newspapers. It had been foolish for him to make such a big deal over Melanie's simple request, especially when he couldn't offer an explanation that made sense to her.

This month marked a year since his arrival in Silver Creek, and until now the town had felt like a haven of security for him. But bumping into Larry Cohen at Melanie's awards banquet that night and then at her office had freaked him out a little. They had warned him during the WITSEC orientation that it wasn't all that unusual for protected witnesses to run into people from their past—even hundreds of miles from home. They'd been coached in how to deal with such a likelihood, and in spite of the panic he'd felt that night, he thought he'd handled it reasonably well. He felt sure he'd convinced Cohen that he was mistaken. But the orientation had failed to inform him of how paranoid such an event might make him in the days that followed.

It hadn't helped matters when Cohen showed up at By Design two weeks ago. According to Melanie, Cohen was there to invite her to present a workshop at a graphic arts conference the Cohen Group was hosting. Melanie recognized Larry Cohen as the man from the Addy awards and had mentioned to Joel that Cohen had been at her office. But from what Joel could gather from her—without asking questions that might have aroused her suspicion—Cohen hadn't connected Melanie to Joel. It was probably just his overactive imagination that made him think Cohen had recognized him in the lobby of By Design.

But his sense of peace had crumbled a little in the face of these encounters with this man from his other life. And in spite of Joel's clean-shaven face and his new haircut, Larry Cohen *had* recognized him that night at the Addys. He hadn't imagined that.

Joel comforted himself with the fact that Cohen had legitimate reason to be at these advertising venues. The man posed no threat. But what if Cohen went back to New York and happened to mention to the wrong person that he had spotted a dead ringer for Joe Bradford in St. Louis? Joel shuddered. If that happened, his safety might be compromised. The odds were remote, but was he willing to stake his life on them? Or Melanie's life?

He had agonized again and again over how much of his past to share with Melanie. WITSEC had pounded it into his head that he could tell no one. In fact, when he'd first been taken into the witness security program, the U.S. Marshal assigned to his case had been furious when he found out how much Joel had told Tim. Tim had quietly changed residences twice since the trial—just to be sure. And whenever he came to visit Joel, Tim took extreme caution to be sure he wasn't followed.

As long as Joel embraced his assumed identity, he felt relatively safe. Still, if he thought about it too hard, it nagged at him to be keeping something so significant from Melanie. But even if he decided to tell her everything now, how could he possibly expect her to understand after all this time? After his deception was so complete? Could she ever forgive him?

He didn't want to find out. Besides, it was Joel Ellington that Melanie had fallen in love with, not Joseph Bradford. No. He'd made his decision, and he'd honestly made it with Melanie's best interests in mind. It served no purpose to second-guess himself now. And the events of these last weeks only confirmed his resolve. God forbid Melanie should ever have to put on the kind of performance he'd been forced to act out in front of Larry Cohen that night at the Addys.

He shook off the unsettling thoughts and picked up the *Dispatch* again. Scanning the sports pages, he checked the scores. The Bulls game was on cable tonight. Maybe he'd call Melanie and suggest they order pizza in and watch the game together.

He shook out the front section of the paper, skimmed the headlines, and turned the page. A New York dateline in a series of national news briefs caught his attention. He read the story three times before it soaked in.

No! How could this be? With a sinking feeling, he stared blankly at the newspaper in front of him. Fear knocked around in his gut and the walls seemed to close in on him. All the qualms he'd dismissed as foolish not ten minutes ago seemed to mock him now, and he felt like a trapped animal with nowhere to hide.

He read the article one more time. How terribly ironic that this story should appear in the very issue in which his engagement was announced. Here, in black and white, lay the incongruity of the joy and the agony of his life: his engagement to Melanie, representing all that was new and redemptive. And a few thin pages away, a revelation that was sure to turn his world upside down: Another witness had stepped forward, and the prosecutor in Victoria's murder case was talking about a new trial.

Why hadn't Toliver informed him? Joel had had no contact with the Justice Department for over a year now. He'd not expected to hear from them again—ever. Now he confronted the awful truth. He would surely be called to testify again. And once again he would have to face the man responsible for Tori's death—the men responsible for his exile.

Oh, Melanie. How could I have dragged you into this mess? And Jerica. Oh, dear Father, what have I done?

Suddenly the truth stood before him in perfect clarity. He would always be a fugitive. He would never be able to ensure the safety of anyone close to him. Already he had imposed deceptions, large and small, on Melanie and on everyone else he'd come to know and respect here in Silver Creek. And as it always was with deceptions, one lie led to another and another and another. He realized now that his dishonesty, however necessary to his safety, however well intentioned, would eventually erode the trust of everyone dear to him.

Perhaps most disturbing of all, Joel now saw that his deception had changed who he was deep inside, as surely as his protective identity had changed who he was on the outside. He wasn't even sure he knew himself any more. He had been mistaken to think that he could hold a position of leadership in the church when his very identity was based on a lie. People had looked to him to make important moral and spiritual decisions, yet their confidence in him—in who they thought him to be—was based on lies!

It was time to ask some tough questions. What if something

went wrong at this new trial? Perhaps, unknowingly, he had already put Melanie in peril. But even if he hadn't, what if, after they married, he was forced to assume yet another identity, another life? If another relocation was ever necessary, how could he possibly ask her to bring Jerica and follow him back into the Federal Witness Security Program? It would be grossly unfair to drag the two people he loved most in the world into his dangerous circumstances. And even aside from the danger, how could he rip them from the small town they loved, the job in which Melanie found such satisfaction and financial security, and most of all, the grandparents who were so much a part of Jerica's life?

How could he even think of taking Jerica away from the LaSalles? She was all they had left of their son—their only child. She and Melanie were the only family Jerry and Erika had in the world, their only hope of carrying on their legacy. How could he be so selfish?

The answer was simple. He could not. As much as he loved them, he could not pull Melanie and Jerica into his deception. *Because* he loved them, he could not ask them to sacrifice everything they held dear for him.

As the realization soaked in, Joel slumped over his desk, putting his head in his hands. And in that moment of utter agony, he made the most difficult decision of his life. He must leave. Now. Before he hurt them worse than he already had.

Trembling, he picked up the telephone and dialed a number from memory. He punched in the extension. The phone rang a dozen times before Joel finally hung up. What was going on? He'd never had trouble getting through before.

He dialed again—a different number—tapping a pencil impatiently on the desktop, sweat forming on his brow. "Come on, come on, Tim…pick up the phone," he whispered under his breath.

As the phone rang again and again on the other end, he grabbed the newspaper and creased it, jamming the New York article deep into the folds of newsprint. He reached for his handkerchief and mopped away the sweat that beaded his forehead.

Then abruptly, Tim's voice came on the line.

"Tim! Thank God you're home!" His voice came out as a strangled sob.

"Joe? What's wrong?"

He paced nervously, as far as the phone cord would allow, like a dog on a short leash. "Something's happened, Tim. I need to talk to Toliver, but I can't get through. He's not answering his phone."

"What happened? Tell me."

"No, not on the phone." He whispered into the receiver now. "I'll…I'll meet you at your place. I'm…I'm not sure what I'm going to do for money until I get hold of Toliver…"

"What's going on, Joe? Has something happened? Do you need to get out of there?"

"I can't talk now."

"Don't worry about money, Joe. You just get here as quickly as you can."

"Thanks, Tim."

He willed himself to calm down, forced himself to think rationally, to make sure his brother had all the information he needed. He spoke into the receiver again. "I'm leaving now…driving. I have to take care of some things here first, but I've got my cell phone. I'll call you when I get on the road."

He dropped the phone in its cradle and ran his fingers through tousled hair. Thank goodness Don Steele wasn't in the office on Mondays. Joel wasn't sure he could have behaved as though everything were normal. Quickly, he scratched out a note to Don, then went into the pastor's office and reached for the top drawer of the desk. It was unlocked, as Joel had known it would be.

He filed through the small stack of paychecks until he found the one made out to him. In spite of the fact that his name was imprinted on the check, he felt like a common thief. Payroll checks weren't actually due to be distributed until Wednesday, but Darlene always cut them in advance. They would just have to understand. He laid the note he'd written to Don on top of the remaining checks, and silently slid the drawer shut.

Catching sight of the file cabinet in the corner, he went to it and tested the top drawer. It wasn't locked either. He slid the drawer open and thumbed through the file folders until he found one labeled with his own name. The papers inside were mostly tax forms and curriculum proposals. But at the back of the file he found a copy of the résumé he'd used to get hired at Cornerstone. He slipped it out of the folder.

He went down the hall to his own office again, where he emptied the contents of his desk drawers into his briefcase. Then, checking the hall to make sure it was empty, he locked his office and went to his car.

At his apartment, he trudged back to the bedroom where he dumped his dresser drawers into a suitcase. Dragging the case to the bathroom, he added the contents of the medicine cabinet. He hauled the bag out to the front door, then went to his desk and pulled out a sheet of paper and an ivory envelope. He wrote for twenty minutes, unsure whether the words he penned even made sense. He folded the single sheet of paper, slid it into the envelope, and wrote Melanie's name on the front. As the finality of what he was doing began to soak in, his hands started to shake.

The doorbell pierced the silence of the apartment and set his heart thumping.

He went to the kitchen window, parted the louvers of the blinds and peered out over the parking lot. None of the cars parked out front looked familiar.

Cautiously he went into the hallway and opened the front door a crack.

John Toliver, inspector with the U.S. Justice Department, stood on the stoop, a jacket over his arm. "Hello, Joe," he said. "We need to talk."

∽

Melanie pulled into the nearly empty parking lot of Silver Creek's small community hospital and found a space near the visitors' entrance. She pulled down her visor and checked her appearance in the small mirror. Rummaging in her handbag, she found a comb and ran it through her hair, fluffing her bangs with her fingers. Then she pulled out a tube of lipstick and slicked it over her lips, pressing them together and checking the final effect again in the mirror.

She hoped visitors' hours would allow her to see Jeanne before supper. Jeanne Hines, Darlene Anthony's mother, had been admitted to the hospital again the previous Friday after tests showed that the cancer had spread to her liver. Melanie's heart went out to Jeanne—and especially to Darlene, who had always been very close to her mother.

Last night, Jerica had spent almost an hour with crayons and glue, making an elaborate card for the elderly woman who had taught Jerica's Sunday school class. Melanie picked up a small gift and the carefully signed card from the passenger seat beside her. Wide flourishes of bright crayon and glitter decorated the front of the card. Her daughter had definitely picked up some of the family flair for design. Inside, Jerica had colored a picture of Mrs. Hines and had penned a cheery get-well message. But sweetest of all, the outside of the card depicted a happy family-to-be—Joel disproportionately taller than Melanie and Jerica—all of them fitting under a rainbow, or perhaps it was supposed to be the St. Louis Arch. The weekend before, she and Joel had taken Jerica on an outing into the city, and they had ridden to the top of the arch. It had definitely been a highlight of Jerica's not-quite six years.

Melanie locked the car and headed toward the wide front doors of the medical center, her thoughts preoccupied with the wedding that couldn't get here fast enough to suit her. Everything was on schedule, and she and Joel had been enjoying the planning process, in spite of the stress caused by the mounting list of things that needed to be done before the big day arrived.

Her dress, a simple street-length shift of satin and lace, had gone in for alterations weeks ago and had finally come back. To her relief, it fit perfectly. Jerica's dress was a miniature version of Melanie's— pale pink-tinted beige with creamy lace overlays. Melanie refused to let Joel see his bride-to-be in the dress, but she had finally given in and allowed Jerica to model her dress for Joel. They had dissolved in joyful laughter when the little girl gazed approvingly at her reflection in the mirror, then sighed dreamily and exclaimed, "Oh, I just can't wait till our wedding."

Smiling to herself at the memory, Melanie checked in at the receptionist's desk, then took the elevator to the second floor. Knocking quietly on Jeanne's open door, she tiptoed to the bedside.

The woman stirred in the bed, opened her eyes, and smiled when she saw Melanie. "Hello, there."

"Hi, Jeanne. I'm sorry if I woke you. How are you feeling?"

"Like I was run over by a truck. But don't tell Darlene I said that. I am starting to get antsy to go home though, so I guess that's a good sign."

Melanie reached out and took her frail hand, squeezing it lightly. "Well, I hope it's not long before you *can* go home." Melanie laid the card and package on the nightstand. Jeanne scooted up in the bed to look at them, while Melanie helped her adjust the firm hospital pillow behind her back.

"How are those wedding plans coming along?" Jeanne inquired. "It's just a few weeks away now, isn't it?"

"Five weeks, three days, ten hours and"—she looked at her watch playfully—"thirty-seven seconds."

Jeanne gave a weak laugh. "I'm so happy for you, Melanie. And Jerica, too. Joel is all she could talk about in Sunday school last time

I was there… Her new daddy. Speaking of whom"—her voice held a question mark—"you don't happen to know where Joel was today, do you?"

Melanie wrinkled her brow. "Why, he was at work as far as I know…at the church."

"Oh…well…Darlene was here just a few minutes before you came in. She said Joel hadn't come in to the office today. It's Pastor Don's day off, so Darlene called Pastor at home, and he didn't know where Joel was either. They were kind of concerned."

"Really?"

"Oh, I wouldn't worry. Pastor told Darlene that he thought maybe Joel had told him last week that he was taking the day off, and he just forgot to mark it on his calendar." Jeanne Hines leaned forward in the hospital bed. "Just between you and me, Darlene thinks Pastor Don is getting a little forgetful in all the hubbub over this building project."

"Hmmm," Melanie said, ignoring Jeanne's disclosure, perplexed over the revelation that Joel hadn't shown up for work. "I didn't think Joel had any other plans today. I haven't seen him since church yesterday, but he didn't mention anything then. I hope he's not sick."

"Well, I didn't mean to worry you. I just thought you might know where he was…" Jeanne's voice trailed off. An uncomfortable silence followed as Melanie racked her brain to remember if Joel had said anything about taking today off.

"I shouldn't have said anything," Jeanne said finally. "He's probably out buying you a wedding present or something, and now I've gone and spoiled the surprise."

Melanie brushed off the apology. "Oh no. Don't worry about it." She looked pointedly at her watch and stood to leave. "Well, I'd better go pick up Jerica. You take it easy now, Jeanne. We'll be praying for you."

"Thank you. And thanks for coming, Melanie. Tell Jerica I'll treasure her little card."

Melanie backed out of the parking lot, her mind turning over Jeanne's news about Joel. It wasn't like him to miss work without calling. In fact, now that she thought about it, he had mentioned that he had an especially busy week ahead, because they were going to be finalizing the curriculum for the coming Christian education session.

Instead of going straight to the LaSalles' to pick up Jerica, Melanie swung by the church. The parking lot was empty except for Don Steele's battered VW. She drove by Joel's apartment, but his car wasn't there either.

Fifteen

"What are you doing here?" Joel stood with one foot against the partially open door, his right hand rigid on the doorjamb. It was a stupid question. He knew exactly what Toliver wanted.

The burly man shifted his weight and stared at Joel. "Can I come in?"

Joel moved his foot and opened the door. Toliver stepped into the entryway and started for the living room, but Joel stood in his way.

"There's been a new development."

"Yeah. Thanks a lot. I read about it in the paper."

Toliver seemed to miss the irony in Joel's voice. "You moved on us, Joe. It took awhile to track you down. That's good."

Joel ignored the comment and waited for Toliver to deliver his news.

"We have a new witness, Joe. A girl who lived next door to the house that burned. She was in a bit of trouble with the law herself back then. She was afraid to step forward. But she's ready to testify now. She ID'd you going into the house that night. She never saw you come out, but she witnessed Difinni going in some time after midnight. The prosecutor thinks we have a case again. But we need you to testify. We won't lose this time, Joe."

His head was spinning. "But…they think I'm dead. If I show up now, the game starts all over again…"

"If you *don't* show up, Difinni will walk again. We have a real chance of getting a conviction this time," Toliver said. "We need you, Joe."

Joel's heart sank, and he glared at the inspector. Toliver may as well have sentenced him to the gallows.

It was obvious Toliver knew he had him. "It'll take a few months is all. You can stay put for now. Nothing has to change. You're secure. We just need you to be ready when we call. Find a way to take a sabbatical when the court date comes up. When it's over you can pretend this never happened. Pick up where you left off."

"That's not possible."

"It is possible. I don't think you have a choice."

Joel fought to rein his anger in. "You don't understand. I have commitments here. I have…I have a fiancée…with a little girl." But he knew in his heart that it was a last-ditch plea against a destiny that had already been decided.

Toliver puffed out his cheeks and released a stream of breath, leaving no doubt that he saw this as a complication. But he shrugged. "Okay. If we need to, we can bring them in too."

"No."

"It's highly unlikely we'd even need to do that, Joe. We've got a solid case. The guy won't get off this time. Chances are this'll all be a distant memory by Christmas."

Christmas was ten months away. And he knew these things sometimes strung out for months beyond the original trial date. "No, John. I won't drag Melanie into this. I can't."

"Then you'd better tell her good-bye for a while."

Joel brought his fist down hard on the counter and gritted his teeth. "I want out! I don't want anything to do with this! You guys already own half my life. Just leave me alone."

"They'll slap a subpoena on you. You know they will, Joe. My hands are tied. I have my orders." He glared at Joel, then his eyes softened. "Besides, you don't want that scum to get away with what he did, do you?"

Toliver's words hit their mark, and Joel knew that he could never refuse an opportunity to put the man behind bars forever—the man responsible for Tori's death and his own exile.

He pressed the palms of his hands hard on the countertop and slumped in resignation. "What do I have to do?" he breathed.

With Toliver's instructions implanted in his brain, Joel moved quickly, packing a few boxes and loading them into the trunk of his car. His gaze panned the small apartment. How easily he had removed every trace of himself from this place. In a few short minutes, it was as though he'd never set foot in Silver Creek, Missouri.

He closed the door and locked it behind him, leaving his keys and a final check for the rent in the mailbox. The tinkle of wind chimes broke through his rising distress, and impulsively he yanked Melanie's gift from the nail on the eaves. Would there be anything to celebrate on the next tenth of May? Or would he have yet another false date to eschew by then?

In the Taurus, the cord that hung from the rearview mirror caught his eye. A symbol of his faith in God—and more important, of God's faithfulness to him. Could he still believe that? Even now? He slipped the cord from the mirror and tucked it into the envelope with the letter he'd written Melanie. He had never told her exactly what the cord meant to him—he never would now—but somehow, it seemed important that Melanie have it. She did know that it represented a scripture that comforted him. Perhaps it would remind her, too, to seek solace in God's Word.

Joel's heart broke as he realized that, because of him, Melanie would have desperate need of solace in the days to come.

He turned the key in the ignition, and the engine sprang to life. Turning out of the parking lot, he glanced in his rearview mirror. Toliver's unmarked car followed him at a distance. The inspector would wait while Joel dropped the envelope in Melanie's mailbox. By the time she discovered it, Joel would be a hundred miles away.

∿

Melanie picked up Jerica at the LaSalles', then ran by the grocery store for milk and eggs. It was after 6:30 when she pulled wearily into the driveway.

Jerica ran back to her room to play, and Melanie changed out of her business suit.

While she put the groceries away, she absently dialed Joel's number. It rang four times before the answering machine picked up.

Even filtered through the phone lines in the form of a recording, Joel's voice stirred something inside her. She listened with a soft smile on her face until the tone prompted her to leave a message.

"Hi," she said softly into the receiver. "It's me. Just heard you were missing in action. Hope everything's okay. Give me a call when you get home. I love you."

She dropped the phone in the cradle and went to the front door to check the mail. As she pulled a pile of catalogs and other junk mail from the box, she noticed a long ivory envelope with her name on it—no address, no postmark. She recognized Joel's handwriting.

She dropped the mail on the hall table and took the letter to the kitchen table. Her hands were trembling as she opened the envelope.

Later, she would wonder why she had somehow known—even before she opened the envelope—that the letter within would change her life forever.

Joel sat on the edge of a sagging mattress in a hotel room on the out-skirts of Chicago. Another safe house. He almost laughed at the irony of the name. Nothing about this dingy room felt safe.

He put his head in his hands. He had never felt so alone. He'd thought he had experienced the ultimate loneliness when he'd en-tered the Federal Witness Security Program the first time. But this was worse. With the advent of Melanie and Jerica into his life, his dreams had been handed back to him beyond anything he could have prayed for. He had experienced restoration, and now, unbeliev-ably, it had been taken from him as cruelly as his very identity had been wrenched from him in the beginning. Even the biblical Job had not had to suffer the loss of his restored life.

How could he ever trust God again? The only thing that kept a spark of hope aflame within him was the thought of another chance to testify against the man who was responsible for Victoria's death and now for this exile from everything and everyone he had come to love in Silver Creek. From the day that vile criminal had stolen his past from him, Joel had lived a lie. Against his will, he had been made into someone he was not. Now he didn't know who he was anymore. It was almost as though he didn't exist.

Yet he *must* exist. For only a living, breathing man could feel this pain that was a physical ache in the region of his heart.

He picked up the Gideons Bible from the stand beside the bed. Through the veil of his tears, the words rippled and melted into a language he could not interpret.

He sank to his knees and tried to pray, but the words caught in his throat. A low moan—a voice he didn't recognize as his own—came from somewhere deep within him. Had God, too, been lost to him?

If that were so, he wasn't sure he wanted to go on living.

∽

Melanie unfolded the letter and something coiled out onto the table—the thin, red satin cord that had always hung from the rearview mirror in Joel's car. She twined the braided cord between her fingers, her mind spinning. What was this all about? Trembling, she sank into a chair and tried to make sense of the words on the page in front of her.

Melanie,

> *I don't know where to begin or how to make you understand what I am about to tell you. I love you with all my heart, but something has happened that makes it impossible for me to stay here. You must trust me that for reasons I cannot explain to you, it is for the best that I go away and that we end our engagement.*
> *As difficult as I know this will be, you must not hold on to any hope whatsoever that my circumstances will change. Please don't worry about me. I will be okay, but I will never be free to share your life, and I beg you to go on…even to find happiness with someone else. I don't know what you'll tell people, but whatever you do, you must not come looking for me.*
> *I know you believe you knew me, Melanie, but there is so much you don't know about me because I have not been totally honest with you. I ask your forgiveness for that. I can't explain except to tell you that too much of my life has been a lie. But Melanie, you must believe this: My love for you was the one true thing in my life. My feelings for you were never anything but*

*honest and true. My love for you and my faith in God
were the only things I could ever count on.*

*I am so sorry for disappointing you in this way. And
Jerica—I love her as though she were my own daughter.
I don't know how you will explain this to her, but please
let her know that I will always love her and pray for her.
It would have been a sacred privilege to be a part of
your lives. I am so sorry that I have hurt you both…so
sorry that it has to end like this. But there is simply no
other way.*

*You told me once that time heals all wounds. I
know now that there is some truth to that, and I pray
that time will go quickly for you in the next weeks and
months and that you will soon come to a place where
you can remember our short time together with a measure of happiness.*

*There is nothing more I can say except that I will
never forget you. Your love has been a blessing beyond
words, and your name will be in my prayers every day
for as long as I live.*

> *With all my love,*
> *Joel*

She let the letter fall to the table and tried to stop her hands from shaking. It seemed unthinkable that this could be happening. What could possibly have caused Joel to abandon her like this? Especially when he claimed that he still loved her. It didn't make sense.

She felt panic rise in her throat, and she willed herself to remain calm, to think things through rationally. But no matter how many times she read the letter over again, no matter how she tried to read between the lines, she could not understand what it meant.

She picked up the satin cord and ran her fingers along its length.

Why had Joel given her this now? Why, when he never would explain its meaning to her beyond telling her that it reminded him of a passage of Scripture that comforted him? She couldn't imagine what was so personal or secret about it that he would continue to deny her an explanation. She'd always suspected that it had something to do with Tori. That he hadn't wanted to tell her for fear it would hurt her feelings or make her jealous. But if that were so, why had Joel given her the cord now?

She felt sick to her stomach. She had to find him, had to talk to him, and find out why he was doing this. But she needed help. Whom should she tell? To whom could she go?

He had said in his letter that he hadn't been totally honest with her. What did he mean by that? She remembered the night he had asked her to marry him and how he had struggled to tell her about Tori and his former engagement. Had he lied to her then? Was there more to the story than he'd told her?

And what did he mean that she must not come looking for him? Suddenly nothing in her life made sense anymore.

Sixteen

Melanie sat woodenly, staring across the kitchen but seeing nothing. Her thoughts were a confusing swirl of senseless words. Her mind swam with sordid possibilities—some too ugly to entertain. She didn't know what to believe now.

What if Joel was in some kind of danger? Yet nothing he had ever said gave her a hint of what it could be.

Suddenly a small voice broke into her musings—

"Mommy?"

Jerica! Oh, dear God, how will I ever explain this to her? How could she ever make this precious child understand that she had been robbed of another daddy?

"Hi, sweetie," Melanie said, swiping at tears she hadn't realized she'd shed.

"What's wrong, Mommy?"

"It's okay, Jer. I…I just got some bad news." She struggled to control her voice.

"What happened?"

"I'm…not sure yet, baby. I need to call Uncle Matthew and talk to him. I'll tell you about it after I talk to Uncle Matt, okay?"

Jerica nodded silently, her eyes round.

"Can you do me a favor and go find a video to watch for a little while? I need you to be very quiet and not interrupt me while I'm on the phone, okay?"

"Okay, Mommy."

Melanie was barely aware as Jerica shuffled off to the family room. She took the letter to her bedroom, slumped onto the mattress, and dialed her brother's number.

"Hello?"

"Karly?"

"Melanie! We were just talking about you. We got our airline tickets today. Oh, I am so excited that we're finally going to meet your Joel. How is everything going?"

"Oh, Karly, it…it's not going so good."

"Mel? What's wrong? Has something happened?"

"Joel's…left, Karly."

"What? What do you mean?"

"He broke our engagement."

"Oh, Mel, what happened? Are you okay?"

She started crying. "I'm just really confused right now. I… I'll tell you all about it later, but…right now I need to talk to Matt. Could…could you get Matthew? Please…" She heard Karly put the receiver down and call Matthew to the phone, her voice on the other end echoing Melanie's urgency.

"Melanie?" Her brother's deep voice came on the line, and Melanie tried to draw some of the strength from it. "What's wrong? Are you okay?"

"Oh, Matt. Joel's gone! I…I got a letter from him, and he's gone. I don't know where he went. I don't know what happened. He just left."

"What? Melanie, what are you talking about? Joel left? I don't understand. He broke off your engagement? Why?"

"I don't know," she moaned.

"Well, what did he say?"

135

"He wrote a letter, Matthew. It…it says something has happened that makes it impossible for him to stay here." She smoothed the letter out on the quilt, but the words blurred through her tears. "It says that…he loves me, but he can't marry me…that he'll always pray for Jerica. It says… Oh, Matt, I don't know what it says." She beat a fist impotently on the mattress. "None of it makes any sense at all. Everything was fine yesterday."

Matthew swore softly into the phone. "How could he do this to you, Mel? How could he do this to that precious little girl? So help me—"

"No. That's just it… He *wouldn't* do this. You don't understand. Something is wrong. Something is terribly wrong. There has to be a reason. There has to be an explanation."

"Then, why didn't he give you one? Is he… Do you think there's someone else, Mel?"

"No! Of course not." In her confusion, she had actually considered the possibility, but she'd put it out of her mind immediately. She smoothed the letter out again and read parts of it to Matt. Hearing the words aloud hurt more than she thought she could bear.

"This is just plain weird," Matthew said when she'd finished. "Something is very wrong here. This guy sounds heartless."

"No, Matthew!" She felt compelled to defend Joel against the thoughts she suspected were going through her brother's mind. "You never met him, or you'd know that Joel isn't cruel. He would never do anything to hurt us unless…unless there was a good reason."

"I'm having trouble thinking of a good reason. Can you think of anything…any reason…anything at all?"

"I can't, Matt. I'm…I'm at a loss. Joel didn't talk much about… his past, but nothing he ever said gave me any reason to think he was anything but good and honest."

"Do you want us to come?" Matt's tone softened. "Karly's telling me our tickets are open-ended. We can come now since…well, since the wedding is…called off. Do you want us to come?"

"I don't know." She sighed and combed her fingers through her hair. "Let me think about it. Maybe you could help me find him, help me find out what happened... I just don't even know where to start."

"You can't go looking for him. You have no idea where he might be or what kind of trouble he might be in. I don't like the sound of this at all, Melanie. We don't know what you're messing with here."

"That's just it! Maybe he *is* in some kind of trouble. Maybe he needs me."

"Melanie, promise me you won't do anything until I get there."

"You're coming, then?"

"I'll be on the next plane to St. Louis," he told her. "And I'll call Mom and Dad and tell them what's happened. Do you want them to come too?"

Melanie sagged. She hadn't thought of her parents yet. They would be devastated. "No, Matt. No. Not yet. Not until we know what's going on. There's nothing they could do anyway. They'd just worry. I don't want Dad getting upset... His heart..."

"So you don't want me to call them at all?"

"Yes... No... I'm sorry... I don't know what to say." She felt on the edge of panic and knew she wasn't making sense. "Yes. Call them. Please. But just...tell them the engagement is off. Don't tell them Joel is gone. And tell them *not* to come. I'll...I'll call them later."

"Okay." Matt was silent on his end, and Melanie could tell that he was trying to gauge her emotional state. She must sound like a raving maniac.

"I'll be okay, Matt." She tried to put conviction in her tone.

"I know. I know you will. We'll be praying for you."

"Thank you, Matt. Tell Karly I'll call her tomorrow."

"I will." He took charge now, his voice assuming the authoritative tone of the attorney he was. "I'll be there as soon as I can arrange a flight. I'll get a car at the airport. I'll call you and let you know what time to expect me. You just hang tight and wait for me to get there, okay?"

"Okay," she squeaked. She hung up and slumped to the floor, flinging up a jumbled prayer for her parents. Her father was in fragile health, and her mother had enough to worry about just looking after Dad.

She heard the video blaring in the family room, and her mind ricocheted to Jerica. She couldn't tell Jerica about Joel. Not yet. Maybe this was some huge misunderstanding, and it would all be worked out by tomorrow. Maybe she would never have to tell her daughter anything. Maybe tomorrow everything would be clear. Joel would come back, and they could pretend none of this had ever happened, pick up where they left off.

She struggled to her feet and went into the family room. Jerica had fallen asleep in front of the television. Melanie scooped the little girl up and carried her into her bedroom, took off her shoes, and tucked her under the covers still dressed in jeans and sweatshirt.

The phone rang, and she ran across the hall to her bedroom and grabbed the receiver. "Hello?"

"Melanie?" It was Jerry.

"Hi, Jerry."

His voice was tight. "Mel, I just got a call from Don Steele. Joel didn't come into the office today...and then Don found a strange note from Joel in his desk drawer. And Joel's paycheck was gone... It's been cashed. Have you seen him? Do you know what's going on?"

"Don got a letter? What did it say? Oh, Jerry, I got one too." The words came out like lead.

"What is going on?" he repeated.

"I— I'm not sure, Jerry. All I know is that Joel said he had to...to go away. Oh, Jerry," she sobbed. "He broke off our engagement. What am I going to tell Jerica?" She fell apart now.

"Oh, dear Lord. Are you okay, honey?"

"No...I'm not okay," she choked.

"We'll be right over." The line went dead.

Fifteen minutes later, Jerry and Erika were sitting in Melanie's living room trying to make sense of a senseless letter.

The LaSalles sounded as worried as Melanie was. "Could he have been in some kind of trouble with the law?" Jerry asked.

"No! Of course not."

"Did he have a problem with an addiction or—"

"Erika, he never had so much as a glass of wine as long as I knew him. He didn't even like to take an aspirin."

"Well, what else could it possibly be?" Erika said. "Do you think maybe he was sick? Maybe he found out he had some…disease or something, and he didn't want you to have to go through losing another husband?"

She hadn't considered this possibility, but if it was true, it made her angry. Her voice rose a pitch. "Well, then he was pretty stupid to think this was a way to spare me the grief!" She took a deep, shuddering breath and willed herself to calm down. "I'm sorry. I didn't mean to yell at you."

It helped just to be sitting here with people who loved her.

In her mind, Melanie replayed every conversation she and Joel had ever had, desperate for anything that would give her a clue to his behavior. A sickening feeling came over her when she remembered how pale he'd looked the night of the Addys. And how he'd left her office feeling ill the day they'd stayed in and eaten the instant soup. Maybe he *had* been covering up a serious illness, as Erika suggested.

But why would Joel leave her when he, of all people, understood what it was like to lose someone he loved? Suddenly it struck her that perhaps that was the answer. Maybe Joel saw himself as some kind of jinx. Maybe his motivation for leaving was about his fears of losing her, the way he'd lost his mother and father…and Tori. It was irrational, and yet somehow the thought offered a measure of comfort.

Another thought came to her, and she turned to Jerry. "Would Pastor Steele have an old address for Joel? Or maybe Tim's address?"

"Tim?"

"Joel's brother."

"Oh yes. I don't know if Don would keep those on file or not, but it's worth a try."

Jerry went to the phone and explained to their pastor what had happened from Melanie's end. Melanie heard him tell Don Steele that he intended to go to Joel's apartment and see what he could find there. But Melanie knew in her heart that they would find nothing. Joel was gone. Somehow, she knew it.

Melanie turned to Erika. "Thank you for being here for me, Erika. You don't know how much that means."

"I'm just so sorry this happened, Melanie. It's all so strange."

"Would you...mind staying here with Jerica for a little while? I'd like to get out of the house for a little bit. I need to think this all through and—" Her throat closed up, and she couldn't finish.

"Are you sure you should be alone, Mel?" Erika asked, squeezing her shoulder lightly.

"I just need a few minutes to myself. I'll be okay."

Erika looked to Jerry, as though asking his permission to allow Melanie to leave. "You go," she said. "We'll answer the phone and make sure Jerica's safe."

"Please don't tell her what happened. If she wakes up, don't tell her anything yet."

"We won't say anything. But you be careful, Melanie. You're upset... Don't have an accident."

"I'll be careful."

Seventeen

A light rain had started to fall. Melanie drove over wet streets to the east end of town and pulled into the parking lot at Joel's apartment. As she'd known it would be, the numbered space in front of his building, where his Taurus usually sat, was empty. She eased her car into the space and sat looking up through the windshield. His kitchen window, where he'd always kept a tiny lamp burning, was a gaping black hole. The wind chimes that had swayed musically from the eaves over his deck—her birthday gift to him—were gone too.

Somehow, none of this surprised her. She found things as she had expected to find them. Empty and void of any sign that Joel had ever been in Silver Creek, had ever been in her life.

Feeling numb, she backed out of the lot, and as though on automatic pilot, she drove out of town, turning off on the country road that led to the old stone church where Joel had taken her the day he'd asked her to marry him. Easing into the overgrown drive, she saw the sturdy steeple silhouetted against a darkening sky. It comforted her somehow. She shut off the ignition and sat there in the car with the muffled sound of the rain outside a background for her thoughts.

She replayed every moment of her blossoming romance with Joel. She thought of the way she had always teased him about his Eastern accent. Oh, how she'd come to love that low, masculine voice. She could almost hear it in her ear now as he whispered words of love to her. She remembered the affection and devotion reflected in his eyes as he explained some mystery of nature to Jerica.

The tears came, and she choked out the words that had played over and over in her mind since she had received Joel's letter. Words that she had not yet spoken aloud. Words that she had not yet translated to prayer. "Oh, dear God. Why did you let me love him when you knew this would happen? Why did you let him love me? Why, God? Why? Oh, Joel…I love you. I love you, and I didn't even get to say good-bye."

She wept and railed and finally poured out her heart to her heavenly Father in a way she hadn't since the morning she had held Rick in her arms and watched helplessly as he took his last breath. And though she didn't understand the whys, she discovered that she was not angry with God. Instead, she felt sheltered in his arms, surrounded by a tentative peace.

She sat that way for half an hour, and finally, she wiped her tears and turned the key in the ignition. The motor purred, and Melanie maneuvered the car onto the muddy road and turned toward home.

There had to be a reason why Joel had done what he'd done. And somehow, she would discover what it was. If it took the rest of her life, she would search until she found an explanation. Because she wasn't sure she could live not knowing.

～

The blare of an unfamiliar alarm clock jarred Joel awake. He rolled over in the narrow hotel bed and fumbled blindly with the buttons until the noise stopped.

He stretched and swung his legs off the side of the bed. Immediately, the news he had received yesterday was foremost in his thoughts. It was almost more than he could process.

Last night he had sat in this dingy room for hours, head in his hands, thinking about what he would do now, contemplating all that the years had stolen from him. Somehow it seemed that if he could start at the beginning, he could untangle the knots. Now, for the millionth time, his mind traveled back to the day Victoria had died and the nightmarish revelations that had followed.

He'd spent most of that morning in the hospital, having his face stitched up. Absently, he ran a finger over the welt of the scar. Another secret he had kept from Melanie for too long.

He shook off the image of Melanie, but it was replaced by one more disturbing: the house that Victoria had lived in, alight with flames.

He had felt nothing while they closed the gash, putting more than a dozen stitches into his cheek. The shock of Tori's death—especially coming on the heels of the murder they had witnessed the night before—was all the anesthetic he'd needed to numb the pain.

He had felt nothing later when he went home to an empty house and tried to absorb the reality that she was gone. He had not even been allowed to view her body, to prove to himself that it was true. The authorities assured him that Tori had died quickly of smoke inhalation. But by the time firefighters had reached her, the flames had done their cruel work, and Victoria Payne's casket had remained forever closed.

But he had not laid eyes on even that final symbol of Tori's short life. For U.S. Inspector John Toliver had appeared on his doorstep that evening, much as he had yesterday. Toliver delivered overwhelming and gruesome news: The body of a man had washed up on a New Jersey shore that morning. It had seemed insignificant—an unfortunate drunk, a sailing casualty perhaps. But the bullet holes they discovered in the man's head boded something more sinister. And then, very quickly, the dead man was matched to the description of a waiter reported missing just hours after he had witnessed the execution-style murder of a reputed drug lord in Ciao!, a posh New York restaurant.

Results weren't conclusive yet, Toliver had told Joel, but they were confident that they would discover that the fire that killed Tori was no accident. There were only four known eyewitnesses to the murder. The dining partner of the dead man was the third. He had disappeared. Joel was the fourth.

In the years since, Joel never had been able to recall the exact chain of events that followed. The Justice Department needed him alive…needed his testimony to convict a crime boss who had eluded them for far too long, at a cost of life far too great. They promised him protection. With only a small suitcase of clothes, he was whisked away to a safe house. Over the next nine months, a succession of safe houses became his home.

Finally the trial date came. And then the unthinkable happened. After fourteen days of testimony, the jury in the case announced that they saw no possibility that they would reach a unanimous decision. Astonishingly, the jury was split nine-three in favor of the defendant. The judge declared a mistrial. Two weeks after Joseph Bradford had sat in the witness stand and looked Stanley Difinni in the eye, fingering him as the murderer of Antonio Sartoni, the case had blown up in their faces like a bomb. The shrapnel had left Joe lethally vulnerable. In light of the fact that two witnesses were dead before the trial even commenced, the Justice Department believed there would be retribution.

Learning that he now had to disappear for good, Joel had confided in his brother. It was against every rule they'd imposed. But he had to talk to someone. Unbelievably, Tim had taken matters into his own hands. Worried that his brother's disappearance would attract too much attention in Langston, Tim fabricated a fatal accident that conveniently happened after Joe Bradford was called to Connecticut to help Tim with an unnamed family emergency. The letters Tim sent to the college, and the obituaries he had published in the local papers, provoked an outpouring of sympathy for the popular young teacher. Though the newspapers reported that the funeral was in Connecticut, back in Langston, Foxmoor College had held their own memorial service in Joe Bradford's honor.

After a few weeks, Tim showed up at Foxmoor, conspicuously in mourning, to retrieve Joel's belongings from his office at the college.

Even Toliver admitted that Tim's ruse had worked. If it didn't fool Difinni and his ilk, at least it squelched the possibility of rumors in Langston about Joe Bradford's sudden disappearance. Though to Joel's dismay, Tim's actions spawned new rumors that his death had been a suicide. Toliver had warned that any further involvement on Tim's part would be considered interfering with the legal process. Tim backed off.

And Joe Bradford *became* Joel Ellington. They transferred him to a secret location near Washington, D.C., and he went through an intense time of orientation at the WITSEC center there. He completed the process in a haze of delayed grief over Victoria. And one day he and WITSEC Inspector John Toliver boarded a plane bound for St. Louis, Missouri. The city was the Justice Department's choice because Joe Bradford knew not one soul within five hundred miles.

Joel remembered the flight as though it were yesterday. He had sat in the window seat. With his head against the partially open shade, he watched the city of St. Louis appear below the clouds. Thousands upon thousands of houses and hundreds of apartment buildings sat on a maze of nameless streets. He would dwell in just one of those residences. He bore a new name, a new birthdate, and a new Social Security number. He'd shaved off his mustache and cut his hair. The chances of anyone finding him here were almost nonexistent. And for a brief moment, he had felt elation.

Toliver had rented a car at the airport and driven Joel to an apartment on the south side of the city. Now the streets had names, the houses were numbered, and the world didn't seem so large anymore. His sense of elation collapsed, and he knew fear as he'd never known it before.

Toliver and a WITSEC inspector whose name Joel could no longer remember were his only contacts with the legal system. His brother was the only link to his old life, the only contact he was allowed from his past—and that was limited to arranged, secure phone calls and letters exchanged through a blind post office box set up by Toliver. At that point, it hadn't mattered much to Joel. Tori was dead, and with her his whole world had crumbled.

The Justice Department paid his expenses until he found a job, but they strongly advised against a teaching position. "You cannot be anything that Joseph Bradford was," Toliver told him. The orientation reinforced the need to remake himself completely. If Difinni and his henchmen learned that Joe Bradford was a handball player, they had the means to circulate Joe's photograph to every major athletic facility in the States. Joel gave up handball.

If Joe Bradford was a teacher, Joel Ellington could not be. It was a small matter to access NEA membership file photos, or to obtain information from other professional organizations. Besides, according to Toliver, Justice drew the line at providing false references—too easily checked out, too many other people to involve. They would fund a new education or job retraining, but beyond a certain point he was on his own.

Five months after his move to St. Louis, Joel finally began to feel relatively safe in the obscure Midwestern area. He was off WITSEC's dole and out of touch with the inspectors. He enrolled in classes at a small college, took business courses, and worked at a library at night, trying to decide what he wanted to do with the rest of his life. But the longer he studied, the more he knew what he wanted to do. He *was* a teacher. It was in his blood. It was his calling. He had taught English and literature and even Sunday school classes in his church —and he was good at it.

One morning as he'd sat in his small St. Louis apartment, poring over the newspaper with his breakfast coffee, a classified ad caught his eye. A church in the suburbs was looking for a Christian education director. The job description said the position involved some teaching. It wasn't academia, but it was a start.

Joel applied for the job and, after a congenial meeting with the leaders of the church, thankfully found the committee rather uninterested in his references. They had been looking to fill the position for a long time. He later learned that they'd made a requisite call to the first reference he listed—a Tim Bradford, who had vouched that Joel had indeed worked with him at Foxmoor College, and that a finer teacher could not be found. Joel had been hired practically on the spot, and in spite of the deceit, his fortune had seemed to change that very day.

These last twelve months, life had seemed a sweet gift. And then the past had risen to haunt him again. He'd told Melanie things about his past that were lies. But they were lies that had strangely mutated into half-truths. They were Joel Ellington's truth, designed to save Joe Bradford's life. Sometimes he wasn't sure what *was* truth anymore. And he couldn't afford guilt. With Melanie in his life, it was almost as though his identity had been handed back to him. Though she knew him only as Joel Ellington, *he* was the man she had fallen in love with. What she knew of him went deeper than a name. She knew his spirit. And she loved him for it.

Now none of it mattered. He'd lost Melanie and Jerica. Everything that had made it all worthwhile had been taken from him.

Melanie barely slept that night, her thoughts a cacophonous jumble that she couldn't seem to set aright. Joel was gone. What did it mean? What had gone wrong? She tossed and turned and finally got up and wandered through the house, scarcely aware of what she was doing.

But when Jerica came into the kitchen the next morning, she was waiting.

She stretched out her arms. "Come here, sweetie, Mommy needs to tell you something."

Jerica climbed up onto Melanie's lap, still smelling of sleep. Melanie combed her fingers gently through the tangled hair and hugged the little girl close.

"Are you awake?"

Jerica looked up at her and nodded solemnly.

Melanie took a deep breath. "Honey, I have some very sad news." She pressed her lips together in a futile effort to quell her emotions.

"What's wrong, Mommy?" Jerica cupped Melanie's face in her small hands, and Melanie thought her heart would break.

"Oh, sweetie… Joel…Joel had to go away."

"Go away? Where did he go?"

"I don't know, Jer. He sent me a letter to…to tell us good-bye. Joel's letter said that he loves you very much, and he will always pray for you."

"But why? I don't want him to pray for me. I want him to come and see me. Why did he go away?"

"I…I don't know, Jerica. I truly don't know."

"Did Joel go away forever—like my other daddy?"

"Oh, sweetheart, I'm not sure. Maybe… I just don't know." A sob caught in her throat and she bit her lip to try to stop the tears, but they came anyway. Jerica wrapped her arms around Melanie's neck and patted her gently. They sat together that way for a long time.

Finally Jerica climbed down from her lap and went back to her room. When she didn't return after a few minutes, Melanie went to check on her. She stopped short in the hallway outside of Jerica's room. Quietly she peered into the room.

The little girl was curled into a ball at the foot of her bed, rocking back and forth, gulping back great hiccuping sobs, whimpering over and over again, "My daddy…my daddy. I want my daddy."

Melanie went to her and sank to the floor beside the little bed. She wanted to curl up into a ball beside her daughter. Instead, she put a helpless hand on Jerica's head and sat motionless, her back against the cold bedroom wall as she fought the pain that clawed at her chest.

Eighteen

Matthew Mason pulled into the driveway of his sister's house in Silver Creek and parked the rental car in front of the garage. It had been a long flight with a two-hour layover. He turned off the ignition and expelled a deep breath, steeling himself to face his sister.

It killed him to think about what had happened to Melanie. Hadn't she had enough pain in her life?

He rang the doorbell and immediately heard hurried footsteps on the entryway tile inside. The door creaked open an inch, then two. A dark little head appeared in the gap.

"Hey, Miss Jerica! It's your Uncle Matt."

Jerica gasped and raced back into the house, leaving him standing outside. He heard her voice echo through the foyer.

"Mommy! Mommy! Uncle Matt's here!"

The door opened again, and Melanie drew him inside, then threw herself into his arms. After a long minute, she pulled away and looked into his face. Her eyes were red-rimmed, but the twinkle they always held for him was still there, even behind puffy eyelids.

"Oh, Matt." She gave him a strained smile. "I'm so glad you came. Come in, please. I've got a roast in the oven."

Later they lingered in the dining room over the remains of dinner. Jerica had left the table to play, and for the first time Matt had a chance to talk to his sister alone. He reached across the table and put his hand over hers.

"You honestly don't have any idea why Joel would have disappeared?"

She shook her head and looked up at him with wounded eyes. "I can't even make a decent guess."

"He didn't give you *any* clue why he might have…done this?"

"Matt, I have replayed every single conversation we ever had. I've tried to read between the lines of his letter. I come up with nothing. I have *no* idea what brought this on. I thought everything was fine. Now…I'm almost afraid to know." She looked at the floor. "But I don't think I can live with not knowing either."

"May I see the letter?" She'd read most of it to him over the phone that night, but maybe he would see something she hadn't.

She nodded and rose from the table. Looking as though she were carrying the weight of the world on her slender shoulders, she went down the hallway and came back a few moments later with a worn ivory envelope. Wordlessly she handed it to him.

He read the letter, then folded it carefully and slipped it back into the envelope. "Nothing seemed different between you during the last few days or weeks?" he pressed.

Melanie hesitated. "Maybe…a couple of things. He… Joel didn't want to put our engagement picture in the papers. He said he didn't care if I put the story in—or even just my photo. But for some reason he didn't want his picture used."

"That didn't strike you as odd?"

"Of course it did. We argued about it."

"Why did he agree to have a portrait made if he didn't want it in the papers?"

"We didn't go to a professional photographer. A guy from work took that picture of us at an awards banquet, and we liked it so well we had copies made. But when I started talking about using it for the papers, that was when Joel went ballistic."

"Ballistic? You mean…violent?"

She glared at him. "No, of course not. He barely raised his voice. But he was insistent… He didn't want his picture in the St. Louis papers."

"What reason did he give?"

"He never really gave a reason…" She thought for a minute. "Well, he said we didn't know anyone in St. Louis. But I told him that *I* knew a lot of people there. Clients and business acquaintances."

"What did he say to that?"

"That was when he said I could put *my* picture in if I wanted."

"But you sent me the clipping, Mel. You were both in that photo. Did you put the picture in against Joel's wishes?"

She looked at him as though he'd just accused her of grand theft auto. "No. Joel finally relented. In fact, he apologized and said I could put it in any paper I wanted."

Matt shook his head. "Melanie, how much do you really know about Joel? This…seems extremely strange."

Melanie ignored his question and ran her hands through her hair. "I…I just want to know that he's all right, Matt."

"I know," he said. "I know."

He would never have admitted it to Melanie, but he was not altogether sure he wanted to find the man. He had never met his sister's fiancé, but now he wasn't sure he trusted himself not to do something foolish when their paths finally crossed. The guy obviously wasn't on the up and up. Or else he wasn't playing with a full deck.

Matthew thought back to the only time he had talked to Joel on the telephone. He and Karly had intended to come to Silver Creek a few days before the wedding and spend some time getting to know Joel before the newlyweds left on their honeymoon. They had discussed the plans with Joel on the phone, arranging for Matt and Karly to take Jerica back to New Jersey with them while Joel and Melanie honeymooned. Then Joel and Melanie would fly in to Newark and stay with them for a couple days before they flew on home with Jerica. Matthew had found Joel immensely likeable—and he certainly seemed sane enough. But wasn't that the way most con artists appeared?

"Melanie," he said now, deliberately keeping his tone gentle, "I need you to give me some information, if you can. Tell me everything you know about Joel. Anything he ever told you about his past—even if it seemed insignificant at the time. I need a place to start."

His sister looked up at him with hopeful eyes. "Okay." She thought for a moment, then recited a litany of facts. "His parents were part-time missionaries, so he moved around a lot when he was young, but mostly they lived on the East Coast...in New York. When Joel was eighteen, his parents were killed in a plane crash on the way back from a mission trip."

"Do you know their names? His parents?"

"Um...I think his dad's name was Randall... I think that's right. And his mom..." She put a hand to her forehead, obviously distressed at her inability to remember. "I don't know, Matt. I...I know he told me though. I know he did. But I can't remember. He had a picture of them—in his apartment. And another in his wallet. I could tell you exactly what they looked like, but...I honestly couldn't be sure about their names."

"Was he close to them?"

"Yes, very. He was devastated when they died. He was still in high school. It left him completely alone, since his older brother—Tim—was off at college."

"What else? There has to be something that would give us a hint of what could have happened."

Melanie opened her mouth, then snapped it shut. Then, she sighed and closed her eyes. "Joel was engaged once before," she breathed.

"What?" He struggled to keep the anger from his voice. "Why didn't you tell me that before?"

"There was no reason to say anything before, Matt. It...was in the past."

"Do you think maybe there's still something between them?"

"No. She...she's dead."

He waited. This was getting stranger by the minute. When Melanie didn't offer more, he pressed her. "Tell me about her, Melanie. This could be important."

"Her name was Tori. It... I think it was short for Victoria, but he always called her Tori."

"He talked about her a lot?"

She shook her head. "Almost never. He... I didn't even know about her until just before we got engaged. She died in a fire. That's how Joel got the scar on his cheek"—she brushed the side of her face absently—"trying to rescue her."

"What was her last name? Maybe we can talk to her family... Maybe they'll know more about Joel's past. They might be able to shed some light on all this."

"I...I don't know what her name was." She said it as though she were confessing some unspeakable sin.

"You never asked?"

"He didn't like to talk about it, Matt." Her voice took on a defensive whine. "Joel had a lot of tragedy in his life. He didn't try to hide it, but it was hard for him to talk about it. I respected that."

"Are you sure this Tori—or whatever her name was—are you sure she's dead? Are you sure she even existed?" This whole heroic rescue story smelled to high heaven.

For a moment, Melanie's gaze bored a hole through him. Then she pushed back her chair and started clearing off the table. She carried a stack of dishes into the kitchen. Matt could hear the clatter as she loaded them into the dishwasher. He prayed she wouldn't break something.

Jerica came in from the family room where she'd been watching a video. Without a word, she climbed onto Matt's lap and put her arms around his neck. She laid her head on his chest, and he thought his heart would break.

She looked up at him, her deep brown eyes glistening. "Are you gonna help us find Joel, Uncle Matt?" she asked. "He was gonna be my daddy."

"I know, sweetie."

As long as he could remember, Jerica had talked about having a daddy the way her cousins, Brock and Jace—Matt's own sons—did. Matthew wondered what kind of man Joel Ellington was that he would do this—not just to Melanie, but to the precious little girl who sat on his lap now. Melanie had always been a good judge of character. How could she have been so wrong about this man? He decided the man must have been one smooth actor.

Jerica tugged at his sleeve, forcing him from his reverie. "Are you? Are you, Uncle Matt? Are you going to help us find my daddy?"

He bit his lip and nodded. "I'm sure going to try, honey."

～

"I admit I am completely baffled," Pastor Don Steele told Matt the next day. "If I hadn't seen the letters with my own eyes—in Joel's handwriting—I'd be utterly convinced there's been foul play. But those letters make me feel certain that Joel had good reasons for doing what he did." He tapped a pencil absently on his desk, shaking his head. "But I can't for the life of me imagine what those reasons might be."

Matt sat on the other side of the desk in the pastor's study. He'd barely met Don Steele, but already he trusted the man's judgment and integrity implicitly.

Once more, he picked up the note Don had shown him. The handwriting was the same as in the letter Melanie had received. Both she and Don Steele had no doubt that the letters were written in Joel Ellington's hand. Matt read the brief message once more.

Don,

*I can't explain right now, but something has happened
that makes it necessary for me to leave immediately. I
am deeply sorry for having to tell you in this way and
for leaving on such short notice. I can't say more.*

*I have broken my engagement to Melanie, and she
will need your counsel in the weeks ahead. Please assure her
that my reasons for leaving have nothing to do with her. I
love her deeply. I wish I could explain, but I simply can't.*

*I've taken my paycheck. I hope it won't be a prob-
lem if I cash it a few days early.*

*May God bless you and help you to understand and
forgive me.*

Joel

"You showed this to the police?" Matt asked.

"Yes. But if anything, it hurt my cause. Like I told you, the officer said that unless he's committed a crime, they can't conduct a
search for someone who left of his own accord. I...I didn't make an
issue about Joel taking his paycheck. Maybe I should have. Maybe
they would have taken some action then. But...well, he had the pay
coming. It was rightfully his."

Matt shook his head, racking his brain for the missing piece to
the puzzle. "Do you have the list of references Joel gave when you
hired him?" he asked suddenly.

"You mean from his résumé?" Don stood and went to the file
cabinet in the corner of his office. He pulled out a file folder and
leafed through the papers inside, then spread them on the desk for
Matt's perusal. The thin file yielded Joel Ellington's tax and insurance
forms, curriculum lists, and an assortment of what appeared to be
handwritten sermon notes.

"Hmmm, that's strange," Don Steele said, scratching his chin.

"His résumé doesn't seem to be here." He went back to the file cabinet and riffled through several other folders, but returned to the desk empty-handed.

Matt remembered that Joel had left the note in Don's desk. "You don't keep your drawers locked? Or the file cabinet?"

Don shook his head.

"Who has access to the files besides you?"

Don gave a mirthless laugh. "Just about anybody in the building. But no one else actually uses this filing cabinet...well, besides Darlene, the secretary. I lock my office at night, but I suppose during the daytime anyone could come in here. Why? What are you thinking?"

"I'm not sure yet. Are you positive Joel's résumé was in that folder?"

"Reasonably sure. We keep a copy of each employee's application and résumé on file. But I can't say for certain that I've seen Joel's since we opened a file for him a year ago."

"I just wonder...if for some reason Joel didn't want anyone to have access to the information in his résumé. He was here to get his check and leave that note in your desk the day he disappeared. Is it possible he also cleaned out his file then?"

Don shrugged. "I suppose. But why would he take the résumé and leave all his financial information?"

"I don't know." Matt thought for a minute. "Do you remember who you called for references when you were considering hiring Joel?"

"Well, I didn't make the calls. It would have been someone on the personnel committee that hired him. Probably Bill Randolph or Jerry LaSalle or maybe Ruth Dutton—"

"Jerry was on the board?"

"Yes. He was."

The following day, while Melanie was at work, Matt went to visit Jerry at the LaSalles' home on the Silver Creek golf course. Matt thought that, with his ponytail and ear stud and still wearing his jogging clothes, the man couldn't have looked more out of place in the elegantly appointed home.

Jerry showed him to a butter-soft overstuffed leather chair in the living room. Jerry and his wife sat on a matching sofa across from him, while their little bichon frise flounced annoyingly at their feet.

Matt cut to the chase. "When the church hired Joel, do you remember who you called for references?"

Jerry thought for a minute. "Actually, I made that call. I couldn't tell you the name of the guy I talked to, but it was someone from that college back East where Joel taught. I do remember that the man gave Joel a glowing report. I honestly don't know that we called any other references. I rather doubt we did."

"What are your suspicions, Matthew?" Erika asked, uncrossing her legs and leaning forward on the sofa.

"I don't know," Matt told her, "but something is incredibly fishy here."

Erika nodded vehemently. "I know what you mean. Joel was as nice as they come, but there was always something I couldn't put my finger on. Between you and me, Matt, I think it's a blessing that Melanie's rid of him."

Jerry put a hand on his wife's knee as if to quiet her.

Matt ran a hand through his hair. "I didn't know Joel, but I know that Melanie loved him. It bothers me that she could have been so wrong about him."

"Love does funny things to a person, Matt," Erika offered.

"Well, I suppose that's true, but something just doesn't fit. I don't know what to make of this whole mess," Matt said in defeat.

Neither did Matt know what to make of the scarlet cord that had been in the envelope with the letter Joel had left for Melanie. She hadn't shown it to him until last night. It was strange, to say the least—especially since Melanie seemed to have no inkling of its meaning either.

During the next four days, Matt and Don exhausted every avenue they could think of. Matthew made phone calls and searched the Internet. He spent hours interviewing people in Silver Creek who had known Joel. Without exception, they spoke highly of Ellington. Yet everyone also admitted that they really didn't know much about him personally.

Privately, Matt and Pastor Steele tossed around possibilities they would never have voiced in Melanie's presence: Maybe he was already married or had fallen in love with someone else. Or he had a secret drug or alcohol addiction, or he was caught up in a gambling habit. They speculated about things that had no basis in any fact they knew—that he was dying of some fatal or contagious disease and had just enough decency not to expose Melanie and Jerica to such a situation. They briefly entertained the notion that he was a government informant or a protected witness or that he was a convict on the lam, but those speculations seemed the stuff of Hollywood.

And yet Don Steele—who had known Joel better than anyone besides Melanie—could not point to one thing that even hinted at the mildest of these verdicts. "The Joel Ellington I knew was a man of genuine faith and integrity. I would bet my life on that," Steele told Matt, pounding a fist into his open palm.

Either that, or he was an Oscar-caliber actor, Matthew thought.

Every trail Matt followed led to a dead end. The last action of Joel's that could be documented was his withdrawal of the balance of his bank accounts—in cash—on the same day he'd left the letters and cashed his paycheck.

Tim Ellington, Joel's brother, seemed to have disappeared along with him. Melanie didn't have an address for the man and remembered only that he lived in Connecticut and that he was in the real estate business, but the only Tim or Timothy Ellington in that state was a long-retired auto mechanic. Matthew began to wonder if perhaps the brothers were involved in some kind of scam together. It did seem strange that Melanie didn't know more about Joel's brother—or Joel's former fiancée. But the truth was, Matt couldn't have recited the street addresses of his own wife's siblings—or their birthdays, for that matter. So maybe it was nothing.

A week after his arrival in Silver Creek, Matthew was no closer to an answer than he'd been when he arrived. It was time for him to go back to Karly and the boys in Bergen County and to his job in New York.

Before Jerica was even up for school, he brought the last of his luggage from the guest room and set it by the front door. He'd told Jerica good-bye last night, but he crept into her room to plant one last kiss on her cheek before Melanie walked him out to the rental car.

They stood together on the driveway in awkward silence. "Well," he said finally, reaching out to embrace her. "I better go."

"Thanks, Matt."

"I haven't given up, Mel," he told her. "I'll keep trying to find out what happened."

"I know. I know you will. Thank you so much for coming. Give those boys a squeeze for me. And give Karly my love."

"I will. You come and see us too. Okay?"

"We will." She gave him a brave smile, but her voice held the heaviness of unshed tears.

"I mean it, Melanie. It would do you good to get away. And Karly would love to see you."

"We'll come soon. I promise."

Matt released her and moved slowly toward the car. "Well...I guess I'd better go," he said again.

He got behind the wheel and waved as he backed slowly out of the drive. She followed the car to the edge of the street. When he took one last look in his rearview mirror, she was still standing in the street, small and alone.

He had never felt so helpless in his life.

Nineteen

The hotel lobby was crowded with conference-goers. Melanie shifted her attaché case on her shoulder and studied the agenda spelled out on the placard in front of the main meeting room.

"Melanie!"

She turned to see Doreen McGrath, a designer with the Kieffer Group. "Hi, Doreen! I was hoping you'd be here." The two shook hands over their awkward burdens of computer cases, notebooks, and handbags.

"Are you teaching workshops today?" Doreen asked.

"Just one. Larry Cohen asked me to teach one management session this afternoon. But the rest of the day I'm just a student. How about you?"

"Just a lowly attendee."

"What's your first session?"

Doreen balanced her briefcase against her leg and pulled a schedule from the outside pocket of her purse. "Design and the Law," she read.

"Oh, me, too. Sounds like a fascinating subject, doesn't it?" She rolled her eyes.

"Sounds like a perfect opportunity for a nap." Doreen laughed. "Come on, I've already scouted out the meeting rooms."

Melanie followed the perky redhead down the carpeted corridor of the hotel, grateful to have found a friendly face in the crowd.

"So how have you been, Mel?" Doreen asked when they'd settled at a table near the back of the room. "Busy with wedding plans, I'm sure. Did you bring that handsome man along?"

Melanie felt her cheeks burn. "Oh...Doreen... You haven't heard. We...um... The engagement has been called off."

Doreen's face paled, and she put a hand to her mouth. "Oh, Melanie, I'm so sorry. I didn't know. What happened?"

To Melanie's dismay, tears sprang to her eyes. She swallowed hard, struggling to regain her composure. "I'm not sure, to tell you the truth. I guess Joel...just wasn't ready to be married."

"Oh, Melanie...I feel terrible," Doreen said.

They were words Melanie had heard a hundred times in the last month. The humiliation of trying to explain her situation had been almost unbearable, especially when she wasn't sure what had happened herself.

At Erika's suggestion, she had mailed a note to everyone on the guest list, informing them briefly of the situation and asking for prayers. It had helped prevent many painful questions. But of course, even two months after Joel's disappearance, there were those, like Doreen, who still hadn't heard the news.

She'd given Doreen the same pat, rehearsed response she'd given everyone. And though she feared it made her sound jaded and perhaps bitter, at least it kept her from being bowled over with grief every time she had to explain it yet again. Or did it? The lump in her throat felt monstrous.

The workshop presenter tapped on the mike, and the buzz of conversation around them died down.

"Do you want coffee?" Doreen whispered, bobbing her head to the side of the room where several steaming carafes sat on a linen-covered table.

"Oh...sure," Melanie said, pushing back her chair and following Doreen to the table, deeply relieved for a graceful end to this conversation.

Melanie walked briskly through the doors of Cornerstone and headed down the hallway that led to the day care facilities, anxious to see Jerica after an especially grueling day at By Design.

She passed the secretary's office and waved through the doorway. "Hi, Darlene, how are you doing?"

"Oh, hi, Melanie. I'm doing okay. How are *you?*" The tone in her voice was one of unreserved pity. Darlene brought up the subject of Joel every time Melanie saw her. Not wishing to appear rude, she stepped into the office for a moment. Ignoring Darlene's question, she asked, "How is your mom doing, Darlene? I haven't heard any news for a while."

Darlene sighed heavily, and immediately tears welled in her eyes. "She's about the same. She still can't keep anything down. And let me tell you, she didn't have any weight to spare before she got sick."

"I'm so sorry to hear that. This must be awful for you." Melanie felt guilty that she didn't really care to hear the details. She knew she had become too wrapped up in her own little world of grief. She forced herself to listen now, nodding sympathetically, earnestly trying to feel empathy for this hurting woman.

"I wouldn't wish this disease on my worst enemy, Melanie. I… For a while I had some hope that they might find something that would help her, but I'm…I'm afraid it's spread too far too fast now." Darlene sighed again. "As if that isn't bad enough the insurance companies don't cover half of what they should. They won't even consider paying for some of the new treatments that are available now." Her voice rose. "These are promising treatments—some people are calling them miracle cures. I read an article the other day that sounded exactly like Mom's situation—and this treatment cured the woman in the story! But do you think Mom's insurance company would even consider it? For what they charge, they ought to be ashamed." She bit her lip and stood there, shaking her head.

"I'm so sorry, Darlene. I wish there was something I could do."

"Just keep praying," the woman said.

"You know I will." She patted Darlene's arm and changed the subject. "How is the new building project going?" She couldn't help but remember how involved in the project Joel had been. She shook off the thought. It seemed that everywhere she turned, there was a reminder of Joel.

"Well, they haven't set a firm date yet," Darlene told her, "but I don't imagine it'll be long now before we break ground."

"That's exciting. I suppose it means more work for you, doesn't it?"

"Oh, I don't mind. It helps me keep my mind off my troubles," the secretary said. Abruptly she lowered her voice and asked, "Melanie, have they found out any more about Joel? Do they have any idea where he might have gone?"

Melanie held back a sigh. "No...they haven't, Darlene. I...don't really expect that...we'll ever know."

"But they're still looking for him, aren't they? I mean, surely there has to be some way to locate him."

"I don't think they look too hard for people who don't want to be found, Darlene."

Darlene reached out and touched her hand. "Well, I'm so sorry this had to happen to you...you of all people, Melanie. I tell you... you think you know somebody..." She clucked her tongue. "It's a crying shame, that's what it is."

Melanie forced a smile and squeezed the thin hand. "Well, I appreciate you thinking of me, Darlene." She glanced pointedly at her watch. "I'd better call it a day. I was supposed to pick Jerica up ten minutes ago."

"It was nice to see you. I'm glad you're doing so well." Darlene patted her arm and held up a hand in farewell.

Melanie headed on down the hall. *Was* she doing well? Some days she thought so. Other days she felt as though she were starting from the proverbial square one. She *had* overcome some of the obsessive behaviors that had marked the early days of Joel's disappearance. The hours she had spent on countless Internet searches, entering Joel's name—and Tim's, and any other flimsy clue she could summon—had proven futile anyway. Somehow her efforts only served to prove how little she had actually known about Joel, how fragile a thread their relationship had hung by.

But just as surely as a night of fruitless searching could dash her hopes, so a marathon of daydreams—remembering the precious, tender moments with Joel—could send them soaring again. She couldn't so easily let go of the memories. Whatever else was true, he *had* loved her. And Jerica. Of that, she was certain. And so hope dipped and jounced like an errant kite, dragging her after it on the tails of vague possibilities.

She approached the doors that opened onto the day care wing. The bubbly laughter of children drifted through the hallway. For Jerica's sake, she had to stay strong, stay positive. She forced the corners of her mouth into a smile and walked into the noisy room.

⁓

The April morning dawned clear and sunny, and Melanie tried not to think how perfect it would have been for a wedding. Two weeks ago, knowing that she would need a heavy-duty distraction on this date, she'd invited Jerica's friend Ami Dixon to go with them to the zoo in St. Louis. When Erika learned of their plans and hinted that she would love to come along, Melanie had invited her, too. Now in spite of the poignant significance of this day, Melanie was looking forward to the outing.

Erika offered to drive, and while the two little girls chattered and giggled in the backseat of the SUV, she and Melanie visited in the front.

"I'm glad we're doing this," Erika told her, reaching across the vehicle's console to pat Melanie's knee. "It was a good idea to make some fun plans for today."

"Well, I didn't want to sit home and mope. I've had about all the moping I can stand."

Erika offered a sympathetic smile and, thankfully, changed the subject. By the time they arrived at the zoo, they were excitedly discussing ideas for redecorating the sunroom off Jerry and Erika's kitchen. They parked the car and unloaded the wagon they'd brought for the girls to ride in when they tired of walking. Melanie loaded sweatshirts and a cooler full of snacks and drinks into the wagon, and the four of them headed down the trail to the children's zoo.

Jerica and Ami pranced from exhibit to exhibit, leaving Melanie and Erika breathless trying to keep up. The little girls squealed with delight as noisy lorikeets flew to them and perched on the edge of the cups of nectar they bought. Melanie had forgotten what fun it was to see the zoo through the eyes of a child. They meandered through Discovery Corner and the River's Edge exhibit, saving Jerica's favorite—the otter exhibit in the children's zoo—for last. The girls ran to watch the playful creatures through the Plexiglas display window, then hurried to get in line for the clear tube slides that allowed them to feel as if they were swimming with the otters.

The sun grew warm as it climbed the blue ladder of sky, and when the girls finally tired of the slides, Melanie and Erika found a spot in the shade on a bench near the edge of the walkway where a forest of water geysers spouted randomly from the ground. The women watched and laughed while the two girls danced and splashed in the cool spray.

The zoo was crowded on this first warm weekend of the year. Melanie leaned back on the bench and observed the other children and families who had come to enjoy a day at the zoo. She battled to keep her thoughts in check as everywhere she looked couples strolled arm in arm, and fathers hoisted daughters onto their shoulders for piggyback rides. Perhaps the zoo hadn't been such a good idea after all. She squeezed her eyes shut, grateful that the dark sunglasses she wore veiled the threatening tears. *Help me, Lord. Don't let me ruin this day for everyone else. Help me to dwell on the blessings you've given me. Thank you that Jerica seems so happy. I have so much to be thankful for.* When she looked up a few minutes later, she felt better.

Until she saw him.

He stood not ten feet in front of them with his back to her, watching a group of rowdy boys. His arm was draped over the shoulder of a leggy blonde, but the familiar sway of his back, the way his hair curled into the collar of his shirt, were unmistakable. Melanie's heart beat a tight staccato, and the blood pounded in her temples. *Oh no!* She could not risk letting Jerica see him.

She sat upright on the bench, and she must have gasped, because Erika turned to her with alarm on her face. "What is it, Mel? What's wrong?" Erika followed her gaze to where the couple stood. Just then the young woman laughed, and the couple turned to face the bench where Melanie and Erika sat.

The man's eyes held hers for a second, then in the absence of recognition, swept on to another stranger. Behind wire-rimmed glasses, his eyes were a deep, burnished brown, and his face bore little resemblance to Joel Ellington's—nor did his cheek bear Joel's distinctive scar. Relief and disappointment flooded her in concert.

"It's...nothing..." she told Erika, who was still watching her carefully. She shook her head and took a deep breath, entreating her heart to slow its pace. "I think I...fell asleep for a minute." It wasn't really a lie, was it? Perhaps it had been a wisp of a dream that caused her to conjure Joel from a complete stranger. It was understandable that on this day that was to have been her wedding day, Joel would be in her thoughts.

"I'm exhausted," she told Erika now. "Are you about ready to call it a day?"

"Whenever you are, dear." Erika began to gather up their things and load them back into the little wagon.

"Jerica...Ami." Melanie hollered for the girls, giving the stranger one last longing glance as he and the woman strolled on down the path arm in arm.

∽

The following Tuesday evening, the shrill ring of the phone split the air. By the time Melanie picked it up in her bedroom, Jerica had already answered in the kitchen. Answering the phone was a new privilege, and Melanie listened in to see how the little girl would handle the call.

"Hello, this is Jerica LaSalle speaking," the little voice chirped.

"Well, hello there, Jerica LaSalle," Jerry boomed on the other end, obviously amused by his granddaughter's well-rehearsed spiel.

"Grampa!" she squealed.

"Can I talk to your mommy, please?"

Melanie moved her hand off the receiver. "I'm right here, Jerry. What's up?"

"Hi, Mel." His voice softened for a minute. "Jerica, can you hang up the phone please? I need to talk to your mom."

The silent breathing continued on the other end. "Jerica, hang the phone up right now," Melanie scolded.

They listened for the click on the extension, then Jerry's voice became serious. "Melanie, I got a call from Don Steele this afternoon. There's some bad news that might...well, it concerns Joel."

Her heart stopped beating, and she tightened her grip on the phone. "What is it, Jerry? What's happened? Have they found him?"

"No... Some money from the building fund is missing."

"What? What are you talking about?"

"Just under fifteen thousand dollars is missing from the fund for the new addition. Darlene wrote a check to the contractors for the down payment, and the church got an overdraft notice today. When they checked the account, they discovered that the money was missing."

Slowly, the implication of what he was saying began to soak in. She was immediately defensive. "What? Jerry, what does that have to do with Joel?"

"I don't think I have to tell you, Melanie. It looks like we've found Joel's reason for disappearing."

"What are you talking about? No. I don't believe that!" Her voice rose a pitch, and her hands felt clammy on the receiver. "Joel would never do something like that, Jerry. No… I don't believe it."

"I'm sorry I had to be the one to tell you, but the news will be out soon enough, and I wanted you to be ready for what people will be saying."

"Is there any way they can prove it was Joel?" She tried to rouse that defensive spirit again, but in the space of a minute it had shriveled like an airless balloon.

"I don't know, Melanie. I haven't heard all the details yet, but it… Well, it does make sense. Joel was in charge of a lot of the fundraising. He made some of those deposits—or at least that's what he told Darlene. It looks like the cash deposits from several fund-raisers and donations never made it to the bank."

"I don't understand."

"The correct deposits were all there on paper—on the church's records—but when Darlene compared it with the bank's balance, they discovered that some of those amounts weren't included. That money never got deposited," he repeated. "At least not in Cornerstone's account."

Melanie sank down to the bed, unable to speak.

"Mel, I'm sorry. I am truly sorry…but at least now you know. Now you don't have to spend the rest of your life wondering what went wrong."

"Jerry, I'll...I'll call you back. I can't talk about this right now." She hung up the phone and tried to cry, tried to feel a sense of relief that she finally had her answer, but the tears refused to come. Instead, she felt only a dull ache where her heart used to be.

$\backsim$

All the papers carried the story the following weekend. It ran alongside a photo of Joel, cropped from their engagement picture. KMOV Channel 4 ran a tongue-in-cheek spot on the ten o'clock news that made Melanie sick to her stomach. The media apparently loved the idea of a mysterious disappearance, a jilted lover, a large sum of missing money, and of course, Joel's close connection to the church's building project.

Melanie lived the humiliation all over again. None of the stories accused Joel outright of the theft. The words *alleged* and *suspected* were carefully inserted in all the appropriate places, but Melanie knew there would be no doubt in anyone's mind that Joel was guilty.

And in spite of the defenses that had come to her so readily when she'd first heard the news, in spite of the fact that she simply could not believe the man she loved was capable of such a thing, one nagging thought kept coming back to her: There didn't seem to be any other explanation.

Twenty

Joel Ellington threw the newspaper down on the bed in disgust. "What are we going to do now?"

John Toliver leaned back against the low dresser in the shabby hotel room and eyed him thoughtfully. "*Do* you have the money?"

"You know I don't." Surely Toliver knew him better than that by now. The inspector had seen how frugal he'd been with the funds WITSEC had provided.

"Do you know who does have it?"

"I can't imagine." Joel paced the filthy, matted green carpet, his mind whirling at this turn of events. "Only three or four people have access to the church's bank accounts, and I can't imagine any one of them taking it. Unless they've hired someone new since I left… The bank only had one account. All the different funds were separate on paper only. The building-fund line item had been there for probably five or six years before I came to Silver Creek and it was never drawn on."

"You mean the money could have been missing for a while and nobody discovered it until a check bounced?" Toliver scratched his chin.

"I suppose so. The donations could have been recorded, but the money just never got deposited." He picked up the newspaper again and skimmed the article. "But this makes it sound as though they can trace the missing money right to the time I left."

Toliver actually smiled. "Apparently someone took advantage of your disappearance."

Joel still couldn't fathom who at Cornerstone was capable of such a thing. He put his head in his hands and rubbed his face. "I hate it. I hate this whole thing. No one is going to question this story, and I can't even defend myself. And who could blame them? It...it seems logical that it was me—even to *me*."

"And that's why we're not going to do one thing. We're just going to be grateful for the alibi it gives you. "

"Alibi!" Joel wheeled to face Toliver. "What's going to keep them from starting a manhunt for me?"

"I hate to break it to you, but in the whole scope of things, fifteen grand from the coffers of a small-town church isn't going to be a high priority. From where I stand, the alibi is worth more than that."

"I don't need an alibi! I need justice."

"For now, you're going to have to settle for the alibi, Joe."

Joel glared up at him. "Quit calling me Joe. Joe Bradford is dead."

Toliver waved a hand in resignation, slid from his perch, and rose to his full height. "I'm gonna head out. I'll be back in the morning. With any luck, by the end of the week we'll have a permanent place nailed down."

Silence.

"Joe...Joel...if this goes like it's supposed to, it'll all be over in a few months, and you can have your life back."

"Which life?"

The inspector acknowledged Joel's query with a grimace and a slight bow of his head. Then, jangling his keys in his pocket, he went to the door and let himself out.

∽

While Melanie sliced the last of the tomatoes from Jerry LaSalle's summer garden, Jerica sat in the middle of the kitchen floor surrounded by fresh new boxes of crayons and markers and crisp tablets of writing paper.

"Can I go to school tomorrow, Mommy?" she asked as she restacked the pile of school supplies for the tenth time.

Melanie sighed and rolled her eyes. "No, sweetie. Three more days."

"Not tomorrow, but the next day?" her daughter asked hopefully.

"No. Not tomorrow, or the next day, or the next, but the day after that. *Then* you can go."

"But I'm too 'cited," she whined. "Can't I go a little early?"

"I'm excited too, honey, but you'll just have to be patient. If you went tomorrow, you'd be the only one there. Besides, Thursday will be here before you know it."

Melanie could hardly believe her baby would be starting first grade—in school all day for the first time. And she *was* excited for Jerica. Autumn had always seemed like a time of new beginnings for Melanie—more even than the advent of spring or the start of the new year. Something about the pungent smell of pencil lead and erasers, and the crisp bite in the evening air, had always held the promise of a fresh beginning and exciting possibilities.

Life had gone on. Each day took her a little farther from the heartbreak of Joel's disappearance—his deception—and a little closer to hope.

Cornerstone Community Church had recently hired a new director of Christian education. Most of the financial losses had been recouped through donations and insurance, and the addition to the church building had begun to rise from the vacant lot. Even the news media had forgotten all about the scandal as more exciting new stories broke.

Melanie had resigned herself to never fully understanding what had gone wrong with Joel—not because she knew resignation was the right attitude to take, but because she had no other choice.

She still questioned God sometimes—especially when she saw a faraway look come to Jerica's eyes as the little girl watched her friends climb onto their daddies' laps in church or play catch with their fathers before a T-ball game.

But finally, more from exhaustion than altruism, she surrendered her will to God. He, after all, had never promised that life on this earth would be carefree or just or easy to understand. She took great hope in the promise of a life beyond this one, which had brought her mostly heartache and sorrow. For her daughter's sake, she would go on with her life. She would not again expect it to give her joy. Then, maybe, it would not disappoint.

⌒

The first day of school came and went in a whirlwind, and unexpectedly, as the days went by, little joys began to work their way into Melanie's life. Jerica adored school. Within weeks she was picking out words in newspaper headlines and sounding them out on her own. Melanie started finding little notes that Jerica had left for her around the house. Sometimes it was a challenge to decipher the phonetic spelling—what Jerica's teacher called "kid writing." But the "good nit mommy" or "wak me up urly" messages reminded Melanie what a delight the discovery of this form of communication had been for her when she was small, and what power there was in the written word.

"Mommy, look what we made in school today," Jerica said, as she scrambled into the car one September afternoon. Her eyes were shining, her face alight with pride as she took the paper-towel wrapping off her treasure. She lifted up a string of macaroni painted with bright tempera colors. "It's for you, Mommy. Mrs. Layton said we could keep it if we wanted, but I made mine for you."

"Oh, honey, it's beautiful! Are you sure you don't mind giving it away?"

Jerica shook her head solemnly.

"Well, thank you. I love it." A horn tooted behind them. "Oh dear, we're holding up the line. Buckle up, honey…hurry."

Jerica fastened her seat belt, chattering away about her adventures at school. Melanie pulled onto the street, smiling. It seemed that every day brought something new they could share together. It was a gift to be able to savor it all through Jerica's eyes and Melanie was grateful for each diversion that kept her eyes on the future and put gentle blinders on what was past.

Yet each morning she awoke with a lingering awareness of a sorrow so deep that she ached—physically ached—from the raw power of it.

On a chilly October night Melanie and Jerica cuddled on the sofa in the family room reading from Johanna Spyri's *Heidi.* One of Melanie's most treasured memories of her own mother was the winter they'd read the classic novel together—a chapter each night. Now she sat in front of a crackling fire reading aloud to her daughter and realized with joy that she was handing a tradition down to the next generation.

> "Yes, and do you know why the stars are so happy
> and look down and nod to us like that?" asked Heidi.
> "No, why is it?" Clara asked in return.
> "Because they live up in heaven, and know how
> well God arranges everything for us, so that we need
> have no more fear or trouble and may be quite sure
> that all things will come right in the end. That's why
> they are so happy, and they nod to us because they

want us to be happy too. But then we must never
forget to pray, and to ask God to remember us when
He is arranging things, so that we too may feel safe
and have no anxiety about what is going to happen."

Jerica tugged on the sleeve of Melanie's sweatshirt. "That's what
the grandmother told Heidi," she whispered with a knowing nod.

"That's right," Melanie said, feeling her throat close over the
large lump that had suddenly settled there. *Oh, Father, I know you
are arranging things for me according to your plan. Thank you for
reminding me of that.* Not sure she could trust her emotions, she
stalled, leafing back a few chapters as though looking for the page
Jerica meant.

"Remember, Mommy? Heidi told the grandmother that she
stopped praying because God didn't listen to her prayers. But that
wasn't right, was it, Mommy?"

"No, it wasn't." Melanie brushed a strand of hair off Jerica's forehead. Love for her daughter welled up inside her. "You have a good
memory, squirt," she said, her voice cracking.

"Keep reading, Mommy. You can read and cry at the same time.
Grammy does it all the time."

Melanie grinned sheepishly, cleared her throat, and flipped back
to their bookmark.

The two children now sat up and said their prayers,
and then Heidi put her head down on her little
round arm and fell off to sleep at once, but Clara lay
awake some time, for she could not get over the wonder of this new experience of being in bed up here
among the stars. She had indeed seldom seen a star
for she never went outside the house at night, and the
curtains at home were always drawn before the stars
came out. Each time she closed her eyes, she felt she

must open them again to see if the two very large stars were still looking in, and nodding to her as Heidi said they did. There they were, always in the same place, and Clara felt she could not look long enough into their bright sparkling faces—

Melanie and Jerica were both sniffling a little when the jangle of the telephone broke the mood. They each grabbed for a Kleenex from the box that sat on the coffee table in front of them, dabbed at their eyes in unison, then broke into giggles at their seemingly choreographed movements.

"This better be important," Melanie sniffed, blowing her nose and disentangling herself from the afghan that had covered them.

She went to the kitchen and checked the caller ID. Smiling, she picked up the phone. "Matthew! Hi, there."

"Hey, Mel. How's it going?"

"We're doing good. How about you guys? Everybody okay?"

"More than okay." Her brother's voice held a huge grin.

"Oh? Why's that?"

"We just found out that we've got another baby on the way."

"You're kidding? Oh, Matt! That's wonderful! But I thought you guys were done with babies."

"Well, so did we. But then, what do we know?"

Matt's excitement was contagious. They laughed and rejoiced over the news for several minutes before Melanie insisted that he put Karly on the phone.

"Oh, Karly, I am so happy for you! Maybe this will be your little girl!"

"Well, I'm not going to carpet the nursery in pink just yet, but it is nice to think about. Hey, when are you going to come and see us?"

Suddenly Melanie missed her sister-in-law and friend like crazy. Matt had been to Missouri after Joel disappeared, but it had been almost a year since she'd seen Karly and the boys.

"You know," she said, thinking aloud, "I have three weeks of vacation coming… Maybe I'll just use some of that time and fly out there."

"Oh, Mel, I'd *love* that. How soon could you come?"

"Well, I hate to take Jerica out of school…but I guess your boys will be in school too. Maybe it would be best to leave her with Jerry and Erika. I know they'd be thrilled to have her to themselves for a few days. If I can get away the first week in November, would that work for you?"

"That would be perfect. I'll miss seeing my favorite niece," Karly said, "but this way we can make it a whole week of girls' days out. We can shop and do some sightseeing while the boys are in school and just have a chance to catch up on everything. Oh, I can hardly wait!"

Melanie caught Karly's enthusiasm, and her heart soared at the prospect of seeing her dear friend and spending some time with her brother and nephews in Bergen County. She said good-bye to Matt and Karly and immediately dialed the LaSalles' number. She felt a too-familiar twinge of guilt at the thought of leaving Jerica, but it would be good to get away for a while.

That night, after she climbed into bed, Melanie reached for the drawer of her nightstand, looking for the little book of devotions she'd been reading each evening before falling asleep. It was a habit she'd developed at Pastor Steele's suggestion, and she had to admit it did help to take her mind off the worries of the day and the nagging reminders of all she'd endured the past year.

The drawer caught on something, and when she finally yanked it open, she sat up to sort through a month's accumulation of junk. Removing a nearly empty bottle of lotion and a stack of church bulletins from the front of the drawer, she dug further, unearthing some drawings Jerica had made that she hadn't had the heart to toss.

Absently she swung her feet over the side of the bed and got serious about cleaning out the drawer. Making little stacks to file and others to toss, she reached in one last time and drew out a long envelope with her name on it. *Joel's letter.*

She had read the single page three times a day in those first weeks after its arrival in her mailbox, looking for answers that weren't there. But over the past few months she had nearly managed to put it out of her mind. She hesitated. Finally, she let out a shallow breath and lifted the worn flap of the envelope. As she slid the letter out, the silken cord coiled into her lap, and she felt herself spiraling into the abyss of confusion that had marked too many months of her life. It still puzzled her why Joel had chosen to leave her this silly piece of braided cord as a remembrance of him—a token whose meaning he had refused to explain to her.

Perhaps it was time to throw it away. And the letter, too. They certainly weren't mementos she wanted to hold on to forever.

Almost against her will, she unfolded the letter and read the words she knew by heart—gentle, loving words that didn't match the cruelty they'd inflicted upon her heart. And upon Jerica's. Slowly, she wrapped the cord around her hand, then slipped the tidy loop from her fingers and tucked it back into the envelope with the letter. Carefully, she placed the envelope in the back of the drawer, purposefully burying it beneath other books and papers.

For reasons she didn't fully understand, she couldn't destroy these reminders of Joel. Not yet. Not when they still evoked such deep feelings in her heart…of having loved, and been loved by, him.

Twenty-One

Clutching Matt's arm, Melanie jostled her way through the crowd that bulged at the seams of the expansive Port Authority Bus Terminal. Even as she tried not to look like a gawking tourist, she felt excitement rise within her. Energy seemed to pulse like blood through this vein into New York City. She watched the weary faces of commuters and wondered how people could ever become immune to the amazing sights and sounds of this place.

Melanie fell in step with Matthew's long gait and endeavored to blend in with the flow of the midmorning crowd. They hurried past benches where vagrants slept undisturbed, and she watched in fascination as the masses dispersed into seemingly choreographed queues in front of ticket booths and storage lockers, onto escalators, and finally, like water from a dam, flowed with the throng out onto 42nd Street.

Yellow Cabs zoomed past, some stopping, others moving on. The prospects of getting a taxi right away looked good, but even if she had to wait a few minutes—or walk several blocks up the street where it was less congested—she was in no hurry.

"You go on, Matt," she insisted, when he offered to hail a taxi for her. "I'm perfectly capable of getting myself a cab."

Her brother's office was within walking distance of the terminal, but Melanie was headed for an art museum a mile in the opposite direction. Karly had intended to come into the city with them today, but five-year-old Jace had awakened with a fever and a nasty cough, so Karly had stayed home with him. Though Melanie offered to remain behind with her, Karly had insisted, "This is the last day that watercolor show will be in the city, Mel. Besides, it'll be nice for you and Matt to have some time alone together. You hardly ever get to do that."

It was true. And now Melanie was glad she'd come with Matt. They'd had a wonderful visit on the bus ride into the city, and they planned to meet later for lunch.

She waved him away. "Go on, big brother. I'll be fine."

"You're sure?"

She caught him sneaking a glance at his watch.

"I'm positive. I know my way around pretty well by now."

"Are you sure you have enough cash for cab fare?"

"Matthew!" She laughed. "In case you hadn't noticed, I am not a little girl anymore. And it's not like this is my first trip to New York. I will be fine. Now get moving… You're going to be late for work."

"Well, if you're sure…"

"Get out of here," she commanded, giving him a playful shove.

Matthew stepped aside just as her hand connected with his shoulder and she lost her balance, teetering on the edge of the curb. "Watch it, there," he warned, reaching out to steady her. But as he did so, the heavy satchel she carried slipped from her shoulder, propelling her into Matt's arms. He nearly lost his balance then, and they both got the giggles.

When they were both on firm footing again, Matthew arched one eyebrow skeptically. "And I'm supposed to believe that you're a big girl who can take care of herself?"

She laughed again and reached up to give his cheek a sisterly pat. "Get out of here. Before I do something really stupid."

He smiled and gave her a quick hug. "I'll meet you at The Raven at 1:30," he reminded her. "You have the address?"

She patted her bag where the restaurant's address was safely tucked away. "Got it. Quit worrying. I'll be fine."

He shrugged and headed down the street.

Still smiling, she stepped to the curb and held her right hand aloft, watching as her brother's broad back disappeared into the horde of pedestrians. It had been good to have this time with him and Karly.

With a pang, Melanie thought of Jerica and wondered how her daughter was getting along. Melanie missed her, but they'd spoken on the phone each evening, and it was clear that she was having a wonderful time with Grammy and Grampa.

In the midst of the New York traffic, a new wave of Yellow Cabs appeared. Melanie raised her arm higher. Half a block up the street she watched a tall man reach for the door of the cab that had pulled up beside him. At first glance, the man looked so much like Joel Ellington that for an instant her breath caught in her throat.

Stop it! she chided herself. It had happened often right after Joel's disappearance. As it had that day at the zoo, and too many times since, her heartbreak caused her imagination to conjure Joel out of any male who happened to be tall or sandy-haired or athletically built. She'd hoped that phenomenon was a thing of the past, but she couldn't take her eyes off this man. She watched him climb into the cab and was startled that even in profile, he looked remarkably like Joel.

His cab was moving toward her now, pulling out into the flow of traffic. She craned her neck and resisted the need to blink, lest she lose sight of this cab in the swarm of other taxis that crawled along the avenue.

The car rolled by not ten feet from where she stood, but the glare off the windows prevented her from seeing inside. Then it moved into shadow, revealing the face of the passenger inside. He was staring back at her, recognition obvious in his stricken expression. The thin scar that marred his right cheek was clearly visible.

It was him! It was Joel!

Her knees went weak and her hands began to tremble.

After so many months, so many sleepless nights wondering if he was even alive, there could be no mistake. Even if the scar on his cheek had not confirmed it, there was no doubt that he recognized her as well.

The man—*Joel*—turned away quickly, leaning forward to speak to the driver. As she watched his taxi melt into the river of vehicles on 42nd Street, another Yellow Cab eased up to the curb and stopped beside her.

Behind her, a man groused in a thick Brooklyn accent, "Hey, lady, you want the ride or not? 'Cause if you ain't in a hurry, I am…" He snorted and heaved an exaggerated shrug.

"I'm sorry," she mumbled over her shoulder. Opening the heavy door, she climbed into the cab.

The driver's gaze met hers in the rearview mirror. His dark eyes snapped. "Where to, miss?" he asked in a heavy accent she couldn't place. Her mind drifted.

The cabby put his arm on the back of the seat and asked again. "Hey, miss… Where you want to go?"

"Oh…I'm sorry. Here…" In a fog, Melanie dug in the side pocket of her satchel for a business card. For a fleeting instant, she entertained the idea of having the driver follow Joel's taxi. But one glance out the windshield at the sea of yellow ahead of them, and she came to her senses. "This…this is the place," she said, handing him the card with the museum's address.

The driver held it to the windshield, as though he might be farsighted. He studied the card for a moment, glanced down at a map spread open on the seat beside him, and put the vehicle in gear. "Yes. Yes, I get you there."

He eased the cab into the flow of traffic, and Melanie fell back against the dusty seat. The city that rose up on every side ordinarily aroused intense excitement within her. But now she was oblivious to it. One thought pelted her mind again and again: *He recognized me. He knew it was me, and he drove off anyway.*

Like a bucket of icy water, deep pain and humiliation poured over her, and a lump of old grief swelled in her throat. Trembling and powerless to stop the rush of memories, she leaned her head back on the seat, only vaguely aware of the erratic swerving and braking as the driver negotiated the busy streets.

Finally, the taxicab rolled to a stop in front of the museum. Melanie rummaged in her purse for the right change, paid the driver, and stepped from the vehicle in a daze.

Still shaken, she slowly mounted the steps to the massive building and went inside. Soft strains of Vivaldi floated from the ceiling speakers, muffling the street sounds behind her.

She checked her coat and satchel with the attendant and took the elevator to the basement where her favorite gallery was located. She spent an hour wandering through a maze of muted watercolors and richly textured oils. But she barely saw their beauty. Finally, she stopped in front of a large nineteenth-century canvas depicting a father and child. The curly-haired girl in the painting gazed into her father's eyes with rapt adoration. Melanie's throat tightened as she recognized the expression of her own daughter. Jerica had often gazed at Joel Ellington with the same longing affection. Her eyes misted, and she felt strangely lightheaded.

Why, after all these months—just when her heartache had begun to dull and she felt as though she had rejoined the living—had she seen him again? That brief moment, when their eyes met and recognition was acknowledged, had awakened a gnarled tangle of emotions that could not rationally coexist.

She felt something near euphoria at knowing for certain that Joel was alive. Often, in the weeks after she had received his letter, she had imagined that he was ill...even that he'd died. Or that he had amnesia and could not remember anything about their life together, about the love they shared. Never mind that neither delusion made sense with what his letter said. She had been desperate for some explanation, however absurd, for why he would have left her even while declaring that he loved her.

But side by side with her joy now was despair—and anger. For knowing that he had recognized her but made no effort to speak to her, she had to face the fact once and for all that he had fully meant to leave her.

Yet wedged between those extremes of emotion smoldered a frail spark of hope. He was here in the city. Maybe she could talk to him, plead with him to tell her what had happened. Perhaps yet she would find answers that, if not easily understood, at least could offer some closure on this dismal chapter of her life.

"Excuse me…ma'am? Are you all right?"

Melanie started at the light touch of a hand on her shoulder. She looked up into the face of a museum guard, feeling as though she were awakening from a deep sleep. She scrubbed her face with her hands. "I'm…fine. Thank you." Standing, she stretched her muscles and gathered her purse and the museum's guidebook from the bench beside her.

She looked at her watch, puzzled. "Do you have the time, please?" she asked the guard. Surely it was not as late as her watch indicated.

The guard pulled back a sleeve of his uniform jacket. "I've got 12:35."

"Oh…thank you." She was stunned. She had sat in front of this painting for nearly an hour. In a strange trick of time, it seemed she had been here for only a few moments.

She retrieved her coat, hurried out the front doors, walked a few blocks down the street, and summoned a taxi. She gave the driver the address of The Raven.

Her brother was sitting on a bench in front of the restaurant when she stepped out of the cab. Smiling, he rose and came toward her. "How was your morning?"

That was all it took to bring the tears. "Oh, Matt. I saw him!"

"What? Saw who? What are you talking about, Melanie?"

"I saw Joel, Matt."

"You're not serious? Where? Did you talk to him?"

"No. I   "

A boisterous party of four came out of the restaurant just then, bumping into Matthew. He took his sister's elbow and steered her toward the entrance.

"Let's get a table, and then we can talk."

In the sparse crowd of early afternoon, they were seated almost immediately.

When the waiter had taken their order, Matt reached across the table and touched her hand. "Okay, tell me what happened."

"I saw him...in a cab. It was him, Matt. It was Joel."

"Melanie..." His tone told her that he was more than a little skeptical. "Are you sure? You know this has happened before. You've told me yourself that you've thought you spotted him before, and it's always turned out to be a mistake."

"No, Matt. This time was different. I saw the scar on his cheek...I was only standing a few feet away. He saw me too. It was obvious that...he recognized me."

Her brother studied her as if her face might reveal whether he could really believe her incredible claim. "Well, what did he do? Did he stop the cab? Did he say anything?"

She shook her head. "He...he spoke to the driver and then the cab pulled away. I...I was too stunned to try to stop him." She twisted the linen napkin in her lap. "I spent the morning at that art museum I told you about. I've been there all morning...just thinking, trying to figure out what to do. Oh, Matt, we've got to find him. He's here...in the city. I have to know what happened."

Matthew's forehead creased with deep lines. He sighed and shook his head slowly. When he finally spoke, his voice was hard, "I wish this had never happened. You were doing so well, Melanie. I finally felt like I had my sister back. So help me, I don't know what kind of hold that man has on you—"

He stopped short, and Melanie recognized in the clench of his jaw that he was struggling to control his temper. "I'll never forgive him for what he did to you, Melanie. Forget about him. He's not worth it."

"But…"

"Melanie, think about it." His voice rose several decibels. "What in the name of all that is holy do you have to gain by tracking him down now? He destroyed the faith you had in him, he crushed Jerica's little heart…and for what? A lousy fifteen grand?"

"Matthew, that's not fair," she cried. "You don't know that Joel took that money. He…he wasn't like that. I just can't believe he did it. He wouldn't—"

Melanie cut off her words abruptly as the waiter appeared at their table. She cast her eyes downward while Matthew ordered for both of them. When they were alone again, Matthew leaned across the table and spoke deliberately, clearly struggling to keep his voice low. "You have built Joel up in your mind to be some kind of hero. You've romanticized this whole sorry affair until you can't see the truth when it's staring you in the face."

Matthew dropped his head. "You ask anyone in Silver Creek—anyone at all—if Joel Ellington took that money. Ask them," he challenged. "You know what they would say, Mel. Do you honestly think everyone else is wrong and you are right? That doesn't even make sense. You're deceived! You've let your emotions and your pain make you totally blind to the truth where Joel is concerned."

Her brother's words cut deeply. Tears pricked her eyes, and she couldn't keep them from falling.

"C'mon, Mel, I'm sorry. I didn't mean to make you cry." His voice softened, and he leaned across the table to swab clumsily at her cheeks with his dinner napkin. "I know it was hard for you to see him like that. It's just… This is so unlike you. You've always been so strong. You've always been such a good judge of character. I don't understand why you can't see what is so obvious to everyone else."

She closed her eyes and shook her head at him, begging him silently not to push her further.

The waiter brought their food. Matthew ate while Melanie picked at her salad, scarcely eating anything.

Once their meal was done, they walked back to Port Authority and stood on line for their bus, still not speaking, her long-anticipated day in the city ruined.

At the bus stop back in Bergen County, Karly met them with the family minivan, kids in tow. "Hi, guys! Did you have a good time?" she chirped.

Melanie didn't miss the warning glance Matthew shot his wife. Karly looked at Melanie and back to her husband. "Is everything okay?"

Matthew tipped his head pointedly to the backseat where the boys were buckled in. "Later."

Karly threw Melanie one last questioning glance, but Melanie could only give her a tight-lipped smile in return.

When they got back to the house, Karly sent the boys outdoors to play and came into the living room where Matt was poking at the logs he'd put in the fireplace. Melanie was huddled on the sofa, her legs curled underneath her.

"So what happened? You guys look like you've seen a ghost."

"Well put," Matthew said dryly.

"Matt..." Melanie chided.

"Melanie saw Joel in New York," he explained to his wife.

"What? Joel Ellington? Are you serious?"

Melanie told Karly the whole story then.

But her friend seemed as skeptical as Matthew was. "Mel, I know you want to believe the best of Joel. And I love you for that, I really do. But you've got to think about what's best for Jerica now...what's best for you. A lot of time has passed. If Joel ever intended to offer an explanation for what he did, it would have happened by now. He knew where you were. He could have called—or written. He didn't do that, Mel. And he didn't stop…today."

The humiliation of that fact washed over her again. Melanie sat silently, feeling like a chastened child.

"You've seen him now," Karly went on. "You know he's all right physically. Maybe *this* was what you needed…to have some closure on this whole thing. Maybe this is a sign that it's time to put it all in the past and move on."

That night in bed, Melanie mulled over the things Karly and Matt had said. She could admit that they were right on some accounts. Joel could have at least let her know that he was all right.

Most important, they had a point about her needing to think of what was best for Jerica now. Maybe, as Karly said, it was significant that God had allowed her to see Joel one last time. Maybe she should choose to view this as the finale to a very sad chapter of her life.

Twenty-two

Joel Ellington guardedly scanned both ends of the street before he locked the door to his apartment. The brisk November breeze caught the wind chimes that hung on his porch and set them jangling. Adjusting his backpack over one shoulder, he tucked his keys into his pocket and set out on the twelve-block walk to the school where he taught.

The last of autumn's leaves swirled along the sidewalks and crunched beneath his boots. Ducking his head against the icy air, he pulled his jacket tighter around his waist.

Three days had passed since the shock of seeing Melanie again. Those seventy-two hours had seemed interminable. He would never forget the startled expression that had come to her beautiful face when she recognized him, nor could he erase the vision of the pain that etched her brow as he'd turned away from her. That image had been his constant companion since the moment he'd stared out at her from the window of the cab in front of Port Authority.

That, and the vision of Melanie in the arms of another man.

Although he was no freer to be with her now than he had been the day he left Silver Creek, it hurt deeply to realize that Melanie perhaps *had* found love again, that she was free to make a new life for herself, to have another chance at love. He felt a fresh stab of pain at having seen her in the playful embrace of the tall, dark-haired man. He hadn't gotten a good look at the man's face, but he'd carried himself with the suave assurance of a successful businessman. Probably someone she met through By Design. It must be serious if she'd traveled to New York with the guy. A startling thought pierced his heart—maybe Melanie was married. Now that he thought about it, her manner with the man had seemed like the easy and familiar playfulness of a happily married couple. And why wouldn't Melanie be married? She was young and attractive. He'd been out of her life for many months now. He'd left her with no hope whatsoever for a future with him. Why would he dare to think that she might wait for him?

He shook away the feelings of guilt and jealousy and loneliness for the hundredth time, and forced himself to pray that she was happy. It seemed the only prayers he prayed these days were out of obligation. But he did pray that the man he had seen her with was a good and decent person, that he truly loved Melanie, and that he would give Jerica the love and devotion the little girl deserved.

He ached with longing, thinking of Melanie and of Jerica. But he could never hope to be a part of their lives again. It was too late for that.

Help me, God—but the prayer caught in his throat before it could be given voice. Truth was, he had put his faith on a shelf since leaving Silver Creek. He wondered how many times a man could do that and get away with it—do that, and still have the option of returning to God.

He thought of his parents and Tori and the part they had played in the strong faith he'd once known. Their deaths had nearly ripped the last threads of faith from the fabric of his young life. But his brother had pleaded with Joel not to let their parents' death cause him to become bitter. Joel had taken his brother's pleas to heart and had begun to live out his faith in a way he never had before. And he'd thought Melanie had been the reward for his faithfulness. That God would allow her to be taken from him too had brought him to his breaking point. He'd felt yanked about like a puppet on a string, and now the knowledge that Melanie had gone on to find happiness without him threatened to snap that string completely. He could never deny God's existence, but was this how a loving God treated his children?

He rubbed his hands together and pushed the dark thoughts from his mind. Turning onto the street where the school was, he focused on the bright young students he was privileged to teach. His accelerated English classes were beginning an important literature unit, and they needed to stay on schedule in order to finish it before semester finals.

King's Collegiate was a small prep school that catered to academically talented low-income students. Though many of them suffered significant family hardships and dysfunction, the kids in this school were mostly dependent on scholarships and grants and therefore highly motivated to stay in school. It made his job a breeze. In the advanced classes he taught, especially, these were kids who wanted to be here, wanted to excel, to make something of their lives.

He was grateful for the job, grateful to be teaching again. This private school had few connections to the teachers' unions and national organizations that might have made him vulnerable to scrutiny, so he'd convinced Toliver to approve the position. He had despised living on WITSEC money anyway. It was good to be earning an honest living again.

In the three months since he had come to the school, he'd found a measure of contentment in his work. For that, he was truly grateful; not everyone in his circumstances had an opportunity to work at something they loved. When Joel stood before a classroom of eager, gifted students and helped open up the world of literature for them, he did feel that he was doing what he had been created to do. He was determined to put the past behind him, make up for all of it somehow, and pour his passions into his calling as a teacher

It wasn't easy. Melanie LaSalle had never been far from his

thoughts. But Joel had resigned himself many months ago to the realization that he would probably never be free to love again. And now, with the trial finally imminent, it seemed that even if everything went exactly right and he gained his freedom, it wouldn't matter. He no longer held a claim to Melanie's heart.

A light mist began to fall. He shivered and turned up the collar on his jacket. He should have worn a heavier coat. It seemed winter had arrived in earnest in New York. It would be a long one. He kicked at a stone on the sidewalk, faintly aware that his jaw had tightened and his fists were clenched. *Just get through another day. Just dwell on the good things. Find some small happiness, and be grateful for that…*

⁓

"Let's go make art, Mommy."

Jerica slid off her chair, grabbed her mother's hand, and tugged her toward the sun porch.

"Hang on, sweetie," she laughed. "At least let me put the leftovers away."

On this cold January night, she'd come home late from a meeting at the office. She wanted nothing more than to take a long bath and fall into bed. But she knew it was more important than ever that she spend time with her daughter.

While she cleared the table, she heard Jerica rummaging through the markers and crayons in her art kit, then tearing off a new sheet of drawing paper. Melanie had returned from her visit with Matthew and Karly determined to move forward and make a new start for herself and for Jerica. She'd enrolled Jerica in art classes and had taken up a brush and palette herself. She had loved painting when she was in college, but except for an occasional design job, her artwork had fallen by the wayside after she married Rick, and even more so after Jerica had come along. But now she had set up an easel for each of them on the enclosed sun porch off the kitchen, and she was trying her hand with watercolors—rather successfully, if she did say so herself. Her renewed pastime offered a brief escape from the dark thoughts that had threatened since her encounter with Joel Ellington in New York.

She covered the fruit salad from supper and put the bowl in the refrigerator, then went to join Jerica. As they worked side by side, she couldn't help but smile. The little girl traced the line of her paintbrush with her tongue. Her intense concentration was apparent in the set of her brow. "What are you working on there, squirt?"

"A picture."

"Well, I guessed that, silly. A picture of what?" she asked, going behind Jerica's easel to look at the colorful rendering.

"A family," Jerica said without looking up. She turned her brush expertly and pointed with the handle. "There's the mommy and there's the daddy and that's me." She turned the brush again and dabbed the bristles in bright turquoise paint.

Melanie cleared her throat. How should she respond? It had been several weeks since Jerica had asked about Joel. It was difficult to know if this was prompted by the whole situation with him, or if this was one of those things that would have come regardless of Joel's impact on their lives.

She decided to treat it as the latter. "It's a beautiful painting, honey. You know, I bet your daddy is looking down from heaven right now thinking the same thing."

"This daddy's not in heaven." Jerica continued to apply strokes of paint to the heavy paper.

"Oh? Where is he?"

"I don't know."

Melanie bit her lip. "Do you know his name?"

Jerica looked up at her, eyes luminous, paintbrush poised. "Just Daddy." She swept a streak of pale coral across the sky above her little family, turning from Melanie's gaze.

"Oh, sweetie." Kneeling beside the miniature easel, Melanie

brushed a wayward curl off her daughter's forehead. "I know you miss Joel. I...I miss him too. But I don't think he's coming back, Jer. We need to get used to that, you know?"

"I'm just drawin' a picture, Mommy."

"Okay...okay..." She let out a sigh.

She took up her own paints, and they worked together in silence. She knew how Jerica felt. It didn't matter how much time they spent with friends, how full they filled their calendars, how many paintings they rendered. Each of these could only postpone that moment at the end of each day when she crawled under the blankets and tried to shut out the thoughts of Joel that were always just a blink away.

Involuntarily, she sighed again with exhaustion. "Time to put our paints away and get ready for bed, sweetie." As she helped Jerica clean up their brushes, then get ready for bed, the vague thought crossed through her mind that maybe for once sleep would come easily tonight.

But an hour later, she lay under the quilts staring at the ceiling. Even as she grew drowsy, she found herself hoping that she would dream of Joel. In the early weeks after he left, she had shut out the unbearable reality by reliving through her dreams—both waking and sleeping—every moment she had ever spent with Joel. It was an unhealthy fantasy life, and she knew it was wrong to continue to seek such an escape from reality. But even now—in spite of his betrayal—dreams of Joel were sweet dreams for her.

She resisted the desire to feed the fantasy, praying silently. *Lord, take away this awful pining I have to live in the past. Fill my mind and my heart with your thoughts.*

In spite of her prayer, Joel's face appeared in that hazy state between awareness and sleep. Her memory was stirred as if by an unseen hand, and an image floated to the surface. It was the day they'd gone to the carnival when Tim was in Silver Creek. The scene played like a movie behind her closed eyes. The four of them were having a wonderful time, laughing, soaking up the sun, walking down the midway. Jerica was starving, so they headed for the food pavilion. Joel bought hot dogs and Cokes for all of them. But when they sat down, he realized the vendor had given him back too much change. He dug two dollars from his pocket, and Melanie and Tim sat watching him weave his way through the crowd toward the hot dog stand.

Melanie sat up abruptly, the memory strikingly vivid in her mind. She rubbed her eyes, struggling to recall every detail. She could see Joel's back as he stood in line for the second time that day, to make things right with the cashier. Tim's voice echoed in her mind: "That's Joel for you. Honest as the day is long." It wasn't just a dream. It was a memory. The incident had actually happened that day at the carnival. She had completely forgotten it until now.

She lay beneath the quilts, contemplating what this could mean. Troubled, she reached up and flipped the switch on her bedside lamp. Sliding the drawer of her nightstand open, she reached into the back and withdrew the envelope—the one that held Joel's last words to her.

She slowly lifted the flap and let the braided satin cord spill onto her lap. A red satin cord. Why had this been so important to Joel? What had it meant to him? She could only guess that he had left it with her as a token of comfort. After all, the only hint he had revealed to her was that the cord reminded him of a scripture that comforted him. But what was the scripture? If it was just a generic verse offering reassurance, why would he have been reluctant to share it with her?

She picked up her Bible from the nightstand. A red ribbon marked the place she'd been reading. She was struck by the similarity between the ribbon attached to her Bible and the one Joel had given her. Was it possible Joel's cord had once served to mark a certain passage in his own Bible? Was that what he meant about it reminding him of a scripture that comforted him? She leafed through the New Testament, not having the slightest idea what she was looking for, merely seeking consolation herself. When nothing stood out at her she flipped to the concordance in the back. On a whim, she turned to the word *ribbon*. Nothing. She paged back to see if there was an entry for *cord*. She ran her finger down the column.

Two words stood out as though they were printed in iridescent ink: *scarlet cord*. She looked at the cord in her hand. *A scarlet cord.* Her heart pounding, she turned to Joshua 2:18, the reference given. She leafed back a page to the beginning of the chapter and began to read. The passage told the story of a prostitute named Rahab. The account was vaguely familiar to Melanie, though her excitement waned as she realized that it was unlikely Joel's scarlet cord had any relationship to a story about a prostitute. At least she certainly hoped it hadn't.

The verses told of Joshua, who sent spies to scout out the occupied land near Jericho, which God had promised to give to the Israelites. Rahab gave shelter to the spies, acknowledging that she recognized Joshua's God as "God in heaven above and on the earth below." She begged the spies to show kindness to her and her family, and to spare their lives when Jericho was inevitably conquered. The men swore they would do so, but only if she tied a scarlet cord in her window as a sign.

Intrigued, Melanie scanned the annotation at the bottom of the page. One commentator compared the scarlet cord in the window to the lambs' blood the Israelites were instructed to put on their doorposts during the plagues of Egypt. According to the footnote, the blood-colored cord could be seen as a representation of Christ's atonement.

Melanie ran the thin rope through her fingers again and again. Had that been its meaning for Joel? Simply a symbol that reminded him of his own salvation? That would certainly have been a comfort to him. But what possible reason could he have had for being unwilling to share that with her? He had spoken freely of his conversion as a young boy, won to Christ by his missionary parents, then recommitted after a time of doubt when those parents were killed. No, there had to be something more.

Returning to the commentary, she noticed a cross reference that pointed to the book of Hebrews in the New Testament. She paged forward until she found chapter 11. Rahab's name appeared again in verse 31. Again Melanie had to go to the beginning of the chapter to understand the context of the passage. The writer was citing Old Testament heroes who had exhibited remarkable faith. It seemed odd. Here was a prostitute who had lied to her country's leaders to protect a couple of spies whom she knew planned to ravage her homeland. And yet she was deemed worthy to go down in history as a woman of great faith. Why was that?

Melanie almost forgot her reason for seeking out the story in the first place as she studied verse after verse. From what she could discern, it appeared that Rahab was honored for her actions because they stemmed from her faith in the one true, living God and from her desire to protect spies she knew would soon occupy the land in the name of that God.

A strange thought occurred to Melanie. *Was Joel a spy?* She dismissed the idea immediately. How absurd. What could a spy possibly hope to accomplish working as a Christian education director in a small church in an obscure Missouri town?

Still, the thought niggled at her. Something did not fit with the entire scenario. No matter how objective she was, no matter how logical the facts seemed, she could not make the Joel she knew into the kind of man who embezzled money from his church while he went out of his way to return two dollars to a hot dog vendor. It certainly wasn't enough to exonerate Joel. She could almost hear her brother's derisive laughter if she were to relay that idea to him in an effort to clear Joel's name. Matt would probably tell her that Joel's action was just another way he had deceived her into believing that he was someone he was not. And perhaps that was so. Why then, did a measure of peace fill her heart now? Somehow, she knew—knew in a place deeper and more trustworthy than her human mind—that Joel could never have done the things they accused him of.

Besides, as she'd told Matthew more than once, if it really was about money, the truth was that Joel had stood to gain far more than fifteen thousand dollars by marrying her. With her comfortable salary and her share in By Design, they would never have wanted for anything.

But if it wasn't the money, it had to be something else. *Something* had compelled him to leave Silver Creek. Something she couldn't begin to imagine. And in that moment, she knew that whatever it took, she must find him and learn the truth.

Twenty-Three

Joel Ellington lay in the too-soft bed of his furnished apartment staring at the ceiling. Outside, a January wind howled and the furnace kicked on with a *clank*. How much longer could he live this way? He'd spent months in a hellish limbo, going through the motions, waiting. Waiting to testify at a trial that might as well have been his own.

Exhausted, he closed his eyes and tried to sleep. But slumber came with difficulty. Vivid pictures from the past swirled before him. And as she had in so many nightmares, Victoria appeared again.

In a half-conscious stupor, his mind followed a snarled thread of disjointed memories from a long ago night. Finally he slept, and the memories melted into the dream.

He was back in the restaurant trying to comfort Tori in the aftermath of the brutal murder. Everything around them was chaos.

"It's all right, Tori. They'll get him. He couldn't have gone too far. But…they'll probably want to question us." He swung his head in the direction of the police officers who were directing emergency crews to the table where the dead man sat, still eerily upright in his chair.

A policewoman began steering people to the front of the restaurant. They were like sheep being herded into a pen, some bleating loudly, others mute, obviously still in shock.

He led Tori along, guiding her with one hand at the small of her back. Her dress was damp with perspiration, and he could feel her shudder with each breath she took.

The interrogation took place in the restaurant's small office, and it lasted for almost two hours. Only four people had actually seen the gunman. The dead man's dining partner had still not appeared, but each of the other witnesses had been asked to recount their story separately, away from the hearing and influence of the others. No one was allowed to leave until each had privately given his or her version of the events of the gruesome evening.

By the time he and Tori got back to his car in the nearly empty parking lot it was after midnight. A long black limousine was parked near the curb in front of the restaurant. The dead man's car? Or his fellow diner's? Even the rich aren't immune to tragedy, *he thought as he turned his little Mazda onto the city street. The thought of the restaurant's wealthy clientele reminded him that his wallet still held the wad of cash he had been saving for weeks to pay for this dinner. He held the steering wheel with one hand and retrieved his wallet from his back pocket. With a morbid attempt at humor, he riffled through the bills. "Do you think I should go back and pay our tab? Maybe leave a nice tip?"*

Victoria burst into tears.

"Oh, Tori! I'm sorry. I shouldn't be joking about it." He glanced at her and saw that she was trembling and pale. Easing the car to the side of the road, he shifted into park, and took her in his arms.

"Hey, hey…" he crooned, holding her close. "It's all right. Everything is fine now. God was watching over us. We're safe. Everything's okay."

When she finally calmed down, he drove her back to her apartment. He put the kettle on for tea while Tori showered. Dressed in flannel pajamas and a thick terrycloth robe far too warm for the balmy June evening, she emerged from the steamy bathroom. She was shivering in spite of her attire.

They sat together on the sofa in her living room and talked for hours, going over and over the nightmare they had lived, remembering buried fragments of the evening's tragedy, offering prayers of gratitude that they had been kept safe.

Finally Tori convinced him that she would be fine. "You've got to get some sleep." She looked at the clock on the end table. "You have to teach a class in just a few hours," she laughed nervously.

He took her hands and pulled her up from the sofa. Leading her back to the small, femininely decorated bedroom, he turned down the blankets for her and waited while she climbed in. He tucked the quilts tightly around her shoulders and kissed her cheek.

"You're sure you'll be okay?"

She yawned and waved him away. "I can hardly keep my eyes open."

"I'm going to go out through the back. I'll lock the door when I leave," he told her. "You sleep as late as you want. I'll come and get you for lunch. Okay?"

"Okay," she breathed sleepily. "This bed feels pretty good right now. I love you."

"I love you, too."

Eyes still closed, she smiled up at him. He reached for the lamp on the night table and switched it off.

"Good night, sweetheart," she whispered, as he kissed her again.

Suddenly it was a horror movie playing on the screen of Joel's mind. Tori's face shifted and changed until it was Melanie lying in the bed. "Good night, sweetheart," she said in her sweet Midwestern accent. The face shifted again, and the bed became Tori's coffin.

Joel jerked to consciousness, clawing the air in an effort to shake off the horror of the nightmare that was still to come. Struggling in his mind to sort the reality from the dream, he lay paralyzed in his bed, remembering how he'd heard Tori's steady, sleepful breathing even before he left the room that night.

It wasn't until he was driving home from Tori's apartment that he remembered her diamond. He had just taken it from his coat pocket when the chaos had broken out in the restaurant. He decided to go back to the restaurant the next day to get it back. But by then Tori was dead, and the diamond no longer mattered to him.

And then it had happened all over again with Melanie. He had found love once more, had the promise of a wonderful life with a warm, loving woman and a little girl he loved like a daughter. He had truly felt that he'd been offered a new chance at life and at love. But then Toliver had shown up on his doorstep, and the nightmare had started all over again.

Hot tears seeped from under his eyelids. "Why, God?" He said the words aloud, then again louder, shouting at the ceiling above him and feeling that the words never went beyond the mildewed tiles over his head.

"Why, God? Why?"

∾

Melanie unbuckled her seat belt and stretched as far as the plane's close quarters would allow. She reached into her handbag and pulled out her itinerary. She should be in Hartford, Connecticut, by 10:00 A.M. That would give her time to make a few calls today.

She felt a twinge of guilt about the deceit it had taken to get here. She had left Jerica with her in-laws, telling them that she was visiting a college friend in Boston. That much was true. She'd spent an enjoyable day with Candice Powers. But she hadn't told anyone of the remainder of her plan.

Now that she was actually on the plane, she felt a little foolish—like a grown woman playing at Nancy Drew. But she had thought long and hard about her decision. And she *had* prayed about it. She couldn't say that she felt divinely led to do what she was about to do, but she did feel strongly about the need to find Joel. When Rick had become ill she'd been powerless to do anything to bring him back.

But Joel was alive. And she intended to do everything within her power to find him.

Please, Lord, she prayed, *open the doors you want opened, and close those that you don't desire me to walk through. Don't let me do anything foolish, Father.*

Her first destination was Hartford. Joel's brother worked in the real estate business somewhere in the state. She didn't know if Tim was still there, or whether he actually owned an agency or was just employed as a Realtor in one of them, but it was a place to start. She'd hit a dead end with an Internet search. A Hartford area phone book had shown no listings for a Tim or Timothy Ellington, and the few agencies she'd called hadn't known an agent by that name. But, armed with a snapshot she had taken of the brothers when Tim had visited Silver Creek, she hoped to track Tim down.

The plane touched down at Bradley International just outside of Hartford three minutes ahead of schedule, and by 10:45 Melanie was in a rental car headed for downtown Hartford.

She easily found the agency that the chamber of commerce had listed as Hartford's largest, but no one in that office knew of anyone by the name of Tim Ellington. At their suggestion, she went to another agency nearby that dealt in commercial real estate.

Five agencies later, she got her first lead.

The receptionist at Bel Aire Realty was friendly and talkative and seemed eager to help. "Tim Ellington? No, I don't think I know anyone by that name."

"He might go by Timothy. Here." She produced the photograph and pointed to a tanned and smiling Tim.

The woman's eyes lit with recognition. "Oh, sure, that's Tim Bradford. He occasionally does business in Hartford, but most of his properties are in the Manchester area now. He's with one of the smaller agencies there... I can't think which one right offhand."

"Tim Bradford? You're sure it's Bradford?"

"That's the only name I've ever known him by, honey," the receptionist said.

"Well, thank you... I...I appreciate your help."

"Here, hang on..." The woman went to her desk and pulled a business card from a stack and handed it to Melanie. "This is our branch in Manchester. They can probably tell you which agency he's with."

Melanie left the office in a daze. Back in the rental car, she checked the route on the map. Manchester looked to be about a thirty-minute drive. She should be able to get there before the office closed.

After a wrong turn, she located the Manchester branch and was surprised when an agent there knew Tim Bradford's name immediately.

"Sure, I know Tim," the pleasant, middle-aged man told Melanie. "I think he's with Webber & Wright these days. Do you know your way around town?"

"No, I'm sorry."

The man gave her quick instructions, and by three o'clock she was sitting in the waiting room of Webber & Wright Realty.

The receptionist dialed an extension. "Tim, there's someone here to see you."

A few minutes later, a door opened at the end of the hallway, and a tall, blond, familiar figure strode to greet her. Melanie had forgotten how much Tim looked like Joel. The sight of him reminded her what a risk she had taken coming after Joel this way. Her hands grew clammy, and she wiped them on her slacks.

When recognition came to Tim's face, his expression registered mild shock. "Melanie?"

"Hello, Tim."

He glanced around as though he didn't wish to be overheard. "Why don't we go into my office where we can talk."

She followed him to the dark, paneled office, and he closed the door behind them.

"I guess I don't need to ask what brings you here…"

"I have to know what happened with Joel, Tim. If he doesn't want to see me, I understand, but I think I deserve some answers."

Tim stood beside his desk, rubbing the carpet with the toe of his shoe as though trying to erase a small stain.

"Do you know where Joel is?" she persisted.

"I'm not sure what to tell you, Melanie…"

"You can tell me why you go by the name of Bradford. I don't understand what's going on, Tim. The way Joel told the story, you two had the same parents." Bitterness and confusion had crept into her voice, and she struggled to remain polite. She didn't want to blow her best chance of finally locating Joel.

Joel's brother sat down in his chair and looked Melanie in the eye. "Joel's legal name is Ellington, Melanie. He didn't lie to you."

She felt a headache starting. "Then…Bradford isn't *your* real name?"

"How did you find me?" he asked.

She explained how she had tracked him down, ending by waving the photograph at him.

He slumped in his seat and ran his hands through his hair, taking in a ragged breath before speaking. "I can't give you any details, Melanie, but if you care anything about Joel, you will not flash that picture around here."

"I don't understand. What is going on, Tim? Is Joel in trouble?" Her voice rose a pitch.

He hung his head over his desk and wrung his hands. "Melanie, I can't talk to you about Joel. I…I just can't."

Heartsick, she asked the question that begged to be asked, "Did he take the money, Tim?"

"Money?" Tim's expression was unreadable.

"I—I assume you heard about the money that turned up missing after…after Joel left Silver Creek."

He would not meet her gaze.

"Do you have any idea what agony I have lived through this past year? Do you know what it's like to have your life pulled out from under you like a rug, and to have no clue whatsoever why it all happened? Do you?" She couldn't hold back the anger in her voice any longer.

"Melanie, I am sorry this happened to you. But Joel...it... couldn't be helped. And there's nothing you can do to change it. All I can tell you is that Joel...has gone on with his life. You can't ask me any more questions. There's nothing else I can say."

"This doesn't make sense, Tim. Is Joel in some kind of trouble?" she asked again.

He hesitated, then finally said, "You could say that. And if you flash those pictures around, he'll be in a lot more trouble."

"It must be about the money. I want to help, Tim."

"I'm telling you, the only thing you can do to help Joel is to go back to Missouri and forget you ever met him. I'm sorry. I... I'm going to ask you to leave now."

She was crying now, from sheer frustration and exhaustion. "I know he's in New York, Tim. I saw him."

Tim Bradford's eyebrows shot up, and he sucked in a short breath. "You talked to...Joel?"

She shook her head. "He was in a cab...driving away. But I know it was him. Please, Tim, you don't have to tell me where he is. You don't even have to tell Joel you talked to me, but I've got to have some answers... I can't live like this anymore!" It came out in a sob. "I just don't think I can go on until I know what went wrong."

His tone was compassionate, but steady and determined when he told her, "Melanie, what happened had nothing to do with you. I can tell you that Joel is all right. He is a good man. He would never have hurt you if he had any choice at all in the matter. Now he is going on with his life, and that's what you have to do."

Tim stood and moved toward the door. It was obvious from his staid demeanor that Joel's brother was not going to give her any other information.

Dejected, and more confused than ever, she left his office and drove back to Hartford to find a hotel. Oblivious to the stark beauty of the wintry New England countryside that whizzed by her car windows, Melanie drove on, deep in thought.

Tim's admonition not to show Joel's photograph around frightened her. She couldn't imagine what reason he might have for such a warning. Had Joel taken the money after all? Was he a wanted man? She had already shown the photograph to many people, including the secretary at the agency in Hartford. That woman's reaction hadn't seemed to indicate anything beyond the simple fact that she recognized Tim. Besides, Joel had known she had the photo. He'd never seemed to care if she showed it to anyone.

Then it struck her: Perhaps Tim was trying to protect himself. Was he part of something shady that he was trying to cover up? Maybe it was his own picture that he didn't want shown around the area. But that didn't make sense either. He was working in the Manchester office for anyone to see. Maybe *he* was somehow involved in Joel's disappearance. Had Tim taken the money himself? Yet he seemed trustworthy, and nothing Joel had ever said about Tim indicated that he was anything but a good man.

She remembered the warm and friendly Tim who had come to visit in Silver Creek that summer. He'd seemed different today—suspicious and cool and anything but friendly. She wondered what had caused him to change so. Could Joel have changed like that too?

That night, she tossed and turned in the unfamiliar hotel room. Finding Tim hadn't answered any of her questions. If anything, it left her more perplexed and bewildered than ever.

And infinitely more determined to find Joel and uncover the truth.

~

After the sleepless night, Melanie showered and dressed and pon-dered what her next step should be. Before she'd left Silver Creek, she had assumed that she would find Tim and that he would lead her to Joel. Now she had to come up with another plan.

The fact that Joel had talked about so few people from his past caused her to realize how little she had actually known about him. Had she been to blame for that? she wondered now. Had she never asked him about the most important parts of his life—or worse, had she never listened when he told her? And yet, his openness and hon-esty where the present was concerned—and especially where their relationship was concerned—was one of the things that had attracted her to him, one of the things she missed most about him.

She remembered that Joel had occasionally talked about the col-lege where he'd taught before coming to Missouri. Perhaps someone there might know where to find him. And if not, maybe they could at least shed some light on who Joel Ellington really was.

Melanie couldn't remember many details about the small private school, but she knew it was in New York, and Joel had used the name Langston. Whether that was the name of the college or the town, she wasn't sure. She recalled him commenting on the ice sculpture at the Addy awards. He'd told her there was a fountain on campus like it, a likeness of a dragon that spewed water instead of fire. He had also spoken of a woman named Barbara, a professor in the English department whom he had admired greatly. She thought the woman's last name was Andrews—or maybe Anderson. If she could contact a chamber of commerce or department of tourism in the general area, she might be able to locate the school.

She brought a stale sweet roll and coffee to her room from the continental breakfast the hotel served, then she got out the phone book and her atlas and set to work. The atlas showed a Langston, New York, near Poughkeepsie just over the Connecticut border. For some odd reason, directory information didn't have a listing for a chamber of commerce there. It seemed that a town large enough to support a college would also have some type of tourism department. A call to Poughkeepsie's chamber of commerce confirmed that there was a small private school in Langston—Foxmoor College. She couldn't remember Joel ever using the name Foxmoor, but she jotted down the number and dialed it.

"Foxmoor College, how may I direct your call?"

"Yes, I'm...I'm looking for a professor named Barbara... Andrews, I believe it is...in the English department?"

"That would be Barbara Anderson."

"Um, yes, that's it."

"I'm sorry, Mrs. Anderson won't be in her office until classes resume. May I take a message?"

"Till classes resume?"

"Yes. We're on our winter break. Second semester doesn't start until the nineteenth. None of the teachers will be back until the Monday before."

"I see. Do you... Do you happen to know if Mrs. Anderson lives there in Langston?"

"May I ask who's calling?"

"Well..." She hesitated. Tim's warning had made her cautious. "Mrs. Anderson doesn't know me. I'm kind of a friend of a friend. I'm going to be in Langston this week and I just thought I'd stop by and say hello. You don't need to leave a message."

Melanie hung up and called information for Langston, New York. There were five pages of listings for Anderson. The operator gave her the most likely possibilities and she jotted them down and started dialing. She reached two answering machines and hung up without leaving a message. Two other calls proved to be dead ends, but when she dialed the next number a rather gruff female voice answered on the first ring.

"Is this Barbara Anderson?"

"Who's calling please?"

"Mrs. Anderson… Is this the Barbara Anderson who teaches at Foxmoor College?"

"Yes… Who's calling, please?"

Suddenly Melanie had no idea what she should say. If Joel truly was in trouble, it could make things worse for him if someone connected him to her. But Joel had spoken of Barbara Anderson as a friend and mentor. Maybe she could help. She decided to take the risk. She hadn't given her name yet. She could always hang up. "I'm…I'm very sorry to bother you at home. I'm calling about someone who taught at Foxmoor several years ago in your English department. I wonder if you might know where I could find him."

"Well, I may. Who is it you're looking for?"

"His name is Joel Ellington. He taught English there four or five years ago…"

"Joel Ellington, you say? No, I'm sorry. I've been at Foxmoor for twenty-eight years, and we've never had anyone by that name in the English department. Or in any department for that matter. Who did you say was calling?"

"I'm sorry. Joel is…a friend of mine. This is…Mary Jones." Her heart thumped at the artless lie.

"Well, Ms. Jones, this is a very small college, and I can't recall anyone by that name ever teaching here."

"Are you certain? Joel would have been in his early thirties, tall, light brown hair, a scar on his cheek…"

There was a pause and then a voice full of curiosity. "In his thirties? Oh my, no. Most of our teachers are much older. I can only think of one man in the department in the last five years who was that young. But he was killed in an accident…such a tragedy."

"You can't think of anyone else that age who worked at the school? Maybe an assistant or a fellow?"

"I'm sorry, no. I really can't."

"Is…is there by any chance a fountain on Foxmoor's campus? A dragon?"

A hint of suspicion crept into the woman's voice. "Yes…there's a fountain in front of the administration building…a dragon. I'm sorry, how did you say you knew this man?"

"Well, uh, thank you for your help. I'm sorry to have bothered you." Melanie hung up quickly, her heart pounding.

How strange. She knew that Joel must have been connected to the school somehow in order to know Barbara Anderson and to be familiar with the unusual fountain. He couldn't have made those things up. But why didn't she remember him?

Pondering, she looked at the atlas. Langston was less than a hundred miles from Hartford. The library on campus would have Foxmoor's yearbooks on file. If she hurried, she could be there before everything closed for the day.

Twenty-Four

Melanie stood by the fountain, mesmerized, feeling strangely elated to be standing in a place from Joel's past. A stream of water gurgled from the bronze dragon's mouth, producing a steamy mist in the air. As Joel had said, the fountain on Foxmoor's campus did indeed look remarkably like the ice sculpture that had been the centerpiece on the banquet table at the Addy awards a year ago.

But when she walked across the empty campus to the library, Melanie was disappointed to find that it, like most of the buildings on campus, was closed until the students returned after the winter break. A receptionist in the administration office told her that Langston's public library might have the college yearbooks in their collection.

She returned to her car and drove to the business district of the small town. Housed in a two-hundred-year-old stone building that was as dim and cold today as it likely had been two centuries before, the library held the charmingly musty smell of old books, pencil shavings, and oiled wood. An impressive collection of books lined the sturdy shelves around the main room's perimeter.

"Yes, I think we have a few," the librarian said when Melanie inquired about the yearbooks. "What years were you looking for?"

Melanie told her.

"Wait here. I'll see what I can find."

The woman returned with a stack of the slim Foxmoor annuals, and Melanie took the books to a quiet corner of the high-ceilinged room. She opened the issue of the last year she thought Joel would have been at the college and flipped to the faculty pages. She could tell at a glance that his face was not among the predominantly female, predominantly senior-citizen staff of the college.

She turned to the index, scanning the columns for his name, with no luck. A quick glance through the student photo pages confirmed that his picture was not in that section either. On a hunch, she returned to the faculty pages and found the "not pictured" section at the end. There were only four names on that list, but one of them grabbed her attention: Joseph Bradford.

There was that name again. Was it possible that Bradford—not Ellington—was the family name? Tim had said that Ellington was Joel's legal name. But she'd thought that a rather odd way to put it. His legal name? Had *Joel* changed his name for some reason, then?

The librarian helped her set up the outdated microfiche reader where the town's old newspapers were on file. Melanie scanned the issues of the weekly *Langston Advisor,* going back five years. The images whizzed before her as though she were seeing them from a fast-moving automobile. But nothing on this highway of film looked familiar. Until she came to a large headline on a front page dated January twenty-sixth, three years earlier: *Local teacher killed in motorcycle crash.*

Barbara Anderson had mentioned a teacher at Foxmoor who had been killed in an accident. Melanie focused on the story, which continued on an inside page. Finding the section, she stifled a gasp as Joel's face appeared through the viewer. The photograph, a poor quality snapshot reprinted in black and white, was still sufficiently clear for there to be no doubt in Melanie's mind that it was Joel. His hair was longer and he sported a mustache. Though his right side was facing the camera, there was no sign of the distinctive scar on his

cheek, but of course, the picture had probably been taken before he
acquired the scar.

Most disconcerting of all, the photo caption read *Joe Bradford*.
Melanie sat in stunned silence.

So it *was* Joel who was using an assumed name. Not Tim. Joel
Ellington had lied to her about everything—even his very name. No
wonder all the Internet searches she and Matt had done when Joel
first disappeared led to dead ends.

Her senses numbed by the shock of what she had discovered, she
turned back to the microfiche and read the newspaper account:

> LANGSTON, NY—Foxmoor College suffered a
> tragic loss Friday with the death of English profes-
> sor, Joseph (Joe) Bradford. Bradford was killed in a
> motorcycle crash in Connecticut. Bradford came to
> the English department of the four-year private
> school two years ago, and according to Barbara
> Anderson, head of the department, the thirty-four-
> year-old teacher was a favorite with students.
>
> "It's a terrible tragedy. I am deeply saddened to
> hear of Joe's death. He will be greatly missed," Ander-
> son said when contacted at the school yesterday
> morning.
>
> According to Anderson, Bradford's life was
> marked by tragedy. His parents died in a plane crash
> when he was a teenager, and his long-time girlfriend
> had died in a house fire just weeks before his death.
> Bradford had reportedly received minor injuries while
> attempting to save Victoria Payne from the burning
> building.
>
> Private graveside services were held Monday in
> Kingston. A memorial service in Wilkes Chapel on

the Foxmoor campus will be Sunday afternoon at
2:00 P.M. Memorials are suggested to Foxmoor College Scholarship Fund.

Bradford is survived by one brother, Timothy
Bradford of Manchester, CT.

It was eerie to read this obituary beside Joel's picture. It was no
wonder Tim didn't want her showing Joel's photograph around the
area. People in Langston thought he was dead! Suddenly, she remembered Joel's encounter with Larry Cohen at the Addy awards. Hadn't
Cohen mistaken Joel for someone he thought was dead?

She scanned the obituary again, her heart hammering. Why on
earth would someone have falsely reported Joel's death? She was sure
this somehow explained why he had used an assumed name when he
came to Silver Creek. But she couldn't begin to fathom why he
would have needed to conceal his identity.

The story said burial was to be in Kingston. Why there? She had
never heard Joel mention the town before. She was tempted to go
back and confront Tim Bradford with what she'd found, but she was
beginning to suspect that Tim played a major part in this whole
twisted plot. He definitely knew something he wasn't telling her.

She made a copy of the news article, gathered her belongings, and
went out to the rental car to consult the atlas once again. Kingston
wasn't far. Maybe the newspaper files of that library would yield more
clues to a mystery that was becoming stranger by the hour.

Armed with a new name for Joel, Melanie entered the small but
modern Kingston Public Library and searched the computer files for
newspaper stories about the Bradford family. She started by looking
for the obituaries of Joel's parents. She could figure out the approxi-
mate dates the death notices would have appeared from information
Joel had given her about the age he was when his parents had been
killed—if she could trust anything Joel had ever told her.

Half an hour staring at a computer screen finally yielded what she was looking for. The story of Randall and Patricia Bradford's death in a small plane crash had been front-page news two decades ago. And apparently Kingston was the Bradfords' hometown. She was certain Joel had never mentioned that fact. She glanced up at the elderly librarian who was perched on a high stool behind the circulation desk, working at the computer. The woman would probably recognize the Bradford name if Melanie inquired.

With Tim's warning ringing in her ears, Melanie got up from the computer and went to the desk. "Excuse me," she said, clearing her throat.

The librarian slipped her reading glasses from her nose and let them hang from the gold chain around her neck. "Yes? May I help you?"

"Um, yes…well, I hope so. I'm looking for information about a family who used to live in Kingston—the Bradfords? Randall and Patricia were the parents' names."

The woman put a hand to her throat. "Oh, my, yes…the Bradfords. Such a tragedy. That whole family…" She clicked her tongue, then studied Melanie's face for a moment. "Did you know them, dear?"

"Oh no… I just heard about them from…from a friend of mine."

"Oh? Who would that be? Perhaps I know them?"

She decided to hazard the truth. If what she'd discovered so far were true, there would be no harm in using Joel's alias. "His name is Joel Ellington, but I doubt you'd know him. He's…not from around here."

The librarian wrinkled her forehead. "No…no, I don't believe that name is familiar."

"No. He's…a friend of the Bradfords' son—Tim," Melanie risked.

"Oh. Well, I certainly knew little Timmy. And Joe—his brother. That was a sad story too. I assume you know about that?"

Melanie shook her head, feigning ignorance. The woman gave

her a gentle smile, which only made Melanie's deceit more difficult. She had told more lies in the past two days than she had in the rest of her life put together.

"Joseph was killed in a cycling accident just a few years ago—a motorcycle," she harrumphed. "Dangerous machines, if you ask me. Such a waste! He was a fine young man, Joseph was. Taught English up in Langston. Foxmoor College."

Melanie nodded and inclined her head toward the woman. "Well, it was a loss. A huge loss…" The woman seemed absorbed in the past for a moment, then shook her head as if to erase the tragic memories. She eyed Melanie curiously. "Now, just what was it you were looking for?"

"Oh, well…my…my friend is…helping Tim do a family history. When he found out I was going to be in town, he suggested I see what I could find." Melanie's heart pounded erratically. The lie had come so easily, but had it given her away? It was very possible that this woman knew Tim lived in Manchester. Perhaps Tim still visited Kingston on occasion.

But the woman seemed oblivious. "How thoughtful of you," she said. "Well, I'll see what I can do. We have quite an extensive archive of the local newspapers."

"Yes…yes, I've already found the obituaries."

"Oh…well…" The librarian seemed taken aback, and Melanie worried that she was growing suspicious.

"I'll keep looking through the papers," she said. "I just thought you might know somewhere else I could look. Thank you so much."

Melanie went back to the computer and found a shorter version of Joseph Bradford's obituary. There was one more item in the local news section in an issue of the newspaper dated four years after the plane crash—a small notice of Timothy Bradford's graduation from a Christian college in California. But there didn't seem to be anything else about Joseph Bradford. Feeling nervous and guilty about her lies, she quickly searched a few more issues without success. She printed out the stories she'd found, then gathered her things, thanked the librarian once more, and went out to the car.

She wasn't any closer to locating Joel. Nevertheless, Melanie found a tiny seed of hope in reading these news accounts. They matched the stories of Joel's life and family that he had told her.

Some part of their relationship, at least, had been based on the truth. And they proved that what Joel had told her about his fiancée was true. If he was going to lie about anything, wouldn't that have been the one thing he would have kept from her? She had a full name for Joel's Tori now—Victoria Payne. Maybe she could find out something through the woman's family.

She wasn't sure what her next step should be. She didn't dare go to Tim for answers. And if Joel was indeed in trouble with the law, she didn't want to open him up to further scrutiny by going to the local police. She shoved aside a thought that nagged at her: Tim had said Joel was in trouble. That lent credence to the possibility that he was guilty of taking the money from Cornerstone's building fund.

She desperately needed advice, and the only person she trusted to help her was her brother. Gathering her things from the library desk, she set out on the three-hour drive to Bergen County.

$\sim$

"It seems pretty obvious what this is all about, Melanie!" Matthew knew he was shouting, but his sister's naiveté appalled him, frightened him even.

"Matthew, calm down...please..." Karly pleaded with him.

Karly was seven months pregnant now. He knew she didn't need the stress, but he had to try to talk some sense into Melanie.

"Matt, I know it looks bad," Melanie pleaded now. "I know it does. But I—I can't explain how strongly I feel this... I'm just certain Joel did not take that money." Conviction punctuated her words.

She had told him a ludicrous story about some incident at a carnival when Joel had gone out of his way to return change to a food vendor who'd undercharged him. She was grasping at straws. He understood her need for closure, but this had been going on for too long. She should have moved on by now.

"Besides, Matt," Melanie was saying, "why would Joel go to all that trouble—changing his name and moving a thousand miles across the country—for less than fifteen thousand dollars? That doesn't make sense at all. He could have had twenty times that if he'd just married me!"

"He was probably on the run from some other heist! He *had* to move and change his name! People like that are professionals, Mel. Their talent is convincing people that they are trustworthy. Don't you get it? For all you know, Joel set up that whole carnival vendor scenario."

Melanie sat staring out the window, her face a mask of misery.

He sighed, willing himself to calm down. "Think about it, Melanie. Joel obviously changed his name shortly before he came to Silver Creek. This probably isn't the first time he's pulled a scam like this. Did you check the papers in Langston for similar stories? Maybe he took money from the college too. That would explain why he had to fake his death and disappear from there. Did you check on that? I'd be willing to bet the brother is in on this whole thing."

Matthew shook his head in frustration. What had his sister gotten herself involved in? She was playing detective, and if she didn't have a nervous breakdown first, she was going to get herself killed. He wouldn't be surprised if this Tim Bradford had had her tailed after she left his office. He'd even suggested the possibility to Melanie, but she seemed convinced that she hadn't been followed. But if these men had the power to fake a death and create a new identity, who knew how far they would go when faced with the threat of being exposed?

Melanie had come to him for help, yet if he did what he felt needed doing, she would surely think him a traitor. Melanie had become totally irrational where Joel Ellington—or whatever the man's name was—was concerned. Someone needed to save her from herself.

He went to her now, resting his hands on her shoulders. "Melanie," he said, "I'll do everything I can to straighten this out. Please just promise me that you will go back to Silver Creek and wait there. You're in over your head here, Mel. I don't want to see you get hurt. Let me see what I can find out. Maybe somebody at work has some connections in Manchester or in Langston."

"Oh, Matt. Would you really do that?"

He looked at her and wondered how he could ever live up to the expression of longing and hope and trust he saw reflected in his sister's eyes.

"I'll try," he sighed. "That's all I can promise."

∽

"Mommy!"

Melanie heard the precious voice before she spotted Jerica running down the concourse at the St. Louis airport. She quickened her pace and let her carry-on luggage slide to the floor as her daughter rushed into her arms. "Hi, sweetie. Boy, did I ever miss you!"

"I missed you too, Mommy."

The airport was crowded on a Sunday evening. Jerica skipped happily among the rows of seats while they waited for Melanie's luggage to show up on the carrousel.

"How was your trip?" Erika asked.

"It was…okay. It's good to be home, though," she said, anxious to change the subject. She hadn't yet decided how much she would tell the LaSalles. If they weren't any more sympathetic than Matt and Karly had been, she wasn't sure she wanted to tell them anything.

Maybe it would be best to wait until she found out what Matt might discover. "Was Jerica good for you?"

"Oh, goodness," Erika said. "When has she ever *not* been good for us?"

Melanie forced a laugh. "Oh, I can think of a few times."

"Well, she was good as gold," Erika said. "She missed you, though."

"Not as much as I missed her."

Finally her two large bags rolled into view. Jerry grabbed the heavier one; Melanie took the other. With Jerica under her grandmother's watchful eye, they made their way to the parking lot.

As they drove toward Silver Creek, Melanie's mind swirled with all she'd discovered in the past days. She'd learned more about Joel in the past week than she had during the entire year she'd known him.

And she was more confused than ever.

Twenty-Five

"The State calls Joseph Bradford."

The courtroom was warm, the air oppressive, and as he walked down the aisle that split the gallery, Joel tugged at his tie, fighting off the sense of panic that threatened to cut off his very breath. Stanley Difinni sat beside his attorneys at the defense table. Joel avoided looking in his direction. Soon enough, he would have to look into the eyes of the man responsible for Tori's death.

The case had been a year in the making, with delay after delay. But finally everything was going exactly as the prosecutor had hoped. As planned, Constance Green, Victoria's neighbor, had positively identified Difinni as the man she'd seen going into Victoria Payne's apartment early that Sunday morning. Even in the dim light of the streetlamp, the port-wine stain on the man's face had been distinct—and memorable, Green had said.

Speaking privately with Joel, Toliver surmised that Difinni had waited outside the restaurant the night of the murder—apparently with at least one accomplice—and followed the witnesses home. Because Joel had parked on a side street and left through the back door of Tori's apartment, Difinni apparently believed he was still in the house. The fire he'd set was meant to kill them both, but by the time the newspapers reported only one fatality in the fire, Joel was in protective custody.

Now a court officer summoned Joel into the courtroom. Holding open the gate that separated the gallery from the bench, the officer waited for Joel to pass through. *Help me, Lord. Let justice be done this time. Please, Father.*

The court clerk held a Bible in front of him. At the clerk's instructions, Joel placed his left hand on the smooth black cover and raised his right hand.

"Do you solemnly swear that the evidence you shall give the court and the jury in the people of the State of New York versus Stanley Difinni at the bar, to be the truth, the whole truth, and nothing but the truth, so help you God?"

The last four years of his life had been nothing but lies, but it had all been for this moment of truth. He made his voice strong when he answered, "I do."

"Please state your full name for the court."

"Joseph William Bradford."

Joel took his seat on the witness stand.

For the next two hours as the events were chronicled in vivid detail, Joel was forced to relive the murder he and Victoria had witnessed, to relive the night Tori died.

The prosecutor thrust a grisly photograph in front of him—the man's corpse, still sitting upright at the table in the restaurant that night. "Mr. Bradford, do you recognize this photograph?"

"Yes sir." Joel cleared his throat, struggling to keep his voice steady. "It was taken the night…the night of the murder at Ciao!"

"And you were there, were you not? You witnessed this murder."

"Yes."

The prosecutor slid another photograph from a manila envelope. "And this one? Do you recognize this?"

Joel's breath caught as he was confronted by an image of the house where Tori had lived—a photo taken after the house had been gutted by the flames that took her life. The prosecution had not wanted Joel to see these photographs beforehand. They wanted his reactions on the witness stand to be honest and emotional and gripping. Now he had no problem giving them what they wanted. Blood rushed to his head, and his throat filled, threatening to choke him.

"Mr. Bradford? Do you recognize the house in this photograph?"

"Y-yes. Yes, I do. Tori—Victoria Payne—lived in an apartment above the house."

"And what was your relationship to Ms. Payne?"

"She was my—" He swallowed hard and started again. "She was my girlfriend. I took her to Ciao! to...to ask her to marry me."

"And she died in the fire that destroyed this house before you had a chance to propose to her?"

"Yes. She did." Joel hung his head and blinked away sudden tears.

While the prosecutor expounded on the events of that fateful night, Joel found himself swamped in regrets over Tori's death all over again. If only he had insisted that she come home with him that night or that she stay at a friend's house. If only he'd watched to see if they were being followed when they left the restaurant. If only the police had told them what kind of criminals they were dealing with. *If only...if only...if only...*

The testimony dragged on, and with each piece of evidence the prosecution presented, another agonizing memory was dredged up—the most horrific days of Joel's life reconstructed before his eyes. Justice had been frustrated once by a jury unable to reach a verdict. He prayed with everything in him that this jury would open their eyes to the truth.

Finally, at three o'clock, with his testimony finished and court adjourned for the day, Toliver drove Joel back to his apartment, taking a circuitous route through the city as a precaution.

"You did well today," Toliver told him as the car idled in the street in front of Joel's place. "He won't get off this time."

Joel nodded and got out of the car.

He let himself into his apartment and locked the door behind him. After he hung up his coat, he went to the entryway where his briefcase sat. Pulling a stack of term papers from the case, he took them to the shabby desk in the kitchen.

He'd done everything that was in his power to do. If justice was thwarted again, he wasn't sure he ever wanted to know about it.

Methodically, he started reading his students' essays, desperate to put the grueling day out of his mind. But one image fixed itself in his brain and wouldn't let him go: Melanie and Jerica, forever lost to him now…lost to someone else.

The trauma and distress of the day gathered steam and rolled over him like a freight train.

And finally he broke down and wept.

~

Melanie cradled the cordless phone on her shoulder and watered the plants on the sun porch as she talked. "Are you sure, Karly? I'd love to come help with the baby, but I don't want your mom to feel like I'm butting in." Karly and Matt's baby was due late in March. Jerry LaSalle had already offered to fill in for Melanie at the office.

"Actually, you'd be an answer to her prayers," Karly replied. "With my sister in Iowa due the same week I am, Mom is going crazy trying to decide which direction she should go. This is Kelly's first baby, and I told Mom she really ought to be with her. But Mom's worried about who will take care of the boys. If she knows you'll be here with Brock and Jace, she can go to Des Moines with a clear conscience. Besides, I'd love to have you here."

"And you're sure you don't mind if Jerica comes with me?"

"Are you kidding? The boys will be ecstatic. It'll make the time go so much faster for them if Jerica's here."

Karly's enthusiasm now was all the convincing Melanie needed. "I'll call about tickets tomorrow," she told her friend.

Melanie set the watering can down and pinched a yellowed leaf from a philodendron, rolling it absently between her finger and thumb. She cleared her throat. "Karly...I don't mean to nag, but... do you know if Matt has heard anything? About Joel? I know he promised to call me the minute he had any news, but...I just thought I'd ask."

Karly hesitated on her end. "I'm sure he would have said something if he had news, Mel. But I'll tell him you asked... I know you're anxious."

"Thanks. Well, I'd better let you go. I'll call you as soon as I have our flights booked."

She took the phone into the kitchen and replaced it in its base, then went to wash the pungent scent of the leaf from her fingers. The last weeks of her life had been lived in a state of limbo. While she waited to hear what Matt's investigation might turn up, she was merely going through the motions—putting in her hours at By Design, giving Jerica as much attention as time allowed, and trying not to drive her brother crazy with her frequent phone calls.

Melanie thought Matthew had seemed nervous and detached the last time she'd spoken with him. She understood. He was afraid of what his search might turn up. And to be honest, she was fearful too.

Trying for the thousandth time to put the whole situation out of her mind, she went to her computer to search for airline tickets for the last week in March. She would have to work overtime to get things in order at the office before she left. And even though Jerica's school had a spring break during that time, she would still miss a few days of school. But how much homework could there be in first grade?

As she finalized the details of the trip, her excitement grew. It would be good to get away and spend some time with her brother and his family. But there was something more—a vague feeling of anticipation that she couldn't quite explain.

Joel wiped the blackboard clean, dusted the chalk from his hands, and turned to face his class. "Why do you suppose that four hundred years after it was first performed, *Romeo and Juliet* remains so popular—especially with young people?"

"Because teachers like you are always forcing us to read it?" Gina Salvatore deadpanned from a slouch behind her desk.

"I'll give you that," Joel said, tossing the plump girl a grin that said *Touché*. "But think about it. This story has been produced as a new movie every generation in the history of film. How do you explain that?"

Five hands shot up. Joel called on Danny Barrientos, pleased that the boy was prepared for once. "Twenty words or less, Danny."

Good-natured laughter rippled through the room. Danny Barrientos was not known for brevity. "Probably because it's about kids our age."

Joel nodded. "I'd buy that. Any other ideas?"

"Because it's got the same issues we deal with?"

"Like?"

"Love, suicide, intolerance," Danny offered.

Again Joel nodded his affirmation. Several other students offered their opinions.

"Okay, good. Great thoughts. Now who can give me a quick synopsis of the play?"

Danny stood, bowed ostentatiously, and gave a creditable review of the plot.

"Good," Joel said, then winking, "Straight out of *Cliffs Notes* but good nevertheless. Okay. You can take a seat, Danny. Let's give someone else a chance. Somebody name the major protagonists in the story."

"Duh. Romeo and Juliet," Gina muttered from the back of the room.

"Well, I see somebody did their homework," he said dryly. "Okay, major antagonists?"

Again several eager hands went up.

The conversation grew lively when he asked them to think of modern comparisons to Shakespeare's theme. As ideas flew back and forth across the room, Joel came around and leaned on the front of his desk, arms folded. He listened, letting the students carry the discussion, stepping in occasionally to steer them toward the next level of analysis.

After a long semester struggling with Shakespeare, it seemed these kids were finally getting the hang of it. "You guys are something else," he said now, slapping his copy of *Romeo and Juliet* on his thigh. "If I didn't know better, I'd think you were actually enjoying this unit."

A few sheepish smiles hid behind notebooks. A few more broke into full grins.

He looked at the clock. "Well, let's stop there for today. Tomorrow we'll discuss Act Two. If you haven't read it, get—"

The old building's clangorous bell cut him off abruptly, and the classroom emptied like salt from a funnel into the noisy hallway.

Smiling to himself, he tidied up the room. That finished, he chalked some sentences on the board for tomorrow's first-hour English class, then headed down the hall to the teacher's lounge to get his coat.

"Hey, Joel! How's it going?" Elaine Waring was at the sink rinsing coffee grounds from an ancient coffee maker. Her blond hair fell softly over her shoulders.

"Fine, Elaine. Hey, how was your vacation?"

"It was fantastic. Seventy degrees the whole week I was there."

"Well, I hate to tell you, but it wasn't far from that here." He grinned.

"So I've heard," she said, hands on hips in mock indignation. "Why does everybody insist on telling me that?"

"Ah, we're just jealous. Don't pay any attention."

She gave him a grateful smile, put the clean carafe back on the burner, and grabbed her coat in a none-too-discreet effort to walk out with Joel.

Elaine had been flirting with him for weeks. He knew she would go out with him in a second. All he'd have to do was ask. And he had to admit that he was attracted to her outgoing personality. She was cheerful and thoughtful, and extremely pretty besides. And he was so lonely.

But there was only one woman he was lonely for. Only one woman for whom his heart ached. *Oh, Melanie.*

He reminded himself again how unfair it would be to put someone else through the torture he had put Melanie through. Trying not to be rude, but not wanting to encourage the young teacher in any way, Joel headed the opposite direction when they reached the end of the sidewalk. "I need to run by the grocery before I head home," he explained. "See you tomorrow, Elaine." He waved over his shoulder.

Obviously disappointed, Elaine walked away with a glum good-bye.

Joel brushed away the feeling of depression that threatened to blanket him. He gave himself the familiar pep talk: He had made a new life for himself.

In spite of the circumstances that had brought him here, it was actually rather good to be back on his native East Coast. And he was teaching again and finding his job ever more rewarding.

Though the shock of seeing Melanie on the streets of New York had caused him a serious emotional setback, he was finally beginning to feel he'd been given a chance to start over once again. He forced himself to dwell on the small happinesses of this new life: the bright students who had opened up their lives to him, a clean apartment in a decent neighborhood, access to all the opportunities and entertainments this vibrant city had to offer.

Not wanting to make himself a liar, he stopped off at a small corner grocery and bought a few things he needed. Putting the small bag on one hip, he turned west toward his apartment.

The sun was low in the sky on a February afternoon, but the air felt almost balmy after a week when the thermometer had climbed high into the fifties. Feeling more lighthearted already, he whistled a cheerful variation of "Danny Boy" as he strolled up the street to his apartment.

He was almost on his porch when he saw them.

The two figures were partially hidden in the shadows of the porch overhang, smoking cigarettes, not speaking. His heart leapt to his throat, and he fought the instinctive urge to turn and run.

The heavier of the two men stepped into the sunlight and extended his right hand with a half smile. "Hello, Joe."

Twenty-Six

Joel's heart thudded in his chest as he eyed the two large men who stood, waiting, on his porch. He glanced at the street and saw a hulking black sedan parked half a block down. One of the men stepped off the porch and started toward Joel, his hand outstretched. Joel had never seen the man before. The blood pounded like a jackhammer in his ears as he considered taking flight.

Then the taller man moved into the light and relief surged through Joel's veins, followed quickly by apprehension. It was John Toliver. There must be some news about the trial. "What's going on?" He hurried toward the apartment now, not wanting his neighbors to overhear. "Toliver? What is it?" Joel heard the tremor in his own voice, and he despised it.

John Toliver motioned toward his companion. "Joe, this is Marshal Harvey Denton...Justice Department. Can we come inside?"

This must be significant if they sent a U.S. marshal. Joel dug his keys from his pocket and, without a word, let the two men inside the apartment. He led them to the small living room and motioned for them to take a seat on the threadbare sofa.

"Anybody care for something to drink?"

Both men held up their hands, declining the offer.

Joel grabbed a can of Coke from the refrigerator and returned to sit across from them on the edge of the old vinyl recliner. The heavy coffee table formed a barrier between them.

"We have some good news for you." The marshal took a stack of papers from the briefcase on the floor beside him and handed them wordlessly across the coffee table to Joel.

Joel leafed through them, noting what seemed to be copies of court dockets, and other legal rhetoric he didn't recognize. One name jumped out at him though: Stanley Difinni, listed as a defendant in the case. He looked at Toliver now, waiting for the explanation he knew would come.

"The sentencing took place yesterday. Difinni got forty years...without parole."

Joel slumped back in the recliner, surprised at his relief, trying to figure out just what this news meant to him. "No parole?"

"No parole. No hung jury, no technicalities, no appeals, no nothin', Joe...this guy ain't goin' nowhere. And they hauled the alleged accomplice in on another charge a couple weeks ago. I think his case'll go the same way." The inspector's voice had taken on the streetwise inflection of the New York detective he had been before joining the Justice Department ten years ago.

Joel couldn't speak for a minute. Finally he asked, "So what are you telling me?"

Harvey Denton fielded the question. "You're a free man, Mr. Bradford. As far as we can tell there aren't any other important connections to the Sartoni murder on the outside."

"As far as you can tell?"

"There isn't anybody, Joe," Toliver reiterated firmly. "We're confident of that. You have no value to them now."

"So...what does this mean?"

Toliver looked around the apartment. "Well, that's up to you. You got your job fair and square now. You've been paying your own way for a while. You're free to go."

"You're telling me I'm out of the program again?"

"You've been secure for months now anyway. These new convictions pretty much sew it up."

"So I'm out from under your protection? Just like that? Don't I have anything to say about it?" His voice sounded hollow, not unlike the feeling in the pit of his stomach. "What about retribution?"

"We don't think that's a threat, Joe. Not with these two locked up. Their thugs are small potatoes. They don't have the power they once had. La Cosa Nostra is a dying breed… The Mafia's a dinosaur."

Joel snorted. It hadn't felt like a dying breed that night in the dining room of Ciao! It hadn't felt like a dinosaur while he watched the flames rise from Tori's apartment.

Toliver shifted in his seat. "C'mon, Joe. Most people are overjoyed with this kind of news."

"You make it sound so easy."

Harvey Denton looked at Joel with sympathy. "Hey…you've got credentials with the school, so if you want to relocate, you can go anywhere, and good references will follow. You can keep the ID you're using. Everything's legit…Social Security, the driver's license, all of it…" His words trailed off as if he knew he hadn't convinced Joel.

Toliver cleared his throat. "It's a tight case, Joe—um, Joel. From the top down, everyone's confident you're home free. Enjoy it."

Denton handed him yet another collection of papers. "There's some information here that'll help with the adjustment. Most people in your shoes make a pretty smooth transition."

For the next twenty minutes the marshal answered Joel's halting questions. Finally he snapped the briefcase shut and stood to leave. Toliver followed suit.

"You call that number if you have questions." Denton indicated the sheaf of papers they'd left on the coffee table. He and Toliver went to the door, shook Joel's hand in turn, and stepped off the porch, leaving him to absorb the news.

~

The Continental 747 glided onto the runway at Newark International and rolled torpidly toward the terminal gate. Finally, the seat-belt light flickered off, and Melanie reached over to help Jerica unbuckle. "You can stand up and stretch a little, but let's wait until the aisle clears out," she told her daughter.

Jerica scrambled to her knees in the seat, turning to rest her chin on the high seat back behind her. "Are all these people going to Uncle Matt and Aunt Karly's house?" she asked, eyes as wide as the open cabin windows that overlooked the tarmac.

Melanie laughed. "No, sweetie. Just us."

"Then hows come they all came on our airplane?"

"Well, they're probably visiting other people who live close to Uncle Matt," she explained.

Jerica watched for another minute. "How much longer?"

"Just a couple of minutes. We need to get your sweater out of the carry-on bag. It's colder here than it was back home." Outside the window, she could see the steamy breaths of the ground crew as they worked to unload the luggage.

Melanie waited for the stragglers from the back of the plane, then stepped into the aisle and gathered their belongings from the overhead compartment. She unzipped the flight case, found Jerica's sweater, and helped her put it on. As they left the plane and made their way to the baggage claim, the little girl chattered away about her cousins and all the things she intended to do while they were in New Jersey.

After they collected their bags, Melanie steered Jerica to the car rental desk. While she filled out the paperwork, Jerica tugged on her jacket. "Where's Uncle Matt, Mommy? And Brock and Jace?"

"Shhh. Just a minute, Jer. Mommy's trying to concentrate." She finished signing the rental forms and knelt to explain. "I told Uncle Matt that we'd rent a car and drive to their house this time. I didn't want him to have to leave Aunt Karly to come and get us. The baby could come any day now, so they need to stay close by the hospital."

They got caught in rush hour traffic, and by the time she and Jerica pulled into the Masons' driveway, it was nearly suppertime. Brock and Jace came racing around the side of the house to greet them, sweaty and grimy, typical little boys. Jerica squealed with delight when she saw her cousins, and she scrambled over the backseat and out her mother's door.

Karly waddled out the front door, and she and Melanie embraced—or at least they tried to over the mound of baby. Melanie held her friend at arm's length. "Karly! You're big as a barn!"

"Gee, thanks," her sister-in-law laughed.

"You know what I mean. Are you just miserable?"

"A little," Karly admitted. "But it'll be worth it. At least that's what I keep telling myself. Oh, Mel, I'm so glad you're here. Come on in."

Leaving the luggage in the trunk of the rental car, the five of them went up the steps and into the Masons' sprawling split-level.

Karly put Melanie to work slicing carrots for a salad while the boys dragged Jerica off to meet the neighborhood kids.

"Don't be too long, Brock," Karly hollered after them. "Dad will be home in half an hour and we're going to eat right away." Her warning was lost in the slam of the screen door.

"So, how are you doing, Mel?" her friend asked, as quiet settled over the house. Karly lifted the lid from a pot of spaghetti sauce that sat simmering on the stovetop and stirred it with a large wooden spoon. The kitchen filled with its savory fragrance.

"We're doing okay. It's…it's been hard. I won't say it hasn't."

"I can't even imagine. You must still wonder…what happened. Where Joel is now."

Melanie picked up a large carrot and sliced furiously, not wanting to meet Karly's gaze. She merely nodded, afraid words would give way to tears.

"Have you…dated anyone else, Mel?"

"No!" It came out harsher than she'd intended. It was an effort to change her tone. "No, Karly. I'm…not ready for that. I'm not sure I ever will be."

"Of course you will! Oh, Mel…don't wait too long."

She shook her head. "No, Karly. All…all my dreams died with

Joel. There isn't anyone else out there for me. I don't think I...could ever really trust anyone again."

"Oh, Mel...don't say that." Karly tapped the spoon clean on the lip of the pot and replaced the lid, then came to Melanie's side and put a hand on her shoulder. "There are a lot of wonderful men out there."

Melanie looked at the floor and shook her head.

"Just think of all the great men in your life...Matt and Jerry... and your pastor...I forget his name. Don?"

She nodded.

"Mel, there is someone for you. I just know it. Don't let this make you bitter."

Melanie swallowed back the tears and risked looking Karly in the eye now. Her friend had enough to think about without worrying over Melanie's problems. "Hey, I'll be okay. Don't worry about me. It's just going to take some time..."

A twinkle came to Karly's eye. "Well, you know what they say, don't you?"

Melanie shook her head, waiting for the punch line.

Karly giggled. "Men are like wet firecrackers. Just when you think every last one is a dud, you come across a good one."

"Yeah...and just hope it doesn't blow up in your face."

"Ooh, touché," Karly said with a comical grimace.

Melanie turned to give her an appreciative hug. It was a comfort to laugh and joke with her best friend. She hadn't realized how much she'd missed her long-time confidante until this moment. And with the new baby on the way, this was a time full of hope and promise for her brother's family. She wasn't going to ruin it with her melancholy outlook. Standing there in the warmth of the Masons' kitchen, she resolved to put aside her own unhappiness and focus on enjoying this special time with people who meant the world to her.

Twenty-Seven

Joel watched Toliver and the marshal drive off, then went back into the house and dialed Tim's office, scribbling meaningless shapes on a notepad while he waited for the receptionist to put him through.

"This is Tim Bradford." His brother had on his no-nonsense business voice.

"Tim? Hi, it's me."

"Joe...Joel, what's up?"

"You won't believe it... I'm out..."

"What?"

"I'm out of the program."

"Again? What happened?"

Joel recounted Toliver's visit. "So now that Difinni is behind bars, they don't think I'm in any danger," he concluded.

Tim was silent on his end. "Do you believe them?" he asked finally.

"I don't really have a choice, Tim. I'm out. They didn't lay out many options."

"So what *are* your options? You can't go back to being Joe Bradford."

Joel had already pondered that. "No. Joe Bradford is dead. I'm proud of our family name, our heritage. Giving my name up was one of the hardest things about disappearing in the beginning. But—

Well, I like my job at the school. I think I'll probably stay there for a while, and I have no desire to get into all this with them."

"I can understand that," Tim replied. "So you...can keep your identity? As Joel Ellington."

"Yes. But I figure it won't hurt anything to lay low for a while. Stay where I am, play it safe. I'd rather not take any chances just in case Difinni's got a vengeful streak...just in case he still has friends out there. It's been a pretty good cover. I haven't had anyone looking for me..."

"Joe...actually there was—" Tim stopped abruptly, as though he had suddenly changed his mind about what he was going to say.

"What, Tim? What is it?"

It remained silent on the other end of the line. He could almost hear his brother collecting his thoughts, sorting out what to say. Finally Tim sighed. "Somebody *is* looking for you."

"What do you mean?" He didn't like the tone of Tim's voice.

"Melanie LaSalle came into my office a few weeks ago."

"Melanie?" The name struck him like a thunderbolt.

"Yeah, she tracked me down somehow. She was showing a snapshot around...one of those she took of us at that festival when I came to see you in Silver Creek."

He wondered how much erratic beating a man's heart could take before suffering permanent damage. "What did she want?"

"She asked if I knew whether you took the money that was missing from the church."

"What did you tell her?" He held his breath.

"I didn't tell her anything, Joe. I just told her that I couldn't talk to her about you and that she had to stop looking for you. She said...something about needing to go on with her life, but she couldn't do that until she knew what had happened."

So that's the way it is, then. She wants to forget me, wants to move on.

"You didn't tell me you saw her." Tim waited, accusation in his voice.

"Yes…in New York. We didn't talk. She…was with someone else."

"Oh." Tim cleared his throat. "I'm sorry, Joe."

"No, don't be sorry. I'm…glad. She should go on with her life. She deserves that." Joel had covered the notepad in front of him with harsh geometric figures traced over and over again until the pencil lines cut through to the sheet below.

"You don't sound happy about it."

Anger crept into Joel's voice. "Should I be happy about it? I loved her, Tim…with all my heart. If I'm honest with myself, I'm still in love with her."

"Then tell her."

"No!" He hadn't meant to shout. "I'm sorry. But…that part of my life is over. I can't go through this again, Tim. And like she told you, she needs to get on with her life. I've hurt her enough…hurt her little girl enough too." A lump lodged in his throat, and silence again filled the wires between them. He wasn't sure he was ready to accept the things he was telling his brother. It still hurt even to utter Melanie's name. "It's time I let it go. No sense complicating things any more."

"She thinks you took the money from the church, Joe. At least you could set that straight."

He shook his head vigorously, though he knew that, across the wires, the action was lost on his brother. "No, Tim. Let it lie. What purpose would it serve?"

"It would clear your name. At least with Melanie."

"And then she'd have to wonder all over again about why I left. No…let it lie," he repeated.

"I… I'm sorry about all this, Joe. If there's anything I can do, you know you just have to call me."

"I know that. Thanks, Tim."

They said their good-byes and hung up. Joel slumped over the desk, raking his fingers through his hair. They'd preached at the WITSEC orientation that the adjustment going into the program was horrendous—often almost too great to be borne. He'd experienced that and knew it was true. But Harvey Denton had said that most people made the adjustment out of the program without difficulty. He wasn't so sure.

A picture formed in his mind—the glimpse of Melanie he'd had in front of Port Authority that cold November day. A picture of her, laughing in the arms of another man. That day he had forfeited any right to a life with her again. His freedom now did not negate that fact. Still, the truth of his loss sent a chill of despair down his spine.

∼

Over the next few days, Joel went through the motions. He showed up at school each day and walked back to his apartment each night. He rarely left the house otherwise. And if he slept, he dreamed of flames and gunshots, of Victoria's tears and Melanie's. Waking or sleeping, his mind conjured menacing images and bizarre scenarios that had no basis in any real threat. He was out. He was free. Why couldn't he get his subconscious mind to believe that? Why did he so often wake to his own hot teardrops seeping from under swollen eyelids?

He could not seem to shake the sense that he was still a hunted man. He felt as though he'd been left defenseless in the middle of a jungle, abandoned without any means of security or protection. Over the preceding months, knowing that his identity was protected, hidden within the Witness Security Program, he had come to feel relatively safe here in his New York apartment and in his classroom. Now, though nothing had changed—except on paper—he felt vulnerable everywhere he went. Reason told him that a common street thug presented more peril to him now than the people who had threatened him before. But the dreams persisted.

Four days after Toliver and Denton's visit, Joel climbed out of bed, still shuffling the disjointed thoughts and fears in his mind and finding no place to lay them down. He had to get out of here…out of the house. After a quick shower, he pulled on khakis and a denim shirt. He was determined to face his fears, to go out into the city where he felt most vulnerable.

The sun was bright, reflecting off morning dew that frosted brown and grey patches of grass and concrete. The sidewalk was slippery in places, and Joel slowed his pace.

He walked aimlessly, block after block, until his gaze was drawn to the spire of a chapel rising into the blue-grey winter sky a few blocks ahead. Strangely, but undeniably, he felt drawn there. He had not attended church since he'd left Silver Creek. Oh, he had lived out the morals of his faith. He'd tried to keep himself from sin—though he knew in his heart that this overwhelming fear *was* sin. But he had also tried to pray—and felt nothing, heard nothing in reply. Now, strangely, the cathedral drew him like steel to a magnet.

It was Sunday morning, a day that had become like any other over the past months. He climbed the wide, shallow concrete steps and entered the building. The foyer was empty, but a cappella music drifted through open doors on either side of him.

He straightened his coat and walked inside. The sanctuary was massive. A few dozen worshipers filled the front pews. Joel slid unseen into a pew many rows behind the others. The melody filtered from the choir loft above him. He closed his eyes and listened, allowing the music to soothe him.

The choir chanted the words in Latin, but then the lyrics changed to English, and the words of the song pierced his heart. Soft, stringed instruments joined the chorale, and the haunting harmonies rose on a crescendo of soprano and alto voices that wove themselves skillfully around one another as the choir echoed the beautiful words from the Psalms in a round.

"You are my hiding place…when I am afraid, I will trust in you."

He didn't want to spend the rest of his life in fear and anger and disbelief.

"You are my hiding place."

The melody played on, and suddenly he was overwhelmed by a thought—one that burst so clearly that the knowledge of its truth seemed to have always been a part of him. His freedom and safety had never had anything to do with his physical circumstances. Instead, they had always depended on whether he was trusting God with every detail of his life.

He was finally, truly free to live as God intended him to. Not just free from fear, or free from threat of the evil in the world—because there would always be that. But his heart had been set free, and there was genuine liberty in the knowledge.

As though the words of the psalm had come true in his own heart at that very moment, Joel was flooded with peace. He finally understood that his life was hidden in Christ's. Death itself could not change that.

The music faded away, and the minister rose to speak. But the eloquent words droned beyond Joel, a mere background to his thoughts.

He thought of his parents. He wasn't sure he would ever understand why God had taken them from him at a time when he still needed them so profoundly. It didn't seem fair, and it didn't make sense that God would allow the deaths of people who were working so sincerely for his cause.

And Victoria. She had been as close to a saint as one could be on this earth. Of all those in the restaurant the night of the Sartoni murder, she was the most innocent. Yet she had lost her life because of another man's evil.

None of it made sense. And yet the peace remained. Somehow he no longer needed to understand. What he did understand was that this evil world was like a vapor. In an instant he could be wiped from existence. And what mattered then?

He knew that his parents and Tori had known the answer. Each of them had understood that this life was over in a blink of an eye, whether one lived ten years or a hundred. But there was a life far more precious after this one. That was where they had stored their treasures. That was where they had placed their hopes. He knew now that it was where his own hope lay as well.

Melanie came to his mind, and he felt not the seething anger he half expected because he'd lost her—only a deep regret, and a sadness that his freedom had come too late for her to share in it.

Twenty-Eight

Sunday morning, Melanie and Jerica went to church with Matthew and Karly. After lunch Melanie volunteered to make a run to the grocery store. She went through the motions, filling a cart with the food and toiletries from Karly's list, but her thoughts were far from her task. She had lived in a peculiar haze of anticipation and dread since the day she'd promised Matthew that she would wait for him to seek out information on Joel. She knew her brother was preoccupied with Karly's imminent delivery. But she wished he would do something. This limbo of not knowing was driving her mad.

She paid for the groceries and started back to the Masons' house. When she pulled into the drive and walked through the garage door, Matthew and Karly were headed out the same door.

"Her water broke and her contractions are only five minutes apart," Matt told her. His voice held a quaver Melanie had never heard before.

"Oh, Matt! I can't believe my timing! Why didn't you call me? I had my cell phone."

"It just started fifteen minutes ago," Karly said, as Matt loaded her bags into the car.

Matt went back into the house, and Melanie helped Karly into the passenger seat and pulled the seat belt around her. "I'll be praying for you, sweetie."

"Thanks, Mel." She grimaced and gripped the dashboard. "Tell Matt he'd better hurry."

Melanie ran into the kitchen. Matt dismissed the neighbor woman who'd come to watch the boys, and began a litany of instructions about the boys and the pets and the house.

"Just go. Go!" Melanie said, giving him a playful shove. "Between the kids and me, I think we can figure it out."

Matthew kissed each of his sons and Jerica, and ran to the car where Karly was waiting. Melanie and the children followed him and stood in a knot in the garage watching until the car disappeared around the corner.

"Okay, guys," Melanie said, herding the little boys and Jerica back into the kitchen. "Anybody hungry?"

"Is our mommy gonna be okay?" five-year-old Jace asked, a worried frown creasing his freckle-strewn forehead.

"Oh, honey. She'll be fine. Before you know it, she'll be home with a brand-new brother or sister for you guys to play with."

"I hope it's a girl. I already got a brother," seven-year-old Brock declared.

"Yeah," Jace echoed his big brother. "It just gots to be a sister."

"Well, sister or brother, you'll love this baby all the same," she told them.

"Is Jerica gonna get a new baby, too?" Jace wanted to know.

Melanie could feel Jerica's eyes on her, waiting for her answer. She tried to keep her tone light. "Oh...I don't know. Maybe someday, buddy. Now what about that snack? Let's make something really creative."

"Cool," Brock declared.

She parked the three of them on barstools at the kitchen counter, and they told her which cupboards held the ingredients for peanut butter and crackers and banana slices.

Melanie spent the evening doting on her nephews and enjoying their interaction with Jerica. She was amazed at how vastly different two rambunctious boys were from one little girl—even one as energetic as Jerica.

Melanie scarcely had a moment to think until the kids were tucked in for the night. Just after nine o'clock, Matthew called to announce that Karly had delivered a healthy seven-pound boy named Parker.

"Mother and baby are both doing fine," he announced proudly.

"Oh, Matt, I'm so happy for you," Melanie rejoiced with her brother. "But you better be here in the morning," she joked. "I'm not sure how you're going to break the news to the boys. They had their hearts set on a sister."

"They'll get used to the idea," Matt told her with a chuckle. "Just wait till they meet this little guy." The pride in her brother's voice brought a lump to Melanie's throat.

The next days were full of activity. Karly and the baby came home, and no one in the house got much sleep after that. Little Parker seemed perfectly content to sleep all day long, but when night fell, he was ready for action.

Melanie relished caring for the baby and watching Jerica's joy over little Parker. The possibility that her daughter might never know the joy of welcoming a new brother or sister home from the hospital filled Melanie with sadness. Yet she was grateful that Jerica could enjoy this time with her cousins. Jerica seemed to feel right at home here. She and the boys spent sunup to sundown playing in one yard or another in the Masons' close-knit neighborhood.

The following Thursday, during the quiet of morning, Melanie and her brother were eating breakfast at the kitchen table while Karly nursed the baby in the rocking chair across the room. The boys and Jerica hadn't yet crawled out of bed.

"Mel, I… There's something I wanted to tell you." It was obvious that Matt was trying to sound casual, but the self-conscious way he cleared his throat gave her a hint that something important was coming.

"What?" she asked. "What is it?"

"I've had some news…about Joel." He glanced toward her, but seemed to be making an effort to avoid her eyes.

She sucked in a sharp breath. "What is it?" she repeated, her heart pounding.

"The sheriff called from Franklin County yesterday."

"Franklin County, Missouri?"

He nodded. "There's been an ongoing investigation, and they've located Joel living in New York. It sounds like… Well, it sounds like they'll be bringing him in for questioning."

"What!" she exploded. "They're going to arrest Joel? Oh, Matt! Why didn't you tell me? Where is he?"

"Shhh," he reprimanded, looking down the hallway where the children slept. "It doesn't mean they're going to arrest him. They just want to question him."

"But, Matthew, they don't have proof Joel took the money… They couldn't!"

"What more proof could you possibly need, Melanie? A man disappears from sight, and two months later fifteen thousand is missing from an account that he was supposed to have made deposits to? You're in denial if you think this man isn't guilty as sin!" Now Matthew was practically shouting.

For a moment she sat in stunned silence. Then the reality of what her brother had told her began to soak in. "I can't believe this," she moaned. "Why didn't you tell me? Why didn't you at least let me talk to him first?"

"Melanie, you act like I'm personally arresting Joel. I'm just reporting what I found out."

"But you never did believe me all the times I tried to tell you Joel was innocent. It's as though you *want* him to be guilty…you want him to get caught."

Matt leveled his gaze at her. "Maybe I do, Melanie. Maybe then you would get over this and get on with your life."

She pushed her chair away from the table and ran out through the French doors that led to the deck off the kitchen. She plopped into a cushioned lawn chair and sat there, too angry for tears yet feeling guilty at her outburst.

She heard Matthew rustling about in the kitchen, rinsing dishes. He knew her well enough to leave her alone for a while. After a few minutes, he poked his head out the door. "I have to catch the bus, Mel. I…I'm sorry. We'll talk tonight, okay?"

She merely nodded. He started to say something, then apparently thought better of it and lifted a hand in a halfhearted farewell.

A few minutes later Karly came out onto the deck and sat down beside her. Karly reached out and put a hand on Melanie's arm. "Mel," she said quietly, "You know Matt's just trying to help. He only wants what's best for you. He's worried about you. We both are."

"I know… I know that. But why can't you and Matt support me in this? You're treating me as if I'm crazy. Why can't you trust my judgment? I know Joel. If he did take that money, he had a good reason. And I know he loved me—and Jerica. I saw his face. I don't think I was imagining that there are still feelings there for me. Oh, Karly, I still miss him so much. Sometimes I just want to walk out that door and go up and down streets until I find him."

"Mel…we've talked about this before. I know it's hard, but you might have no choice but to accept that you will probably never know why this happened. I wish I could tell you—" She turned her head abruptly. "Jerica! Good morning, sweetie." Karly cut a quick warning glance back at Melanie. "Are you ready for some breakfast, Jer?"

Jerica stood at the door, already dressed. Her forehead was furrowed, and her eyes held a wounded glaze.

Melanie turned away quickly and scrubbed at the tears that

dampened her cheeks. She faked a cheery smile and faced her daughter with an outstretched hand. "Hi, sweetie. I didn't know you were up." How long had Jerica been standing there? Melanie looked to Karly, who was obviously wondering the same thing. But she only frowned and shrugged.

"Mommy?"

"What's wrong, punkin?"

Jerica's gaze seemed to pierce through her, and she studied Melanie with an intensity far beyond her years. But quickly her expression changed, and she was a little girl again. "Can I play in the Goldsteins' yard with Brock and Jace?"

"Don't you want some breakfast first?"

"We already had Pop-Tarts."

"Oh. Well...Is that okay?" Melanie deferred to Karly.

"Sure. It's just two houses down," Karly told her. She turned to Jerica. "Just tell the boys to make sure it's okay with Tad's mom first, okay?"

Jerica nodded soberly.

"You stay with the boys, okay?" Melanie said. "And if you want to come home you ask Brock to walk with you. Don't come back by yourself."

"Okay."

Brock stuck his head through the open door. "C'mon, Jerica. Hurry up. Tad's waiting for us."

She started through the door, then stopped and cocked her head in her cousin's direction. "Does Tad have a dog?"

"No, dummy. C'mon!"

"Brock!" Karly chided. "You do not speak to Jerica like—"

"Sorry."

Jerica shrugged him off.

"Hurry up!" Jace's voice echoed from just inside the door.

"Okay, but wait a minute," Jerica told her cousins. "I gotta get something first. Bye, Mommy."

"You be good," Melanie called after her. Her words were drowned in the slam of the door as Jerica followed her cousins into the house.

"Is she still afraid of dogs?" Karly asked.

"Terrified. Except for Erika's little Biscuit. She tolerates him." Melanie was preoccupied, remembering Jerica's bewildered look. What had they been talking about when she came out to the deck? She frowned. "Karly, how long do you think Jerica was standing there? Do you think she heard us?"

Karly shook her head and cringed. "I don't know. I didn't even see her come outside. But I think she was okay, don't you? Maybe she was just worried about the dog situation."

"I hope that's all it was," Melanie sighed. Still, Jerica's distressed expression wouldn't leave her. "Oh, Karly, I'm so tired of this." She bit her lip and pounded a fist impotently on the upholstered deck chair. "I'm so sick and tired of this whole thing. Matt is right. It's been a year. Why can't I get over this? Why can't I get over *him?*"

Karly patted her arm gently, tears welling in her eyes. "Because you loved him, Mel."

The insistent cries of a newborn wafted from inside the house. Karly offered Melanie an apologetic smile, rose from her chair, and went inside.

Melanie stayed on the deck, thinking about what Karly had said. Her friend had spoken in the past tense, but the truth was, her love for Joel was as strong as it had been that day she had tearfully cleared the last of Rick LaSalle's shirts from her closet.

I still love him, she thought. *In spite of everything, I still do.*

Twenty-Nine

It was a cold, grey day in Silver Creek, Missouri. Darlene Anthony sat enjoying a cup of coffee and a break from her secretarial duties at Cornerstone Community Church. She took a final look at the master copy for Sunday's bulletin, satisfied that she'd banished every last typo and grammatical error from the pages. A shadow crossed her desk, and she looked out through the office window to see an officer, dressed in the uniform of the county sheriff's department, heading up the sidewalk to the church's entrance.

Startled, Darlene quickly dialed Don Steele's extension. "Pastor, there's someone here. I…I think he's from the sheriff's office. Should I send him in?"

"Do you know what he wants?"

She heard the wide front doors creak open, then close again. Within seconds, the towering man stepped into Darlene's office, removing his hat as he ducked through the doorway.

Darlene covered the receiver with her hand and gave him a nervous smile. "I'll be right with you."

Before she could say another word, Pastor Steele opened the door to his adjacent study and stepped into Darlene's office. He extended his hand to the lawman. "Hi, I'm Pastor Don Steele. How can I help you?"

251

Darlene quietly replaced the receiver in its cradle and busied herself with some paperwork on her desk.

"Tom Stanton." The man introduced himself as he accepted Pastor Steele's outstretched hand. "Deputy Stanton, from the county sheriff's office. I'd like to speak with you for a moment if I could, Reverend Steele"—his eyebrows leaned in Darlene's direction as he finished—"alone."

"My office is right this way." Pastor Steele led the deputy into his office, pulling the door partially closed after the officer had ducked inside.

From her desk, Darlene could barely hear their muffled voices. Quietly, she got up and went over to the copy machine in the corner behind her desk and switched it off. Without the hum of the copier, the two men's voices carried quite clearly.

Darlene sat back down in her padded desk chair and pretended to proofread the bulletin.

"…what we discovered after talking to Mr. Ellington's brother is quite interesting," Officer Stanton was saying.

"You're sure about this?" Pastor Steele asked.

"Well, we have a couple more leads to follow up on. We don't want to scare him off before we have the evidence we need to convict, but I think we are just days away from bringing him in."

Darlene sat perfectly still, straining to hear the rest.

She heard defeat in Don Steele's voice. The minister sighed heavily, and Darlene could almost picture him hanging his head the way he did when one of his flock went astray. "I'd always hoped they were wrong about Joel."

"I didn't know him, of course," Stanton said. "Read the stories though. Seemed pretty cut and dried to me. Just a matter of finding the guy."

"Will he be brought back here to the county for trial?"

"Well now, he hasn't been officially charged, but if—"

The rest of Stanton's sentence was lost as the motor of the water fountain down the hall kicked on. Darlene could feel her heart galloping, and a fine film of perspiration beaded her upper lip. They must have found Joel. And now it sounded as if he was going to be charged with taking the money for the building fund.

It was awful to think of him being found guilty. She wondered if it would make any difference when the authorities learned that the money had long since been replaced by the insurance and several generous donations, including a contribution of three thousand dollars that she herself had given from her mother's life insurance policy.

Her shoulders sagged at the thought of her mother. Not a day went by that she didn't weep over the senseless death of the wonderful woman who had given her life.

<hr />

Melanie's thoughts drifted, and she succumbed to the warmth of the morning sun and the comfort of the deck chair. She started awake when Karly came back out with the baby in her arms.

"Oh! I must have fallen asleep," Melanie said, yawning and stretching. "Here, let me have him." She held out her arms, and Karly transferred little Parker into them. "Does he need to be burped?"

As if on cue, the baby emitted a rumbling belch.

"Not anymore," Karly laughed.

Melanie stretched Parker out on her lap and cooed senseless baby talk to him. There was something so hopeful and reassuring about a tiny new baby.

"I'm going make a pot of coffee," Karly said. "Do you want some?"

"Sure, I'll take a cup. Are the kids back yet?"

"No. You apparently haven't seen Tad's backyard." Karly described the Swiss Family Robinson–like tree house Tad Goldstein's father had built in the neighboring yard. "I think Brock and Jace would just move in over there if we'd let them."

"Oh, Jerica will think she's died and gone to heaven."

While Karly rattled dishes in the kitchen, Melanie watched the infant with fascination, trying to remember when Jerica could possibly have been this small. Parker's bright little eyes already tracked the exaggerated movements of her head, and he seemed to be mimicking the faces she made at him, working his round O of a mouth with furrowed forehead. Amazing. What an incredible miracle babies were.

Karly brought a tray out, and they sipped coffee and admired the baby, soaking in the rare spring sunshine. The sun was high in the sky when their reverie was interrupted by the distant slam of the front door and the clatter of sneaker-clad feet across the kitchen tile.

Melanie looked at Karly with a knowing smile. "It must be lunch time. Here, I'll go fix some sandwiches." The baby was dozing now. She gave him back to Karly, then gathered the coffee mugs and magazines that had collected on the deck before going into the kitchen. The boys were standing in front of the open refrigerator jostling for front and center.

"Hey, guys. You hungry?"

"Starving," Jace declared. "Can we have pizza?"

"I think your mom and I decided on sandwiches. Can you handle that?"

"Sure," Brock said, with a tough-guy shrug. "PB and J?"

"If that's what you want. Where's Jerica? Did she like the tree house?" Melanie asked.

"I dunno," the boys said in unison.

"What do you mean… She came back with you, didn't she? From Tad's house?"

They both shook their heads matter-of-factly. "She never went to Tad's," Brock said. "She said she had something else to do."

"What? You mean she's been here all this time?" Melanie hadn't heard a peep out of Jerica all morning. She glanced at the digital clock on the microwave, and her heart lurched. It was 11:30. It had been almost two hours since the boys had gone to play at the Goldsteins'.

"Hmmm," she said, pushing away a spasm of alarm. "She must have fallen back to sleep. Would one of you guys go back and tell her that we're making lunch?"

The brothers raced each other down the hallway yelling. If that didn't wake Jerica up, nothing would.

But just as quickly, they came back out to the kitchen. "Jerica's not there."

"What?"

"She's not in the bedroom."

Melanie's stomach clenched. "Are you sure?"

"Yup. She's not there," Brock declared.

"Well, she has to be somewhere." It came out as a bark, and she could see by the crestfallen expression on Brock's face that she'd spoken too harshly. But now her fear took over. She hurried back to the bedroom. It was empty. Retracing her steps down the hall, she looked into the bathroom and poked her head into each of the other bedrooms off the hall. All were empty.

Panic pumped adrenaline through her veins. She raced down the steps to the basement family room. The lights were off and the television screen was black and silent. *Where else could she be?*

Melanie took the stairs two at a time back to the kitchen, shouting Karly's name.

Her sister-in-law came in from the deck, cradling Parker in her arms. "What's going on?"

"I can't find Jerica, Karly!" She heard the hysteria rising in her own voice. "The boys said she never went with them to the neighbors'—to Tad's."

Karly looked from Brock to Jace. "Jerica didn't go with you?" she repeated.

They shook their heads again, faces solemn now, as if they were afraid they were in trouble.

"Let me put Parker down," Karly said, her face grim. She took the baby back to the nursery, and when she came back a minute later she knelt in front of her eldest son. "Brock, this is important. Do you know where Jerica is?"

"No, Mom. I haven't seen her since this morning."

"Jace?"

The five-year-old's eyes were wide. "I don't know where she is, Mom. She was gonna go to Tad's with us, and then she said she had to do something."

Melanie bent to join Karly at the boys' eye level. "What, Jace? What did she have to do?"

"I dunno. She didn't tell us."

Melanie looked at Karly. "Where else could she be?" She rose to her feet and started down the hall again. "Jerica? Jerica Beth! Can you hear me?" Karly and the boys followed suit, parading through every level and room of the house shouting for Jerica—to no avail. They gathered back in the kitchen several minutes later, quiet and sober.

Karly took charge. "Brock, you and Jace go look around the neighborhood. Maybe she tried to follow you guys to Tad's and got lost. I'll check the yard. Mel, you go through the house one more time. She's got to be somewhere."

When they'd left, the dead silence of the house told Melanie with certainty that Jerica was not inside. She walked through the house again, this time listening for a telltale sound instead of shouting Jerica's name. Finding not so much as a clue, she began to search in ridiculous places. She opened cupboard doors and rummaged through clothes hampers. Macabre images swarmed her mind like angry hornets.

She remembered that Matt had caught the kids making forts out of the bunk-bed mattresses a couple nights ago. Melanie went to the boys' room, cleared away the lumpy quilts and lifted the mattresses off the platforms, dreading what she might find. She went to the other bedrooms, doing the same.

She walked into the guest room where Jerica had slept last night.

The quilts had been pulled up in a lumpy heap, and the decorative pillows were propped neatly against the headboard—Jerica's feeble efforts to make the bed after she'd crawled out of it that morning.

Melanie went to the end of the bed, spread her arms wide, and grabbed two corners of the quilt, giving it a shake to make sure that none of the lumps in the blankets were child-sized. The comforter settled back onto the bed, and at the edge of her vision, she saw something flutter against the pillows.

She took a step toward the head of the bed and held her breath as a tentacle of raw terror snaked up her spine.

Thirty

A smudged sheet of ruled paper rested against the pillows, one side ragged where it had been ripped from a spiral notebook. Melanie picked it up and slumped onto the bed at the sight of the childish scrawl. She read her daughter's sweet misspelled words. As their meaning soaked in, her hands began to tremble violently.

> Der Mommy,
> I am ging to fine Jole for you.
> Love,
> Jerica

Melanie's breath caught in her throat. *Where* in heaven's name would Jerica have imagined Joel might be found? Her thoughts raced as she tried to think of the conversations she'd had with her daughter. Had Jerica overheard her or Karly say something this morning, before they'd realized she was standing on the deck? What had they said that would make Jerica think she could find Joel? Desperately she replayed her conversation with Karly, trying in vain to imagine how her own brain might have processed things when she was Jerica's age.

How far could a determined little girl get in two hours? What if someone had picked her up? The thought sent a blade of ice through

Melanie's heart: What was she doing sitting here? Every second was critical now. Clutching the note, she stumbled blindly down the hall and into the kitchen where Karly was on the phone calling the neighbors.

She thrust the paper into her friend's hands.

"Oh dear God!" Karly whispered as she read her niece's scribbled words. "Let me call you back, Ann. We just found…a note from Jerica." Karly pressed the End key and set the phone on the counter, inspecting Jerica's note more carefully.

"We need to call the police, Mel," Karly said in a hushed voice.

Her palms clammy, Melanie nodded numbly and grabbed for the phone.

Karly took it from her. "Let me call." She punched in the emergency number.

Melanie stood nearby, the blood draining from her face, her hands trembling. She threw up a desperate prayer while Karly told the dispatcher what had happened and gave a description of Jerica. "No, ma'am, we've already checked all the nearby neighbors. Like I said, she left a note. We're pretty sure she's run off. Yes, that's right. She's six. Jerica." Karly spelled the name into the phone. There was a long pause while she listened, then, covering the receiver with one hand, she looked at Mel. "What was Jerica wearing today?"

Melanie's memory came up utterly blank, and she felt herself edging over the brink of panic. Shaking uncontrollably, she racked her brain trying to picture what Jerica had looked like as she'd stood on the deck just hours ago. What kind of mother couldn't remember what her child had dressed in that morning? "I…I can't remember! Karly, I can't remember!" By the sound of her own voice, she knew she was losing it.

"Hang on just a minute," Karly said into the phone. She put a warm hand on Melanie's arm. "It's okay, Mel. I can't remember either. We'll think of it. It'll come. Just stay calm. Was it…was it that little pink corduroy set?"

"No. No, I just put that in the washer last night. Oh, Karly, I can't remember. What's wrong with me?" She put her head in her hands, trying to block a barrage of terrifying thoughts. She willed herself to be calm. And there it was: She remembered tying ribbons in Jerica's pigtails last night. Bright orange ribbons. Jerica had been so taken with the new hairstyle that she'd insisted on leaving them in when she went to bed. This morning she'd put on the outfit that matched the ribbons.

"It was her orange overalls," she told Karly now. "Remember? The ones Jace teased her about? He told her she looked like a pumpkin. Remember? And she probably had that little orange-and-yellow striped T-shirt on with it. It has *Oshkosh* embroidered on it. So do the overalls. That's what she usually wears with them anyway." She knew she was rambling, but thankfully Karly was already relaying the information into the telephone.

"And she had ribbons in her hair. Orange ones. Bright orange ones. Be sure and tell them that. Pigtails."

"That's right," Karly confirmed, her head bobbing. "Oh, good. That'll make her easy to spot." Karly finished describing the outfit to the dispatcher, and answered a few more questions. She hung up and put an arm around Melanie. "It's going to be all right, Mel. The police are sending a car out right away. We'll find her. Don't worry."

"I want to go look," she said.

"Okay. Maybe…maybe one of us should stay here. In case the police call back. I know the neighborhood, Mel. I know where the kids play. I'll take the boys with me, and we'll drive around for a while… You can stay here with the baby and answer the phone. And…talk to the police."

The reality of the words felled her: *The police.* They'd had to call the police to search for her daughter. She crumpled into a chair and slumped over the kitchen table.

"We'll find her, Mel," Karly assured her, rubbing gentle circles on Melanie's back. "I promise you, we'll find her."

Karly went to check on the baby, then herded the boys out to the car. Melanie dragged herself up and followed them out to the driveway, the cordless phone clutched in one hand.

As they drove off, she felt as though they'd left her behind in a shark-infested ocean. In a daze, she went into the house and walked back to the guest room again.

A sob rose in her throat. "Oh, dear Jesus," she prayed, her voice rising in hysterics. "Help us, Lord. You have to help us find her. Please, God. Please."

A dozen grizzly newspaper accounts swirled through her mind—stories of lost children that had ended in unspeakable tragedy.

Keep her safe, Father. Oh, please, God. Please. Don't let me lose her, too.

∼

Darlene Anthony had just taken off her coat when Pastor Steele called her into his office.

She hung her coat on the back of the door and went into the adjoining office. "Did you have a nice lunch, Pastor?"

"Hello, Darlene. I have some rather bad news, I'm afraid. I just got a call from Jerry LaSalle. Melanie and Jerica are out in New Jersey visiting Mel's brother, and Melanie just called him to say that Jerica is missing. Apparently she ran away."

Darlene gasped. "Oh no! How awful!" She forced herself to swallow the lump in her throat and blurted out, "Why would she run away? How long has she been missing?"

Don Steele took off his glasses and wiped them on the sleeve of his oxford shirt. "Jerry didn't really have any details, but apparently, Jerica…well, she went looking for Joel."

"Joel Ellington? Oh, my goodness!"

"Yes. They had a neighborhood search organized when I talked to Jerry a little while ago, but so far…nothing. Naturally they're all pretty scared."

Darlene put a thin hand to her mouth as the seriousness of the situation registered. "Oh, that poor little girl. Melanie must be worried sick."

"Jerry said they'd call back here as soon as they have any news. But they wanted to get it on the prayer chain right away this morning. Would you get those calls started, please, Darlene?"

"Of course. Of course..." Flustered by such dreadful news, she went over the information again with Pastor Steele to make sure she had the details right. She tried to jot down some notes, but her fingers wouldn't seem to cooperate. Finally, she gave up and went to the phone in her own office. Trembling, she managed to dial the first number on the prayer chain.

By noon people all over Silver Creek and beyond were praying for Jerica's safe return. As the day wore on, the phone in Darlene's office rang repeatedly. She could only tell the callers that Jerica was still missing and that they would let the prayer warriors know the minute they had something new to report.

At 1:30 that afternoon the phone rang again. "Cornerstone Church. This is Darlene."

"Darlene? Jerry LaSalle here." Darlene hardly recognized the elder's voice. He sounded terrible.

"Jerry. Oh, we've all been praying for you. Do you have any news?"

"I'm afraid not. They've been searching for two hours now, and...nothing. Is Don there?"

"Of course. Just a minute, I'll get him."

Pastor Steele seemed anxious and upset after talking to Jerry. Darlene watched him pace the hallway in front of his office. He was short with her, and he jumped a foot in the air every time the phone rang.

As concerned as Darlene was about Jerica, the grim news was overshadowed by the thing that had weighed heavily on her mind long before she'd walked into the office this morning—the thing that had weighed her down for months on end.

Today had been the day that she was finally going to talk to Don. This situation with little Jerica changed things. Maybe this made it even more crucial that she tell Don what she should have told him months ago. She knew he was preoccupied with concern for the LaSalles. But she wasn't sure she could bear the weight of her burden another minute.

With knees threatening to buckle beneath her, she rose from the desk and went to knock softly on the door that separated her office from Pastor Steele's.

∼

The strobing lights of the patrol car parked outside the Masons' home strafed the family room walls in rhythmic revolutions, piercing Melanie with a stark reminder that Jerica was gone. She and Karly and the boys had answered the two young policemen's questions until she didn't think the officers could possibly come up with one more question to ask.

Matthew had received Karly's frantic message and had taken the first bus home. Now he sat in his big leather recliner by the fireplace and patiently answered Sergeant Riordan's questions even when Riordan and his partner, Officer Marcus Pilsen, interrogated him as though they suspected he had kidnapped Jerica himself.

Finally Pilsen stood and shook Matthew's hand. "I think that's all I need right now."

"Thank you, officer. Will it be okay if my wife and I go join in the search around the neighborhood?" People from all over their housing development had been looking for Jerica since before the police arrived.

"Sure, that would be good. Do you have a cell phone where we can reach you if we need to?"

Matt patted his breast pocket. "Yes. Melanie has the number."

"No!" Melanie jumped up from the edge of the chair she'd been perched on. "I want to go too, Matt. I want to help look for her. Maybe she'll answer my voice." Melanie kept her eyes on the officer.

Marcus Pilsen shook his head. "I think it would be best if you stay. Your daughter may come back home, and if she does it would be best if you were here. And someone needs to stay and field any phone calls. If the girl calls here, it needs to be a familiar voice that answers that phone."

It had now been more than five hours since anyone had seen Jerica, and with each passing second Melanie's fears ballooned. She knew everyone's chief concern was finding Jerica before the sun went down. New Jersey nights were still frigid, and after dark the dangers grew exponentially.

Sergeant Riordan gave Melanie detailed information about how the search would be handled throughout the day. "We'll be in contact with you at least every hour to update you," the sergeant said, moving toward the door.

Melanie felt the panic mount at the thought of being left alone in the house again. But she walked the two men to the front door. They were halfway down the steps when Riordan's pager sounded. He motioned for his partner to remain with Melanie and walked out to the driveway to answer the page. Melanie watched him carefully, and her heart quickened when she saw him turn and start back up the drive. He was actually smiling.

"Looks like your little girl's been found, Mrs. LaSalle," he said. "Sounds like she's fine."

Melanie's knees buckled, and she slumped down on the front porch steps.

Officer Pilsen rushed to sit down beside her. "Are you okay?"

Barely able to speak, she held up a hand. "I'm okay," she finally managed to choke out. "I...just want to see my daughter."

"Of course," Sergeant Riordan assured her. "Apparently an elderly couple saw her walking near the Marta Vista County Park. They're staying with her until the police arrive. We'll probably want to take her to a hospital"—he held up a hand at Melanie's gasp—"just as a precaution…to check things out. It sounds like she's in fine shape."

He let out a kind chuckle and shook his head in apparent amazement. "I'll bet she's exhausted, though. That park is up in the foothills of the Ramapo Mountains. It's almost three miles from here."

Thirty-One

The ride to the park seemed an eternity. Melanie wept silently, gratefully, in the backseat of the police cruiser, watching the terrain as they drove, imagining her daughter trudging along the sidewalks and roadsides they passed. The thought of Jerica walking such a distance all alone sent chills up Melanie's spine. And the knowledge that she'd done it for Melanie's sake—to find Joel for *her*—nearly broke her heart. It was a miracle Jerica hadn't been hit by a car or picked up by someone with sinister intentions.

She'd left a note for Matthew and Karly, and now she gripped her cell phone and punched in Matt's number, anxious to relay the wonderful news. Busy. He was probably trying to call her.

"We're almost there, Mrs. LaSalle," Sergeant Riordan said over his shoulder.

Her excitement rose as the signs that marked the entrance to Marta Vista County Park came into view. But a new twinge of alarm surged through her veins when she saw the emergency vehicles in the parking area—an ambulance, two police cruisers, and what appeared to be a park ranger's vehicle. Bright red, white, and blue lights flashed over the scene. A few civilian vehicles were leaving the park slowly, drivers and passengers craning their necks toward all the activity.

Melanie watched the two policemen's faces, and she could see that they, too, were concerned. "What's wrong?" she asked, trying—and failing—to keep her voice steady. "What's happening?"

"I'm not sure," Sergeant Riordan said. "Stay here," he told Pilsen, then looked at Melanie. "Sit tight a minute. I'll see what's going on."

He scrambled out of the car and jogged to where two other officers stood with their backs to Melanie. One of them stepped aside briefly, and she could see that they were talking to an elderly woman who sat alone on the bench of a picnic table. The woman was too far away for Melanie to get a good look at her face, but by her bent posture Melanie guessed that she was in distress.

Melanie was trying to figure out how to open her car door when Sergeant Riordan loomed outside her window. Pilsen reached to the driver's side and pushed a button. Melanie's window rolled down a few inches.

Riordan put his arms on the side of the car and leaned to speak to her through the window. "Mrs. LaSalle," he said calmly, "I don't think there's anything to worry about, but it seems your daughter's run off again."

"What? What do you mean?"

Riordan motioned toward the woman on the bench. "The old woman and her husband are the ones who found your daughter. According to her, the little girl was sitting calmly between them, and they were reassuring her that we were on our way. All of a sudden, she just jumped up and ran off again."

He pointed toward a wide sidewalk that disappeared into a hilly, wooded area. "She went into the woods. The woman's husband went in after her, but I guess he doesn't get around too well. That was"—he glanced at his watch—"probably ten minutes ago. The park is under the jurisdiction of the sheriff's department. They have a command center set up over there." He inclined his head toward the group of emergency vehicles. "They've already got some citizens and park personnel searching for Jerica and the old man. I'm sure they'll find them in no time."

Melanie looked toward the wooded area beyond. "What... What's in there?"

"Hiking trails. It's rocky, but nothing too treacherous, although there are a couple of bridges that—" He seemed to think better of whatever it was he'd started to say and tilted his head toward the clear sky. "We can be thankful it's still daylight and the weather's good."

Melanie's stomach twisted. "Can I go look for her? Maybe if she hears my voice..."

"Possibly. In a few minutes. I want you to talk to the woman first. Maybe she can give us a better idea of which way she went and what her state of mind was."

Melanie nodded numbly. Sergeant Riordan opened her car door. Melanie scrambled out and followed him across the parking lot.

As they got closer, Melanie noticed that the grey-haired woman appeared to be much older than she'd first guessed. The woman sitting beside her wore a badge that said BERGEN COUNTY SHERIFF'S DEPARTMENT. She stood and walked toward the approaching pair, and Sergeant Riordan introduced Melanie to Lieutenant Shawna Kiley.

"Hello, Mrs. LaSalle," Lieutenant Kiley said, putting a comforting hand on Melanie's arm. "I'm sure your daughter is going to be fine. We're doing every—"

"Did you see her?" Melanie asked, clutching at the young woman's hand. "Was she okay?"

"No, ma'am, I didn't see her. We didn't get called out until she'd already run off. I'm sorry. But Mrs. Phelps here"—she indicated the elderly woman—"said the little girl didn't seem to be injured or sick. Just a little dirty and agitated. Oh—" The lieutenant dug in her pocket and held out a small plastic bag. "Someone found this on the walk. Is it hers?"

Melanie reached out and took in a sharp breath when she saw the orange ribbon coiled inside the bag. She'd tied the ribbon into Jerica's pigtail last night. It gave her hope somehow. At least it proved that it *was* Jerica the elderly couple had seen. "Yes. It's Jerica's. She was wearing it in her hair."

"Okay. Good. I'd like to have you talk with Mrs. Phelps. Maybe you'll pick up on something that we didn't. Something she said to them that might help us."

"What *did* she say? What did she tell them?" Melanie was desperate for any piece of information about her daughter, any morsel to assure her that Jerica was unharmed.

Melanie hadn't realized how hard she'd been squeezing the young woman's hands until Lieutenant Kiley pried herself from her grasp. The lieutenant took her elbow and steered her to where Mrs. Phelps sat. "She's very hard of hearing," she told Melanie quietly. "You'll have to really speak up."

Melanie nodded and held out her hand to the elderly woman. "Hello, Mrs. Phelps."

The woman nodded an acknowledgement, but did not speak.

Lieutenant Kiley stepped in. "Mrs. Phelps," she shouted, "this is the little girl's mother."

"Oh, of course, I can see the resemblance," the woman said in the slow, quavering voice age had bestowed on her. She wiped at a rheumy eye. "Me and Mac just finished a little picnic, and we saw her walking all by herself. Came up that road right over there." She pointed an arthritic finger toward the main entrance to the park. "Your little girl was just as sweet as she could be. We could tell she was lost so we asked her where her folks were. She said she was looking for her daddy. We told her we'd help her find him, but while Mac was lookin' for the ranger, she said, 'I gotta go find my daddy.' Then she ran off again."

Melanie's heart lurched.

"Mac—my husband—tried to catch her," Mrs. Phelps said, "but she was just too fast for him. My goodness, I've never seen a little girl run so fast in my life."

Lieutenant Kiley turned to Melanie. "Is the girl's father on the way?" By the way she said it, Melanie could tell she'd already been informed that she was a single mom.

"She… Her father is dead. But…I know who she's looking for."

Sergeant Riordan stepped closer, took Jerica's note from his pocket, and handed it to Lieutenant Kiley. "She left this for her mother to find. I've already made the other officers aware of it."

Riordan excused himself and walked toward the command center while Lieutenant Kiley studied the note in her hand. She looked to Melanie. "Who's 'Jole'?"

"It's *Joel*. We were engaged," she explained as simply and truthfully as she knew how without going into the details. "He…called the wedding off, but Jerica called him Daddy."

"Have you contacted him?"

"No. I…I don't know where he is."

"Any idea why she'd think she could find her dad—er, find this guy in there?"

Melanie shook her head grimly. Why on earth *did* Jerica think Joel would be here? Had she just gone out the Masons' front door and started walking up and down streets?

The thought slammed into her like a punch in the stomach. Melanie gasped. The words echoed the very thing she'd spoken to Karly this morning, just before they'd discovered Jerica standing there—listening. *Sometimes I just want to walk out that door and go up and down streets until I find Joel again.* That was what she'd told Karly.

"Are you all right?" Lieutenant Kiley bent slightly to peer into Melanie's face.

"Please," Melanie choked out suddenly, clenching her fists at her sides. "We're wasting time. Can I go look now? She'll know my voice."

There was sympathy in Lieutenant Kiley's voice. "I don't think it'll take them long to find her. There's five or six miles of trails in the park, but they cross back on each other, and it's pretty well self-contained."

"Please," Melanie pleaded.

The lieutenant looked at her watch. "Ms. LaSalle, when they bring her out, we'll most likely want to get her to a hospital just to have her checked over. We don't want to have to come in looking for you. It's best if you stay near the command center so we can reach you the minute they find her. We've got plenty of time before the sun goes down. I don't think you have anything to worry about. There's a good team already searching, and lots of volunteers besides."

She looked at Melanie with deep compassion in her eyes. "I'll tell you what," she said, putting a hand on Melanie's shoulder. "Let's go talk to my captain…and Sergeant Riordan. We'll see what they think about your going in."

The young lieutenant turned away from Margaret Phelps and made her voice a whisper. "To tell you the truth, I'm more worried about Mrs. Phelps's husband right now."

Melanie felt guilty that the simple statement comforted her as it did.

Matthew Mason's heart nearly stopped when he saw the knot of emergency vehicles gathered at Marta Vista County Park. Surely they wouldn't all be here unless something terrible had happened.

He pulled into a parking space and jumped from the car. Spotting Officer Riordan and Melanie, he raced across the paved road toward them.

"Matt!" Melanie ran to meet him and fell against him.

"What's going on?"

Melanie's face was drained of color. "Oh, Matt, they still haven't found her!"

"What? But…I thought someone *had* found her…here at the park."

"They did. Over there." Melanie pointed to an elderly couple sitting under a picnic shelter. "But Jerica ran away from them. She told them she had to…find her daddy. The man went in to look for her, but— Oh, Matt…look at him. He can hardly walk. They ended up having to send people in after *him*."

Matthew followed her gaze to where ambulance personnel were working with an elderly man. He was sitting upright and seemed to be talking to them.

"But they're still looking for Jerica?"

"Yes. Twenty people or so are in there looking—mostly people who were here at the park and offered to help with the search. Why aren't they finding her, Matt? It's been almost an hour. Where could she be? Something must have happened. And they don't want me to go in…in case they find Jerica. They want me to be here."

"I've hiked those trails before. I'm going in. Maybe she'll answer my voice. What made her come here?"

Melanie started crying again. "I think she overheard me tell Karly that…sometimes I just wanted to walk up and down the streets until I found Joel. I think she just started walking and…ended up here…"

He could hear the near-hysteria in his sister's voice. He grasped her shoulder, trying to convey a strength he didn't feel. "We'll find her, Mel. Don't worry… We'll find her."

Sprinting toward the trailhead, he began to climb the stone stairs cut into the side of the rocky crag. He'd forgotten how quickly the elevation rose. He was winded within five minutes. A sheriff's deputy met him at the place where the trails divided. "You here to help with the search, sir?"

"Yes. I'm Jerica's uncle."

"Okay. Good." He pointed to a sign that mapped out the four different paths that wound through the acreage at the base of the Ramapo Mountains. "We've got people on every trail already. Probably not as many on this northwest one. These trails cross over each other at several junctures. These two"—he pointed to two short marks on the map—"are easy, half-mile treks. These others are two-and three-mile hikes, a little more advanced. Of course, that probably didn't mean anything to the little girl. Kids usually climb upward when they're lost—it tends to be warmer the higher they go, and they're looking for light, so they go up."

Matt nodded, grateful for some advice.

"Call her name," the deputy continued, "she might recognize your voice. But don't forget to listen, too. If she's hurt she might not be able to make herself heard."

"Thanks," Matt told him. He started up the trail, trying to think the way Jerica might have. This two-mile trail seemed a continuation of the path that led to the trailheads. She would have stayed on the path, wouldn't she? Yes, he decided, if Melanie was right about what Jerica had overheard her saying.

He walked slowly, looking from side to side as he went, keeping his eyes peeled for a flash of orange and his ears tuned for any sound at all. He could hear the faint cries of the other searchers calling out Jerica's name. The voices bounced off one another and echoed through the woods, making it hard to determine where each sound had originated.

"Jerica!" he shouted, then waited for a response. The poor kid was probably scared to death, with everybody yelling at her. "Jerica!" he cried again, attempting to make his voice as friendly as he could at such high decibels.

Though it was unseasonably warm for April, Matt felt the humidity rise and the temperature drop by at least ten degrees as he climbed in the shadow of the trees. He shuddered involuntarily, thinking how cold it would be in here once the sun went down.

When he'd gone half a mile or so, he met a teenage couple coming down the trail. "Are you helping look for that little girl that's lost?" he asked.

"Yeah," the boy said. "We went all the way to the end of this trail and didn't see anything."

"We're going to do the three-mile route next," the girl offered.

"Good," Matt said. "Thanks…thanks a lot. She's…my niece."

"Oh. Sorry, man," the boy said. "I hope you find her. It'd be the pits to have to spend the night out here."

Matt nodded and started on up the trail, then turned back and shouted after them, "Was there anyone else searching this trail?"

"We didn't meet anyone," the girl said, shaking her head. "But somebody was probably here earlier. They had people start looking about an hour ago."

"Okay, thanks. I guess I'll stay on this one, then." He waved and started back up the trail. He was glad Melanie hadn't come into the woods. He was feeling a little panicked himself now that he was up here. The park might be less than seventy-five acres, but with the tangle of trees and vines and trails that wound back and forth over several miles, the task was daunting. He stopped and looked up at the trees, grateful to see the sun still peeking between the dense mesh of branches, well above the horizon.

Half an hour later, Matthew reached the end of the trail and started back down. He prayed with every step that he would not have to emerge from these woods to see disappointment and despair on Melanie's face.

But when he reached the junction of the shorter trail, he came upon another searcher who confirmed his fears. Jerica still had not been found.

Sweat-soaked and exhausted, he went to meet Melanie, who by now was beside herself with panic.

"She's probably fine, Mel," he panted. "I wonder if she's frightened with so many people calling for her. Maybe she's hiding."

Melanie grabbed at his arm. "Matt, they've got to let me go in. Maybe she'll answer my voice. Maybe I can explain what's happening."

"Melanie, you don't know what it's like in there." The terror on her face deepened, and he was immediately sorry he'd said anything. He put a steadying hand on hers. "I just mean that there's a lot of territory to cover. And the acoustics are weird in the woods. She wouldn't be able to understand much more than her name unless you happened to be within a few feet of her when you yelled." He let that soak in for a minute. "Let's go talk to Riordan and see what he thinks."

"Wait, Matt." Something in her voice grabbed his attention.

He turned back to face her. "What?"

"Maybe if Joel went after her. Maybe she'd answer him."

"What are you talking about?"

"What if she *is* hiding? You know how stubborn Jerica is. She went looking for Joel; maybe she's decided she's not coming out until she finds him."

"And how do you propose to get Joel here before…dark?" He could not keep the frustration out of his voice.

"Hear me out, Matt. I think…if I tell Tim what's happened, I think he could talk Joel into coming. I know it sounds crazy, but Joel's in New York. He could get here in an hour. I am not"—her voice broke, and she bit down hard on her knuckle, then turned her hand into a fist and shook it at him—"I am *not* going to let my little girl spend the night in those woods."

The determination and strength that had come into her voice now encouraged Matthew. Maybe it was worth a try. A thought played at the edge of his consciousness. If on some wild chance Joel did come to help with the search, the local law enforcement agencies probably had the authority to take him in for questioning right here. He brushed the thought aside. Finding Jerica was all that mattered right now. "Do you have Tim Bradford's number?"

Melanie dug through her purse and finally held up a worn slip of paper in triumph.

Matthew took it and keyed the Connecticut area code into his cell phone.

Thirty-Two

"I just got a call from a Matthew Mason."

Even through a hundred miles of telephone wire, Joel Ellington heard the tautness in his brother's voice.

"Matthew Mason? Melanie's brother?"

"Yes."

"What did he want? When, Tim? When did he call?" Joel sank onto a chair in his tiny apartment kitchen and nervously wound the phone cord around his wrist, unwrapped it, then wound it again.

"I just hung up from talking to him. Melanie is visiting him in New Jersey. I guess her daughter has run off—Jerica, isn't it?"

"Run off? What do you mean 'run off'?" Joel sat up straight and instinctively reached to the desk behind him for a pen and notepad.

"She's lost in some park near where the Masons live. Just a minute...I wrote it down..." Joel heard the rustle of papers on Tim's desk. "Yes...it's Marta Vista County Park in Bergen County."

Joel's heart raced. "How long has she been missing? And...why did they call *you?* I don't understand."

"Apparently the little girl left a note saying she was going to look for you, Joe."

"Oh dear Lord," Joel kneaded his temple as the implication of his brother's words soaked in.

"I guess they've had searchers looking for her for several hours, and she still hasn't turned up."

"Several *hours!*" His heart lurched again, and he pushed his chair back and stood. *Oh, Father, take care of her... Help them find her.* "How big is this place?"

"I don't know. Mason didn't give many details. He sounded upset. Apparently they're thinking now that she might be hiding from the searchers. This place is in the Ramapo Mountains, but they—"

"In the mountains! What can I do, Tim?" Joel paced the kitchen, as far as the phone cord would allow.

"Melanie thinks she might respond to your voice. You know... since it was you she went looking for."

Joel's mind raced. He went to the desk drawer and yanked it open again. Propping the phone on his shoulder, he pulled out the atlas and flipped to the pages that showed New Jersey. "Where'd you say this park was again?"

"In Bergen County. The Ramapo Mountains...or near there anyway." Joel traced a finger over the map's grid until he found the thin, black letters that spelled out the name of the mountain range. He found a more detailed map of the area and located Marta Vista County Park.

"Yes, yes...here it is. I found it," he told Tim. He did some quick calculations. "If I don't run into any traffic, I can be there in less than an hour. I'll have my cell. Call me if you hear any news. Anything at all."

"I will. I promise. I'll let Melanie's brother know you're coming. You be careful, Joe."

∽

Joel stepped hesitantly out of the car, taking in the scene around him. Half a dozen people milled about on the asphalt road that ran in front of the entrance to the walking trails. A uniformed policeman and a middle-aged man in suit and tie seemed to be in charge. Another group—apparently curious bystanders—hung out across the street near a playground.

The policeman took a step to the side.

And then Joel saw her.

Melanie was talking to the officer, gesturing in a way that was so familiar to Joel that it made him ache. Her face was a mask of grief. Her hair was matted to her forehead and spilled to her shoulders in disarray. Dark circles ringed her eyes, and her face was devoid of the usual carefully applied cosmetics. It had been so long since he'd seen her. Yet even weary and tattered by grief and fear as she was now, to him she was beautiful.

His eyes never left her face as he got out of the car and walked toward what was clearly a command center for the search team. His heart went out to her—she who had suffered such loss already—and for the thousandth time he sent up a silent prayer for her and for Jerica.

He quickened his pace, anxious to see her, anxious to help. Just then, a tall, dark-haired man moved to Melanie's side and put a protective arm around her. Something about him was vaguely familiar. And then Joel knew. It was the same man Melanie had been with in front of Port Authority bus station that day in New York.

Melanie looked up at the man now, an expression of trust and love on her face. Seeing her with him felt like a knife in Joel's soul. He hesitated at the edge of the walk, not sure how welcome he would be, even though he'd been summoned here.

No one seemed to notice him as he walked toward the group of searchers assembled at the edge of the woods. He cleared his throat and stood just outside the circle, waiting for a lull in the sober conversation.

Then Melanie turned slightly, and their eyes met. She gave a little gasp. "Joel…oh, Joel. Thank goodness, you came." The look in her eyes was unreadable, but his name on her lips moved him as it always had.

"I'm so sorry, Melanie." The words were ripe with meanings that stretched back far beyond this day. He marveled that he was beside her again after so many months of aching to be with her. He reached out and gingerly touched her hand, trying to focus on his reason for being here. "What can I do? How can I help?"

Melanie turned to an older man who seemed to be heading up the command center. "This is...Joel Ellington." Her voice broke. "He... He's the one Jerica went looking for."

Joel heard it as an accusation, but this was not the time or place to ponder it, or to defend himself.

The older man extended a hand. "Detective Clark Nathanson."

Joel shook his hand and acknowledged the man beside Melanie with a brief nod. Melanie moved back to the man's side.

Nathanson took Joel aside. "From the things the child told the elderly couple who found her, we think maybe she can hear us, but she's just too frightened to respond. The mother said she's stubborn—and apparently on a mission. She went looking for you?" He made a question of it.

"Yes," Joel acknowledged. He didn't explain. How *could* he explain?

"We're going to want you to stick around. You might be able to talk her into—"

A sharp bark split the air, and from the edge of his vision, Joel saw a blur of fur. He turned to watch a K-9 van unloading two German shepherd search-and-rescue dogs across the road.

The detective turned away from Joel and sprang into action. "Okay, people!" he shouted, "The dogs are here. Let's go!"

Volunteers and emergency personnel began to congregate around Nathanson. Joel followed the man back into the circle, in uncomfortable proximity to where Melanie and her friend were standing.

But Joel's concern was for Jerica. He reached out and put a firm hand on the detective's arm. "You're taking the dogs in there?" he asked, indicating the wooded area.

"Yes, sir," Nathanson said.

"That little girl is terrified of dogs," Joel said firmly. "If you think she's hiding now…not answering because she's frightened, you'll never get her out of there if she hears those dogs."

"He's right," Melanie's friend agreed.

"Oh dear God, why didn't I think of that?" Melanie turned to Nathanson, her hands fluttering in front of her face. "Jerica gets hysterical around dogs—especially big ones. Can't you wait? Just a few—"

Nathanson waved the dog handlers aside. "Hold off a minute," he yelled. He pulled Joel from the knot of searchers. "Okay, we're going to send you in…have you walk the main trails. We'll keep everyone else out for now. Maybe she'll respond to your voice." The older man shaded his eyes and looked up at the sky. "We're losing daylight quickly though. You're going to have to get in and get out in a hurry. If what you say is true, I don't want to have to send the dogs in after dark."

Joel nodded, feeling energized by the assignment.

Nathanson showed him a map of the trails, pointing out the ones they thought were most likely for the little girl to be on. "Call out to her every few minutes," the detective told him. "Your voice will be muffled in there, so make it loud and clear, but keep it friendly, too. Make sure she knows you're not angry with her. Use her name often, and if you have a pet name for her, or something that only you would know about her, use that, too. If the mother's hunch is right, it's *your* voice that will get a response."

Nathanson lowered his voice. "There's a lot of rough terrain in there if she went off the trails. A couple of bridges with pretty steep drop-offs. There's a chance she's fallen. She could be unconscious. I don't know the child, but she must be a pretty determined little girl to have gotten this far from home. It could be—like her mother said—she's just decided she's not coming out until she finds what she went looking for."

The detective paused and eyed Joel. "That would be you," he said finally. "I hope you were worth it."

Joel acknowledged his judgment with a nod. The detective walked with him to the edge of the woods. "Unless you hear or see something," Nathanson told him, "don't veer too far off the paths—we don't want to lose you, too. It gets dark in there sooner than out in the open." He glanced up at the sky and his brow furrowed. "Stop to listen for a reply every minute or so."

Again, Joel nodded soberly.

Nathanson looked at his watch. "I'm gonna to give you half an hour—forty-five minutes tops. After that we're sending the dogs in. The volunteer crew has already combed the woods twice, but we're talking close to seventy-five acres, so it's likely we could have missed something. Oh—" The detective handed him what looked like a hair ribbon, knotted and crumpled. "The little girl lost this. She was wearing overalls this color. That should make her easier to spot."

Joel took the ribbon and curled it into his fist. "Do you need this?" he asked. "In case you have to use the dogs?"

Nathanson shook his head. "No. Someone brought some of her clothing. We'll get a better scent off that."

The detective turned away, and Joel started up the trail. Something about that orange ribbon got to him. Made it all too real. He wanted to fall to his knees on the side of the trail and weep. But he couldn't afford that luxury. He had to find her. He had to.

For the first two hundred yards the path was wide, and the overgrowth was well contained. But as he went deeper into the woods, the trail rose and tapered, and there were places where it dropped sharply into a narrow ravine. Fortunately the gully was dry in most places and shallow in the rest. Still, he couldn't help but recall an old warning that a child could drown in half an inch of water.

"Jerica!" he shouted, his imagination urging him on. "Jerica!" He wondered if Melanie could hear him in the park below. Over and over, he called the little girl's name. And while he listened for a response, he sent up a silent, anguished prayer. *Oh, Father, help me find her. If only I could find her and give her back to Melanie…that would be something…something that might make up for what happened. Make up for my leaving them. For the pain I've caused.*

Joel glanced at his watch and was surprised to see that its phosphorescent face was glowing in the dusky half-light. He hadn't realized how dark it had gotten. He looked up at the trees above him and saw through the lacy branches of red oak and dogwood that the sky beyond was still bright and blue. But deep in the woods the tall pines and the tight-knit foliage and vines blocked out much of the sunlight. The air was cooler here, dank and mossy smelling. The nascent leaves rustled overhead, and all around him there was a constant creak and rasp of branch rubbing branch. Myriad insects and birds added to the eerie symphony.

Joel shivered involuntarily. He called out her name again with greater urgency. "Jerica! Jerica, it's Joel! Can you hear me? Jerica? C'mon, babe, answer me…please!"

He looked at his watch again. He'd been in the woods for twenty-five minutes. He'd probably covered over a mile on the winding trails. It would take him fifteen, maybe twenty minutes to get back out if he didn't stop to holler or listen. He wanted so desperately to be the one to find her. He trudged on, kneading the limp orange ribbon in his fist.

"Jerica!" he shouted again. *Please, God. Please. She's got to be all right. Help me find her. Please.* He stopped again to listen. The *chirrup* of insects answered him, building to a deafening crescendo. He needed to start back, but what if she was just around the next curve in the trail? What if she was injured—or even dying? He walked faster. "Jerica!"

He walked a few yards and stopped again. Suddenly the woods fell silent.

Dead silent.

The cicadas stopped singing, as though they ran on electricity and someone had pulled their plug. The breeze that had caused the hemlocks to whisper was stilled. For one fleeting moment there was not a sound in the entire woods.

Except for a faint, mournful wail that Joel heard from behind him. It seemed to be coming from a secondary path he'd just crossed. He heard the sound again—briefly and below him, it seemed. He strained to listen, willing nature to hold its breath one minute longer.

There it was again. The mewling sound came from beneath him. He backtracked and took the lesser trail, peering into the grey-green haze of vegetation that framed the sound. As his eyes adjusted, he realized that some twenty feet off the trail was a rift. He scrambled cautiously over the tangle of tree trunks and dead limbs until he could see into the ravine.

He listened again. Silence. Then a flash of light caught his eye. He glared into the dim light in the ravine, desperate to see what was below. He heard a rustling of leaves, and again he saw a flicker of light, and then a patch of orange. Pumpkin orange. Like the hair ribbon in his hand. He scrambled down the steep terrain and crossed the rocky bottom of the creek bed. He could see the heap of orange on the other side clearly now. It looked limp and lifeless. His heart stood still. He forced himself to breathe.

"Jerica?"

To his amazement, the crumpled heap shuddered and struggled to sit upright.

"Jerica!"

A hoarse whisper-soft voice spoke his name. "Joel?"

"It's me, sweetie." He plowed through the tangle of vines and jagged rocks on the creek bed and hunched down beside her, searching her tiny form for signs of injury. It was hard to tell in the dim light, but she didn't seem to be bleeding. And she was moving her limbs and speaking clearly. Those were good signs.

He reached out and touched her forehead lightly. It felt cool and dry against his palm. "Jerica? It's Joel. Are you okay?"

"Joel?" There was disbelief—suspicion—in her voice. "Is it really Joel?"

"It's me," he repeated. "It's me." He resisted the urge to pull her into his arms and crush her to himself, afraid she might have injuries he couldn't see.

She leaned to peer up into his face. "Oh, Joel. I found you," she cried. "I found you!"

A sob crawled up his throat, and it was all he could do to smother it. "Yes, sweetheart." He laid a gentle hand on her dirt-smudged, petal-soft cheek. "You found me."

Thirty-Three

"Are you okay, honey? Does anything hurt?" Joel eyed Jerica carefully. "Did you *fall* down here?"

The little girl frowned and shook her head. "I climbed. I didn't want those people to find me."

"What people?"

"Those people that were yelling at me. And that old man that was chasing me. I didn't want them to talk to me. They were going to make me go to jail."

She didn't seem to be delirious. In fact her voice—her vocabulary—was far more grown-up than he remembered. She was taller, too. Looking at her gangly arms and legs, it struck him that he had missed out on a whole year of her life. Again, he felt like weeping.

"No, honey. Nobody wants to put you in jail. They're all just worried about you. Your mommy is worried about you."

Jerica rolled onto her hands and knees and struggled to stand.

"Wait a minute, sweetie. Sit down. Let's make sure you didn't break anything. Can you wiggle your fingers and toes?"

She looked at him as if he'd lost his mind, but she plopped back down on the ground. She held up her arms and wriggled her fingers, then looked down at her feet. He could see the outline of her toes squirming inside small, muddy tennis shoes.

"Good…good," he said. He squeezed her feet through the shoes and patted her legs gently. The soles of her shoes emitted a flash of light, matching the rhythm of his pats—the flicker he'd seen from the trail. *Thank you, Lord, for that crazy fad.*

Gently, he palpated her arms and legs. When he was fairly sure that nothing was broken, he helped her stand and brushed the dirt and leaves from her overalls. "Are you okay?" he asked again.

She nodded, her eyes as dark as coffee beans. "Are you going to take me back to my mommy?" she asked solemnly.

"Yes, Jerica, I am. Your mommy is worried sick about you. She's been looking everywhere for you. We were all worried."

She didn't respond.

"Here," Joel said, holding out his arms, "let me carry you." He put his hands around her waist and lifted her into his arms. She wrapped her arms around him and rested her head on his shoulder. He felt her warm, sweet breath on his neck, and he wanted to hold her that way forever.

He climbed up the embankment to the main trail. Jerica felt like a weightless bird in his arms. And he felt as though *he* could fly.

A thousand images swirled through his mind in the twenty minutes it took him to walk down from the trail. Jerica was quiet on his shoulder, and he thought perhaps she'd fallen asleep.

Sweet memories of the times he and Mclanie and Jerica had spent together in Silver Creek filled his thoughts. He remembered a smaller Jerica grinning at him across the T-ball field. He saw her and Melanie, faces aglow from the candles on a birthday cake they'd made just for him. He heard the music of their laughter—mother and daughter—and envisioned their beloved faces that held smiles that were meant for him alone. It was as if his life—the fleeting time he'd shared with Melanie and Jerica—passed before him. They said that happened before you died. He couldn't help but think that when he emerged from these woods it would indeed signify a death of sorts.

But he could not grieve any longer. There was no sorrow left in him. He'd been privileged to help Melanie in one of her darkest hours. He'd been given one last chance to say good-bye. To see their faces. Even to hold Jerica in his arms. And for that he would always be grateful.

As he came closer to the trailheads and began to catch pulses of light through the trees from the emergency vehicles, he found himself torn between slowing his steps to savor these final minutes as long as possible and hurrying to Melanie to ease her agony over Jerica. He shook his head, put his selfish desires aside, and quickened his pace. He grew breathless as he came down the last wide steps carved into the foot of the mountain.

He heard someone shout, and then pandemonium struck. From the corner of his vision he saw the ambulance backing up to the entrance to the hiking trails. He saw the dogs being led back into the K-9 vehicle. A cadre of reporters and television camera crews crowded toward him. He watched Detective Nathanson and several other law enforcement officers jogging to meet him. And then he saw Melanie sobbing for joy in the arms of the tall, handsome man.

Now she pushed away from the man and broke through the crowd, racing toward her daughter, crying out her name. Joel put a protective hand on Jerica's head and hurried toward Melanie.

At the sound of her mother's voice, Jerica stirred in his arms, and he moved her from his shoulder to the cradle of his arms so that Melanie could see her face, see that she was unharmed.

Melanie was only yards away now, arms outstretched, tears streaking her face. Joel kissed the top of Jerica's head one last time, then he held out his offering. Melanie dropped to her knees, and Jerica slid from his arms and ran into her mother's embrace, nearly bowling her over. Mother and daughter knelt together on the rocky ground and held on to each other as if they would never let go.

He did not want to leave them. Didn't want to let Melanie or Jerica out of his sight. But neither did he want to cause them more distress than they'd already suffered.

He reached out and put a tentative hand on Melanie's arm. "I… I'm glad she's all right," he told her.

She looked up, as if noticing him for the first time. Her eyes seemed to reflect all the sorrow and regret that was in his heart. "Oh, Joel. How can I ever thank you? I'm so sorry for…putting you through this."

Her words were ludicrous in light of the fact that it was his fault they were here in the first place. "I'm just…glad she's safe. Everything will be all right now." He wished he could make those words true for Melanie, wished he believed them for himself. He reached out to touch her again, thought better of it, and pulled his hand away.

Just then, Melanie's friend appeared and nodded curtly to Joel. Then he knelt and put a gentle hand on the little girl's shoulder and stroked her face. "Are you okay, sweetie?" He brushed a strand of tangled hair off her forehead.

Joel watched them, feeling invisible. And numb. He turned away and started walking, skirting the perimeter of the command center, which was already beginning to disintegrate.

A firm hand on his shoulder stopped him. He turned to find a policeman eyeing him.

"Mr. Ellington?"

Joel nodded.

"Could you come with me, please? We'd like to ask you a few questions."

If she lived to be a hundred, Melanie didn't think she would ever feel such gratitude as she felt now, holding her daughter in her arms. She wept tears of joy, and then, as she thought again of what could have happened, she felt a flash of anger. She was tempted to spank some sense into her daughter. What had Jerica been thinking, running off like that in a strange place where she knew no one, was familiar with nothing?

Before her emotions could bring her full circle to gratitude again, she became aware of the medical personnel working around her.

A husky, bearded man put a hand on her arm. "Ma'am, we'd like to check her out. Make sure we haven't missed any broken bones or internal injuries."

She let the man take Jerica from her embrace. The little girl whimpered a little, but Melanie gave her a reassuring smile. "It's okay, punkin. I'll be right here."

"Wait, Mommy. Where did Joel go?" She craned her neck to look around the paramedic's bulky figure.

"He...it's okay, Jerica. They... Someone just needed to talk to him. You need to let this man check you out, okay."

"Tell Joel not to leave, okay?"

Melanie bit her bottom lip. "It'll be okay, Jerica."

Matthew helped Melanie to her feet. She leaned against his strong frame, watching as the technicians did an initial check of Jerica. Melanie was vaguely aware that the various law enforcement agencies manning the command center were working hard to keep the media at bay. Melanie heard her name and the shouted questions that followed, and she saw an occasional camera flash, but for the most part the officers' efforts seemed to be successful. She was thankful. She was in no mood to answer any questions.

The paramedic who had taken Jerica from her arms turned to her now. "It looks like your little girl is fine, Mrs. LaSalle, but we strongly recommend transporting her to a hospital to be checked over by a physician. We probably ought to start an IV on her, too. She was out there for an awful long time without anything to eat or drink."

Melanie looked to Matthew who was nodding his agreement. "Yes," she said. "Of course. May I ride with her?"

"Of course."

The ambulance personnel placed Jerica on a gurney and slid her into the vehicle. Melanie climbed up behind them and took a seat on the narrow bench the technician indicated. Jerica was quiet as he checked her vital signs, and she barely flinched when he inserted a needle to start the IV.

As the ambulance rolled past what was left of the temporary command center, Melanie glanced out the window. She saw Matthew standing by himself to one side, his face still reflecting the grim potential their situation had carried. Small contingents of volunteer searchers waved and smiled as the emergency vehicle headed out of the park.

They neared the exit, and Melanie's heart lurched as she caught sight of Joel. He was standing beside Sergeant Riordan's patrol car, deep in conversation with the police officer. With one hand on Jerica's shoulder, Melanie turned in her seat to peer from the window as the ambulance pulled onto the highway. Joel faded from sight, and she took a shuddering breath. How she longed for a chance to express her gratitude to Joel. Just to speak with him once more. She'd been able to tell him thank you when he came down from the trail, but the words were so very inadequate. There was so much that had been left unsaid between them.

She hoped Matthew would seek Joel out before he left and express their thanks for what he had done today.

As the vehicle sped along the parkway, the drone of the engine settled into a constant purr, and Jerica was lulled to sleep. Now the frightening memories of the last few hours rolled over Melanie in full force. She reached for Jerica's hand and ran a finger over the inside of her tiny wrist, desperately needing the assurance of the pulse that fluttered there.

From the jump seat at Jerica's head, the paramedic gave Melanie a reassuring nod. "She's doing just fine." He turned his attention to regulating the IV and checking the little girl's blood pressure again.

Closing her eyes, Melanie leaned her head against the side of the ambulance and shut out everything around her.

Oh, thank you, Father. How can I ever thank you enough for restoring my daughter to me? And thank you, Lord…for using Joel. Now Jerica will always know how much Joel cared for her. Thank you for ending it this way. Her eyes filled with tears. She pressed her fingers against her eyelids, but the tears seeped out anyway. She'd shed far too many tears over the past hours…and weeks, and months. It was time to let go. Time to relinquish everything. Her daughter. Her future. Her very life.

And Joel.

I give up, Lord. I've been trying to figure out this puzzle for so long. I've tried so hard to make the pieces fit the way I want them to fit and I…I can't do it. I realize now that you never intended me to do it. Forgive me for trying to fix things on my own. Oh, Father, I've been searching for so long, trying to find what I lost. Trying to find peace. But I realize now that I've been looking in the wrong places. Only you can give me the things I've been searching for. And…Father, you've been there all along…waiting patiently for me to come to my senses. Forgive me, Lord. Forgive me. I give it all up. I put it all in your hands.

Her breath came easier, and a sweet peace settled over her like a cool sheet on a warm summer night. She could not renounce her love for Joel Ellington. Having been so newly in his presence, she felt her love more strongly than ever. But now she surrendered her right to have him in her life. Surrendered willingly and gratefully. It was far too heavy a burden to carry by herself.

Thirty-Four

The hospital bed dwarfed Jerica. Melanie smoothed the blankets around her slight form again and watched her daughter's face closely. The little girl was engrossed in an old Andy Griffith rerun and seemed oblivious to all that had happened in the last twelve hours.

Melanie released a breath of pent-up stress. Movement in the hallway caught her eye, and she looked up to see Matthew standing just outside the door. In his hands he clutched a bouquet of colorful balloons and a plush stuffed animal.

Jerica's view was blocked by the curtain drawn between her bed and the empty bed nearest the door. Being careful not to bump the IV needle that was taped in place on the back of her small hand, Melanie patted her daughter's black-and-blue arm. "I'll be right back, sweetie."

She went to give Matthew a hug.

"How is she?" her brother whispered.

"She seems to be doing great. She has some pretty good bruises, and she's tired, but she ate like a little pig at supper. I don't think they really needed to admit her."

"Maybe not, but you know you would have worried about her all night if we'd taken her home."

She nodded. "That's probably true. I guess it's good to have her here overnight at least. Come on in. She's awake. She'll be thrilled to see you. And she'll love the balloons. That was so sweet of you,

Matt." Melanie looked up and read the message on the largest Mylar balloon: YOU ARE SPECIAL.

Melanie led the way into Jerica's room, but with a teasing twinkle in his eye, Matt put a finger to his lips and tiptoed to Jerica's bedside. Hiding behind the curtain, he stuck the balloon bouquet around the barrier where Jerica would see it.

Jerica started, then squealed, "Joel? Daddy!"

Where she stood at the end of Jerica's bed, Melanie froze. She watched Matthew's shoulders slump and his smile fade. She pasted a smile on her own face and—trying to ignore Jerica's comment—drew Matthew quickly into Jerica's line of vision. "It's Uncle Matt, Jer. Look what he brought for you!"

Jerica's countenance fell. "Oh…hi, Uncle Matt."

Melanie grabbed the stuffed animal from Matt's hands and thrust it into Jerica's lap, desperate to turn the child's thoughts another direction. "Look, sweetie. Uncle Matt brought you a little"—she picked up the toy again and inspected it—"it's an otter, isn't it? Or is it a seal? Isn't he darling?"

Jerica took the plush toy and hugged it to her face with her right hand, but Melanie didn't miss the slight crane of her daughter's neck toward the curtain.

Matthew gave Melanie a sidewise glance, and she forced another smile.

"How are you feeling, baby doll?" Matt asked his niece, moving to the end of the bed.

"Good. I wanna go home. Where's Brock and Jace?"

"Aunt Karly stayed home with them—and baby Parker." He looked at his watch and winked at her. "It's past their bedtime. What are you doing up so late anyway?"

"Uncle Matt," Jerica huffed, throwing him a long-suffering look, "I'm in the hospital. I been sleeping forever."

Matt laughed and reached out to tweak her toes through the thin hospital blanket.

Jerica yelped, but quickly turned serious. "Do you know when Joel's coming to see me?" she asked. Her question was pointedly directed at Matt.

Melanie pressed two fingers hard against her temple, suddenly aware that her head was throbbing. Jerica had asked about Joel half a dozen times since they'd admitted her to the hospital. After all Jerica had been through, how would they explain Joel's absence to her? No, how would *she* explain? It wasn't fair to drag Matthew into this.

She stepped in to rescue Matt. "Jerica…honey…I'm not sure if we'll…see Joel again. We are so glad he found you, and I told him thank you…back at the park. I'm sure he knows how happy you are that he found you."

"I found *him*, Mommy. I found him for *you*."

"Oh, sweetie. I know you were trying to help, but you need to let Mommy take care of this. I don't know what's going to happen, but…this is between Mommy and Joel. Mommy is fine now. I…I don't want you to worry about it—about me—anymore, okay?"

Jerica shook her head solemnly, her eyes seeming far too old for her innocent face.

"I'd probably better get going," Matthew said now, obviously uncomfortable with this conversation. He squeezed Jerica's toes again. "I'll see you at our house tomorrow, okay, squirt?"

"Okay. Bye."

"What do you tell Uncle Matt, Jerica?" Melanie reminded in a stage whisper.

"Oh! Thank you for the cool stuff. I like it."

"You're very welcome, honey." Matt started for the door.

"I'll be right back, Jer," Melanie told her. "I'm going to walk Uncle Matt to the elevator."

"Okay." Jerica nodded, then turned her attention to the remote control. She jabbed at one of the buttons, and Barney Fife's grating voice crescendoed to fill the room.

"Thanks for coming, Matt," Melanie said as they walked down the long corridor toward the main elevators.

"Sure. She…looks good."

"Yes."

They walked in silence, but at the elevators, Matt turned to Melanie with an expression she couldn't quite read.

"What is it?"

He hung his head for a long moment, then looked up to meet her gaze. "There's something I need to tell you, Melanie."

"What?"

"You have to promise you won't get upset."

"What is it, Matt?" The hallway grew uncomfortably warm.

He took a deep breath and let it out slowly. "They took Joel in for questioning today…from the park."

She wanted to be angry. She wanted to weep and rail. But she couldn't fight anymore. She had deep regrets. She still had a million questions. But underneath it all, the peace she'd found during the ride in the ambulance buoyed her.

Laying a hand on her brother's arm, she willed her voice to remain steady. "Thank you for telling me. I… I'm sorry about this morning, Matt. This whole thing"—she inclined her head toward the hallway that led to Jerica's room—"was my fault. I…I know I just need to let it go. But Matt…would you let me know what happens?"

He stroked a hand down her arm. "I will, Mel."

"I don't know what I'm going to tell Jerica," she said. "She keeps asking about him. I don't know what's going to happen to Joel, but I'd like…to talk to him."

"Let's wait and see what develops, okay?"

She nodded. "I won't do anything stupid," she said, sensing that he needed the reassurance.

He nodded with a slight smile. "I know, Mel. I trust you." The bell sounded, and the elevator slid silently open. "See you in the morning."

She stood alone in front of the doors for several minutes after they closed. Then she went back down the corridor to face her daughter's questions.

⌒

Matthew Mason leaned over the rocking chair to kiss his wife, then stroked the soft down on his newborn son's head. "You need anything?" he asked.

Karly shifted the baby on her lap and reached for Matt's hand. "I'm fine. You look exhausted."

He sighed. "Yes, I guess I am." He lifted her hand to his mouth and kissed her knuckles one by one. In the soft light from the nursery lamp, Karly looked lovely. "I'm glad this day is over."

"Me, too. Do you think this will finally put some closure on things for Melanie?"

He thought for a minute, then sighed. "She seemed to be taking things well at the hospital tonight. I'm more worried about Jerica now. Mel said she keeps asking about Joel."

"Maybe Melanie should talk to him, Matt…and Jerica, too."

"I thought about that. You don't think it would just stir things up more?"

"I think they need to say good-bye to Joel. Both of them. Especially if there's a chance that he'll end up in jail."

He let go of her hand and rubbed his face. Maybe Karly was right. He hadn't been able to get any information from the Bergen County authorities yet, but he'd left a message on Tim Bradford's answering machine.

"Well," he said finally, "I need to go call Don Steele before it gets too late. I promised Melanie I'd let him know that Jerica was okay."

Pulling the door to the nursery shut, he went down the hall to the den. He dialed Don's home number and leaned back in his chair, weariness washing over him.

"This is Pastor Steele."

"Don? This is Matthew Mason in New Jersey."

"Matthew. Do you have any news for us?"

"Yes. That's why I'm calling. Jerica is fine."

"Praise God! We've been praying for her…for all of you."

"Thank you. She's spending the night in the hospital tonight just so they can keep an eye on her, but she's perfectly fine." Matthew relayed a brief account of the afternoon's events. "Joel got there just before they were going to send the search dogs in and—"

"You saw Joel?" Don Steele interrupted.

"Yes. He's the one who found Jerica, actually. I…didn't get a chance to talk to him, but the police were taking him in for questioning about the time I left the park. Apparently the warrant—"

"Questioning? You mean about the…embezzlement…here?"

"Yes…" Matt hesitated.

"Joel didn't do it, Matthew."

"What?"

"He didn't take that money." Don Steele breathed out a long sigh into the phone.

"How do you know that, Don?"

Don sighed again. "Darlene Anthony—a woman who works as a secretary here at Cornerstone—turned herself in a couple of hours ago."

"You're not serious!"

"I am. I'm still reeling from the news myself. I would never have suspected Darlene in a million years. But her mother was dying of cancer, and apparently she needed the money to pay for some experimental cancer drugs. Got them somewhere down in Mexico…saw an ad in some magazine. I guess she was just desperate enough that when Joel left, she saw an opportunity to take the money she needed and pin the blame on him."

"That's incredible. So…Joel had nothing to do with it? You're sure she's not just covering for him?"

"No. Darlene assured us that she acted alone. Everything she told us checks out."

"But—if the money wasn't Joel's reason for leaving, what was?"

"I have no idea, Matthew. I have no idea."

A minute later, Matthew hung up the phone. He found the number for Tim Bradford that Melanie had given him at the park today and punched it into the keypad of his phone, his thoughts spiraling at a speed too fast for him to follow.

Thirty-Five

The classroom was empty and quiet. Joel moved the eraser over the blackboard in wide arcs, wiping away the morning's English assignment. But his thoughts were miles away from the halls of King's Collegiate, reliving the events of yesterday, remembering how it had felt to see Melanie and Jerica again.

Suddenly the ancient intercom over the door crackled to life, and the school secretary's voice broke through the static. "Mr. Ellington?"

"Yes?"

"There's someone in the office to see you. Are you free?"

"Yes. Who is it please?"

"A Matthew Mason?"

Joel's breath caught. *Melanie's brother.* "I'll...be right there. Thanks, Shirley."

He ran a hand through his hair. What could Melanie's brother want with him? Melanie must have told him about what happened at the park yesterday. Had something happened to Jerica? She'd seemed fine when they put her in the ambulance, but he hadn't heard anything since then. And how had Matthew found him here?

Joel hurried down the hall. He stopped short in the office doorway. The man standing at the front desk was the man from the park yesterday, the one from the street in front of Port Authority a hundred yesterdays ago. "What...is this?" he asked warily, his defenses alert.

The man stepped forward and extended a hand. "I'm Matthew Mason. In all the excitement yesterday, we were never officially introduced. Your brother said I could find you here. I hope this…isn't a problem."

This was Matthew Mason? Joel's mind raced to make sense of it. This was the man he'd felt so threatened by?

His thoughts flew to Melanie. "Is Jerica all right? And Melanie? Has something happened?"

Matthew smiled. "Everything's fine. But…we need to talk. Is there someplace—?" There was a note of urgency in his voice. His gaze darted meaningfully to the secretary and two student aides who were working in the office.

"Yes…sure." Joel turned to Shirley, who had been watching the exchange with interest. "I'll be back in a few minutes, Shirley. I don't have a class till fourth hour."

The woman nodded and ostensibly busied herself with something on her computer screen.

Joel turned back to Matthew. "Let's…go outside," he said, inclining his head toward the front entrance just beyond the office.

He held the door open for Matthew and led him across the fenced-in grounds to a small courtyard at the far end of the campus. A group of benches were scattered around the edge of the square.

Matthew put a foot up on one of the benches and rested his hand on its weathered back. Taking his cue from him, Joel remained standing, shifting his weight from one foot to the other, still trying to wrap his mind around the fact that this man he'd thought was Melanie's new love was in fact her brother. What did he want that was so important that Tim would have sent him here?

Matthew cleared his throat. "Ellington…I don't know what your game is. For a year now I've thought you were a con man and a thief. Now at least I know that you're no thief, but I have no idea what to believe about you."

"What are you talking about? I assume you know that the police took me in for questioning yesterday…at the park. I can only tell you what I told them. I did not take that money. I have no idea who was responsible, but—"

"Wait— You haven't heard, then?"

"Heard what?"

"I talked to Don Steele last night. The secretary at the church turned herself in. She took the money."

"Darlene? Are you talking about Darlene Anthony?"

"Yes, that was her name. She told Don that you weren't involved in any way."

"Darlene stole the money?" Joel's mind reeled.

"She took it to pay for cancer treatments for her mother." Matthew went on to relay what he knew.

Joel found it difficult to make the meek woman into a thief, but then, if anyone understood what desperation could do to a person, he did. "Does Melanie know?" he asked finally.

"Yes. I told her this morning. But I don't have to tell you that this turn of events begs the question, Ellington. If you didn't take the money, why did you disappear?" Anger had crept into Matthew's voice, and it rose with each word. "You wrecked my sister's life. And yet a year later she is still obsessed with you, and her little girl apparently aches for you so badly that she'd do what she did yesterday just to find you."

Matthew took his foot off the bench and kicked a pebble across the cement. "I don't know what you did to inspire that kind of loyalty and love. But I want you to hear me and hear me well. It's time for my sister to move on. And I don't think that can happen until she talks to you. Until she knows the truth."

Joel felt lightheaded. Melanie still loved him? He held up a hand. "Wait a minute. Please…Matthew. You're telling me that Melanie still…has feelings for me?"

Matthew hesitated. "I think you have some hard questions to answer before this discussion goes any further."

Joel paced along the edge of the concrete, trying to make sense of all this. If what Matthew said was true, there was no reason to hold back the truth any longer. He'd had enough of lies, enough of deceit. It was only fair that Melanie know the truth now.

He sighed and took a seat on the far end of the bench. Matthew sat down on the other end, waiting, his expression skeptical but open and earnest, Joel thought.

Joel released a short sigh and met the man's gaze. "I'm not even sure where to begin."

"I've got all day," Matthew Mason told him, draping an arm across the back of the bench.

Jerica was released from the hospital the next afternoon with no more serious instructions than to take it easy for a few days. When they got back to Matt and Karly's house, Jerica went out into the yard to play with her cousins. Still a little nervous about Jerica's state of mind and wanting to keep a close eye on her, Melanie took her cell phone out to the deck while she called her parents and Jerry and Erika to let them know how everything was going.

She hung up from talking to Erika, and homesickness billowed over her. She wished she could take Jerica and fly back to Silver Creek tonight, but the doctor had advised her to wait a few days before traveling with her.

Melanie looked across the yard to where the children were playing. Brock and Jace were chasing Jerica. She was squealing like a stuck pig, but Melanie could tell by the ocean-wide smile on her face that she was enjoying every minute of her cousins' attention. A wave of longing swept over her for all the things that would never be— living near her brother and his family, a baby brother or sister for Jerica, the life she'd dreamed of with Joel…

She thought about the incredible things Matthew had learned

from Don Steele last night. Her heart went out to Darlene, but more than that, Melanie was relieved that Joel had been cleared of the crime. Yet it bewildered her more than ever. If it wasn't the money that had caused him to leave, then what was it? Perhaps she would never know all the reasons behind Joel's actions. These weren't easy things to ponder. Still, she had placed her feelings for Joel in the hands of her heavenly Father, and she was determined to leave them there.

She could not deny that she still ached for Joel. But now the familiar yearning was tempered by the inexplicable sense of calm that had anchored her since that defining moment in the ambulance with Jerica when she had turned the rudder of her life over to the God who knew far better than she what was right and good. Somehow she understood that the peace was there to stay this time. "Thank you, Father," she whispered into the breeze.

⁓

Melanie woke the next morning when she heard Matt's alarm clock go off down the hall. She had let Jerica crawl into bed with her last night, and now she watched her for a few minutes, needing the reassurance of her soft, even breathing. Melanie crawled out of bed and padded down to the kitchen where Matt was pouring cereal for Brock and Jace. Karly was nursing the baby in the family room.

Matthew and Karly and the boys were driving upstate to spend the day with Karly's brother and his family, who had not yet met little Parker. The Masons had invited Melanie and Jerica to go along, but she didn't feel Jerica was quite up to the all-day outing. Besides, they had long flights ahead of them tomorrow.

"Are you sure you don't mind being here alone all day?" Karly asked, peering hard into Melanie's face as if she would find her friend's true feelings written there.

"Don't worry about us," Melanie insisted. "A day of peace and quiet sounds wonderful to me. Jerica can sleep in while I finish up our laundry and get packed."

After they'd eaten, Melanie helped Karly get the boys ready. Across the hall from Brock and Jace's bedroom, she heard Matthew talking on the telephone in his office. It sounded like he was discussing business with a client.

"Doesn't that man ever take a day off?"

Karly's back was to Melanie as she diapered the baby on the little changing table under the window. "Not often enough," she replied lightly.

A few minutes later, Matthew herded his little family out the door and to the waiting minivan.

"Enjoy your day, Mel," he hollered on his way down the hall to the back door. "Don't wait up for us… It might be late. Oh, by the way," Matt said over his shoulder as he stepped into the garage, "a guy…a friend might drop something by the house later this morning. Would you mind listening for the doorbell?"

"No problem."

She heard the van pull away, and a delicious silence descended on the house. She went to check on Jerica one more time. The little girl was curled into a cocoon of blankets, her face serene in repose. Melanie wondered if she would ever take Jerica's safety for granted again. She whispered a prayer of thanks and slipped out of the room, closing the door behind her.

Matt had kindled a fire in the fireplace, but the flames had dwindled to nothing and the house had grown chilly. Melanie brought in a log from the woodpile on the back deck and settled it on the fire. She pulled a sweater over her turtleneck and put the kettle on for tea.

She started a load of laundry and tidied up the kitchen. The kettle whistled, and she went to turn off the stove. While her tea brewed, she went to retrieve the newspaper from the driveway. She

was on her second cup of tea and halfway through the tough Saturday crossword puzzle when the doorbell broke the stillness.

The sudden noise startled her so that she broke the lead of her
pencil. Then she remembered that someone was coming by the house.
Legal paperwork of some kind, she assumed. She finger-combed her
hair quickly and went to answer the door.

Joel Ellington stood in front of her, his gaze searching, piercing
her heart.

"Hello, Melanie."

Thirty-Six

Joel waited on the doorstep, hope and longing mingled on his face. "May I come in?"

The sound of his deep voice brought a sharp pang to her heart and assured her that this was not her imagination playing tricks. Unable to find her own voice, she put a hand to her mouth. Suddenly lightheaded, she rocked back on her heels, struggling to keep her balance.

He put out an arm to steady her. "Are you okay? I'm sorry. I didn't want to frighten you."

"Joel? What are you doing here?" Her breath came in a shudder, and she clasped her hands to keep them from trembling.

"Please, Melanie, may I come in?" He stood before her looking a little like a lost puppy hoping to be adopted.

When she remained speechless, he offered, "If it's any comfort, your brother called me this morning to tell me I could find you here. He knew I was coming. We...we talked yesterday."

"Matthew knew? I...I don't understand."

"Please, Melanie. I promise I'll explain everything."

"Yes...of course. Come in." Her mind careened as she led him through the entry hall to the family room. The fire had begun to die down again, and she shivered involuntarily.

"Would...would you care for a cup of tea?"

"Um, sure. Thanks."

Her hands trembled so badly she feared she would drop a teacup or spill the boiling water, yet at the same time she was grateful to have something to occupy them. Joel sat in silence in a corner of the sofa while she finished making tea. She came from behind the kitchen island and handed him the hot mug. Her hand brushed his in the transfer, and a little tremor went up her spine. He was very, very real.

"How's Jerica?"

"She's fine. Exhausted though; she's still sleeping." She eased down on the other end of the sofa, cradling the lukewarm remains of her own mug in her palms. "Why are you here, Joel? I don't understand."

"I know you don't, Melanie. How could you? But I want to explain everything...from the very beginning. If you feel up to it."

She merely nodded.

For the next hour she listened, transfixed, while he told her everything, beginning with the complete truth about Victoria and her tragic death. "I loved her so much, Melanie. When I met you it seemed impossible that I could have found love again. For a while I was afraid that I'd—" He hesitated. "Well," he said finally, "that I'd fallen in love on the rebound. But as time went on, I knew that what we had was real. I hoped that you were the woman God intended for me. Then, when I realized I would have to testify again, I knew I had to leave. I could not drag you and Jerica into that mess..."

He reached out and touched her hand tentatively. "I'm so sorry I wasn't honest with you from the beginning. It wasn't fair of me to ask you to make a decision about marrying me without having all the facts. But you have to understand that there were rules... WITSEC—the Justice Department—was adamant that no one could know my past. I put myself at great risk by telling Tim when I first went into the program, but at that point, I didn't care. I had to have someone to confide in, someone to help me deal with my grief. The loneliness, the isolation... It would have killed me. And I was the only family Tim had too."

"I understand, Joel," she said haltingly, struggling to absorb everything he'd told her. "I know you thought you were doing what was best by…deceiving me."

He put up a hand. "Still…what I did wasn't fair. I should have trusted you, Melanie. I'm ready to do that now. And…well, things have changed. I'm out of the program now. I want to explain everything…if you're still willing to listen."

His eyes pleaded for her permission. She gave it with a slow nod, not trusting her voice.

As the rest of Joel's story unfolded, as the astonishing details of his life came to light, she found herself in tears for the agony he had suffered. How alone he must have felt, waiting all those months to testify again! How horrible it must have been for him to know that he had left her and Jerica feeling abandoned, devastated. And to be unable to explain any of it.

Yet with all her sorrow over the cruel events that had parted them, she felt an incredible spring of hope bubbling up within her. Joel was innocent after all. He *had* had a reason for leaving all along—a reason that was fully justified. Everything he had said in his letter was true. Every good thing she had believed of him was confirmed. *Thank you, Lord!* It seemed too amazing to be true. She was afraid she might be dreaming again.

Joel's voice broke in on her thoughts. He put down his cup of tea and angled his body to face her on the sofa. "You know, I never realized how much our past forms our identity. Once they…took that away from me and I was living a lie, it was almost as though I didn't exist anymore. Sometimes I was afraid you'd fallen in love with a fantasy…with someone who wasn't even real. Do you remember when you and Jerica made me a birthday cake?"

She nodded, not sure where this was going.

"The day you were celebrating for me wasn't the day I was born. It was…an arbitrary day the Justice Department picked out to put on my identification cards."

"I didn't know."

"No, of course not. But do you see why I wasn't even sure who I was anymore? So I had to wonder how *you* could know who I was. Does that make any sense at all?"

She nodded. "I think so." But when he moved closer to her, when he laced his strong, warm fingers with hers and tenderly kissed her forehead, she could only whisper, "Oh, Joel. Every second of this moment in time is as real as anything I've ever known. I'm not in love with a name or a birthday! I'm in love with *you*. With the flesh-and-blood man sitting beside me now." She moved closer to him on the sofa and put a tentative hand on his arm.

He looked at her with tears in his eyes. "When I saw you from the window of that taxi in New York, I thought my life was over. I saw you…with Matthew, and then when I came to the park when Jerica was lost, he was there, too. You were…in his arms both times. I…I was sure you'd found someone else."

"Oh, Joel. No…"

"I realized then how much I had lost. And…" He pulled her into his arms, and she went willingly. His voice came muffled and ragged in her ear. "Oh, Melanie, when Matthew came to see me yesterday and introduced himself as your brother…you have no idea what a gift it was. What a relief." He kissed her temple and whispered huskily, "It killed me to think of you happy with someone else."

"There was never anyone else, Joel. Only you. Only you."

A thought sprang to her mind, and she pulled away from him, jumped up, and ran to the kitchen counter where her purse sat. She reached in and retrieved the envelope and returned to the sofa. Taking Joel's hand, she opened his palm and spilled the contents of the envelope into it. The scarlet cord coiled into the cup of his hand, and she asked the question with her eyes.

He closed his eyes, and there was such tenderness written on his face that it brought her to tears. "Yes, Melanie. I'm ready to explain it to you now."

She waited, her thoughts swimming.

A faraway look came to Joel's eyes, and he lowered his lashes and busied his fingers, twining the cord around his wrist, unwrapping and winding it again as he spoke. "When I first went into the program—became a protected witness—I hated living a life that seemed such a lie. I know this might sound ludicrous to you after all that's happened, but…I've always prided myself on being an honest man. And suddenly it seemed as if everything that came from my mouth was some twisted variation of the truth. The rational part of me"— he looked up for a minute and smiled softly—"the self-preservationist, knew that the lies were a necessity. They didn't just protect me, they protected the people who came into my life as well."

"Even me," she conceded.

"Yes. I didn't want you to have the burden of knowing my situation. Even after I came to Silver Creek…after I was essentially out of the program…it was awhile before I felt safe. But even after I knew I loved you—after I trusted you implicitly—I didn't want you to ever have to cover up for me the way I had to cover for myself. And I…told myself that I'd made a new life in Silver Creek as Joel Ellington. It was Joel you loved. After I fell in love with you…I was afraid that if I told you the truth, then it would all fall apart. I'd lose you. Maybe lose my job. I know it wasn't fair to you, Mel," he said. "I should never have dragged you and Jerica into this. I should have been honest. But I'd already decided never to go back. I was… between a rock and hard place, I guess."

He hung his head and wrapped the silken cord tighter around his wrist, but she put the palm of her hand on his cheek and turned his face to look at her. "Oh, Joel. I would have gone with you. It would have been worth it."

"No." He shook his head, his tone rigid. "Not with Jerica involved. I never should have let our relationship go so far. But I was so lonely, Mel. And you were there, and…I didn't mean to fall in love with you. I just woke up one day and realized that I *had*."

She took his hand and squeezed it, her heart overflowing.

Joel uncoiled the cord and ran its silken length along the inside of her wrist. "About this cord... I was sitting in church one day not long before I came to Silver Creek. The Scripture reading was the story of the prostitute Rahab from the book of Joshua." He shrugged. "I know...it sounds like a strange story to find comfort in." He repeated the story she had read from the Old Testament that night in her room. "When I realized that later, in the New Testament, God counted Rahab's actions as an example of faith, it comforted me in a way I can't begin to describe. I never wanted to deceive anyone, Melanie."

He looked at her, his expression pleading with her to believe him. She put a gentle hand on his arm and waited for him to continue.

"I went out and bought this"—he held up the cord and let it coil back into his hand—"to always remind me of the reason I was living in the circumstances I was. I— I'm not sure why I gave the cord to you, Mel. I guess it was...cruel...when I knew you couldn't possibly understand the meaning it had for me. But I...I wanted you to have something to remember me by."

He ran a hand through his hair and shook his head. "Oh, Melanie. Hearing my own words makes me realize what a terrible thing I did to you. I guess..." He sighed and held up the cord again. "I hoped this would somehow comfort you, too. That it would remind you that I did love you and that I would be praying for you."

"In a way, it did. It did all those things. I found that same passage of Scripture one night, and I somehow knew that it meant something...important. I just didn't know what."

Joel took her right hand and entwined his fingers with hers. "Can you ever forgive me, Melanie?"

"Joel..." She choked on his name and swallowed hard. "I've... already forgiven you."

"It's all over now, Melanie. The trial...everything. I think I'll still use some caution...keep the identity WITSEC gave me just for my own peace of mind. But I'm not afraid anymore. That's all over."

He stopped and stared into the fire. Melanie waited, sensing he wanted to say more. Finally he turned to her and reached out to place a tentative hand on her face. "Do you… Is there a chance that there still might be something between us?"

"Oh, Joel. What was between us never ended, as far as I'm concerned. I've never stopped loving you."

Joel took the scarlet cord and wrapped it tenderly around Melanie's left wrist, then around his own, loosely binding their wrists together. "When I was reading my Bible the other day, I found a new meaning for this cord."

She gazed up at him expectantly.

"In the book of Ecclesiastes it says that a cord of three strands is not easily broken." Smiling down at her, he told her, "Whenever I see this cord from now on, it will make me think of you and me and the way the Lord brought us back together…in spite of everything."

"Oh, Joel." She could no longer stop the tears that had welled behind her eyelids. They coursed freely down her cheeks. Joel leaned over and kissed them away. Then he slipped the cord from their wrists and drew her into his arms. They sat together, wrapped in each other's embrace, basking in the knowledge that their long ordeal was over, and in the end neither of them had lost what was truly important.

Suddenly Melanie pushed away from him, an amazing thought fresh in her mind. "Oh, Joel. Just wait until Jerica finds out! She'll be so happy…so happy to have her daddy back—" She couldn't continue over the sob that swelled her throat.

"Shhh…" He put a finger to her lips and brushed a strand of hair from her forehead. "Don't cry. There'll be plenty of time for tears later."

She sniffed. "I can't imagine ever knowing anything but tears of joy from this day on."

"No," he said soberly, shaking his head. Tenderly, he smudged the dampness from her cheek with his thumb. "There will be tears, Melanie. That is life. But I'll be there to dry them for you. You and Jerica both…for the rest of our lives."

Acknowledgments

For help with research: James Scott Bell, Terri Blackstock, Colleen Coble, Gene Cole, Jim Dailey, Sharon Fox, Angela Elwell Hunt, Martha Johnson, David Keazirian, Carla Long, Gerry Loomis, Crystal Ratcliff, Mary Rintoul, Maureen Schmidgall, Kathie Sprout, and Allison Wilson.

For reading my manuscript in its earliest stages and offering advice and encouragement: Debbie Allen; Lorie Battershill; Erin Healy; Terry Stucky; and my parents, Max and Winifred Teeter, who also provided a wonderful writing retreat in their lovely, *quiet* home.

Special thanks to:

My fabulous authors' groups, ChiLibris and ACRW, for providing encouragement, instruction, research assistance, prayer, love—and tons of laughter.

My prayer partners: Colleen Coble and Lori Copeland, whose friendship, support, and thoughtful prayers mean the world to me.

My wonderful editors at WaterBrook Press: Dudley Delffs and Traci DePree.

My family: Without the incredible love and joy my husband and children give me, this would all be meaningless.

∾

To write to me, or for more information about my books, please visit my Web site at www.deborahraney.com. I love hearing from my readers.